PERSON OF INTEREST

PERSON OF INTEREST

Theresa Schwegel

St. Martin's Minotaur
New York

This is a work of fiction. All of the characters, organizations, and events portrayed in this novel are either products of the author's imagination or are used fictitiously.

www.minotaurbooks.com

"I Got It Bad and That Ain't Good"
Music by Duke Ellington
Words by Paul Francis Webster
© 1941 (Renewed) EMI Robbins Catalog Inc.
Rights for the Extended Term of Copyright in the U.S. assigned to
Famous Music Corporation and Webster Music Co.
Rights for the world outside the U.S. Controlled by EMI Robbins Catalog Inc. (Publishing)
and Alfred Publishing Co., Inc. (Print)
All Rights Reserved. Used by Permission of Alfred Publishing Co., Inc.

Design by Maggie Goodman

Library of Congress Cataloging-in-Publication Data

Schwegel, Theresa.
    Person of interest / Theresa Schwegel.—1st St. Martin's Minotaur ed.
        p.   cm.
    ISBN-13: 978-0-312-36426-7
    ISBN-10: 0-312-36426-1
    1. Police—Illinois—Chicago—Fiction.   2. Chicago (Ill.)—Fiction.   3. Domestic
fiction.   I. Title.

PS3619.C4925P47   2007
813'6–dc22   2007033535

First Edition: December 2007

10 9 8 7 6 5 4 3 2 1

In memory of

Leonard Schrader,

who always believed in my voice

Acknowledgments

This book would not have been possible without the insights provided by two fine police officers: Sergeant Dave Anderson and Officer Dave Casarez. Sincerest thanks.

Thanks also to those who offered expert advice, or directed me to someone who could: Sergeant David Putnam; Edgar Bridwell, Chris Carani, and Eric Patzke; Alex Pappas, Nikki Krohn, and Peggy Quick; Dan Judson, Ken Harvill, and Dan Kauppi; Kevin Stevenson, Wayne Priest, Lauren Anderson, and the Kennicotts. If it seems like I know what I'm writing about, each one of these people deserves credit.

Many thanks to Linda Cessna, Anna Kennedy, Kurt Kitaski, Doug Lyle, and Terri Nolan—writers who inspire me with their own interesting work.

My infinite gratitude goes to David Hale Smith and Kevin Adkins, who never fail me, even when I'm failing on the page, and to Kelley

Ragland, who is always the one pitching when I knock it out of the park.

And finally, as always, thanks to my family—to the Schwegels and the Brawners—and especially to those who put up with me too often: Don and Joyce, and D. Jay. You're my heroes.

PERSON OF INTEREST

1

Springtime hasn't always depressed Leslie McHugh. When she was a girl, she looked forward to the days when the sun would try to stay in the sky just a little longer, signaling everything below to get up and get going: to sprout and bud and bloom. She could even feel herself open up, a blossom, roused by the season's potential. A flower.

And then she started working at Sauganash Flowers and Gifts for ten bucks an hour.

Today she sits at the front counter, flipping through an American Floral Distributors product catalogue, waiting on six o'clock. Behind her, a giant poster of a fresh rose–covered wedding cake fades with each passing year, and there's not much to look forward to. Business has been dead since Easter, so Raylene took the afternoon off, let Leslie close up shop. She sits, her enthusiasm as stagnant as the humid air. She hopes the phone doesn't ring, because if it isn't a customer it's Raylene, calling to make sure she didn't cut out early. Either way, she's stuck.

At twenty to six she ditches the catalogue and gets up to treat the leftover flowers. One by one, she takes the buckets from the cooler: the six varieties of roses, the daffodils and the hyacinths, the tulips. She transfers each bunch into its own new bucket filled with fresh Chrysal solution and, once immersed, draws a sharp knife across the stems of those that look a little peaked.

Afterward, she returns the buckets to the cooler, so that the happy daffodils and the showy purple hyacinths may sit like trumpets and bells, on display at eye level to announce to the customers another glorious day. That's what their positioning is supposed to do, anyway. Leslie, being the one in charge of keeping them alive, finds the whole scene contrived, and very sad. Each flower holds on for dear life here, being treated and temperature-controlled like a corpse until it's bundled or bouqueted and sold to someone who thinks a spray of pastels will brighten up their little corner of the world.

When she's through with the cold-stored flowers, she uses a mister to keep the warm-climate plants hydrated: the zinnias, the completely out-of-season sunflowers. Raylene buys those in the lightest yellow, so customers think of summer instead of fall.

Leslie takes the dirty buckets to the back and cleans them out with bleach and water, the familiar solution no less abrasive to her poor corroded nostrils, her roughened skin. The bleach still stings her thorn-pricked fingers, and she's never away from this place long enough to get the chemical smell from her hands.

At five to six, the front bell rings. *Great,* she thinks: just in the nick of time, some husband forgot his anniversary, or some woman wants to browse.

When she trudges up front, she wishes she'd have closed up early, because it's not just someone. It's Niko Stavrakos, her daughter's newest boyfriend.

Leslie feels like she should check her hair. "Niko, is that you?"

"Mrs. McHugh," he says on his approach, arms out. "*Yassas.*" He addresses her formally, but his kisses to both cheeks are as familiar as those from any one of her cousins. He's twenty, too old for Ivy, she thinks; too polite, in any case.

Leslie hasn't seen him in a few weeks and he seems taller; plus, he's grown his sideburns, shaved them to clean rectangles that cut his jaw. He'd introduced himself to Ivy at the Heartland Café three months ago, and Ivy said he was "nice." He's more than nice.

"What are you doing here?" Leslie asked him.

"I need to buy some flowers."

"Don't tell me you and Ivy are fighting. I was going to ask her why you haven't been around—"

"It's nothing like that. I'm a busy guy."

"If the flowers are for Ivy, I can tell you she will not be impressed."

Niko scratches at one of his sideburns, tolerant, but like he's already had this conversation. "They're for my mother. She hasn't been feeling well; you know the Greek-mother thing, right? She has too much to do to be sick."

Leslie isn't exactly thrilled to be lumped into the Greek-mother category: visions of her own mother, busy and frumpy, ruin any possibility of feeling attractive.

Maybe Niko senses her annoyance because he says, "Ivy suggested I come see you."

"That's a surprise. She doesn't exactly respect her mother the way you seem to respect yours."

"Ivy's young," he says, picking up one of the cheap plush chicks left over from Easter off the front display, turning it around in his hands. "Anyway, my mother is pretending she's not sick, and I thought I would bring her a little something to keep her going." He tosses the chick back on the display and smiles at her like his mother has nothing to do with it.

How thoughtful, Leslie thinks, careful not to let his smile lead. He watches her mouth as she says, "Let me show you what we have available," and she wonders what he's watching when he follows behind, over to the cooler.

She slides open the door, says, "These Casteras are nice, I just clipped them," and takes a bunch of the slender, beautiful brick-red-tipped roses from their bucket.

"They're nice. But what about these?" He points to the bucket of Madame DelBards, the bright, velvety bestsellers.

Leslie puts all but one of the Casteras back in the bucket, keeping it to convince him otherwise; isn't it just like a man to believe the bigger and brighter, the better.

"The Casteras are very fragile," she says, "but they're worth the price."

"You mean they're expensive, and they'll die?"

"Sometimes the beauty of the thing lies in the moment."

"I don't know, these big ones look nice." He turns the bucket of Madame DelBards around on the shelf, checking them out.

"They do last longer, but you could buy them at the grocery store. The Casteras are unique." She twirls the single rose between her fingers.

"But they die."

"Everything dies, Niko."

"Geez," he says, his hands up, surrendering. "What was I thinking? I'm going to buy my mother roses so they'll die? She'll take it as a bad omen. She'll freak out."

"She shouldn't. I can't imagine anyone getting too worked up over a flower."

He considers the Casteras, and reconsiders. "I better get the ones that last the longest. So they'll be alive until she feels better."

"Fair enough." Leslie selects a dozen of the freshest roses and takes them to the counter, all the while feeling Niko's eyes fastened on her. He doesn't make conversation and she doesn't know what to say; there's something between them, but she doesn't know what.

"You talked to Ivy today?" she asks, the best she can come up with.

"No, not today."

Leslie hasn't, either. She pretends wrapping up the roses takes all her attention.

As she's tying the bow around the box, Niko says, "I'll bet you never get flowers, with this job and all."

"This job, yes, that's one reason." She doesn't say that another would be because these days, Craig is about as romantic as a carp. He blames his job, though he's been a cop for more than twenty years and never this much of a jerk. She hands Niko the box, says, "Ivy's father works a lot."

"Well, it would be silly for him to waste money on flowers when they aren't as pretty as you."

She can't look at him but she says, "Niko," her tone dismissive, embarrassed.

"I'm sorry," he says. "You know us Greek men. We can never resist beauty."

"You know us Greek women," she shoots back. "We can always resist your charm."

She still doesn't look at him. Silly boy.

After Niko leaves, Leslie closes up shop, and she doesn't make much of his visit until she goes out to her car. There, stuck between the windshield and the wiper, is a single Madame DelBard rose.

2

It's been said that the Chinese take gambling so seriously that a man would bet his life's earnings on the number of seeds in an unpeeled navel orange. Craig McHugh can't remember where he heard that, but after playing Pai Gow with Mr. Moy and company for a month and a half, he's pretty sure it's true.

Moy shuffles the cards, fifty-two plus a joker. This is nothing like a friendly game with the boys, where the cards give you something to think about between sips of Heineken. Where winning an argument over the Cubs' outfielders or beating a guy to the punchline of a joke you already read in *Playboy* is equally satisfying. Craig stretches his neck to relieve his tension headache, and also to get a subtle look around the room.

Only three men are pressing their luck tonight: Craig, Fish Eye, and Dandelion. Craig hoped for some bigger players, some guys with better connections, but Dandelion said Moy wiped out a whole table that morning with a string of flushes. The fact that Dandelion turned up again, resilient against his own loss, is an obvious indication as to where he acquired the nickname, his round yellow face notwithstanding.

Fish Eye traps a Viceroy between stained incisors and lights up, the only other thing to do here aside from setting cards. He takes a long drag; his right eye swims around in its socket. Craig's never sure where the guy is really looking. Maybe nowhere particular. Maybe everywhere at once.

The den sits at the back of Chu's China Delight, behind the kitchen. From the outside, it's dressed up like a walk-in meat locker; a heavy steel door guards the small, smoky room and its rickety card tables, its precious dice. Plenty of meat in this place, Craig thinks. Fresh, stupid meat.

The locker's cooling system serves to circulate air since there are no windows in the room. No decoration, either; only cards, players and endless minutes between hands. Minutes when someone might get tired of losing. Or of the house rules. Or of being quiet. Craig's spent enough time and money here to know there are plenty of bones to pick with Moy; it can't be much longer before the seams of this carefully set scene spread and fray and he gets a glimpse backstage—back to where Chinatown does its real business with the Fuxi gang. That is the reason Craig is here, waiting on Moy to deal another hand.

Moy pauses like he's listening to the cards. Apparently they tell him to reshuffle.

Outside the Pai Gow den, boxes of wooden chopsticks, soy sauce packets and almond cookies sit stacked against the unpainted wall adjacent to the service door, waiting to be sorted and shelved after the three p.m. delivery. The service door leads to the alley that runs parallel to Argyle Street. The only white men who use this door besides

Craig wear uniforms with logos like Halsted Packing House or Chicago Meat and Produce Market, Inc. Craig doesn't wear a uniform, but he'd say he does business just the same.

Moy is still shuffling.

Craig hears the business of the kitchen in the next room: the chopping of bok choy, the sizzle of egg foo young dropped in hot peanut oil. Craig would never get takeout from this place. He's seen the cooks at work: their eyes on the televised horse races; cigarettes hanging from their drying lips, ashes fluttering into the wok as they stir-fry pork for kung pao. If it is really pork, soaking in plastic buckets of purple-red marinade beneath fluorescent lights softened by the kitchen's general layer of grime.

The customers don't seem concerned with quality as they come in, hurried, to order by number from inaccurately glamorized photographs of combination plates. The front of the place is a well-designed stage. "Number sixteen, no MSG," they may say, and they'll receive an obedient bow, though the latter request won't make it back to the kitchen. The customers won't know any better; they'll love the sticky white rice packed into wire-handled cartons stamped with the Chinese character that represents wealth, fortune, and luck, though it could just as easily signify rat piss. They'll rave about the chow mein noodles, unaware they came prepackaged, as ethnic as a Ritz cracker. And they'll actually believe the cooks are Chinese.

Knowing all this doesn't make Craig feel any better. He's just glad the only thing on his plate at this place is the game and, if he's lucky, another name, another link in the Fuxi chain.

In the den's thick air, Fish Eye's cigarette smoke mingles with the oily smell that sticks to Craig's clothes, his hair, his skin—like he's been glazed with it. It stays with him long after he's lost his allowance for the night, another unappetizing reminder of the job. He'll probably never eat another egg roll.

Finally, Moy deals the cards, seven hands for only four players, four cards to the dungeon, as are the rules. Moy places every card on the table like it's deciding a fate. Then he rattles three dice in a cup and tips them out onto the table to determine the order of play.

Craig thinks the whole ritual is time suckage, as if the motions affect who gets what cards, but win or lose, he can't complain. Not to these men. The odds have to tip in his favor eventually, don't they?

Craig's dealt his cards last: a pair of aces, the joker, a jack; the rest slop. He could set three of a kind with the aces, or split them. It's a toss-up; worst case, he'll wind up with a push, which means he doesn't win or lose, save for the house's ten percent. He takes an impatient breath.

Mr. Moy's thin lips stretch horizontally across his face, his smile all lines like a stick figure. "It('s a) good thing (there's) no bluff(ing) in Pai Gow," he says, Craig mentally fixing Moy's broken English as he speaks. "You('re a) terrible bluff(er), Mickey."

"Yeah," Craig says, unnecessarily rearranging his hand, playing the role of the malleable whiteface, the unlucky Irishman known as Mickey. That his badge and his gun are in the glove compartment of the unmarked, GIS-monitored car down the street is concealed quite well, he thinks. And that he's here, running his own game on the Kuang Tian tong, Moy's upfront "community" organization that will be his link to the Fuxi Spiders gang, is the real bluff. When he nails the Fuxis for handling the bad China White—the heroin cut with fentanyl—that's been killing junkies from here to 187th Street, Moy won't be so certain about his bets.

Craig splits his aces.

Mr. Moy shows his cards: low hand is an ace-jack; the high hand, three deuces. The house wins. Again.

And now Craig has to wait some more while Moy goes counterclockwise around the table, comparing his hand to Dandelion's, then to Fish Eye's, and finally to Craig's, all as precisely as he calculates how much more each man owes. Gives Craig plenty of time to figure out he's down a little over two grand.

Moy snatches Craig's cards and begins the whole ritual again, his face listless, despite the fact that he just raked in another couple hundred bucks.

Craig pushes back from the table, his irritation an inevitable tell. He can't help it; he feels like he forked over some sensibility with that last twenty dollars. "Mr. Moy," he says, "I want to know something: how come the house always gets lucky?"

Moy's expression doesn't change. Like he isn't even listening.

Craig catches the back of the chair as he stands up to keep it from tipping back and clattering to the floor. "I'm just saying, maybe it's fate. But tonight? The cards are playing like your command of English. Convenient."

Moy looks up at him, through him. A dare.

Craig didn't plan to be the one to pick a fight; he promised he'd keep cool, let the others' losses get the best of them. But damn this game: there's no strategy. No skill. It isn't fate, and it isn't fair.

And it doesn't matter. It's work.

Craig sits. Moy has no idea what they've both got to lose.

Moy resumes shuffling, and eventually deals. When he gets to Craig he pauses, a card pressed between his fingers like he's second-guessing Mickey's seat at the table. Craig thinks this is the start of something, and he's right, but it's not because of Craig; the next thing he knows, three men dressed in black from hair to heel bust in on the den like a SWAT team.

Maybe he should've, but Craig didn't order the SWAT team.

"Mr. Moy," Craig says, "what's happening?"

Moy says nothing; he meets the intrusion like a man sentenced to death, his face long ago through with emotion.

Craig doesn't know Mandarin or Cantonese or whatever the hell language one of them is yelling at Moy, but the gun the man wields speaks to Craig pretty clearly: he could die here if he doesn't do something.

More men in black, who knows how many, crowd into the room like insects teeming toward the dark. The leader repeats his demand, to Craig it sounds something like: "Ayy doww, Su naaan . . ."

Craig pushes his chair aside and crouches: he's got his backup Walther .380 tucked into his boot and fuck this undercover simple-guy act; if he's going down, he's doing it shooting as Detective Craig McHugh, twenty-three years serving, Chicago PD.

Or maybe not. Because before he can get to the gun, one of the men grabs Craig by his thin hair and yanks him to the floor. Another's knife, a threat at Craig's throat, is a reason to cooperate. When he looks up, he meets a pair of eyes so empty he knows there'll be no negotiation. He shies away from the serrated blade, shielding his face with his hands, and someone else steps on his fingers; his eyes begin to tear and he loses sight of the blade as he tries to jerk his hand away.

He hears Dandelion cry out; he isn't sure he makes any noise himself when someone kicks him in the stomach, stealing his breath. There are black-shod feet all around, and it is futile to think he can go for his gun but he tries anyway, reaches until he is stopped by the blow of a heavy boot to his back, and then he is kicked again, and again, and again.

I'm going to die in this shitty place, he thinks. Die nameless and disappear, without knowing why, accepting this fate on behalf of some crooked Chinamen.

Confusion dilutes the pain and as he slips from clear consciousness, he tries to hold on for his mind's auto-replay of his life. The frames slow to lingering photographs, and finally stop on an image of his wife. It's when she was a girl, about their daughter's age—the way he'll always remember her: long black hair tangled by the lake water; olive skin kissed a shade darker, cheeks flushed by the summer heat, and her eyes, smiling at him like they used to, when things were so good.

And that awful yellow bikini, the one that tied in white strings at the sides, covering just a little of everything he always wanted to protect.

Fate, Craig decides, is a bitch.

3

Leslie dries the crystal bud vase with a hand towel, holding it up to the overhead light to make sure it is streak-free. It is her favorite vase; not an antique, but one she bought for herself last year when Raylene sent her down to Kennicott Brothers to pick up green plastic pots and wet foam for St. Patrick's arrangements. Leslie justified the purchase by figuring it'd be a nice gift for someone. There still hasn't been a someone.

The Madame DelBard rose would not have been her selection. It is too bright, too meaty; it is grown to endure and to show off, rather than to bask in its short life and simple beauty. And it hardly smells like a rose.

Still, the sentiment was nice. For a young man to buy his mother roses—and then to leave one for Leslie—sad to say, but it's the nicest thing anyone's done for her in a while.

And it was so simple. Doesn't her husband know how easy it can be?

She fills the vase with cool water and a dash of preservative, and leaves the water running to clip the stem underneath. Then she puts the rose in the vase and sets it up on the counter. From there, she'll be able to enjoy it when she's cooking, or doing dishes, or sitting at the counter, the place she eats when she's alone.

She puts the plate of feta, pita, and olives she'd prepared up on the counter next to the rose and pours herself a glass of pinot grigio. Craig never showed, and when Ivy came home just after eight—or rather, came through the kitchen on the flight path to her room—she said, "Already ate," and disappeared before Leslie could ask about school, or work, or to find out when she dyed her hair jet-black.

Leslie didn't much feel like cooking or arguing anyhow. She opted for a light meal and now, the quiet: the kitchen clock ticking, the laundry tumbling in the basement. She doesn't feel as melancholy as she did earlier. The wine goes down smooth.

She turns the crystal vase around, admiring the rose. It was nice of Niko. Polite. Smart, too: since he's Ivy's boyfriend, there's an obvious impetus for him to get on good terms with her mother.

She chews a green olive to its pit, the combination of brine and oil perfect on her lips. She thinks of the way Niko's eyes fell just so, watching her.

She tosses the pit on the plate. She's crazy to think Niko's body language read like an invitation. It must be because he was so confident, coming in with his don't-stop-me smile, still unburdened by all the things years do to tamp desire. And hope. When he smiled it was as though he reached for her, soul-first. And his blue eyes next: right there in the flower shop, his flirtatious glances were like whispers of impossibility.

The dryer buzzes in the basement. The Maytags have become a sad soundtrack to her life, spinning without judgment. They wash away stories of Craig's last shift, of his whereabouts. They rinse out all Ivy's time in the mall food court, or whatever coffeehouse of the week. A simple cycle and everything is as it was, though the only thing truly the same is that Leslie is here, doing the laundry.

She goes through the living room, past the baby grand she never plays anymore—she'd been good, once, hadn't she?—and descends into the basement. She puts the clean towels in the wicker basket, colors in the dryer, then begins separating the remaining darks from whites. Craig's brown corduroys, his Bears sweatshirt; half of his collection of black socks, most of them worn thin at the heel. And Ivy's don't-you-dare-put-them-in-the-dryer jeans, tangled up with her little tank tops, sitting here on the basement floor just as they were worn and peeled off, in layers, army green over pink over vanilla.

The typical smells of worn clothes—of fried food and feet and springtime, and of Ivy's too-sweet melony perfume—are no comfort tonight. Leslie doesn't feel at all sentimental.

Even the odor of stale cigarette smoke that finds its way from the pile fails to rouse her. She knows her daughter plans to live to see graduation, and she knows that Craig's clothes—the stupid checkered button-downs he wears over and over like another uniform—are the ones that stink. Like an ashtray. Again. She wonders if he has resumed the habit, though he wouldn't admit it if he had.

She checks all the pockets, removes forgotten accessories: a receipt from Hot Dog on a Stick, thirty-three cents in change, a wayward Excedrin. Would Craig or Ivy really miss any of this stuff? They'd miss her, certainly, if they had no clean underwear.

She goes through the pockets of Craig's faded Levi's and there, tucked into the fifth pocket, she finds a matchbook. A plain white matchbook; no logos to indicate where he got it, or what brand of cigarette he currently prefers. It bugs her, not so much that her husband is smoking again, but that she wouldn't know it from a kiss, or a little time in the same room.

She flips open the matchbook and finds a handwritten phone

number with a 312 area code—a downtown exchange—inside. The lettering is precise, almost decorative, and written only by a woman's hand.

Leslie stands there, something with a zipper making racket in the dryer, the recurring sound the only indication this is real. How strange, she thinks, that the first thing she knows of the other woman is her superior penmanship. The anxious laughter in Leslie's throat dies as she realizes the whole thing is ridiculous, and impossible, and happening just the same. And she knew, in the way a wife can know. In the way a cop's wife *knows*.

The 312 number rings four times and goes to voice mail.

"Can't sleep without me, can you?" the woman at the other end asks, her tone trying for sexy. "If you're hearing this, I'm busy, but I'm always available, if you know what I mean. Leave me a message, or call the arms," she says and gives the number. Then she says, "My arms are always open." Beep.

Leslie's message to the woman is the sound of the phone being thrown across the kitchen, disconnecting when the battery does.

She pours herself another glass of pinot grigio, takes three awful gulps and pours some more. Craig told her he'd been stuck on desk patrol, clearing cases because of the election year. Craig told her the shift change would be a good thing, because there'd be opportunity for overtime, and he knew she was antsy about remodeling the house— *and don't worry, honey,* he said, *I'm moving some of our money around just for that.* And, when he came home late for the umpteenth time, Craig told her that his deviated septum was bothering him. That's why he slept on the couch. Every single night for the past two months, at least.

Bastard. Liar.

There had been endless explanations up until now, hadn't there? For the money that had been disappearing from the savings account.

For Craig's long hours away, and his negative attitude at home. But now, forget explanations. The evidence is clear: Craig is having an affair.

She can't believe it. Who would want him?

The doorbell stops Leslie in her mental tracks. No good news can show up on a cop's doorstep this late at night. Instantly sober and decidedly embarrassed by her condition, she dumps the rest of her wine in the sink, stows the glass in the dishwasher, and reties her hair. She knows she looks a mess, and she is suddenly afraid this is as good as she'll feel for a long time.

A series of harsh knocks at the front door make nausea swirl in her gut. She knows who it must be—

"Mrs. McHugh," a man calls out, voice chilly.

She approaches the door though she doesn't feel her feet touch the floor or her fingers unlock the deadbolt and then she is face-to-face with Officers Stan Denniwitz and John Roscoe, patrollers she knows from Craig's old district, the Twenty-Fourth. They stand there, broad shoulders, somber faces, and she knows something terrible has happened to Craig.

Somehow Leslie smiles while her heart curls up in her chest. "Craig?" is what comes out of her mouth.

"Craig's fine," says Denniwitz.

Leslie's still holding her breath when Officer Roscoe says: "Then again, we didn't tell him about Ivy yet."

Her exhale is a hiss.

"Go get her," Denniwitz tells Roscoe, who turns and makes for the squad, his surly walk a likely testament to his night.

"We wanted to make sure you were here," Denniwitz says. "We busted up a rave, found enough ecstasy to get a head start on world peace. Roscoe spotted Ivy; she danced right into his backseat. I have to warn you, she's high as the Hancock."

Roscoe gets Ivy out of the back of the squad and escorts her up the walk. She's wearing a short black dress that Leslie's never seen. A sliver of skin shows through a run in her stockings, the flesh as white as when she was a baby. She clings to Roscoe's arm and Leslie thinks there is nothing else left of her daughter that seems so young.

"Not only is she feeling the love," Roscoe says, "she was spreading it. We found her with tabs of ecstasy—"

"They weren't mine," Ivy says to him, sounding far less convincing than the girl who announced her bedtime to Leslie some two hours before. Clearly, she's learned the art of duplicity from her father.

Ivy's hands find their way from Roscoe's sleeve to his chest, and she fingers a button on his uniform. "They weren't yours," Roscoe says. "They just happened to be stuffed into your—" He takes hold of Ivy's wrists to stop her.

"I didn't know what they were," Ivy says, mustering some conviction. "I was holding them for someone." Her ink-black hair is matted, sweaty against her forehead; her blue eyes wander behind thick mascara.

"We believe you," Denniwitz says, like he doesn't at all.

"We didn't want her dad to see her this way," Roscoe tells Leslie, his hands still clasped around Ivy's wrists.

"Craig would kill her," Leslie says. "Go inside," she orders Ivy, her tone enough to make it happen, though Ivy grins at her mother like nothing's amiss when she does.

Leslie looks at the cops, both of them standing there like they're waiting for orders. Roscoe, a short man who stands taller with his badge, seems to smile each time his jaw works at a piece of gum. Does he find this entertaining?

Doesn't anyone respect her?

A thought clicks into place, as inescapable as a handcuff's shackle:

if she's going to confront Craig tonight, she's got to have someone on her side. Starting with these two.

She steps out onto the porch so both cops can look down at her. She's sure they'll see the desperation in her own, put-on smile. "Any chance we can leave Craig out of this?" she asks. "I'd really appreciate it if you'd let me handle it. Things have been tough for us lately, and I don't think Craig needs the extra stress." She knows these guys are paid to read between the lines, and by the sad look on Denniwitz's face, it seems like he knows more than Leslie about how tough it's been.

Denniwitz says, "We'll forget it, sure. But get her away from that crowd, Leslie, or things will only get worse."

"And don't let Ivy drink any water," Roscoe says, "unless you plan to let her sweat it out."

She makes sure Roscoe's looking at her when she says, "She's going to sweat it out, I can tell you that much."

"Good night, Leslie," Denniwitz says, the weight of his bond with Craig making the statement heavy.

"Good night and thank you," she says, with equal weight. She is, after all, Craig's wife.

Leslie watches the men return to their squad, dutifully suppressing their take on the situation until they're safely out of earshot. She waits for them to drive off and takes another moment for herself to thank God that her family is safe. Even though she could kill them both.

Then, she steps inside and deadbolts the lock. "Ivy," she calls upstairs. "You're in deep shit."

4

Craig is a lucky man. He knows it when he looks at himself in the dirty mirror above the sink in the locker room: the bags under his bloodshot eyes, the slight jut of his jaw that defies his practiced indifference. He knows he could have been killed tonight.

He also knows he has to hide the pain of the wounds sustained at Mr. Moy's, unless he wants to be the one to put the final nail in the coffin of this soon-dead case.

He rubs his temples, the tension headache returning after adrenaline flushed it out. Every breath he takes is torture, forcing his lungs against his bruised ribs. He was kicked so hard his guts feel like they were yanked around his spine and repositioned. He's hurting enough to wonder if he should tell someone. Not that he will.

Lieutenant Flagherty comes out of one of the stalls behind Craig and the smell of a fragrant dump follows. Flagherty steps up to a sink, washes his hands, meets Craig's gaze in the mirror.

"Detective," Flagherty says. "Tough one, huh." Flagherty could be referring to his bowel movement, or to the shift, or whatever the hell else.

Craig says, "Tough, right." But Flagherty doesn't know Craig is referring to the fact that he was nearly killed. That his cover could have been blown. That he lost the last of the buy money. And there's no way Flagherty could know Craig lost a little over a grand of his own. No one—certainly not anybody in blue—knows he's been putting up his own cash to stay in the game.

Without drying his hands, Flagherty picks up a Glade aerosol can, its rings of rust left on the sink's soap ledge. Flagherty sprays a burst of freshener, asks, "You going to choir practice?"

"Don't think so." Knocking back a couple beers with the boys won't help Craig figure out how to get his money back. And he can't exactly commiserate.

Flagherty leaves the Glade on the sink to drip dry. "Make sure you get squared away with Suwanski before you leave," he says, tone diplomatic, as it should be from a guy giving orders who hasn't seen the street in years. He tucks his tail and turns for the door on the path back to his desk, leaving the place smelling like flowers growing in shit.

Craig turns on the faucet, splashes his face. He wishes he could get a minute where somebody wasn't riding him. And he'll bet Suwanski's in his office right now oiling up his saddle, because when Craig called in to report what went down at Moy's and couldn't think of a more delicate word than *raid,* Suwanski was still repeating the word *fuck* when he hung up.

Craig knows he fucked up this time, and he knows what Suwanski's going to say: he shouldn't have played so long. Nobody worthwhile was at the table and, as behind as he was, he was supposed to cut out. That's the rule: when the night's allowance is gone, Craig is gone.

The other rule, the number-one rule, is for Craig to put his own safety first. This coming from Suwanski, his case agent, the one who advised Craig to go in without backup or a wire. This from the same guy who downplayed the investigation, wrote it up as a small-time gambling case so other agencies wouldn't blow Craig's cover trying to come in at other angles.

No, Suwanski hasn't been following the rules, either. But they agreed at the start that the situation demanded a certain deviance from procedure. No cop, no white man, no outsider had ever played at Mr. Moy's. Craig had worked an in: he had hooked up with a Chinese American named Tse Jin Yuan—"Juan," Craig dubbed him, after about the thirtieth time Suwanski mispronounced his name. Juan's American half kept him from becoming a member of the Fuxis, and his Chinese half was pissed about it, so he agreed to vouch for Craig and get him a seat at Moy's.

Suwanski was the one in charge of making a case out of the connection, so from the get-go, he'd been operating around the bureaucracy. He had to work without the actual infrastructure. He had to appease the bosses with the bare minimum. Document without pertinent details. And, once or twice, not document at all.

As the case has worn on, though, Suwanski has begun to think less like a detective and more like a desk. And after tonight, Craig bets it's going to take one hell of an act to convince him that they need to move the rulebook aside and let it play out.

Craig parks his ass on a bench and takes off his shoes. It's a relief to free his feet from the black socks that have been choking his ankles all night. Fucking Job. In all his years he's never felt so worn out. And he never felt so much like someone else.

But what could anyone expect? Try playing cards day in and out with the players of the Kuang Tian—men whose hearts only beat in order to get blood to their heads. Try playing for months on end in a room full of men who deal in fate and so much honor and no respect. They think you keep coming back for the money; they look at you like you are a fool.

Then, try spending the rest of the shift in another room with different men who are supposed to be your brothers. You play another role for them; you tell them what they want to hear so you can continue to do the Job. They deal in policy and paperwork; they operate by committee. Each time you come back they look at you like you're a fool, just the same.

And then, because the rest of your waking moments carry the potential to compromise your cover or shut down the case, when you finally do go home, you do not talk to your wife. There's nothing worse than when she looks at you like you're a fool.

What would you tell her, though? How would you explain? You've long ago decided that it doesn't do her any good to know the shit you see. The shit you go through. You're supposed to serve and protect her, and your family, above all. You've built mental walls in which to house this shit and it is stowed and it stays. Even if it is so horrible that you have to tuck a little of yourself in there along the way.

This case? It is not so horrible. You have been shut out by people like this before. But not this time. You are not going to give up your seat at the table. You can't. No one in Kuang Tian—not even in the CPD—will believe it when you force Moy's hand against the Fuxi Spiders, the impenetrable crew that, much like the mob, will only fall if their friends turn against them. No one will believe it, because you are a friend. What else could anyone expect?

You are a fool. You are not a fool. It doesn't matter: you are not you.

Craig opens his locker, the first time in months. His old patrol uniform hangs there, dust settled on the shoulders of its plastic dry-cleaning bag. On another hook his old duty belt is like a museum piece, worn to its retirement. A pair of winter work boots sits at the bottom of the locker, crusted with salt and street filth and probably worse on the insides. His old life, shut into the locker like unusable evidence.

Three corners of a photo remain taped to the locker door. It had been a picture of Ivy at her eighth grade graduation; Craig took it down when it yellowed and curled. He never replaced the photo because he never uses the locker anymore. And because Ivy hates him now.

Craig reaches up, feels around the top shelf, comes out with two unspent .38s and sixty cents in change, which isn't even enough to get a pop from the vending machine.

Yeah, he fucked up this time. Real good. But what's worse? Knowing that his own mistakes could take him out of this game while the bad guys keep on playing, no rules, ever.

A single overhead fluorescent buzzes in Suwanski's office. He's at his desk, computer screen bathing his face in a purplish glow, its flicker of activity reflecting in his eyes.

Craig can't see what's on the screen when he taps on the office door, but he can guess when Suwanski double-clicks the mouse, switching the glow to a respectable white.

"Research?" Craig asks, meaning online Texas hold 'em, an activity the stickler Sergeant Kitterman failed to find relevant to their case. The Sergeant met the request with a pamphlet on gambling addiction, which Suwanski conveniently stowed in Craig's glove box.

Suwanski leans back in his chair. "Looking at porn, actually." He crosses his thick, freckled arms. "It's as close as I'm going to get to enjoying myself tonight. Again."

Craig sits, smells the clean odor of hard alcohol. He swivels his chair, rolls to the edge of the desk. "Are you sharing?"

"I don't think so. Mega-free Smut dot com is a very personal experience."

"The tequila, Ronnie."

Suwanski rolls his chair back, bends over to retrieve the half-empty bottle of Patrón Reposado from under his desk. Craig notices he's yet to lose a single red hair on his head. Craig runs his hand through his own hair, on a rapid track to thin and gray, and wonders how Suwanski wears stress so well: growing a beard, losing a few pounds. Maybe it's the tequila; somehow shit rolls off him like he's greased.

Suwanski opens a desk drawer and produces a pair of paper cones that Craig recognizes from the watercooler down the hall. He hands one to Craig and fills it with Patrón; Craig waits while he fills the other. "To the case," Suwanski says, toasts. Then he slugs his share, takes another swig straight from the bottle and says, "It's over."

Craig holds the cone poised at his mouth, afraid drinking would be agreement. "It's not over."

Suwanski takes another pull from the bottle, puts it aside and steadies his gaze on Craig, waiting for him to take the drink.

Craig tips the cup back. He feels the shiver, the alcohol hitting the back of his throat. He suppresses the reaction.

Suwanski doesn't say anything, just watches Craig settle up with his tequila.

"Ronnie, we've come this far," Craig says finally, hating the desperation in his voice.

"They cleaned you out, McHugh. It's over."

"Moy, yes—Moy was cleaned out. But he's going to respect our balances. He said so."

Suwanski sits back. "You get hurt tonight?"

"I'm fine." Craig reaches for the bottle; the alcohol could make him believe it.

"You're not fine," Suwanski says, taking away the bottle. "You're in no shape for this. I can see it, McHugh: you're caught up in it. You played, and you lost, and you think you can get it all back."

"I'm there to collect information. To remember faces and get names. Not to take it personally. Not to make it personal."

"Then how come we're broke and you still seem to think you have some control? We've been at this for months and we don't have a single thing to give to the state's attorney."

"We have plenty to give him if we want the Kuang Tian tong to get a slap on the hand for playing cards. We're on to more, Ronnie: especially now. The Fuxis are going to show more faces and we're bound to find out who's running the China White."

"Now? Are you kidding? It's over our heads. If Moy's going to respect your balance, as you say, then it's time to cut our losses and say good-bye. It's the best way; nobody's going to wonder why you want out after you were caught in the crossfire."

"I don't want out."

"You don't have a choice." Suwanski leans forward, folds his hands on the desk. "What I know about tonight, McHugh? You had a gun and you didn't use it. You didn't protect yourself, and you had no exit strategy. And now you're sitting here, asking me to ignore the risks; I'm telling you no. You should consider this a stroke of luck."

Craig scrapes at the wax on the rim of the paper cone. He's so sick of luck. "Ronnie: I had the situation under control," he lies. "I kept my gun concealed so I wouldn't blow my cover."

"You had the situation under control," Suwanski repeats, without question, and without belief.

"Look, I rolled with the punches tonight because I knew it would change things. Moy knows who hit us—I could see it in his eyes."

"You think he's gonna tell you?"

"People on Argyle are going to be talking."

"No shit people are going to be talking. On Argyle and all the way over to this office. What do you suppose Sergeant Kitterman's going to say? And how about his boss?"

Craig puts up his cone for another shot. Suwanski pours the Patrón and Craig drinks, welcoming the tequila now, hoping courage follows quickly.

Suwanski says, "You could have been killed. We've done a lot of this off the books and I've glossed over most of the rest, but you dead? That's one thing I can't rewrite. There's no more money, and there's no more support. I'm closing the case."

The words hit Craig harder than the alcohol. He stands up. "Ronnie, hear me out. Please."

Suwanski shakes his head no, but he doesn't say it; just bites at his thumbnail.

"Remember the Min Lo case?" Craig asks. "I worked that case. An entire family was wiped off the map and nobody would talk. This community is so shut up they might as well be in China." He squares his shoulders to Suwanski, says, "Except now, Ronnie, I'm in there. *I'm inside.* And I'm not playing the game waiting for the cards to turn; I'm waiting for something like this. I'm waiting for something to happen while I'm there. To be a part of it. So I took some hits tonight—we all did. Moy too. There's got to be retaliation, and I can be right in there. We can get these guys just like we planned—if I can play."

"The money's gone."

"I'll use my own."

"The hell you will."

"I won't bow out."

"Sit down," Suwanski says. He slides the Patrón out of the way so they meet eye to eye when Craig sits. "Why are you so caught up in this." He waits a minute, like he's searching Craig's face for some kind of doubt, but Craig sits, straightfaced and mum.

Suwanski knows they can't quit when their odds are better than nothing. Finally, he says, "Be clear: you will not use your own money."

"I'll just go down there and feel it out. I'll talk to Juan."

"I don't share your confidence in the kid."

"He's taken us this far."

"I'm going to bring in the other agencies. Get the locals up and running in the neighborhood."

"You bring in a bunch of strangers and we're made, Ronnie. These guys don't even trust each other."

"I can't send you in alone."

"Give me two days. Two days to see how it falls out. Then you can bring in the feds if you want to."

"Jesus, McHugh, I don't believe this."

"Don't believe what?" Sergeant Kitterman's heavy phlegm-voice booms from the doorway.

Craig eyes the bottle of Patrón, same thing Suwanski's eyeing. Moving it would only call attention. Craig's glad he drank a little: it's probably the only thing keeping his nerves in check. He rolls his chair back to welcome Kitterman, figures the bottle is Suwanski's problem. "Sergeant."

Kitterman clears his throat and steps inside gut-first; Craig sees "Noise" Dubois behind him, the Sarge's new sidekick. Dubois stays in the doorway, hat in his hand; looks like his mind is somewhere else.

"Jesus you don't believe what, Suwanski?" Kitterman asks again, sizing up the men, the room, the tequila. Kitterman is a big guy, a lot of person; Craig wonders if he finds everyone else small.

Suwanski says, "McHugh's talking about a new lead he has on the case."

Craig nods like he knows where Suwanski is going with this. But where the hell is he going with this?

"How come you're here past your bedtime, Kitterman?" Suwanski asks, always the one to skirt issues with vaguely offensive personal insults. Usually seems to work, but just in case, Suwanski presses on: "We're making some real headway, if you want to take credit." A quick look at Craig seals the deal: Suwanski isn't just blowing smoke for the bosses, he's keeping the case afloat.

Kitterman looks right through the tequila when he says, "This isn't about the case. I've got bad news. They asked me to come and tell you personally, Craig."

Craig feels his body shrink, his breath suspend, and the alcohol is the only warmth in his system. His thoughts flit—*What? Who? Leslie? Oh God, Ivy? A car accident. Mom?* He feels the sting of tears in his eyes that had been so fucking dry from the smoke at Mr. Moy's and whatever floats in the spring air.

"Is it my daughter?" Craig asks, because that's the worst thing he can think of.

"Your daughter—no, she's fine, far as I know—"

"Then for fuck's sake who died?"

Kitterman widens his stance like it'll better support the news. "Rudy Pontecore. He was killed last night."

"Was he working, or . . . ?" Craig doesn't finish when Dubois shakes his head, chin low, ashamed.

Kitterman clears his throat, says, "He made a buy on the west side. Judging by the packaging, they believe the heroin he purchased was what the locals call 'magic.' They found him shortly after, outside Loretto Hospital."

"He was trying to get help?"

"They think he was looking for syringes." The touch of indifference in Kitterman's voice makes Craig want to get up and punch him in his big goopy mouth. "The guys in the Fifteenth thought you'd want to know right away, being his old partner."

"Being his friend," Craig says. He looks at Dubois, knowing a connection between them is pending, since Dubois lost an old partner a year or so back. But Dubois doesn't offer any consolatory gestures. Suwanski, on the other hand, offers Craig the Patrón.

"The service is on Friday," Kitterman says. "I spoke to the Fifteenth's funeral coordinator and he assures me Pontecore will have a proper burial."

"Of course he will," Craig says. "They treated him like dirt; they should have no trouble burying him in it."

"We're sorry, Craig," Kitterman says.

Craig doubts it. He reaches for the tequila. "I'm sorry, too."

5

"Ivy, come out of there," Leslie says to the bathroom door.

Again, no response.

The toilet flushed at least five minutes ago and Leslie's been waiting in the hallway, listening to the on-off of the faucet. The girl's probably washing off her makeup, washing out her mouth, washing who knows what down the drain—

Leslie pounds on the door with the heel of her hand. "Ivy, this is not a suggestion. Get out here now and talk to me or I'm calling your father." She knows it's a terribly worn-out threat, but she'd readied all her fighting words for Craig, and she wasn't prepared for this left-field complication.

As it is, Leslie's concern for her daughter is compromised, because Ivy's no dummy. She knows better than to sneak out on a school night dressed like a tramp to go to some dance party. She definitely knows better than to take drugs. And if nothing else, she knows better than to get caught.

"Ivy, please." Leslie puts an ear to the bathroom door, but now there is no sound at all from inside. She quiets her mind and listens: nothing.

Worst-case scenarios fast-forward to terrible endings: Ivy passed out. Or she's in there choking on her own vomit. Maybe she drank too much water—she could have put herself in some drug-induced seizure. Or a coma.

What if she's dying in there?

Panic shorts Leslie's system like a blown socket.

"Ivy!?" She pounds on the door with both fists until the door is loose on its hinges. When there's no response, fear brings her to her knees, and she buckles to the floor.

Which is where she is, not thirty seconds later, when Ivy opens the door and finds her. Ivy's smile takes up her face like this is the greatest surprise in the world and she says, "Mommy, what are you doing down there?" She helps Leslie to her feet and then, in a shocking move, gives her mom a hug.

Though Leslie is relieved the girl is walking and talking, her reaction is rigid at best; the swell of emotion now gone, she is nonplussed by the fact that it took some kind of wonder drug for her daughter to display this affection. Leslie is unable to remember the last time they'd even touched. Was it her fortieth birthday, back in February? Before that, even? Long enough to make this warm and fuzzy gesture completely awkward.

Still, Leslie clasps her hands around Ivy's waist, embracing the opportunity as much as anything. She feels Ivy's breasts press against her own; the soft bloat of Ivy's belly. She smells her daughter—the very way she's always smelled—beneath the perfume and the hair products and the smoke on her little black dress.

Ivy says, "This is what a hug should feel like."

"What did you take?" Leslie asks, the question muffled by her

daughter's shoulder. Ivy stands two inches taller, four with her plat-
form shoes.

"I need to get out of these clothes," Ivy says. "My body can't
breathe." She twirls away from Leslie and down the hallway like the
platforms float.

Leslie follows, her mood spiked with envy.

From the door, Leslie watches her daughter negotiate with her
outfit: she pulls the black dress over her head, simultaneously tug-
ging at the stockings. She tosses the garments on a pile of clothes
that still wear their price tags: apparently, she did some shopping for
tonight's occasion.

Then, in a black bra and underwear Leslie has never washed, Ivy
turns and moves toward her desk, showing her mother that the new
panties do not, in fact, cover her plump behind. It's a thong, and one
skimpy enough not to bother—and that's her daughter, so sure of
herself, wearing next to nothing.

Ivy wakes her computer with a single keystroke, tapping into her
online world.

"I don't think so," Leslie says to all of it, and enters the room.

"What?" Ivy turns, again reacting as if her mother's presence is a
surprise. The girl's pupils are completely dilated, her eyes colored ob-
sidian instead of baby blue.

"Disconnect," Leslie says.

Back in the bathroom, Ivy's cell phone rings, the sound like a delivery truck's reverse alert, the annoying result of her father's refusal
to let her customize the ring tone.

Ivy makes a move for the call, but Leslie blocks the doorway. "Put
some clothes on."

"Fine," Ivy says like her feelings are hurt.

She finds a pair of too-short pink cotton pajama shorts and a tank in her pile of clothes, rips off the price tags, and dresses. She curtsies to her mother. "Can I get my phone now?" Though her lips twitch intermittently, she's still got the wherewithal to be a smartass, and she seems lucid.

Seems being the key word. "No," Leslie says, "you may not use your phone."

Ivy's computer, still awake and apparently entertaining itself, elicits a series of submarine-sounding blips.

"Can I—"

"No," Leslie says. "Sit down."

Ivy collapses belly-first onto her bed and flips over like an acrobat, swinging her feet around to the floor in one fluid move. She took gymnastics when she was a kid, and though her body is no longer like a gymnast's, the muscle memory remains. "Do you want to talk?" she asks, and pats the cherry-patterned bedspread, inviting Leslie to join her. "Mom, come in here. Let's talk."

Ivy's black lace bra straps show under her cutesy flowered top, the woman trapped inside the girl; and as the girl is currently trapped inside this room with her mother, Leslie assumes her candor is calculated. It's unnerving, and Leslie feels self-conscious as she enters the room.

Ivy's happy face turns. "Are you okay? Are you drunk? Have you been drinking?"

Leslie realizes she might not set the best example, but her behavior is not up for debate. She sits on the bed, dismissing the girl's questions by stating, very sternly, "Ivy."

"Mom? Is something wrong?" She touches Leslie's hair. "It's like silk," she says. "You are so beautiful. And so sad."

"Ivy," said in a tone to shut her up.

"Are you and Dad having problems?" Her eyes are curious, black as an animal's. "I knew it. I've sensed it."

"You're pretty sensitive all of a sudden," Leslie says, sarcastic, since it's a wonder how anybody—especially her own daughter—could fail to notice the complete disconnect between her and Craig. Then again, it's possible Ivy wrote off her parents' behavior, just like Leslie had Craig's. *My arms are always open*, the woman's voicemail said. Maybe Leslie's haven't been.

Ivy says, "I feel good."

"You're high."

"I'm tired." Ivy pulls her hand through her hair, and Leslie notices the black dye that stains her scalp at her hairline. Craig hasn't seen the new color yet. He's going to hate it.

"Your dad's going to be here any minute."

"Oh, shit," Ivy says; apparently the reality of the situation is an instant detox. "He's going to be mad."

"He was mad when you forgot to get an oil change," Leslie says. "He'll be livid when he sees your hair. I don't know the word for what he'll be when he finds out about this."

"Please don't tell him. He'll be so angry . . ." Ivy's gaze falls; she clasps her hands and knees together, her legs bowed: the portrait of a very sorry little girl.

"Ivy, you lost your chance at cute when you bought that dress. You're absolutely right he's going to be angry. *I'm* angry. You scared me half to death."

Ivy looks up at the ceiling like it's the sky and there are stars; whatever drug is left in her system sneaks a smile.

"Ivy. I am not amused. Tell me what happened."

Ivy leans back on her elbows and kicks a leg out on the bed, real casual. Leslie knows she's doing this to make whatever she has rehearsed sound equally so, but the drug won't let her lose that hint of a smile. "It wasn't a big deal. Me and Niko—"

"Niko and I."

"Me and Niko," Ivy repeats, and sticks out her tongue. "We were going to see this band downtown. But we had to drop his brother off by the party. When we got there I heard the music and I wanted to go in. People were passing these pills around. Niko said no, I said yeah. I only got to dance for a minute or two and the cops came."

"How did you end up with the pills?"

"I didn't want anyone else to get into trouble."

"And you thought Stan and Roscoe would cover for you."

"They did, didn't they?"

"The question is, why should I?"

Ivy sprawls out on the bed like she's given up. "I just wanted to try it, Mom. You and Dad are the ones to tell me how I'm going to have to pay for it."

Leslie looks at Ivy's glitter-pink toenails; she looks like such a girl now. Doesn't make it any easier for Leslie; she hates playing cop and court. Usually, she doesn't have to, since Craig is the resident expert. But Craig isn't around. Hasn't been, might not be.

"Ivy, sit up." Leslie takes the girl's hand to help, but her touch is met with a little too much interest, like human contact is some wild new experience. "Let go. Look at me."

Ivy does, with a wasted smile.

"Listen. There are some things I want to know about tonight, and then I'll decide what to tell your father."

Ivy's smile turns conspiratory. "*What* to tell him?"

"Don't think you're getting away with anything. For one thing, you're returning those clothes."

"They had a sale at work. I was planning to return most of it."

"All of it."

Ivy nods, reluctant.

"This is the first I've heard of Niko's brother. What's his name?"

"Rios."

"How old is he?"

"I don't know, I only met him a couple times."

"But he's the one who took you to the rave."

"I already said I'm not going to get anyone else in trouble. I went in there all on my own."

"I don't care: I want to talk to Niko."

"Why?"

"Because you came home 'all on your own.' I want to know why he didn't stay with you."

"There were like a thousand kids there. I got lost in the crowd."

"I want to hear it from him. And don't think you'll be seeing him until I do."

"Okay," Ivy says, her mouth a pout.

Leslie is uncomfortable approaching the next part of the conversation. She's never had a sex talk with Ivy, and it's all the more awkward to think her asking has anything to do with Niko. But she has to ask now, doesn't she? Not for her own sake, but for Ivy's? And for a mother's?

"I want to know if you and Niko," she pauses, afraid she sounded fond at the mention of his name. Ivy doesn't seem to notice. "I want to know if you've been intimate."

A grin sweeps by Ivy's lips. "Mom, give me a break."

"Don't talk to me like I'm stupid. You're dressing up, sneaking out, taking sex drugs; it follows."

"It's not a sex drug, Mom. It's about love."

"Does Niko distinguish between the two?"

"Niko's straight, Mom, but I'm not sprung on him. And anyway, you can't have sex when you're rolling. They say you'll never be able to top it."

"That doesn't exactly put my mind at ease," she says, even though it does.

"I'm so tired," Ivy says. She pulls back the covers, crawls into her spot, and gazes up at the ceiling. "Snuggle with me."

Knowing she may never get an invitation like this again, Leslie climbs in next to her, to lie beside what's left of her little girl.

Above them, a map of the world is affixed to the ceiling.

"Where'd you get that?" Leslie asks.

"I tore it out of a book at the library and blew it up at Kinko's."

Could be worse, Leslie thinks. This could all be a lot worse.

As Ivy's eyes get heavy, Leslie turns to face her daughter, to study her: her unblemished skin and soft mouth; her lineless eyes and peach-fuzzed cheeks. Her only flaws, aside from a barely visible scar that runs across her forehead from a trip down the basement steps when she was seven, result from the things she's done to change herself. The makeup, the hair, the beads of sweat above her brow from the drug—underneath, there has never been a girl more beautiful.

"I didn't sneak out, you know," Ivy says. "You just weren't paying attention."

After a while Leslie says, "I have a lot on my mind."

Ivy closes her eyes and yawns and Leslie catches it easily.

Ivy says, "I have had sex before. Once, with Jeff Yager last year."

Leslie's mouth stops mid-yawn, remembering Jeff's clumsy walk; his pants too big, belted below his boxer shorts. She thought he was a dork. She thought he was harmless. And all the while he was—

"He was an asshole," Ivy says, words sleepy.

Leslie should have known. Ivy thought Jeff was It: the phone bill went up, all her notebooks were covered with his name—she'd even started wearing her pants bigger. Ivy has never been able to hide it: when the girl's got it, she's got it bad.

Ivy takes a deep breath and sighs, long and final. Then she turns to lie on her side, and Leslie watches as she closes her eyes and gives up the fight. She's soon asleep, a faint smile on her face.

Leslie rolls onto her back, looks at Europe up there on the map. At Greece. At all the tiny islands around it, specks of other worlds so far away. There are so many places she'll never see.

As she lies there, listening to Ivy breathe, she wonders what she's missing.

6

"You look amazing."

She knows his voice, the way his accent sculpts the words. She soaks it in like the sun that makes everything sweat and shimmer around them.

She keeps her eyes closed, savoring the anticipation she always feels before their eyes meet. Before they connect.

"I brought you something," he says.

She feels the lightest whisper of a touch near her navel, something softer, cooler than his fingertips. Her skin is so warm, so comfortable, even with so much of it exposed.

"What is it?" she asks him.

"Open your eyes."

She covers her brow with one hand, a visor, as her eyes adjust to the sunlight. Everything is white in the heat and she squints, knowing more than she sees, and knowing that Niko is standing before her, taking her in: her black two-piece and her body, slender and unscarred, just the way she wanted him to see it.

"I found it on the beach," he says, and then she sees quite clearly that in his hand there is a flower, a crisp, asymmetrical gathering of petals and stamen, the blood-red color so vivid it seems to drip. He places it in her hand and it begins to flutter and bud, alive and impossible, but it does not startle her.

She brings it to her face, inhaling. "It doesn't smell like anything."

"It is a carnation."

She believes him, and she knows he is wrong. She spreads her palm and the flower quivers, the stamen like tendrils, exploring. Then the deep red coloring changes, becomes electric, and at once the flower is no longer hers to hold. It floats upward, like a helium balloon, smaller and smaller, into the cloudless sky.

And in the world now, there is so much else in focus. The shape of the sun. The curve of the horizon. The depth of the water. And Niko.

She says, "I never want to leave here."

He kneels beside her. As he moves closer, his face is difficult to see, even to picture. But she can feel him without his touch. All her senses perceive him. Her breath is shallow. She is aroused by anticipation.

"It is unfamiliar," Niko says.

He extends his hand, an offer. She reaches out, ready; ready for this, but she is unable to take his hand, no matter how she tries. And when she cannot, she is no rising flower; instead she falls, and falls, and falls . . .

Downstairs the front door slams and Leslie wakes, sucking in a breath like she'd been trapped underwater. She sits up, registering a shallow ache at the front of her head, and also the fact that she'd fallen asleep in her daughter's room. Next to her, Ivy sleeps undisturbed, probably in the middle of some fabulous dream.

As Leslie gets her bearings, she realizes that Craig is home.

She rolls off the twin mattress and covers Ivy, who's kicked off the sheets in a recovery sweat. She brushes a few coarse strands of hair behind Ivy's ear and watches her breathe just long enough to know she's okay. Her makeup is smeared on her face and pillow, and her awfully black hair makes her skin death-white. Leslie turns off the light and clicks the push-button lock into place before she closes the bedroom door behind her. Craig never looks in on his daughter anymore, but there's no reason to chance it.

She pivots in the hallway, deciding she could sneak into her own bed and pretend to be asleep, talk to Craig tomorrow. But she's wide awake now, and the hall clock ticks past three a.m. Where the hell has he been? In the other woman's open arms? She pivots again, makes a beeline for the bathroom.

In the mirror: tangled curls, flaked mascara, sour mouth. Is this how Craig sees her? Spent, and same-old? She washes her face, rinses with Scope, and tries not to wonder what the other woman looks like.

Downstairs, the house is dark except for the streetlight that offers just enough light through the front window for her to see that Craig is sitting on the couch, his head in his hands.

"Wonderful," she says as she reaches the bottom of the staircase and enters the open room. "You're drunk." She flips the switch on the wall, lighting lamps on both sides of the room, and rounds the couch to face him.

He looks up at her, bleary-eyed and out of it.

"What's the matter, honey?" she says. "Can't sleep? Don't tell me you were expecting open arms."

Craig's expression remains; not even a thread of anger is tied to the way he says, "Fuck you."

Leslie doesn't know which of her defenses go up but they prevent her from saying anything more than "What," and it's a question she doesn't want answered. Does he already know about Ivy?

Craig presses his lips together and his shoulders slump and he holds his breath and this is exactly the way he didn't cry at his father's funeral. He isn't drunk, he's upset. He must know.

"We can talk about this," Leslie says, assertion in her voice though she doesn't feel so righteous now, coming down on him when Denniwitz must have told so-and-so who spilled the beans, or Roscoe couldn't keep his mouth shut and now Craig knows the whole thing, including Leslie's part.

Leslie knows she has to backtrack. "I'd hoped we could handle this privately," she says, an argument as much as an admission.

"Right, Leslie. It was probably on the ten o'clock news."

Great, she thinks: not only did the guys ignore her request, they broadcast it.

"Kitterman came and told me," Craig says. "I'll bet he loved rubbing it in my face. He was so casual about it—like I'm just another jerk off the street."

"Oh, I see," she says. "You're worried that this reflects poorly on you. *You're* embarrassed."

"Did you come down here to bust my balls? Make me feel like this is my fault somehow?" He sits forward to empty his pockets, tosses change and bullets on the coffee table. "It's not my fault."

"We should all take some responsibility for what happened," she says, diplomatic now.

"You, Leslie? What responsibility are you going to take? Getting the fucking flowers to the church?"

"What?" she says, no idea what he means, except to hurt her.

Craig sits back, says, "There was nothing I could do."

"Is that an apology?"

"He was using again and he wanted to die and I let him."

At once the conversation makes completely different sense. The realization hits her. Craig is talking about Rudy. Rudy Pontecore. "I'm sorry."

"Just leave me alone, would you?"

Sickened, Leslie ignores him and sits down on the couch. Rudy Pontecore, a cop, an addict, a corpse. There's nothing Leslie can say here. There is simply nothing to say.

The room is middle-of-the-night quiet, and Leslie feels uncomfortable, exposed with the lights on; they tell secrets to the neighbors.

She wishes she could reach out to Craig, but he won't let her. She wishes he would tell her more, but she can't ask. So instead, they sit in silence, and she is just glad he does not ask her to leave again.

Poor Rudy. Craig had known him for at least a dozen years, but it wasn't until departments branched and ranks changed that they became the best of friends: it was just last summer, when they were assigned to work a murder together. Leslie never knew much about the case since Craig never brought work home. She'd asked, of course, especially since this case had him away from home for days at a time, but when pressed, he said, "It's not something I want you to understand." In the *Trib* she read about the case: some Vietnamese family had been tortured and killed, probably a robbery, maybe personal.

The case was never solved, but Rudy and Craig were suddenly like boyhood friends, years behind them. Or fraternity brothers, secretly bonded.

Brothers. Until Rudy hit the junk. Quick and hard.

Last time Leslie saw Rudy was Christmas. He came by to see Craig, brought his latest wife, Donna, who brought snowman cookies from the Jewel. Rudy said he was clean, and he stood in this very room and drank a club soda. The ladies had afternoon tea; Craig had a cookie. And, like they say, everything was fine.

Except Donna kept eyeing the carpet. Leslie wondered if the woman felt awkward; maybe she was noticing the stains, the wear and tear. Or the way things can be overlooked.

It was after Christmas that things really began to change with Craig—little things, at first. He'd stay out later. Or he'd come home and ignore her, flip on the tube. And now, after some four months, if he shows up it's always late, and he never comes to bed. Earlier tonight, she'd chalked it all up to an affair, but maybe it was Rudy. Maybe he'd been the catalyst for Craig's distance, and difference. Maybe Rudy was killing himself, and part of Craig too.

Ashamed, Leslie moves over to Craig and puts her arms around him. He is resistant, but she stays there, just holding on.

Then, she says, "I'm sorry," and she means it.

Hearing the words, he lets his head fall on her shoulder, and after just a few moments, sitting there together, he slips an arm around her waist and pulls her close. His grasp is needy, she thinks; and the way he nuzzles her is almost desperate, as though he wants to cover himself with her and hide.

He couldn't do this with another woman. Could he?

Rudy's death must be too much for him. Ever since the day they married, Craig had promised he'd take care of her—her boy in blue. But he was never a boy, to Leslie or to any of his friends. He was always a man. And a man takes care of things.

But he couldn't take care of Rudy.

Craig's breathing becomes shallow, as it does when he's about to speak, but Leslie knows he has nothing to say; when things go bad, it's all she can do to sit here, silent, and let him try to feel grief.

Until Ivy appears. She pads down the steps and across the room, behind them, on her way to the kitchen. "What are you guys doing down here?"

"We're talking," Craig says, letting go of Leslie, his walls going up.

"So this is when you two talk," Ivy says.

Leslie jumps up from the couch and ushers her daughter away, praying *Don't turn around Craig don't turn around* . . .

Once in the kitchen, she whispers. "Jesus, Ivy, are you trying to get in trouble?"

"No, Mom, I'm trying to get a glass of water." When she gets on her tiptoes to reach for a glass in the cabinet, the black thong peeks out of the back of her shorts.

"What if your father sees you like this?"

Ivy opens the fridge, its light unkind to her. Getting water from the dispenser apparently requires all her attention, and Leslie can tell her daughter isn't yet sober or fully awake. She takes a long drink of water, in no hurry.

"Ivy," Leslie says, "I didn't tell him about tonight. I didn't tell him anything. Please, go upstairs before he sees you and puts it all together."

Evidently the water is a potion of reason because Ivy says, "Cover me. I'm going in." Said just the way she used to as a kid playing cops and robbers, her favorite game.

But—

"What the hell did you do to your hair?"

—it's too late. The kitchen light comes on and Craig enters, aggressive.

Ivy sets her water glass on the butcher block like she stole it. "I dyed it," she tells him. "Black."

"You look like one of those freakshows at the Village North," he says, referring to the theater where they run *Rocky Horror.* Craig turns to Leslie: "Did you let her do this?"

"Yes," she says, a partner in crime.

Except her daughter inexplicably starts to giggle. Must be inexplicable to Craig, anyway.

"What's so funny?" he asks both of them.

Leslie says, "That's enough, Ivy. Go to bed."

"No," Craig says. "I want to know what's so funny."

"It's a secret," Ivy says. "If we tell you we have to kill you." Talk about inappropriate.

Craig steps forward, Ivy back. "What did you say to me?"

"Honey, she didn't mean it that way," Leslie says. "She doesn't know—"

Ivy cowers as he advances and orders, "Go. To. Bed." The girl is out of there like the room detonated.

Craig asks, "Why is she acting so fucking goofy?"

Leslie shifts on her feet. There is no way she can tell him about tonight, not right now. Not after the news of Rudy. But she's got to tell him something, so she says, "She's got a new boyfriend."

"I've seen boyfriend goofy," he says. "This is not boyfriend goofy."

"You didn't let me finish," she says, though she had.

Craig's face is set the way she imagines suspects see it: like he already knows and it's only a matter of time before you just tell him. Leslie feels like she's bartering the truth.

"This guy, his name is Niko," Leslie says. "I think she's in love with him."

"So what's the secret?"

Leslie picks up the glass Ivy left and takes a sip, buying time. It occurs to her that Ivy wasn't supposed to drink any more water, and she wonders if concern reads like guilt on her face.

"Leslie," he says, arms folded like an unconvinced judge. "I get lied to all day, every day, by everyone. This is, by far, today's most pathetic attempt."

"I don't know why I'm under interrogation."

"Fuck it," he says, throws his hands up in the air. "I don't care what she did. I'll ground her until I'm dead."

"Craig, you're upset about Rudy and you're taking it out on her. On us." She hopes she can shift from questions to conversation, but while Craig works her over with silence, she spots the empty bottle of pinot grigio, the perfect answer, on the counter. "You want to know the secret? I let Ivy have a glass of wine. She came home tonight and we had a glass of wine."

Craig's face turns red against his tough-cop scowl. He believes her, that's for sure. "Underage drinking is illegal," he says, beginning, as he always does, with the law.

"It wasn't a big deal, honey. We just had a glass of wine. We sat and talked. It was harmless."

"Harmless until she gets drunk and wraps your fucking car around a tree."

"Don't blow it out of proportion. It was a onetime thing."

"Rudy is fucking dead because of a onetime thing."

Craig is red from his neck to his forehead, the veins at his temples pulsing. Leslie wonders what he'd look like if he knew the truth.

"I'm sorry, Craig," she says. "It was a mistake."

"Your mistake is thinking you can be friends with Ivy."

"It'd be nice to have one friend in this house."

Craig's response is to take the first thing within reach—the crystal vase—and throw it against the wall. Leslie jumps back as it shatters, water everywhere; Niko's rose lands amidst the crystal shards.

"Good one," she says, though her voice is small, hollowed. He doesn't get angry like this. Not physically. Not at her. She feels the water soak through the toes of her sock and it hurts, the way humiliation hurts. She says, "Impressive argument."

"How can I argue?" He's yelling now. "You don't know what the real world is like. You don't know what's out there—what people do to each other. You're fucking oblivious. And as for us? You'd be just as happy with an alarm system and a weekly check. I don't know why I even come home."

"I wonder the same thing," she says, hoping to return the hurt.

Craig takes his keys from the hook by the phone and Leslie knows the conversation is over. He steps around her to leave and she sees the color has drained from his face, like a man who just lost a fight. Still, if she asked him now, he'd probably say that everything was fine.

She could follow him out. She could be right behind him with other arguments, more ruinous things to say. Instead she picks the rose up off the floor and places it on the counter. Then she gets the broom from the utility closet and sweeps up the mess, hating Craig for letting her have the last word, and wishing she could again dream of butterfly-flowers, of the sun, of Niko. Wishing she really were oblivious.

7

A fire engine's siren wakes Craig from a brief, fitful sleep and he reaches for his gun. The siren wails as the truck runs up Broadway, on its way to whatever probable misadventure.

He puts his gun back on the nightstand and shuts his eyes, resting a minute longer. One noise or another—some woman yelling, the red line train, a car in need of a muffler—turned five hours of shut-eye into a series of naps. He never sleeps well at the Aragon Arms Hotel.

He stretches. His feet, still in his shoes, hang off the end of the bed. He turns over, on his back, but he knows there's no way he can rest now. He had been dreaming about waking up anyway.

When his eyes adjust to the morning light, he wonders how the ceiling could be stained brown by water damage; the bathrooms sit at the south end of every floor, and the room Suzanne put him in late last night is smack in the middle of the building. What a dump.

He sits up and the mattress buckles, its springs having long ago surrendered. Something crunches or snaps or dies when he steps onto the hardwood floor; he doesn't want to know.

The slice of daylight, in through the nappy curtains, doesn't do the room any favors. Calling it a shithole would be complimentary even though Suzanne said this one, the only room she had available, is supposed to be a "sweet." That's how she wrote it on the bill. Cost him twenty bucks extra.

Craig rubs his arms. The paper-thin quilt, which he slept on top of, is threaded with brittle nylon that scratched at his dry skin every time he switched positions. But he wasn't taking his chances; who knows what's gone on before between the sheets underneath.

His stomach growls, sick and empty. He hasn't had anything to eat since his shrink-wrapped White Hen dinner last night, and the tequila he had after hours is sour in his system. The air in this place isn't helping: it sits in the room, old and dusty, like the furniture.

The window opens easily, further inviting the street din, but the fresh air seems content to stay outside, humid and held still by the late morning sun.

Daylight's burning, Craig thinks. Just a couple phone calls and he'll be out of there, get some eggs.

First call: Suwanski. Voice mail, which is good. "It's McHugh. I'm taking a few days for Rudy. Give me the weekend and I'll get back to Moy's." Since the service is tomorrow, this buys him time. He's fairly certain Suwanski won't bug him but just in case he says, "You want to reach me, don't."

Second call: Juan. Voice mail, which is annoying. Juan hasn't been as cooperative lately, and Craig hates smooth talking. He waits for the beep, says, "It's Mickey. Meet me at Mr. Salsa. I'll buy you breakfast. This is mandatory. I eat alone, you pay." He hangs up, half-hoping he won't have to buy the snitch a meal. He's not that hard to find.

Craig pockets his wallet and all that goes with it, pinches the room key between his fingers, and says good-bye to another shitty night.

The bathroom down the hall is occupied, so he decides he'll wait to take a leak at Mr. Salsa. It's cleaner at the hole-in-the-wall restaurant; at least he can count on toilet paper. He's got a stick of deodorant and a different shirt in the car, and he'll spend a long time in the shower later. Who does he have to impress, anyway?

Suzanne.

Craig laughs out loud. She's the hotel's manager-slash-resident. At first he thought she'd be good to know: after a long night at the Pai Gow table when he claimed he needed a place to crash, Moy said, "Go see Sooz(anne) at (the Aragon) Arms (Hotel)." The rest of the guys at the table nodded their heads like they'd all had the pleasure, and Craig thought he'd found another way in.

Since that night, Craig's had more than the pleasure. What started as a ploy to fish for information has developed into a dangerous game of skunk and cat. Pepe-le-Sooz has made more than one very generous offer, and he's afraid that one of these days she won't take no for an answer.

Craig survives another trip in the elevator, a bad ballast in the fluorescents overhead causing the lights to flicker as the car practically free-falls between each floor. He wonders which inspector's signature is scribbled on the operation certificate: if the guy is real, or if he owed the Aragon's owner a favor .

The elevator door opens; all Craig has to do is leave his key and get out the door. It should be so easy.

He steps to the lobby, or what discriminating people might call space for a bench and a perpetual cloud of cigarette smoke: ambiance provided by Suzanne, as she lives in the office that flanks the entrance. Craig is already paid up for the night, his stay rarely more than a few bucks anyway, like a losing gambler whose room is comped. After last night, though, he doesn't feel like he's getting a deal.

The room key is still on its way to the bottom of the box when Suzanne appears in the office window, her cleavage announcing the rest of her. "Mickey, you slept in."

"Yeah, late night," Craig says, caught in long strides toward the door.

"Owner was here this morning," she says, clicking a hand of fake nails on the counter. Craig thinks they call those white tips on her nails French, but that's about as exotic as Suzanne gets.

She sizes him up, a distinct pause below his belt, while she sucks on a Virginia Slim. He notices the sweat on her upper lip when her face brims with a smile. Her extra thirty pounds must keep her plenty warm.

"The owner," Craig says, moving it along. He feels like he should cross his legs.

Suzanne leans out from her perch in the window. "He says if I keep letting you guys stay a night at a time you're gonna have to provide proof of employment like the rest."

Most people rent weekly or monthly, like the sign next to the window says. But the NO SMOKING sign above it is not lost on Craig. "No problem," he says, starting for the door. "Next time."

"Hey, Mickey," she says, "you going to Moy's?"

Craig stops, finding the question interesting. For one, he is amused by the way she casually addresses the man, as Mr. Moy would not approve. For two, Craig knows she's slept with him, because during one illogical attempt to flirt with Craig, she said something derogatory about Moy's egg roll. In the singular. They were not discussing takeout at the time.

Mostly, though, Craig finds the question is interesting because Sooz just might know something about what happened at Mr. Moy's last night.

Craig takes his hands off his hips so he doesn't look like he's interrogating her when he asks, "Moy had a little trouble, didn't you know?"

Suzanne puts out her cigarette and finds the piece of gum she'd had tucked in her mouth somewhere. She chews over the news.

"Somebody cleaned him out," Craig says, but it doesn't look like it gets any of Sooz's synapses firing.

Without looking, Suzanne locates her pack of cigarettes under the counter. She slips the matches from the cellophane, says, "All Moy told me is to free up two rooms for the weekend." She lights a cigarette. "Trouble better not be coming here."

Craig would love to get a look at the registration log, were there one. If his suspicion is correct, Moy's bringing people in to address the situation. Craig has got to be here. "Sooz," he says in a way that lays possibility on thick. "Don't break my heart and tell me you're all booked up."

"There's always room for you, honey." She rolls the skinny cigarette in her fingers while her tongue works its way around her crooked teeth. "I could use you around here to do a little maintenance. There are places Moy can't reach, if you know what I mean."

"I'll be back," he promises, makes for the door. He hopes this case wraps up before she wants more than innuendo.

Craig walks down to Montrose and hits Mr. Salsa before the noon rush. He orders a chorizo and egg burrito and a Mexican Coke and sits against the wall where he can watch them make the chips. The place smells of meat grease, just what he needs to coat his stomach.

Between the green painted letters on the window that read TACO & BURRITO HOUSE from the outside, he keeps an eye on the street. There's no sign of Juan, so when his food is ready, he guesses he can eat in peace.

Maybe not in peace. Rudy keeps getting into his head like another migraine.

Craig dashes hot sauce on his lunch, hoping for the burn, but Rudy is still the winning distraction. He remembers the last time they ran into each other: it was shortly after New Year's. Craig had seen him, clean, just a few weeks before; he'd been all dressed up, trying to smile. The next time he was smiling, all right: he was jonesing hard with a story to sell about needing a little cash for his first anniversary.

Ten bucks doesn't get much of an anniversary gift, Craig had said.

Rudy was wild-eyed, the jitters. "It's cool, Mickey," he'd said, an uncharacteristically ineffective argument. He had sleep caked in his eyes and the corners of his mouth were gummy when they weren't stretched to a smile.

Craig wished his friend had been happy to see him, but he knew Rudy was happier to see the ten bucks. Rudy didn't stick around once he had the cash.

Craig shakes the visual, adds more Tapatío to his burrito. He knows the guy was dead before he died. And everyone knew the junk had turned him into someone else. Rudy blamed the Job. But didn't it get to all of the good ones—the ones who stay in the thick of it—somehow?

Craig remembers working the Min Lo case, the one that partnered them. A Vietnamese family was murdered, their eight-year-old girl tied up, her throat slit so shallow she'd probably held on just long enough to watch her parents die. It was awful. Each of them tortured and killed. Fear caught in their dead eyes, the father's set on his daughter. It seemed they'd been killed for nothing more than the cash they had in the house. And it seemed that the man's fingers and arms had been broken, the woman's hair torn from her head, and the child made to hold the knife that killed her, for no reason at all.

The case was never solved. Rudy and Craig weren't able to locate a single suspect. Nobody in the Vietnamese community would speak up; either they were afraid or they simply wouldn't get involved. The detectives exhausted every angle, and they still didn't have anything more to go on than their own nightmares. It was the worst fucking scene Craig had ever seen.

When they were forced to dump the case, Rudy and Craig went out and got real drunk: their requiem for the Min Los. They went to Hamilton's, the place by Loyola where college kids make fools of themselves and off-duty cops ignore them for a couple free beers after hours.

Over however many bottles of MGD, Craig remembers telling Rudy he felt like they'd flunked Murder 101. It was their job to find the person or persons responsible, he said; the community depended on them to catch the bad guys.

But Rudy argued, "Remember the scene?"

Craig answered by finishing his beer.

Then Rudy said something Craig will never forget: "We deal with this shit, me and you and guys like us, so everyone else can go on believing that monsters only exist in fairy tales."

Rudy leaned back on his barstool to check out a couple underage college girls dressed in their look-at-me best who were sharing gossip and a pitcher of Bud Light. He said, correctly, "They don't need to know."

Craig throws his napkin on his half-eaten burrito and pushes back from the table. There are monsters here, just around the corner.

8

"You don't know how it feels." Mona's voice breaks like a thousand hearts. But what else is new.

"Mom, I know how it feels," Leslie says. "I've been to the eye doctor."

Leslie turns off the Kennedy at Harlem, finally stepping on the gas at the open exit ramp. Traffic on the expressway is terrible: it took them almost an hour from the junction. An hour of this torture.

"I could go blind," Mona says, wiping tears from her cheeks beneath her big black solar shields.

"You just feel that way because your eyes are dilated. The doctor said this is nothing more than regular macular degeneration. You probably see better than I do."

Mona sniffs. "When it comes to this family I certainly do."

Leslie can think of about sixteen rebuttals, but she's been running on autopilot and Dunkin' Donuts coffee since seven a.m. and she doesn't have the energy to bicker.

Challenge ignored, Mona pinches her lips on one side of her mouth, setting her distended jowls askew. When she makes this face Leslie thinks she looks like a disgruntled fish. With the additional oversized eye protection, she could be a cartoon. Leslie prays Craig will look nothing like this when his skin begins to age and hang.

"You just don't care," Mona says. This is her fallback insult, and this is about the fourth time she's fallen back on it since they left the ophthalmologist's.

"You're right, Mona. I don't care." Leslie could agree or disagree; it doesn't make much difference what words either of them uses anymore. The accompanying hostility says it all.

When Leslie signals to turn left on Talcott Avenue Mona says, "I thought we were going to go to Walgreens." The fact that she knows they are not headed north toward the pharmacy in spite of her imminent blindness is a perfect illustration of why no doctor can make a firm diagnosis. Her story always defies her symptoms.

"I already told you I have to get back to work," Leslie says. "And I also told you I'll pick up your Metamucil and bring it by in the morning."

"It's always up to you, isn't it?"

"Oh yes, I run the show," she says, doing her best to leave sarcasm out of the statement. She silently notes the fact that her mother-in-law could indeed use a bowel movement.

Leslie turns onto Talcott, her own relief instant once their destination is in sight. She pulls into the Resurrection Center's parking lot and kills the engine in a fifteen-minute parking spot. "We're here."

"I hate it here. I liked the Lawrence House. I belong in the city."

The other reason it doesn't matter what words they use is that they have some variation of this same conversation every day. Leslie's response is always something like today's: "The Lawrence House was a dump. You said so. We all decided, together, that this is the best facility. And you are still in the city. This is Harlem Avenue. It's not like we committed you to a farm." Leslie unfastens her seatbelt. "I'll help you inside." She gets out of the car, and as she rounds the hood she sees Mona swing the passenger door too wide, its momentum stopped by the silver Lexus parked next to it.

"Jesus," Leslie says, quick to push back the door and assess the damage, hoping there are no witnesses. Luckily, there's no ding on the Lexus, but there is evidence of that intention on Mona's spoiled fish-face.

Leslie palms her keys and shoulders Mona's purse, her patience thin. "Do you need help?" she asks as Mona pulls herself up by the side bar. She seems to know exactly where Leslie's arm is, and she takes it. Leslie resists comment; it's just a short walk now, across the lawn and to the entrance, and then she can pass Mona off to someone who gets paid to deal with her.

"I just wish my son was here," Mona says, "so I didn't feel like such a burden."

The statement goes in one of Leslie's ears but never makes it out the other. *Burden.* The word sticks around while she recalls her post-Easter dinner conversation with Craig. He came into the kitchen and watched Leslie wash the myriad of holiday dishes. The longer he stood there without helping, the more she wanted to break one of the serving plates over his head. Leslie calmly handed him a dish towel—a not-so-subtle hint that he immediately set aside. He had something important to ask, see: he wanted to know if Mona had become a burden. Apparently while Craig had been forced to make idle conversation with his mother in between bites of ham, the good detective got a clue.

At least that's what Leslie thought. But now that she's heard the key word, she doesn't need to read the script to know she's been cast as the villain. Leslie thought Craig had consulted her out of concern for her sanity. She thought he meant to help. She thought he was on her side.

He didn't dry a single dish.

Leslie has no idea whom Craig is sleeping with now, but he has always been in bed with his mother.

"Mona," she says, her tone like it's Sunday and they're in a park. "It *is* too bad Craig isn't here to make you feel better."

Mona's eyebrows peek out from the top of her glasses, expectant.

"But you do know that he would need directions just to come visit you."

"That's not my fault." Mona's gait becomes rigid, slow. Her bony fingers grip Leslie's arm like talons.

Wearing a polite smile until a stranger passes, Leslie coaxes Mona forward, onto the lawn. "I'm not blaming anybody," she says. "I'm just saying, you should appreciate what you've got."

"Next time," Mona says, "I'll take a taxi to the doctor's."

Leslie doesn't know whether Mona can see or not but she can certainly stand on two feet, so Leslie slips from her grasp and steps back.

"Please," Mona says, "don't leave, I can't see."

Leslie flags an orderly at the entrance. "Mom, I've had enough today."

Mona removes her wraparound glasses and glares at Leslie, the expression somehow regal, like she's entitled to disappointment.

The look makes Leslie feel like she's in trouble; as usual, there's nothing she can do. When the orderly approaches, she turns to leave. Mona's vision will be just fine. If only she'd see things a little differently.

.   .   .

From the other side of the street, Craig sees Vergil Walsh in the Lawrence House's storefront window. Nurses and other residents busy themselves around the old man as he sits in his wheelchair, staring out at the avenue through clouds of glaucoma.

Craig figures Juan is working overtime; maybe that's why he didn't answer his phone again, the third time Craig called. He might be upstairs cleaning bedpans, or reminding some old bat to take her pills for the tenth time.

Craig crosses the street, approaches Vergil's window. Someone usually parks him there to distract him when he gets worked up about how things used to be. Nobody can really argue; they were better. Vergil used to be a pilot in the army. He used to be a featherweight boxer. He used to get out of his pajamas.

Now, people pass by on the street unnerved by the sick man in the window, feeling scrutinized by the real-life mannequin, an advertisement for death. But Vergil isn't sick. He wants to die, sure; given that the highlight of his day is watching the world go by through a smudged window, Craig can't blame him.

Craig stops outside and waves. Vergil nods once, an invitation; he must have recognized Craig by his gait.

Even if Juan isn't around, Craig looks forward to visits with Vergil. Maybe it's because he reminds Craig of his grandfather, an opinionated man who died when Craig was young, leaving only other people's opinions of him. Maybe it's because amidst Vergil's scattered ramblings, there exists a clear picture of the old days in Chicago, of a man's long life. And maybe Craig enjoys the visits because he feels like he's returning a favor, because the old man is the one who convinced Juan to cooperate with the police.

The smell of death finds Craig's nose as soon as he enters the building. Surely someone died here today, though life continues on as scheduled: workers wearing various colored scrubs zip from one place to another, needing to be everywhere at once; the few old folks who hang around the main room wander and dawdle, no particular place to be at all.

Craig can't find too much different in here: same trio of dusty plants, bad mauve décor, and Vergil in his spot. Only things that have changed, as they always seem to, are the faces of the help.

"Verge," Craig says, upbeat.

The old man divides his attention, one part toward Craig's voice, the rest out the window. "What the hell are you doing here?"

"He's in a good mood today," Craig tells a young Latino girl in maroon-colored scrubs as she mops up some accident, working her way toward a bucket. She shakes her head, unamused.

Craig gets a folding chair from a stack along the wall, seats for "community events"—when they round up all the old folks and make them sleep sitting up while a junior high chorus sings, or whatever. Craig takes the chair over next to Vergil and they sit, the street's spectators.

"So, Verge, what's going on out there today?"

Vergil swallows, waking up his mouth. "You know, my father, he was born in 1908. Year after the Series. And when he was on his deathbed, in 1976, he said to me, 'Vergil, there's only one thing I wish I'd been able to live to see, and that's for the Cubs to take a series.' He said, 'I pray it happens in your lifetime.'" Vergil tilts his head in Craig's direction, his eyes still set on the street. "Two lifetimes! Two lifetimes, Craig, and the pitching staff is gonna be the death of me."

"Verge, I don't know if I'll live to see it happen either."

"That's no consolation. I'm going to die on Jim Hendry's watch."

"You still have a few years in you."

"Yeah, the worst ones." Vergil finds his handkerchief in the sleeve of his robe, wipes his nose. "Paper says we need a hitter. Somebody who'll put the ball hawks back on Waveland Avenue. But that's not the trouble. The trouble today is the attitude. They give these players all kinds of money and handle them with kid gloves when what they really need is a good whop in the ass."

"It's a prima donna generation," Craig says, which was Vergil's point of contention last time they spoke. That, and he was still ticked by Craig's decision to move Mona from the Lawrence House to a facility out west at the start of the year, even though Vergil agreed it was best for her safety.

"Verge, I'm here looking for Juan. Have you seen him?"

"There's another one who could use a good whop in the ass. He didn't show up last night, and his replacement didn't speak a damn word I could understand—"

Craig's jaw gets tight. Where could he be? He and Juan had a deal.

"—and I'm taking it personally. When he's not around nobody listens to me. Used to be, people listened. Used to be—"

"Hey if you see him again, you tell him I need to speak to him."

"What do you mean, 'if '? Is he running around with that gang again?"

"Last time I checked he was working for me."

"The trouble with half-breeds, Craig, is that they're born without allegiance." Vergil wipes his nose again. "I'm sorry, but I don't know what he's up to. The other night he was on and on about some lady friend. He said meeting her had changed everything." He looks in Craig's direction. "And don't we know that's a trick."

Behind Vergil, the Latino nurse appears, her hands around the wheelchair's handles, silver rings stacked like finger armor. "Time to go upstairs," she says.

"Bath time," Vergil says. "Hey, Lupe, you aren't going to wash my hair, are you? Because yours never seems to dry."

Lupe: unamused.

"Humor him," Craig says, glad that Verge isn't so blind he can't see her kinky, over-moussed hair that's styled to look wet.

Lupe unlocks the wheel brake and shuttles him away.

"Zambrano's pitching today," the old man calls out over his shoulder, leaving Craig with a smile that fades as he sits for a bit longer, in death's waiting room, looking out at the street.

He splits as soon as an old woman teeters by and he realizes they must have served cabbage for lunch.

9

Leslie drives back to Sauganash Flowers and Gifts and, deciding her customer-service skin is worn thin, drives right past it.

She calls the shop from the road and gets Tanner, one of the delivery boys, a kid who's a year behind Ivy at Taft High.

"I'll cover for you, of course," he says. "I owe you."

He doesn't, really; though Leslie did get him the job, it was only partly because Raylene needed someone cheap and the high school had a work-study program. The main reason Leslie got him the job was her compulsion to give him a chance, since Ivy wouldn't. It worked out well: Tanner always agrees to cover for Leslie. He'll do just about anything she asks just to keep his name in circulation at the McHugh house. Too bad he's built like a doughboy with no sign of toughening up. It's been all she can do to keep hope alive.

"I noticed your name on an order form for a sympathy basket, Mrs. McHugh. I read about Detective Pontecore in the paper. I'm sorry for your loss."

"Thanks, T. Tell Raylene I'll be there first thing in the morning."

Tanner's parting shot: "Tell Ivy hello."

"You got it." Leslie wishes she shared his optimism.

Once home, the afternoon in front of her, Leslie is uneasy. Craig never returned, and a sense of loss hangs over the empty house. She tells herself it's all because of Rudy, but she knows it's because of her husband.

True, Leslie never liked a quiet house; when she was a kid and no one was around, she'd spend hours at the piano, practicing everything from Mozart to Mingus. She'd never lived alone, which helped: she went from her parents' home to a college dorm and then here, to this house, because Ivy was on her way, and marriage. From then on, she had a big partner or a little one in tow, always, wherever she went. Leslie loved it; the good times with Craig and Ivy could've filled a hundred scrapbooks. She quit the piano and started a family and it was right: she was meant to be a stay-at-home mom.

Until Ivy started middle school. The mom part became uncool, and it didn't take long before the stay-at-home part was unbearable.

When summer came that year, Ivy went to camp for a much-needed attitude adjustment. Craig was working homicide, an all-hours job; Leslie was alone. A lot. She filled up the time with housework, yard work, busywork. But without a to-do list, she was empty. She hadn't played the piano in years; as a matter of fact, she hadn't done much of anything for herself since Ivy was born. She hadn't a clue.

One afternoon when she thought she'd die from the quiet, she turned on the television. In all her years she'd never before sat down to watch a soap opera; she cried through the entire last segment of *General Hospital.* And when it was over, she relinquished her stay-at-home title and put in her application at the flower shop. She had to get out of the house.

The clock in the kitchen nears three. Leslie decides to eat now;

she doesn't have to make dinner, since Craig is supposed to be working and Ivy's Thursday nights are reserved for the Young Poets Project. It's the only school activity Ivy willingly attends. Leslie suspects the club members spend more time talking about boys than actually writing anything, but when a girl like Ivy quotes Sylvia Plath, albeit in the heat of a mother-daughter spat, it's an extracurricular godsend.

The club does not support readings or performances, a tenet that allows the young poets to flourish without criticism. That's the answer Leslie got when she asked about Ivy's work. Leslie respected the club's secrecy until about a month ago, when she discovered Ivy's poetry notebook. She'd been in Ivy's room strategically placing a college application when she found it. Leslie knew there was no way she could read it. Not objectively anyway.

Okay, she was snooping. But at that time, that day, she just wanted to hear her daughter's voice.

And all things considered—the *lay* and *lie* discrepancy, an average contempt for authority, the girl's affinity for the word *coitus*—the imagery was amazing. In one piece, she'd described a vast and complex landscape that turned out to be nothing more than the tiny wing of a Viceroy butterfly. Leslie suspected the poem was laced with references to some unnamed boy, but overall, the work was good—so good, in fact, that she left the DePaul application on the bookshelf next to the notebook and never said another word about the Young Poets Project.

After last night, Leslie has to wonder if Ivy's still going to poetry club, or if she's been steered toward a different club crowd. Checking up on her now, though, could ruin whatever good thing they have going.

Checking up on Craig, however, is another matter entirely. If Leslie knows her husband, he'll be back tonight after work, like usual. He'll expect they'll regroup, figure out how to handle Rudy's services like a normal married couple. He'll say sorry, he was stressed, everything's fine now; he'll remain distracted and be more distant, and he'll call that grief. But he won't explain why he didn't come home. He won't talk about where he's been. He won't say a word about the woman with the open arms.

Leslie surveys the contents of the refrigerator. She hasn't been to the grocery so everything's already been opened, half-eaten, left over. Conscious of her stress-tendency to make bad food choices—based on an article she read in one of those waiting-room magazines—she decides on a cottage cheese and tomato sandwich. When she discovers the seven-grain bread has gone yeasty, she puts a frozen thick-crust pepperoni pizza in the oven, telling herself they're mostly all the same food groups.

The Madame DelBard rose, now in one of her mother's antique vases, looks a little droopy—probably because Craig threw it across the room. That was some fight: Leslie can't remember the last time Craig lost his temper and she can't ever remember him making her feel scared. What was he thinking?

The other woman's voice echoes in her head. *Call me at the Arms.* Leslie hasn't tried the number again. She'd hoped Rudy's passing would bring Craig around, get him to tell her what the hell's been going on. But he didn't come around. He went ballistic, and he took off. She doesn't like the guess she has about where he went.

"Can't sleep without me, can you?" the woman's voicemail asks. Leslie grabs a pen and jots down the number she advertises for the Arms, then hangs up and dials the number before she second-guesses herself.

"Eggonaams Hotew," is what the man who answers the number says.

"What?"

"Egg-on-aams Hote-o," the man clarifies.

"Hotel?"

"Hoteo." Said in the affirmative.

Bile creeps up in Leslie's throat. A hotel.

"Egon Arms, is that correct?"

"Aa-raa-gaan."

"Aragon? Like the ballroom?"

No answer.

"Can you tell me, is there a Craig McHugh registered?"

"Register? No," the man says and hangs up, an unwilling informant in Leslie's investigation.

A hotel. With some woman. How does a man who says he spends the night shift pushing papers at a desk manage to drain thousands of dollars from a joint savings account and keep company with some bimbo at a city hotel?

She finds a spoon and goes for the half-gallon of fudge marble in the freezer. It takes a number of suggested servings straight from the carton for her to get ahold of herself.

She takes the carton into the dining room where they keep the phone books, gets a Yellow Pages from the bottom drawer of the china hutch, sets the ice cream on the table runner and flips through the fat book's tissue-thin pages with sticky hands. She finds "Hotels." She does not find the Aragon Arms.

She eats another spoonful.

She tries "Motels." Nope.

She shuts the book. Must be the kind that doesn't advertise.

She eats another serving, at least.

Outside on the street a powerful car engine crawls up, revs, and stops. Hell-bent on devouring ribbons of fudge, she's surprised when the doorbell rings.

She leaves the spoon in the carton and sneaks into the front room to look out the window. Outside, Niko is standing at the door peeking in through the stained glass into the foyer.

She crouches down beneath the window, instantly aware that she just consumed half a carton of ice cream and that she's wearing some of it, too.

This is not like answering the door in the middle of some home improvement project, paint on her face. It isn't interrupting while she's at the piano making her way through one of the old jazz standards. This is catching her in an awful moment of truth, red-handed. She should hide.

Niko rings the bell again and Leslie crawls, on her hands and knees, through the front room and into the back bathroom.

What the hell is he doing here? Ivy is still in school. Leslie takes a washcloth to the stain on her shirt. It leaves a sizable wet spot on her tan blouse, right between her breasts. The humidity has done a number on her skin, her hair. She forgot to get her eyebrows waxed and they're unruly above her bloodshot eyes. She looks like a candidate for a nervous breakdown. What will he think?

She wipes her mouth, her hands, notices she broke a nail in her haste crawling over here. A grown woman: a complete mess. But what does she care if he sees her? He's Ivy's boyfriend. He's the one who took her who-knows-where to do who-knows-what. He's the one with explaining to do.

The thought of Ivy's little black thong brings Leslie out of the bathroom.

"Niko," she says, opening the door just a little. "Ivy's not here."

"This is not a bribe," he says, presenting a paper-wrapped loaf of bread. "I swear my mother insisted I bring it. She loved the roses."

Leslie considers him: his faux-hawk salon haircut, button-down shirt open at the collar, expensive jeans, suede sneakers. An American kid would look like he's trying too hard. But he is neither American, nor a kid. He wears it well.

"It's tsoureki," he says, offering the loaf. "For Sunday. Homemade."

She can't shut the door on Greek Easter bread.

"Kali Sarakosti," he says, wishing her a good Lent as he steps inside to greet her, kisses her on both cheeks. She barely smells his cologne, like sophisticated sweat, and wonders what she smells like to him.

When he steps back she's afraid there's ice cream on her face. Did he taste it? She holds the loaf in front of her chest, the wet spot on her blouse.

"Thank you, Niko," she finally says. *"Kali Sarakosti.* I'd forgotten."

"You forgot? At my house you would think Christ himself was going to show."

"I married a Roman Catholic; Easter was last week. The bunny rabbit's work is done this year. And I haven't exactly observed Lent."

"Neither have I," he says, a nod toward the kitchen. "Something smells delicious."

The pizza. Still in the oven. Probably burnt to a crisp. "Be right back."

In the kitchen, Leslie discovers the pie is salvageable, though the crust is charred and the pepperoni is dried out like bacon bits. She sets it on a wire rack to cool, figuring Craig can have it, or not. Good thing she isn't hungry anymore.

"You have another spoon?" Niko asks, inviting himself into the kitchen carrying the carton of melting fudge marble.

"Oh," she says, embarrassed, and utterly so when she realizes Niko's rose is right there, in full bloom, on proud display in the middle of the counter between them. Will he say something? What should she say? "I'm sorry. I'm so scattered."

Niko takes the spoon from the carton. "It's okay. I can just use this one."

Leslie opens the silverware drawer anyway, and roots around for the pizza cutter, which is right there, but he doesn't know that. "Your mother would be appalled," she says, pushing utensils around in the drawer. "Serving frozen pizza on Holy Thursday."

"Don't kid yourself. My aunt's having Easter this year, so my mother will probably spend all day at the salon tomorrow getting her hair and nails done because she thinks she's got to look good for God."

From the corner of her eye, Leslie can see his right hand move when he speaks, the spoon following like punctuation.

"Some day of mourning," he says. "We Stavrakos men have to fend for ourselves." He scoops a spoonful of ice cream, puts it in his mouth, and puts the carton back in the freezer without any question as to why he found it on the dining room table.

"You used to celebrate?" he asks, tossing the spoon in the sink.

"Of course," she says, finally taking the pizza cutter out of the drawer and busying herself, moving the pie to the butcher block. "When I was young. Good Friday was my mother's favorite day. We'd play Diloti and my father would never join us; he said it was a game to be played with men. But really he didn't play because she always won."

"Funny," Niko says, "my mother won't let my father play because he never wins." He pulls out a stool from under the counter. The rose sits right there in front of him, and he ignores it. "Seriously, I'm starving. What do you say, Mrs. McHugh?"

She looks at him, sitting there, so at ease. Why isn't she? She grins, and bears it. "I say *Mrs.* makes me feel old. Call me Leslie."

"Leslie," he says, his accent skimming over the name. "Just one slice. We'll call it the sacred meal of the rabbit." His smile could launch a religion.

Leslie's face feels flushed and she'd like to think it's because she's getting her second wind, her body giving up on any chance of a nap. She divides the pizza and plates a slice. She feels Niko watching her. She wonders what he must think. What is he doing here again?

She'd like to think his charms are unmotivated, but the only reason he can possibly be here is to get off the hook.

"I'm assuming the tsoureki is a peace offering," she says. "Because of last night."

"Like I said, that was my mother. I'm here because Ivy told me you wanted to talk."

Leslie serves him the pizza and leans against the counter opposite him—a little to the left, so his rose isn't directly between them.

"You aren't having any?" he asks, helping himself to the slice.

"I had a big lunch." Part of which she's wearing, but Niko doesn't seem to notice.

"So," he says, "I take it you never got Ivy into the Greek life. I think I'm more impressed with her heritage than she is." He shoves a corner of the slice into his mouth.

"I think it's pretty clear I don't have much influence over her. You, on the other hand: you must have some hold on her. She took all the blame for last night, you know."

He holds a polite hand near his mouth, like he wants to say something, but finishes chewing. Leslie feels like a voyeur watching him, comfortable, chowing down in front of a near stranger. Why is she the one who feels awkward?

"Look," he says, "whatever Ivy told you about last night, that's the truth. She's a good girl, and I'm not going to cause trouble by pointing fingers. I came over here today because I respect her. And I respect you. So, I made a mistake; I owe you an apology. I shouldn't have left Ivy at the rave when the police showed. I know she was trying to protect me, but I should have protected her."

"You wanted to protect her, you should've left her here. At home. In bed. Not traipsing around the city's underground taking god-knows-what kind of drugs."

"I know she told you it wasn't me who had the ecstasy. I don't have any interest in things that dull my mind."

"But you let her take it."

"I am not her mom."

"Eat your pizza," Leslie says. She bites her broken nail, frustrated that he's right.

Niko pushes his plate aside. "Leslie, last night was a bad idea. I want you to know I have no interest in that scene."

"What about your brother?"

"God love him, he's not the smartest guy. Or the luckiest. I'll be straight with you: he's on parole now, and my mother says I have to keep an eye on him."

Leslie feels like she just stepped up to the ledge of a Loop rooftop. "Your brother was in jail?"

"Served six months for a theft charge."

"Niko, my husband is a police officer."

"And my brother is a loser. I'm not proud of it, but what can I do? Trust me, I didn't willingly sign up to be his sitter." He leans over, swipes a paper towel from the roll under the cabinets, and wipes his mouth. "Did Ivy tell you I'm applying to Columbia? I'm going for jazz studies. They have a new thing going with the Chicago Jazz Ensemble. I met someone who is sneaking me in on a late audition. It's Monday afternoon—my god, I'm so nervous. I could get a mentorship, maybe even with the artistic director. I've been playing day and night, practicing, perfecting. You think I wanted to jeopardize my chance of getting in there? Because of my brother, or some kids' dance party?"

"Is that why Ivy covered for you?"

"Like I said, she's a good girl."

"She's still in trouble."

"Am I?" His smirk is a tease Leslie shouldn't be entertaining.

"I appreciate your honesty, Niko, but you have to understand my position. I can't let Ivy go anywhere with you if your brother's involved. And until I say so, she's not going anywhere at all."

"When, do you think, you'll say so?"

"Depends on Ivy."

"Then I won't hold my breath." Niko drums his fingers on the counter. "I've been sitting in at this club—the Green Mill? On Saturday nights. Maybe you'd like to come. Ivy thinks I'm a complete geek about it, but I don't think she gets jazz."

"You're playing at the Green Mill?" Leslie remembers the jazz joint—its long, dark, wooded bar, the hush in the room; the ghosts of old legends, the potential for new ones.

"What do you think?" Niko asks. "I'll put you on the list."

"Ivy would never let me hear the end of it."

"So don't tell her."

Said playfully, Leslie thinks. Right? She doesn't say anything, afraid she'll sound like a mother, or no kind of mother at all.

The rhythm Niko drums on the counter builds, and he gets up to play the final beats on the stool like a bongo. Then he says, "I want to show you something. Come on." His steps around her are close. She watches him walk out of the room, and wonders if following him admits anything.

Then she hears a few mellow chords on the piano.

As she enters the living room, she finds Niko seated at the keys, stretching his hands. Then, as easily as he does anything else, he bangs out a slow, hard-bop version of "He's a Real Gone Guy."

What Leslie remembers as a light tune is only the same in the order of its notes, which seem to come after one another the only way they could. Niko's fingers are all over the ivories, his body channeling reverence, and anger. And control. At certain points in the line he hits a chord that strikes back at him, like lightning, straightening him out.

Leslie knew he played, but she had no idea: he improvises, does a free verse, he even toys with a Red Garland–esque section. And he never misses a note.

When he's finished, he turns to her and smiles, and Leslie wants to fall, and fall, and fall.

10

Craig doesn't figure there'll be any action at Mr. Moy's aside from the business of chop suey, et cetera, but showing up there might be the quickest way to find Juan. The snitch is the only one who can translate what happened last night into a language Craig understands, and while Juan might be able to ignore Craig's phone calls, there's no way he'll ignore Moy's.

During his walk up to Argyle, Craig stops, lifts his sunglasses, rubs his eyes. The afternoon is warm and windy; residents on Kenmore have opened their windows to air out the last vestiges of winter. Though it's been spring, technically, for months, it hasn't seemed like it until the past few weeks. The weeks that have been hell on Craig's allergies.

Argyle Avenue is busy: people buzz in and out of shops and markets collecting their imported wares. Even the produce looks like it went around the world to get here. Along the stretch east of the el, storefront windows offer hair design, oil-fried honey pastries, dime-store junk. Pages of a Vietnamese-language newspaper litter the street at the wind's whim. Craig can't distinguish Vietnamese from Chinese, but this neighborhood is mostly Vietnamese. Some people call this place Little Chinatown. Most people don't know the difference.

Craig ducks into the alley that runs between Kenmore and Winthrop and cuts right, into the delivery drive that backs up to Argyle's businesses. The difference from front to back is like the underside of a bug: the storefronts are hard shells that cover the grotesque, working parts beneath.

Today one of the working parts is standing outside Mr. Moy's back door smoking a cigarette. Craig's never seen the kid before, and as befits both Mickey's paranoid personality and Craig's own cop instinct, he sizes up the kid on approach. Height: five four, give or take an inch. Weight: hard to say; he's compact, but not skinny. Probably a good 150. Age: also hard to say. His black hair is styled young, shaggy around his face; his hard eyes tell a more grown-up story. Craig guesses twenty-five.

When Craig walks up, the kid flicks his cigarette away and squares his shoulders: No Entry.

"I'm here to see Mr. Moy," Craig says, resisting the urge to assume a gun-hand back stance.

"He's busy."

"The hell he is. It was my money that got cleaned out last night too. Tell him it's Mickey."

The kid studies him, no apparent feelings about the matter, and no response.

"Look, kid, Moy and I are gonna settle our bets one way or another, and if I have to deal with you first I will. But you should know that all I got left in my hand is my fist."

"Is that a threat?"

"One of us is going in there," Craig says. "Do you want to keep talking about it or get to the point?"

Unruffled, the kid shrugs. "Wait here."

When he turns to slip in through the screen door, Craig sees the cobweb tattooed on the back of his neck.

Hello, little Fuxi spider.

Craig's heart beats so hard he thanks God for his rib cage. Finally, a stroke of luck. Who else could be inside? How many?

Craig had intended on asking Mr. Moy straight out about Juan. He was going to claim Juan owed him money, figuring it would be in Moy's best interest to wrangle the kid. Given the circumstances, though, name-dropping could be dangerous. He's got to revise his plan, and unfortunately the new one probably includes losing more god damned money.

The spider-boy appears at the door, says, "You're okay."

Craig says, "The jury's still out on you." He has to keep up the big-mouth routine, because as far as Mickey's concerned, this little bouncer is just standing between him and his money.

As he follows the spider-boy inside, Craig tries to burn the image of the cobweb tattoo into his brain. Every member of the gang is supposed to have one; Craig's only seen two, both prison-grade quality, both easily concealable. The one on this kid's neck is showy. Artistic. Done by a pro. He must be new to the gang, and proud of it.

He leads Craig into the Pai Gow den and they stand against the wall, wait for the hand to play out. In here it's business as usual: a table full of expressionless men waits for Mr. Moy to deal the cards. As is custom during play here, nobody acknowledges their arrival, which is fine by Craig—he can get a read on the room.

There are six men. Moy, Fish Eye, and Dandelion; them he knows. The other three he does not. When Moy roles the dice, the three strangers set their cards quickly and in tandem, like they're part of a production line. Craig pretends to watch the cards while he makes mental notes about the new guys. Their wiry builds are equal, their outfits each versions of the others'; young faces similar. Distinguishing marks? No. Craig thinks they could compete in a look-alike contest.

But he bets that underneath those clothes, they each wear different webs.

Mr. Moy sets his hand. Fish Eye's cigarette smoke hangs in the cold-conditioned air against the stir-fried warm front that moves in from the kitchen; the clang and clatter of woks and pans keep time like an irregular clock. So much in the periphery; to the men, all of it irrelevant. All that matters is right there on the table.

When the hand is finished, Moy nods at the spider-boy, who bows and returns to his post outside.

Then Moy says, "Mickey," and tips his head toward the only open seat.

The three new sets of eyes fall around him, all like they're looking at nobody. Dandelion stares at the table in front of him; direct eye contact is considered aggressive. Fish Eye squashes out his cigarette. Who knows where he's looking.

Craig stays on his feet, says to Moy, "I thought you were closing the house for a while."

"No." Moy points at the empty seat.

Contestant number three says something to the others in toneless Chinese. Whatever it is elicits clearly negative responses from everyone but Dandelion until Moy speaks, and silences them.

"What's the problem?" Craig asks.

Moy says, "Cost of play went up."

"How much?"

"Table minimum (is) fifty."

Twice the price. Craig thinks about the hundred bucks left in his wallet and kisses it good-bye. Suwanski would kill him.

So he argues: "I had about three hundred in cash on me last night, Mr. Moy. The house should cover me."

Moy sits with his hands folded, the cards untouched in front of him. He says, "You lose last night, Mickey. You owe the house. Now, (we're) even."

"I was robbed. This isn't even." Craig pulls the chair out from the table and leans over, his hands gripping the back. "I could've kept playing. I could've won."

Moy looks at the space on the table in front of contestant number three, says, "We all have (to) pay now."

Number three looks at Craig, the kid's blank face a canvas for disgust.

Fuck him, Craig thinks. "I'm in." He sits, antes.

Moy picks up the cards, starts the whole process over again.

Craig looks sideways at the three strangers. Who are these guys? They speak to each other in hushed Chinese. Craig wishes he had a clue what they were saying.

The only appropriate time to talk is while Moy shuffles, but Craig knows opening his mouth at this point is a risk. And asking a question would be a certain mistake.

Finally, Moy deals the cards. Of course Craig's cards are shit. Pairless, the very thing the game's named for. Best he can do is set a face card in each hand.

And of course Moy sets a pair of sevens on his front hand, two jacks, ace high on the back. House wins.

One hand down, one to go for Craig. The irregular kitchen clock drags on toward dinnertime.

Craig watches idly as Moy settles with each player. Fish Eye loses both hands; Dandelion pushes with two pairs on the back hand. Contestant one pushes; two loses.

And number three should lose, because he set his cards improperly, the front hand higher than the back. In card clubs, the dealer might reset the cards for the player. In Mr. Moy's den it's called a foul, the player's cards are tossed, and he loses. Moy says if a man's going to pay, he should know (how to) play. But now, nobody says anything, and Moy treats it like a push. What the fuck?

Should Craig say something? He can't let these guys think he's scared. And what about so-called honor? This guy just looked Moy in the face and stole from him. Craig has to speak up.

He holds on to his cards and the fifty bucks he owes and he asks, "Did the house rules change, too, Mr. Moy?"

Fish Eye pushes back from the table. He's out of there; apparently one fight was enough.

"I'm just saying," Craig goes on, "if this is how you're going to play, I'm going to need to get Juan in here to translate the new rules. You will still let him play here, won't you? Even though you've got a new gatekeeper and apparently a new banker?"

"Juan?" contestant number one asks. "Tse Jin Yuan?"

Moy nods a confirmation. The kid laughs, tells the rest of the Chinese at the table something that makes them bust up, too.

"What's so funny?" Craig asks Moy. "Are they laughing at me?"

"No," Moy says. "Ong say(s) Yuan (was) arrested last night. They laugh because no one bailed him out."

So that's where Juan's been. In jail. "Well," Craig says, mostly to number three, "you play like you do, disrespect doesn't surprise me."

"Mickey, go now," Moy says, for Craig's benefit as much as anyone's.

Craig gets up from the table, throwing the cards and his cash toward Moy. "Don't worry, I'm leaving. If I'm going to get fucked, I'd rather lose the money to a toothless whore."

Craig gets one last look at the strangers. Number three's nostrils flare, almost automatically, the way a spider's scopulae would react to the slightest shift in the creature's world.

Craig storms out the back, acting angry, though he can't be: he just made contact with four Fuxis and he has a line on Juan, who should be able to put names to faces.

Outside the spider-boy says, "Just your fists now."

Craig clenches them as he walks away.

In the car, Craig makes a call to Carol, a dispatcher at the district who's no stranger to favors, particularly if they are returned at Hamilton's by way of a Maker's Mark. She's the one nonsworn woman who hangs out at the bar. She likes to commiserate about life, and hers has been more traumatic than any call a cop could take. Craig thinks she smokes a pack a day just to get this whole thing over with.

"What can I do for you?" she asks, her voice hoarse as an old man's.

"I need to find a guy who got arrested last night. Not sure where. Name's Tse Jin Yuan." Craig spells it.

"Just a sec."

Craig hears speedy clicks at her keyboard before she puts him on hold.

He starts his car and heads north on Broadway. If there are no hits on Juan's name, he'll have to go to the station and make the search official.

"Craig," Carol comes back. "He's at the Twenty-Fourth. Brought in on a narcotics charge. There were a whole bunch of those up there last night; must have been a big bust."

"Thanks." The Twenty-Fourth, Craig's old district, is Rogers Park, so Craig's headed in the right direction.

"This sounds to me like work, Craig," Carol says. "I heard you were taking a few days."

"I'm just tying some things up before the weekend."

"I'm sorry about Pontecore." Carol is the first person who has sounded sincere.

Craig doesn't think she knew Rudy, but talking to Carol about death is like consulting the handbook. Her husband was electrocuted at a construction site. Her son died in the Gulf War. Daughter: drunk driving. Her last living son is a schizophrenic who thinks everyone wants to kill him. Carol always says she just might.

Craig says, "It was the Job. The Job got Rudy." And after all this time he feels like he finally exhales.

"One thing or another gets us all eventually," Carol says. "Saying sorry is all someone like me can do."

"You can do one other thing for me, Carol: don't tell Suwanski I called."

"As long as the Job isn't getting *you*."

At the Twenty-Fourth, the lobby looks like the staging area for a parent-teacher conference, except that the teachers in this case are most likely attorneys. The front desk is a war zone, the officers and employees on one side in a flutter of paperwork, the civilians on the other coming at them in demand of explanations and answers.

Craig flashes his star and swipes his ID, bypassing the battlefield and the bureaucracy, busy in its dysfunction.

Downstairs at the entrance to the holding cells, Craig doesn't recognize the officer who's watching the cages. The guy looks like this is his first mustache; his star could've been pinned on by his mommy.

"Afternoon, Spezio," Craig says, off the kid's nameplate.

"Detective," Spezio replies, off Craig's. He sits up straight.

Craig produces the Mr. Salsa receipt from his pocket and pretends to consult it. "I'm here to talk to one 'See . . . Gin . . . Yoo an.'"

Spezio runs his index finger down the roster, looking for the name.

"Denniwitz brought me in," Craig lies. "We might have the kid on a related case." He figures dropping Stan's name might make it easier; they're old buddies, and he's in this district now. If Stan gets word of Craig's visit, he'll play along.

Spezio is at a loss. "Is it under *S* or *U*?"

"*Y*. Capital *Y*, *u-a-n*. It's Chinese."

"Chinese? I know exactly who you're talking about. Moody little guy."

Spezio isn't so big himself, but no matter.

"Can you put him in a room?" Craig asks. "Nobody needs to see us together."

"Sure thing. Go back to holding two, I'll bring him to you."

"Gratzi," Craig says, as Spezio marches down the hall.

In holding room two, Craig tries to get comfortable. He hates windowless rooms. Or maybe he hates interrogation. It's tiring, dragging the truth out of people. Knowing everybody lies.

A few minutes later, Spezio brings in Juan. He's wearing a jumpsuit and cuffs and his mad face. Craig plays tough-cop, staring him down, while Spezio puts him in the chair on the far side of the table.

"Officer," Craig says, a dismissal.

"Buzz me when you're through," Spezio says, and slips out the door.

Once Spezio's gone Craig lets a grin find his lips. "Juan, my man, you look good in orange."

"Fuck you." Juan scowls, his chin and high cheekbones forming points of a triangle.

"Come on," Craig says, "don't be mad at me. I'm the only one who's come to visit."

Juan fidgets; can't do much in the cuffs.

"Tell me what happened," Craig says.

"It was nothing." He shrugs his bony shoulders. "I was at a party."

"You don't get collared for going to a party. I understand there were narcotics involved?"

"They claimed I had MDMA in my possession."

"Did you?"

"Actually the tab had already dissolved in my mouth."

"Why didn't you call me?"

"There were so many people arrested. I was afraid to use your name. What if it would get back to the Fuxis? Anyway," he says, the points of his face pulsating, "I thought Moy would send someone to get me out."

"Shit went down at Moy's last night," Craig tells him. "He was cleaned out. I was there: took a hit myself. There are spiders crawling all over now."

"The Fuxis are there?"

"I had contact with four of them, three at the table. Young guys, punks, acting like they owned the place. Moy let one of them out of a losing hand. I need you in there. I need to know who they are."

"As you can see, I am currently tied up." His face is all angles, a smile.

"Ha, that's very funny," Craig says like it isn't. "You know I'll take care of it. All you have to do is agree to get in there and find out what happened, and to help me figure out how they're going to fight back."

"That's all? You don't want me to strap explosives to my chest and go down to Chinatown to blow your case open?"

"That's not a bad idea." Craig hits the buzzer underneath his side of the table to summon Spezio. "What happened to you last night, anyway? Convince me, so I can convince Suwanski, so he can convince the state's attorney."

"It was a rave. I like to dance. I like to watch girls dance."

"What about the ecstasy?"

"Best I ever had."

"So I should say that you're an idiot kid, but the charges should still be dismissed in the interest of justice."

Seeing Spezio in the door's tiny window, Craig gets up. "Call me when you're out. I'll be in the neighborhood."

Craig meets Spezio at the door. "Take him back to his cell. He's not talking."

With that, Craig runs up the stairs, past the chaos in the lobby, and out the door. It could take days to clear Juan in the court, but a bail bondsman can get him back on the street by tomorrow. All Craig has to do is go home and get the collateral.

11

Leslie runs water in the kitchen sink, recuts the stem of Niko's rose, and repositions it in the antique vase. She wants it to last.

She tells herself the giddiness she feels isn't because of Niko. Not really. Sure, he'd impressed her with his jazz chops; truth be told, he'd impressed her before that. But he also inspired her. He made her want to play again.

After he left, Leslie sat down at the piano and tinkered with what she remembered of *Monk's Blues*. Her fingering was slow, her rendition simplistic—compared to Niko's stint at the keys, she didn't think she could do justice to *Chopsticks*—but it felt good to sit there and play. To remember the notes and to feel her fingers become more nimble, more assured, every time she repeated the A section.

It had been challenging, and she wasn't that bad.

Through the kitchen window, now, she sees her neighbor Meghan Rellinger approaching the driveway on her way to the front door. Even on a casual trip to visit, she pumps her arms like a speed-walker. Who knows what she wants; she's always on some mission—though it never directly involves Leslie, since an attempt to recruit her for the Women's Identity League some fifteen years ago went badly. To overhear Meghan tell it, Leslie just "didn't understand the importance of community service under God." Leslie's version is that she said no because she was unable to identify with any of the women in the league. She wasn't Catholic, she wasn't rich, and she certainly didn't have afternoons available to sit around drinking white wine spritzers, talking about the best place to buy monogrammed towels. She and Craig were house poor. They'd moved in on a loan from his parents and a great interest rate. She had a tight budget and a young daughter to look after. She thought they'd understand.

Meghan didn't. When she couldn't rope Leslie into her ring, she made it a point to keep her out of all things community, completely. It was easy for her to do, being head of the league, and then the board, and then the association. Years later, even, if Leslie ran into one of the ladies at Dominick's or the dry cleaner's, she would be met with an uncomfortable graciousness, as if the woman was slightly suspicious that Leslie would steal her purse. Not much Leslie could do; after all, she and Craig were lucky to live in the neighborhood on a cop's salary. Over the years, she'd become a practically invisible fixture in the community, like the other ladies' gardeners.

Somehow, through it all, she's managed to remain in a neutral relationship with Meghan. Leslie chalks it up to the fact that Meghan thinks Craig's badge is some kind of novelty—like he's a puppy with cute little sharp teeth.

And Meghan's the next-door bitch.

"Come on in," Leslie calls when the doorbell rings.

She meets Meghan in the foyer, the sun in from the front door hardly as bright as the entire Mary Kay color palette she's put on one day's face. "Sorry to interrupt, but after last night I thought I'd better investigate."

"Everything's fine," Leslie says, expertly, a cop's wife.

Meghan steps in past her and invites herself into the front room. Leslie hates the way she makes herself welcome wherever she goes.

Meghan sits at the far end of the couch and crosses her legs at the knee, tight as a knot. She raises her chin like she's sitting for a painting and asks, "So, who's the guy?"

"What guy?" Leslie has to fake the question.

"The one who left here a little while ago. Tall, dark, and hoo-hah?" Meghan kicks her top leg for emphasis.

"Oh. Yeah. Niko. A boyfriend of Ivy's."

"Well, hun, between you and me, I think it's time for the mother-daughter talk. Ya know, birds and bees, abstinence and the fear of God, all that."

Leslie's heart finds a corner in her chest. The thought disgusts her. She manages a "Yeah, thanks."

"I'm no Mrs. Robinson," Meghan says. "But that guy's no Dustin Hoffman, either."

"He's all right, I guess," Leslie says.

"Uh-huh. I can tell by the look on your face."

Leslie wonders what exactly the "look" is. And how to get rid of it. "Are you wearing a new fragrance?" she asks.

"I'll never tell."

"It smells nice."

"I was talking about the boyfriend."

"There's nothing to tell, Meghan." Leslie tenses when she recognizes Craig's car by its AC fan as the vehicle turns into the driveway.

"Well," Meghan says, "I suppose that's your business. But what happens in the neighborhood is of concern to all of us. So I have to ask: is Ivy in some kind of trouble?"

Leslie wonders if she is a terrible liar when she says, "No, there's no trouble."

"Hun, Grant and I saw the cops bring Ivy back last night. She appeared to be . . . compromised."

"Everything's fine, really. But I'd appreciate it if you didn't say anything to Craig. I haven't had the chance to tell him."

"No wonder there's no trouble."

"Listen: he's on his way through the door and you just watch—you'll understand exactly why I haven't—" but then he opens the door so she says, "Trust me."

Once inside, Craig heads straight for the stairs until he sees Meghan there with Leslie and promptly changes course. "Hi, Meghan," he says, coming into the front room.

"Craig, what are you doing home?" Leslie asks, hoping Craig appreciates the way she artfully delivers the question in a way that makes it sound like she cares and also contains an undercurrent of disapproval, as this pit stop is unexpected.

"Have to get something from my office," he says, mostly to Meghan.

"Always working," Meghan says, twirling the hair around her doll face just for him.

Leslie grits her teeth. Everybody loves Detective McHugh.

"I have to tell you, Meghan," he says, "your place is looking great." The Rellinger house, which already casts a big shadow, has been under renovation for months.

"It should," Meghan says, "for what we're paying those morons."

Leslie doesn't envy Meghan's all-around improved existence as much as her ability to get whatever she wants and enjoy it, too. She hates the way the woman looks at Craig, like she could have him, snap of her fingers.

"Whatever happened with the security system?" Craig asks her.

"Grant still can't make up his mind. Will you stop over and talk to him? We need to get something up and running; you never know what can happen in the neighborhood." A glance at Leslie defines her meaning.

"Is he around this weekend?" Craig asks, oblivious to the eye Leslie's giving Meghan.

"Sure."

"Didn't you say you were in a hurry?" Leslie asks.

"No, I didn't, but I am." Craig doesn't look at his wife. "See you, Meghan."

"Soon." Meghan waits until he's on his way upstairs and out of earshot to whisper, "What was wrong with that?"

"Nothing," Leslie says, her hands curled into fists she would love to throw. "One of his best friends just died, he's secretly cleaning out our savings, and he's having an affair, but there was absolutely nothing wrong with that."

"An affair?" Meghan mouths, hands at her heart. "My God."

"You can understand why I'd really appreciate it if you'd keep this quiet. Ivy is the least of our worries right now."

Meghan whispers, "I'm sorry. I didn't mean to pry."

"Yes you did." Leslie hears Craig's footfall on the stairs so she makes sure her voice is conversational. "That's why you came over here, isn't it? I mean, Meghan, come on, if you feel morally obligated to talk to my husband about something you witnessed then please, be a good citizen and report it."

Clueless, Craig comes downstairs, sets a briefcase by the door, and doubles back into the kitchen.

Meghan spins her wedding ring around her finger again and again like she's working up the nerve to say something. Finally, she whispers, "I just wanted to make sure everything was okay."

Leslie considers her own wedding band, says, "I just wanted to lie and tell you it was."

Craig comes out of the kitchen with the loaf of bread Niko brought. "Where did you get this? There are eggs in this bread."

"Bread is made with eggs," Leslie explains, like she's talking to a child.

"Hard-boiled eggs?" he asks. "There are whole eggs in here. Shells."

"It's tsoureki," Leslie says. "Easter Bread."

"Easter was last week."

She gets up and takes it from him. "It scares me that you carry a gun and you would never survive outside an American suburb." She knows it doesn't sound like she's joking.

"I get more respect from criminals," he says over Leslie's shoulder to Meghan: playing to the audience.

"What, Craig, now you won't even fight with me directly?"

"Jesus, I'm here for five minutes and you're all over me."

Leslie stares him down, trying to wipe the stupid attempt at a smile off his face. She knows he's embarrassed. She knows how he feels.

"I should go." Meghan gets up and makes her way around the couple like she's steering clear of a dogfight.

"Lucky you," Craig says to Meghan when she gets to the front door, "you don't have to come back."

Meghan slips out and gets the hell back to her bigger, better life.

Leslie puts the bread on the coffee table, storms past Craig, and catches the door before it closes. Then she picks up his briefcase, and with every hope there's something breakable and important inside, chucks it out onto the driveway.

Then she turns back to him and says, "Neither do you."

12

"Take a look at this." Craig unfolds a Ryne Sandberg Cubs jersey—autographed by Ryno himself—and spreads it out on the counter. He straightens the crew collar, the buttons.

Simon Brugh tosses his toothpick in the trash can and considers the item through wire-rimmed specs.

Doesn't look like much has changed around here, not that a place like this could: Broadway Bonds is much like any office that deals in the business of paperwork, minus corporate or official décor. Not too many corporate types, and not too much official going on: it's essentially a pawnshop, its merchandise documents.

And Simon looks pretty much the same as he did last fall, the last time Craig was here. His lips are still chapped, his mouth hanging open just enough to breathe them dry; the same cluster of moles stains his cheek, like somebody flicked a wet paintbrush at his face.

A phone rings in the back office, disrupting Simon's concentration. He continues examining the jersey's stitching until the third ring triggers whatever beast lives inside him and he unleashes a primordial cry that, in some form of English, is: "Peteranswerthe-fucker!"

After a moment of collection, Simon turns to Craig and kindly says, with regard to the Sandberg jersey, "Five hundred."

"That's it? The guy was an all-star. An MVP. He just got into the hall of fame. He played in this shirt—see the grass stains? It should be worth at least a grand."

"It might be worth more." Simon looks over his shoulder at the back office doorway. "I'll give you five. My brother isn't going to think much of this."

Craig's open hands are a salesman's. "Your brother lacks your genuine sense of compassion."

Simon isn't buying.

Craig dips into his briefcase and comes back with the handle of a baseball bat. "Sosa's," he says. "I have the other half at home. Nine-ninety-five."

"Sorry." Simon shakes his head. "I don't collect empty pill bottles or used syringes, either."

"Nothing was ever proven," Craig says to deaf ears. "There was never even an official accusation."

No dice. Back into the briefcase.

"How come you're so hot for this Chinese kid?" Simon asks, spinning a new toothpick between his two front teeth.

Craig puts his Chris Chelios hockey puck on the counter. "How about this?"

"Don't insult me. Those things are about as valuable as ice cubes since he left Chicago." Simon picks up his Bulls ball cap and sets it back on his bald spot at a new angle. "Is that all you've got? Because this is the same shit you tried to dump on me last time you came in."

Craig looks into the briefcase at his last and most prized item: his Michael Jordan Chicago Bulls Gatorade Slam Dunk eight-by-ten autographed photo—the glass frame cracked now, thanks to Leslie. Is he going to have to give this up too? He supposes he's already come this far. Keeping this stuff is really just holding on to memories that were never his. He doesn't feel much like himself, anyway.

But this picture—Jordan up and over the basket, goddamn it—

Simon scratches his head at the brim of his hat. "This guy Yoon's bail is twenty G's, Craig."

"It's Yoo-an."

"Whatever. Do the math."

"I know how much it is. I'm giving you all I have."

"Can you guarantee this guy will show up in court?"

"I can guarantee this case will never make it to the judge. You just need to get him out. And you can keep the Sandberg jersey."

"I don't know." Simon jerks his chin toward the back office, where Peter the protestor must sit like a conscience.

Craig takes the Jordan photo from the case and puts it on the counter.

"No shit?" Simon says. He looks at the picture: Jordan, up there, magic. He holds the bill of his cap while he shakes his head. "You haven't been this desperate since the last time Rudy was in the can. It's a good thing he cleaned up or you'da been handing over your mortgage by now."

"Rudy's dead."

Simon quits shaking his head, but his face is stuck on *No shit?*

Craig slides the Jordan picture across the counter. "This has got to be worth about six hundred. You know the rest of this stuff is worth decent cash when you turn it around. You can have it—all of it. Just get my man on the street."

"This is crazy. Who is this guy Yoo-an?"

"You really want to know? So you'll have something to confess if the men he's ratting out are partial to torture?"

Simon slides the Jordan picture back to Craig. "I can't take this. Guilt is an unhealthy emotion."

"So you'll post?"

Simon rolls a computer keyboard tray out from under the counter and clicks its mouse here and there, studying the monitor to his left. "I take it cousin Vinny is going to be the person named?" he asks, referring to the fake relative who always bailed out Rudy. It was funny at the time.

"This isn't a joke," Craig says. "These men don't joke."

Simon considers this, and then he takes the Jordan picture back. "Give me the name and get the hell out of here. Your man Yoo-an will be out by morning."

"To Rudy," Craig says, toasting a shot of Jäger to anyone who'll listen. Nobody is listening; nobody's left except the bartender, a guy in a black polo shirt that sports the name *Rabbit's* on the pocket, the *b*'s gold and bubble-shaped, bunny ears.

"Look, man," the bartender says while he rearranges the bottles in the speed rack, "I don't know Rudy and I don't know you."

Craig slugs the shot and puts another twenty on the bar.

The bartender takes the money and says, "I'll give this to the cabbie."

"No, no—hey," Craig says, "I'm juss trying to get drunk enough to go home."

"You've had plenty."

A short, burly Spanish barback who's been running around all night comes out of the kitchen and the bartender opens his register, counts out some cash.

The little big man takes his wages. *"Adios."*

"Later, Nacho," the bartender says; Nacho pushes out the back door.

"Just me and you now, copper." The bartender shuts the register and thumbs the hammer of his imaginary handgun.

"Juss me an you," Craig agrees, but only because he wants to finish his beer. The guy's been giving him shit all night, even when the crowd at Rabbit's was at its rowdiest. Craig just wanted to sit somewhere where nobody knew him—not as Craig, or Mickey, or as a cop, or even a friend. No matter the rest of it, he just wanted to sit somewhere alone and try to feel like himself.

The bartender flips a dish towel over his shoulder. "Tough guy like you, how come you don't want to go home? Your wife carry the whip?"

"Never said I was tough."

"No, you just sit there all night eyeing the rest of us like we're a bunch of losers. Ever look in the mirror?"

Craig could argue; make the bartender sorry. But he knows he is in no shape; he'd probably only prove the guy's point. He decides he'll savor the tail end of his beer, save this fight for another time.

A car horn sounds from out on Foster and his beer is gone, but not because he drank it. The bartender is washing out his glass by the time Craig connects the dots.

"I'll help you," the bartender says. He comes around the bar and lifts Craig off his stool. "Ten years ago I would've let you stumble out of here on your own, but the last thing I need is a lawsuit from some drunk falling on his face, suing me."

Craig feels the world spin around him as his unfriendly escort gets him to the door. Once outside Craig says, "I'd win the case if I accused you of being an asshole."

The next thing Craig sees is the pavement. He's on his hands and knees; behind him the door to Rabbit's is closed and locked and before him, the cab idles at the curb.

He finds it easiest and somewhat amusing to crawl to the taxi. He pulls himself up by the door handle, teeters back and forth, back again, and forward into the backseat.

The cabbie flips on the light; Craig meets his eyes in the rearview mirror: they are shadowed and tired and unimpressed, like his own. The cabbie punches whatever buttons on his meter so Craig says, "Forest Glen and . . . and . . ." He thinks about home. About going home. About Leslie. "Fuck it," he says, "take me to Argyle and Broadway."

The driver pulls out onto the street and heads east through the red light at Elston.

Craig lets the vehicle's forward motion set him back against the seat. His head lolls toward the window and he watches the streetlights skip by. The city, block by blurry block. As they pass Swedish Covenant Hospital Craig feels like saying, "My daughter was born there."

The driver keeps his eyes on the road.

"She's a good girl," Craig says. "Smart girl." He remembers the day she was born, and he is happy to let his mind wander toward the good stuff. They used to be pals, when Ivy was younger. Once, when she was about eight, Leslie wanted to see the opera. Craig and Ivy objected; Leslie made it a family outing anyway. They all dressed up and got in the car and Craig almost missed the beginning looking for a garage with a reasonable rate. Then, during the first act and a shrill high note, Craig and Ivy took one look at each other and another at Leslie, who was mouth-ajar into it. Craig nodded, excused himself. A minute later Ivy was there with him in the lobby. At intermission, Leslie caught them outside the coatroom eating six-dollar Hershey bars.

"Do you have kids?" Craig asks the cabbie.

The driver looks at him through the mirror, doesn't answer.

Craig leans forward to read the cabbie's identification placard on the divider. "Ahman Asaad," he says out loud. "Ahman, ya have kids?"

Again, the driver doesn't respond.

"Maybe you don't speak English," Craig says. "That's okay, I talk to plenty of guys who do, but they juss don't listen."

Craig can't tell whether the driver's eyes either say *Yes, I understand* or *No, I don't,* but they definitely say *I don't give a shit.*

"Jesus Christ," he says, agony pressing out the words: "My best friend just died and you look at me like I'm nothing but the money in my wallet."

Nothing from the driver.

"You look at me like you will never see me again and you could care less."

As the meter turns over another eighth of a mile Craig realizes, "You look at me just like everyone else does."

And finally, the tears.

Craig sobs all the way back to the Aragon Arms Hotel.

13

"Amen," Leslie says in unison with the rest of the mourners, an embarrassingly scant group. Craig showed up halfway through the service, took a seat in the back and sat dry-eyed; he didn't even bother to speak up when the pastor asked if anyone had a few words.

Leslie can't believe he was late. Or maybe she can, and that's why she's pissed. One thing's for sure: the Xanax she lifted from Mona before she came here isn't doing the trick.

"And now," the pastor announces, "Mrs. Pontecore would like to invite you outside to the garden for refreshments, and a little sunshine . . ."

Leslie looks sideways at Denniwitz's wife, Annabelle, seated to her left. She gets the same look back: *That's it?* No flag-fold? No rifle salute? Under the circumstances, Donna opted for a quiet wake-slash-service at the funeral home, but this is so streamlined that Leslie wonders if God even knows Rudy is dead.

". . . on behalf of the Pontecore family and Drake and Sons, thank you for coming," says the pastor. "May peace be with you." He bows his head and squeezes between his lectern and Sauganash Flowers' standing spray. Leslie guessed she overdid it when she could barely fit the arrangement in her backseat; now that it sits in the chapel, it dwarfs everything else—including the casket. But how was she supposed to know? Usually, at a cop's funeral, the church has more flowers than a poppy field. And Rudy's Mexican. Where are the flowers? Where are the people?

"This is an atrocity," Annabelle says in Leslie's ear.

Leslie looks over her shoulder at where Craig had been seated. "Agreed," she says; her husband is gone.

As the others in their row begin to file out, Leslie sees Annabelle and Stan holding hands and feels as sad as she has all day. Sitting next to the couple was a strategic move: Leslie wanted to be close to Stan so she could reinforce the importance of his discretion. She'd planned to tell him she'd yet to break the news to Craig, but when Craig didn't show, she'd decided to be less on-the-nose. She explained his absence was due to his difficulty with Rudy's death. Said she was afraid Craig couldn't handle any more grief. Made a very grievous face of her own. Stan nodded like he knew her secret code, but now that she thinks about it, Annabelle had the same reaction: *poor Leslie*. They both know what she was really saying. They've all seen marriages crumble.

She follows the Denniwitzes to wait in line to pay respect to Rudy, then to offer condolences to Donna, and then to continue out to the garden. In front of her, Annabelle's second chin disappears when she turns up her first one to whisper in Stan's ear. Leslie wonders how she's become so comfortable with her extra weight. And with Stan's.

Annabelle's dress, with its untailored lines and busy shell pattern, must be straight off the discount rack. The chunky beads double-looped around her neck are nothing special, either, though she probably went directly to the mall with her MasterCard when she heard about Rudy. Still, she wears the outfit, a wife's uniform, and with it a sense of duty that is impossible to criticize.

Annabelle catches Leslie watching her and smiles like a courteous stranger. Leslie feels like a jerk.

Hesitant to make eye contact with anybody else, Leslie looks down at her shoes, the scuffed two-inch pumps she's hated wearing to so many funerals. She fingers her Phos Zoe cross, the Orthodox charm she inherited from her mother that she dug out of her jewelry box this morning. The clasp of its chain is caught in the embroidered overlay on the bodice of her dress, the stitching already frayed from other such snags. Last time she wore this dress she never wanted to put it on again. *Not much new about you,* Leslie thinks. Except the way she feels, this terrible awareness.

As they move ahead in the consolation queue, Leslie hears Craig's stupid laugh and wonders who doesn't. She locates him by the back corner opposite the chapel doorway yucking it up with some uniformed cop she's never met.

"He puts on quite a show," Leslie tells Annabelle.

"That's the truth," Denniwitz says over his shoulder.

Leslie excuses herself and approaches the men, her strides across the room long, so as not to appear rushed.

"Craig," she says, hoping she doesn't sound as if she means to shush him. It isn't until she's right next to him that she smells the hangover: she recognizes the way he sweats it out, the way beer ferments his breath. She forces a smile and sticks out her hand for the officer next to him. "I don't believe we met, I'm Leslie McHugh."

"Jed Pagorski," the young cop says, like nobody died, and shakes her hand. "I'm with Craig in the Twentieth."

"He's on the Hamilton's case," Craig says, his cop slang for getting drunk at the bar where the district boys hang out.

"You too?" Leslie asks.

"I'm driving," Craig says.

"I can smell it on you."

"The driving?" he snaps.

"I suppose I know why you were late."

"I needed a ride."

"You just said *you* were driving."

"His car," Craig says, a thumb toward Jed.

"Where's *your* car?"

"Which one of you's the detective?" Jed asks. He elbows Craig in the ribs, but Craig doesn't flinch, and the look he's giving Leslie could break down peace talks.

"I would appreciate it," she says in her best customer-service voice, "if you would join me and speak to Donna."

Jed is not too far gone to figure out he isn't invited. "I'll be in the garden."

Leslie watches the drunk cop find his way errantly out of the chapel.

"Rudy would be proud," she says sarcastically, leaving Craig to get in line where mourners wait to stand before the casket, and then before the widow.

"Let it go, Leslie," Craig says, having followed her to the back of the line. "Jed's doing me a favor."

"How about you do me one," she says, and slips him her wintergreen Tic Tacs.

"You know I don't like the blue ones," he says.

"Don't be a child."

"Don't be a bitch." He hands them back.

Leslie doesn't understand why every word out of her husband's mouth is a challenge. She tucks the mints back in her handbag and vows silence, no matter how uncomfortable.

Hushed death-talk works its way around them in the chapel as they inch forward in line. Leslie turns a cold shoulder to Craig and surveys her flowers again: the alstroemerias from Peru, the white roses from Ecuador, the Mexican palm fronds. All shipped cold-to-cold, from grower to customer, to ensure long life. She wonders if anyone else in the room realizes how far these flowers traveled, how much care was taken so that they'd arrive, ready to bloom, to show their magnificent faces, to light up the room. Even she had been selective: she chose each alstroemeria and every rose; she arranged them in tiers and threaded palm sheets between. The process had been therapeutic, and also sad, as she was preparing the flowers to die.

It took her most of the morning. It should have cost a fortune. And now the standing spray is only something to be sidestepped as people say their *sorrys* and escape out to the garden, the fresh air, the cheese puffs and coffee.

At their turn, Leslie and Craig approach the closed, unadorned casket. They bow their heads. When Leslie closes her eyes, though, her prayers are immediately trumped by the thought of what it would be like if it were Craig in there, dead. Killed during some gang case, shot during a standoff. What if, just like that, he was gone?

She impulsively reaches for his hand, wanting to be together through it all. Wanting to feel that sense of duty. And hoping he'll return the gesture.

He holds her hand, but she can't find any meaning behind it as he guides her away from the casket, past her flowers, without comment. When they rejoin the line, his hand goes limp in hers and she feels the cold sweat on his palm. She wonders if the clammy hand is a result of his hangover or part of his attempt to be cool through this thing.

They wait, just a handful of people between them and Donna

now, and Leslie wants to bail. She hates this; she never knows what to say. A simple *I'm sorry* is appropriate if she does not assume responsibility, which she doesn't. But Craig does, doesn't he?

She peeks at her husband from the corner of her eye. She has no idea what he must be thinking as he stands there, waiting to talk to his dead friend's widow. Remorse is as real as the space between them. Leslie has been selfish. Reactive. And not very nice.

She whispers to him, "Come home, after this. Will you?"

"I have to work."

"Your mother is there with Ivy. They're making dinner. You must have time for dinner."

"I'm with Jed."

"Bring him along."

Craig sticks his hands in his pockets, looks around the room, probably for another excuse.

"Craig, I want you to come home."

He finds an Excedrin in his pocket, swallows it dry. "Let me talk to Denniwitz first."

And Leslie swallows the anxious lump in her throat. The Xanax isn't doing a damn thing.

The couple in front of them says whatever anyone says to a widow and bids her adieu. Leslie lets Craig take the lead.

"Donna," he says as formally as he delivers his handshake-hug.

Her hair is parted in the middle, held back with barrettes like a curtain, parted for the stage that is her face. "Hello, Craig," she says. "Leslie."

Leslie nods, steering clear of direct eye contact. She doesn't want the urge to evaluate the widow's appearance to be construed as exactly that, either, so she defers most of her attention to her husband.

And so does Donna. She says, "Thank you for coming," mostly to him.

"If there's anything I can do . . ." is the condolence Craig goes with.

"Funny enough," Donna says, "for the first time since I met Rudy I finally feel like I have it all under control." Donna's not much of an actress, because Leslie detects evidence of a true smile beneath the dispirited one on her lips.

"I have something for you," Donna says to Craig, and she finds a flat police badge in her pocket. "Rudy would want you to have it."

Craig takes the badge, holding it as though it's much heavier. "Thank you." And at that moment, it seems to be all he can handle.

Leslie says, "Let me hold it for you."

Craig hands it to Leslie, and she sees the pain in his eyes and knows he's sincere when he says, "Thank you."

"We did everything we could," Donna says. "Now we can only move on."

Leslie tucks the badge in her purse. As she stands here, on the periphery of the conversation, she decides the panic she felt just a moment ago over the mere thought of Craig's death had something more to it—something like curiosity.

Sudden tears find their way from her eyes because this is the very same thing she felt the night Denniwitz brought Ivy home. For a moment that night, she thought something had happened to Craig. For another moment, she might have hoped something happened to him.

"I'm sorry," Leslie says. "Excuse me."

Locked in a bathroom stall, Leslie wipes her eyes with toilet paper, wondering why she's hiding at an establishment where it's okay to be sad and Kleenex abounds. It takes her a good cry and all of two minutes more to pull herself together, and with the clarity that follows tears, she realizes she's in here boo-hooing and Craig's out there, very much alive, and on his way to talk to Stan Denniwitz. She still hasn't said a word about Ivy, and the last thing she needs is for good old Stan to be the bearer of new bad news.

She flushes the tissue, tucks her bag under her arm, and heads out to the garden.

Outside the crowd is split into likely circles: Donna's family, Rudy's family, Craig's "family." The boys in blue are closest to the near-empty buffet tables; the last of the mini-quiches is on its way to Jed Pagorski's mouth.

Leslie finds Craig in the mix of uniforms and sure enough, Stan is right there with him. Leslie works her way around the other circles and into Craig's, but Annabelle cuts her off with a paper plate full of veggies and an, "Are you okay?"

"I'm fine," Leslie says and moves to get Stan and Craig in her sightline. They've split off from the group to the edge of the patio; Stan looks like he's been holding his breath since the last time she saw him. "What's wrong?" she asks Annabelle.

"With those two? You know—same old, who's got the bigger gun." Annabelle snaps a carrot in half with her front teeth, chewing while she says, "Craig says Stan arrested one of his informants the other night." She says her husband's name like it has four *a*'s.

"Always on the Job," Leslie says, for once thankful Craig's cop mind works the way it does, with so many degrees of separation from his loved ones.

"I'll bet you're glad they've given Craig some time off to deal with this," Annabelle says. "From what I hear, he was very close to Rudy."

"Depends on how you define *close*," Leslie says. She's supposed to be close to him and she just caught him in another lie. Where will he spend tonight while he's "at work" again?

"I don't know why Stan's so upset," Annabelle says. "He told me he arrested a bunch of kids that night. Said the squadrol made two trips—they busted up some kind of party."

"When was this?" Leslie asks, anxiety finding its way to her skin in a sweat, her own lies looming.

"Wednesday. Stan's been acting funny ever since. But we all know how our men deal when one falls."

Wednesday, Leslie thinks: the same night Stan brought Ivy home. So what, Stan thinks he busted Craig's snitch at the same party? It's a big city. Too big for this kind of coincidence. Right?

Over Annabelle's shoulder, Stan's face tells Leslie otherwise. Stan's face tells her she'd better get the hell over there. She wipes her brow.

"Did you catch the informant's name?" she asks, praying the informant never caught Ivy's.

"I think it was Spanish," Annabelle says. "Was it Julio? Juan? Jesus? Something like that. What's with all the questions, Leslie?"

"You're talking about how they act when one falls?" she says. "I'm afraid mine is about to go off the deep end. Come on."

When the women join their husbands Stan is saying, "You were expecting a riderless horse?"

Craig looks disgusted. Apparently Rudy's service didn't meet his standards, either.

"This whole thing makes me sick," he says. "I don't recognize any of these people. Except maybe the ones who killed him."

Leslie knows Craig has always blamed Rudy's case agent on up the bureaucratic chain for the way things went bad for Rudy. Judging by the direction in which Craig is giving his middle finger, Leslie guesses one or both of the uniformed men conversing by the knishes are Rudy's former bosses.

Leslie covers her husband's hand and says, "I think it's time to go."

"Yep," Stan says, "I think I'm real familiar with grief at this point. Thanks, Craig." He's trying to keep it light, but—

"Fuck you too, Denniwitz." Craig rips his hand away from Leslie's and points to Stan. "If I lose this kid, I'm taking it up with you."

Stan doesn't say anything: just looks at Leslie.

Leslie doesn't say anything: just looks anywhere else.

Annabelle says, "Honey?"

Craig says, "I'm leaving. Nobody wants to listen. And nobody has to, since we can just bury the problem and enjoy the fucking nice day."

Craig storms off and leaves the three of them standing there, Annabelle with her vegetables, Stan chewing his lip, Leslie watching the various circles intertwine, fearing the degrees of separation have become too few.

Especially when she spots Donna talking to the two men by the knishes. Her eyes are covered by big, dark sunglasses; her smile is no longer covered at all. And those are the men who are ultimately responsible for letting Rudy fall.

"It *is* a nice day," Annabelle says, because someone should.

14

"You sure you don't want to stop in for a beer?" Jed asks as he drives by Rabbit's, turns the corner onto Elston Avenue, and stops behind the '91 Caprice Craig's driving while he's undercover.

"Wish I could," Craig lies because the last thing he wants to do is face that bartender, especially with a bigger, badge-happy partner. "I have to go home."

"Your wife won the last round back there?"

"She invited my mother for dinner."

"Ooh: a sucker punch. You do not mess with Mom."

"Nope." Craig hates that Leslie knowingly baited him to return home. During the ride over here he thought about inviting Jed, like she offered, just because she didn't mean it. But Jed is not one for quiet reflection, and at this point, Craig has heard all he needs to about what it means to be a brother in blue.

"Well, thanks for the ride." He opens the passenger door.

"What are brothers for?" Jed nods, a kid who gets by on faith.

Craig nods back, a man who wishes he had more.

He gets out, approaches his beater. He wishes he had his Tacoma, the black beauty that's collecting dust in his garage. He doesn't understand why the desks ordered installation of a top-of-the-line GIS tracking system in this car and couldn't bother with a basic radio. He keys the Caprice's lock, leaves the parking ticket on the windshield.

Inside, he powers up the UC phone he uses for the case—the bat phone, as Juan calls it.

He loosens the knot of his tie. The sore spot on his conscience is familiar: he always feels this way when someone he's supposed to trust rubs him wrong. This time the one rubbing is Denniwitz. Because Craig dropped his name during his visit to the Twenty-Fourth's jail, he thought it common courtesy to let Denniwitz in on the sham. But, right from the hi-how-are-ya, Denniwitz was clearly miffed. Short. Tight-lipped.

"What's the trouble?" Craig wanted to know after he pulled Denniwitz aside—or more correctly, away from his nosey wife.

"No trouble."

And when Craig asked him to keep the business with Juan under wraps, highlighting some of the life-and-death reasons for secrecy, Denniwitz just said, "Small world," under his breath, like an unfair joke.

Craig couldn't get a read on the guy. Why did he seem like there was something else he wanted to say? Maybe he was just a little wrecked, like everybody else, on account of Rudy, but he seemed about as comfortable as a guy passing a kidney stone.

"I didn't mean to bring you into this," Craig said, "but you're the only one I can count on up there."

"Don't count on me," Denniwitz said. "I don't give a shit about your snitch and I don't want to talk about work." Then he looked around the outdoor patio like he needed air and said, "Some memorial service."

Some guy.

When the bat phone gets a signal Craig dials Juan's cell, lets it ring once, hangs up. He starts the car and rolls down the windows because the AC is mostly noise—it needs coolant. He's been meaning to pick some up for a few weeks. He's been meaning to do a lot of things. Pretty soon, summer will make him regret his priorities.

He supposes he could head south, hope Juan calls on the way. But he's not too far from home. And he really could use a decent meal, a shower. A nap. Especially if he's got to spend another night at the Aragon.

He pulls a U-ey, turns east on Foster, north on Cicero. Cars whiz past him in the left lane; it seems like Craig is never that eager to get where he's going. He turns off at Forest Glen to cut through the neighborhood, though it'd take half the time if he kept to the main streets.

He crosses Peterson and continues on toward home, past the noncohesive mix of homes connected only by a sidewalk. Some of the houses here already display historical markers; others, while architecturally sound, are ugly and should have been knocked down soon after they were built. All of the places are large, stately; they boast, test property lines. Further up, the homes become more petite but no less sophisticated—until Craig's house, that is.

He slows to a stop when he reaches the Rellingers' house. The renovations have made the place appear double its size; by now it must be worth quadruple what they paid for it. The stacked-stone façade that runs along the bottom half of the first story looks like it fortifies the rest of the structure; helps it stand taller, tower over the surrounding homes. Craig's, which was built by the same developer some fifty years ago, sits next door, an ugly, undeveloped twin.

He parks at the curb. The sun has bid the sky good night, leaving a residual blue rendered black by the streetlights. The digital clock on his dash reads 6:58, so he shuts off the engine and decides to give himself a few minutes. Just two minutes, to hide out here.

Through the Rellingers' new front window, light flickers, probably from a candle. Craig can only imagine what goes on in there, in Meghan's sanctuary. She talks too much, sure, but what woman doesn't? At least she always has something nice to say.

From this angle, he can't see into his own front window, but he can guess what's going on inside. Leslie's trying to save the dinner his mother started; she's sneaking chili powder or salt or whatever into the bland side dishes, and making some kind of au jus for the overcooked meat. Mom will argue she's just doing it the way she's always done it, since 1942, and Leslie will say yes, fine, why don't you plate your Jell-O mold; Mom will do so while throwing herself a pity party. Then, with Craig's pending arrival, which Leslie can count on, she will begin the process of extracting Ivy from her room. She'll tell Ivy to set the table; she will say her father's on his way. Ivy will find the one reason why the task is impossible: she can't find matching napkins, or the silverware is dirty. Leslie will then look for napkins and clean forks while the vegetables become limp and the meat sits on the butcher block, as dry as the bones it began with. The only thing that will turn out as it should will be the Jell-O.

Craig sympathizes with his wife; he just doesn't understand how, inevitably, by the time he sits down to eat, he will have yet again become the problem.

At seven o'clock the Rellingers' yard lights come to life, spotlights on a masterpiece. Seconds later the yard's sprinklers are activated, click-click-clicking water onto the new, healthy green sod. His own anemic lawn cowers in the shadows. Craig rolls up his passenger window to avoid the spray and decides that's his cue.

He starts the car and turns into his driveway, the meek yellow porch light detecting movement and offering a dim hello. As he collects his things—jacket, wallet, paperwork, pills—his stomach growls.

As soon as he admits to himself that a home-cooked meal is never bad, the bat phone rings. Of course.

He throws his stuff on the passenger seat, gets back into the car and answers the phone. "Juan. I'm on my way."

"You can't come here, Mick," Juan answers. "Listen: the guys you saw? They were Fuxis, all right. Sent for protection. They worked me over, man: what happened, where I been."

"And you told them you were in jail, and that your girlfriend posted bail, right?"

"I told them."

"So what's the problem?"

"They been talking to Chinatown."

"The Triad?"

"Yes. They are very upset that the north side is unprotected. They've been making good money down south, and think maybe they lost a foothold up here. They think there's competition."

"And the competition hit Moy's."

"Says Chinatown. Fuxis say they have it under control. They think there's a rat in the pipes, and they're going to flush him out."

"Do you have a name?" The gearshift in reverse, Craig looks over his shoulder, backs down the drive.

"You're not going to like it."

"I don't like any of this."

"There's a Fuxi, they call him Silk—he's the nephew of one of the big men in the Triad. You met him yesterday. He was at the table."

"The one who cheated?"

"Probably."

"They think he's the rat?"

"No. He thinks you are."

Craig hits the brakes, coming to a dead stop in the middle of the street.

"But I was there during the raid. I took the hit too. What about Moy? Didn't he vouch for me?"

"Moy didn't say anything. Old man sat there like Hu Jintao himself came in and took his backbone."

"Fuck," Craig says, and then he says it again when he sees Grant Rellinger trekking through his thick sod in flip-flops, making a crisscross path to avoid the sprinklers. Craig hopes he's just getting the mail.

Juan says, "You know how a spider stuns a fly, waits for it to dummy up before he spins it into his web?"

"Yeah," Craig says.

"The Fuxis are pretty good at that."

"Shit, Juan. What the fuck is that supposed to mean?"

"I'm just saying: you're tangled up."

"I'm coming down there," Craig says, the car in drive.

"I wouldn't."

The brakes. "What am I supposed to do? If I don't show they'll think I'm hiding."

"I don't know, Mick."

"What's my way around this? To find the guys who hit Moy?"

"If I were you," Juan says, "I'd let Chinatown straighten it out. I heard they're coming for a sit-down. Tomorrow afternoon."

"No shit?" The car in park.

Craig offers a neighborly wave to Grant when he opens his mailbox. "Chinatown," he says to Juan. "It's about fucking time."

"If you're smart, you'll stay away from Moy's until tomorrow, then play dumb and show up, try to get in on a game."

"For once, Juan, I think you're right. How about you meet me at Our Lady of Lourdes tomorrow, noon." The Catholic church is their Uptown safe house. Not too many Fuxis praying to Jesus.

"I'll be there," Juan says, "but after this I'm going as far away from the web as I can get." He hangs up.

Sitting in his car in the middle of the street, Craig can't believe it: Mr. Moy's little den, its mama spider–gang, and now the fucking grand pooh-bahs in Chinatown: the Triad. And here he was beginning to think he wouldn't get much farther than the Pai Gow table. He considers dialing Suwanski, to let him know what's up, but there's no way he'll get into the game without some considerable cash, and there's also no way Suwanski will give it to him. Craig tosses the phone on the seat, wishing there was one person in the world he could talk to.

Too bad it isn't Grant Rellinger, who's been standing outside looking through his mail in the dark. What's he stalling for? Probably that damn security system.

Craig rolls down the passenger window. "Grant: what's up?"

"Hi, Craig," he says, coming over to the window like he'd been waiting for an invitation. "How are you?" Judging by his tone, Grant's talkative wife must've told him all about yesterday's fight.

"Bumps in the road," Craig says, "but everything's fine."

Grant pushes his square-framed glasses up the bridge of his nose and leans in the window. "Maybe it's none of our business," he says, "but your daughter had a little party this afternoon. We thought you should know."

For the first time today, Craig feels the hair on the back of his neck bristle. "How little?"

"A few cars. It probably isn't a big deal. It's just that the kids seemed . . ." Grant looks around the interior of the car like he'll find the right word, but apparently he doesn't. "Meghan says she's seen one of the boys around lately—he was here yesterday, in fact, with Leslie."

"With Leslie," Craig repeats.

"To tell you the truth I didn't want to say anything. It's Meghan who's concerned." Grant looks back toward his house, straightens the collar of his golf shirt.

"My mother is here," Craig says, an objection.

"No offense," Grant says, "but if your mother is babysitting, she should be fired."

Anger clouds Craig's thinking; this time he doesn't feel like keeping it in check. "Thanks for the tip," he says, and puts the car in drive; the tires squeal before they grab the pavement and leave Grant behind with his mail and his opinion and a taste of burnt rubber.

The car bottoms out at the curb when Craig turns into his driveway. He parks, leaves all his shit on the passenger seat, and goes inside to sit down to another overcooked dinner, and to once again become the problem.

15

"Craig, more Jell-O salad?" Mona asks.

"I'm just about stuffed, Mom."

As he should be, Leslie thinks: Craig's been fork-to-mouth since he sat down at the table and loaded his plate. Twice. Leslie supposes there's no room service at his hotel.

She watches him chew a thick chunk of the pork roast that Mona killed with caraway seeds and a 450-degree oven. He drinks his ice water in gulps, and with some of the pork reserved in his cheek, resumes chewing. Whatever compassion she felt for him at the funeral is mired in disgust. He makes her want to stick her fork in her own eye.

Leslie knows her expression is telling, because every time Craig looks up from his plate, he grips his knife a little tighter. And every time he looks at her, she finds it more impossible to eat. She doesn't know which of his problems is her fault this time, but after his behavior at Rudy's funeral, she's finished. She folds her napkin, and then her arms, and sits back.

"I just don't know what happened to the au gratin," Mona says. "I guess I'll never get used to your kitchen, Leslie."

To which Craig says, "I like the au gratin."

To which Leslie says, "I like my kitchen." She hates the way Craig sits there, slob-king of the dining room, the hair left around his head a cheap crown; and worse, his family before him, competing like jesters.

To Leslie's right, Ivy pushes an unwanted helping of flaccid French-cut green beans around her plate. For most of the meal, she'd been game to answer Leslie's soft-lobbed questions about her day at school and her afternoon at work, albeit with the grace of a pissed-off teenager. She played along brilliantly, as if they had scripted it, until Leslie ran out of unspecific inquiry.

Leslie is thankful her daughter decided to cooperate. When she'd arrived home from the funeral, the first thing she did was corner the girl to find out if she knew anything about her father's snitch. After a covert discussion about it in the linen closet, Leslie was relieved when Ivy claimed she didn't remember meeting a Julio or a Juan or any other Mexican at the rave. Leslie decided the snitch's presence must have been a terrible coincidence. Ivy, on the other hand, had just finished reading *1984* in English class, and so perceived absolute tyranny. She found the mere possibility of having run into Craig's snitch a violation of her freedom, and believed her father must have had her followed. Leslie explained they'd both be in trouble if Craig had gone to such lengths; she also warned the girl what kind of trouble she'd be in if she called him Big Brother at the dinner table.

Now, Leslie hopes Craig finds the girl's behavior average, however impressive it's truly been. Ivy and her mother are in this together, and almost through.

Ivy pushes her plate aside. "May I be excused?"

Leslie feels the first signs of relief but then Ivy says—

"The movie starts at nine."

And at once their delicate show is cancelled, due to creative differences.

Leslie could reach over and smack the girl. There had been no discussion of a movie while they were in the linen closet; there had been no indication given that she was allowed to go anywhere yet. And she knew it, the little snit.

She also knew how to use the situation to her advantage. If Leslie tries to prevent the girl from going, Craig will want to know why, and Leslie's not about to start that battle. Ivy just advanced on her supposed ally, and Leslie has to concede.

"Help me clear the table first," she says, hoping Ivy intends to follow her into the kitchen and explain herself.

Ivy pushes away from the table but Craig says, "You're not going to any movie."

"What?" She looks at her mother like she's been thrust onto the witness stand without counsel; the paranoia in her voice could convict her.

Craig throws his napkin on the table. "I said: you're not going anywhere. I'm still eating. Sit down."

"Unreal," Ivy says, and sits.

Mona nods at her son. "It's nice to have a family dinner."

Tyranny, Leslie thinks: her daughter is right. "Let her go to the movies, Craig. It's Friday night."

"I know it's Friday night," he says like she's an idiot. "Ivy, pass the Jell-O."

The green stuff wobbles and slips around the dish like it's nervous in the girl's hands. Craig spoons a helping onto his plate. Then he reaches out to Mona, squeezing her vein-marbled hand, and says, "This is delicious, Mom."

"Lime and pineapple: your favorite."

"How was your afternoon?"

"Oh fine, honey," Mona says, ready to shine in the spotlight. "I spent most of the day in the kitchen."

"Thanks, Mom, there's nothing like a home-cooked meal."

It's all suddenly sweet enough to make Leslie gag. She knows Craig is either working his way to a point or proving one. She hates him for making them sit here.

"I'm happy to cook," Mona says, "though this wasn't my best effort."

"Everything tastes great." Craig spears a canned pineapple ring and bites it in half, his mouth puckering. He abruptly stops chewing to watch Ivy check the display on her cell phone, a litmus test with a clear result. He doesn't say anything; he doesn't have to. She puts the phone away.

"I had a late start," Mona goes on, of course: she's her favorite subject. "I wasn't feeling very well."

"I'm sorry to hear that," Craig says. "I wish one of the girls had been around to help you."

"Well," Mona says, "Ivy was here when I woke from my nap."

"Oh really." Craig is clearly not surprised. Is this what he's been getting at?

Ivy sinks in her seat. "I got off work early," the girl says, her gaze low, a liar's: she hadn't mentioned anything about it when Leslie asked her over dinner, and Mona sat there, on the lie, until just now. Conniving bitch.

"I'd already dressed the roast and peeled the potatoes," Mona says, "and she said she had homework to finish."

"Homework," Craig says. "On Friday night."

"I think everything turned out okay," Mona tells whoever's listening. "Except the au gratin."

"Ivy," Craig says, "you want to tell me what you were really doing this afternoon?"

"Don't treat your daughter like a suspect," Leslie cuts in.

"What a surprise," Craig says, "the mother of the year sticks up for her little angel."

Leslie sits back. "You are so mean."

"I just don't know how it ended up with this consistency," Mona says, dragging her fork over what's left of the potatoes.

Leslie sees that Ivy's face has flushed a striking pink against her black hair. The girl stares at her half-empty plate, her mother's hurt reflected in her eyes.

But she lied. To all of them. "Ivy," Leslie says, "you're excused."

"No she's not," Craig says.

"Ivy," Leslie says, "go to your room."

"She'll sit right there until I'm through," Craig says, a forkful of quivering Jell-O on its way to his dead-set mouth.

They all sit there, for a moment, listening to him chew, and swallow. Leslie studies the knife resting on the rim of her plate, its handle tarnished, blade dull after so many years of use. Still, she could probably kill her husband with it.

Mona says, "You want to play cards? I'll go get the deck." She gets up, leaving her plate, as usual, for someone else to bus.

"Talk about mother of the year," Leslie says.

"Let's play cribbage," Craig calls after his mother, all the while his eyes on Leslie.

"I didn't do anything wrong!" Ivy bursts out, tears from her eyes. No one stops her when she runs upstairs.

"Nice going," Leslie says to Craig. "Make everyone as miserable as you are."

He says, "Pass the potatoes."

16

Some months before a child is born, ridges develop on the skin of its fingers and thumbs. These ridges form a pattern so unique that at birth she can be identified apart from all others. Throughout life, she carries with her this tangible proof of self, right at her fingertips.

Unless the child becomes a criminal, she won't worry too much about the fact that her fingertips also carry a coating of perspiration and oil which, when in contact with any relatively smooth surface, becomes evidence: a human stamp.

And chances are, if the child turns out to be dumb enough to throw a party while her detective father attends a funeral, she wouldn't have bothered to get rid of all the evidence.

Craig waits until the rest of the family has gone to bed to retrieve his fingerprint kit from the garage. It's the only thing he took with him when he left a brief stint with the crime scene team some five years ago—an assignment he immediately hated, being the sort of cop who would rather go after Colonel Mustard than calculate the trajectory of the blood spatter caused by the lead pipe. Give him a living, breathing liar over a math problem any day: he's a guy who gets truth from talk.

Usually. Not tonight.

Yeah, he could have put the screws to Ivy, since Grant sold her out; he could have played hardball with Leslie, since she's apparently crawled into the girl's back pocket. But there are subjective problems with eyewitness accounts: there are inaccuracies. Biases. Assumptions. There are agendas.

There is nothing subjective about a fingerprint. Which means whoever Ivy had over this afternoon better hope he didn't touch anything.

In the front room, Craig shakes out the Zephyr brush until its bristles spread apart and fluff. He tests the brush on the coffee table, though he won't dust in here, since this is where his mother naps in the afternoons. She'd have been asleep in the recliner, head back, throat open; hearing aids in her lap, so she wouldn't hear herself snore. Ivy and her friends would have steered clear of the room, though they may have stopped to look in for a laugh. Asshole kids. If they're prints are in the system, they'll be sorry they set foot in this house.

Craig takes the kit into the living room, beginning his investigation as any father would: the room where the hard liquor is kept.

He sets up shop on the piano bench, laying out his materials on its slim cloth cushion. He creases a piece of paper and taps out a few dashes of black magnetic powder into the fold, dips the brush into the powder palette and starts with the living room light switch. He carefully brushes the plastic panel in quick, uniform strokes.

A partial print from just one finger may be all that's necessary to identify someone, but there are too many prints smudged and overlapped on the panel to make a decent distinction. Jemma, his CSI connection at the lab, owes him this favor, but she's been by the book since she got burned on a case over sloppy forensics. She matched a crook to a crime; the crook's attorney got him off on a single questionable point of comparison. Now she won't even run prints if she can't get them clean.

Craig called Jemma about this earlier, while Leslie did the dishes and his mom spent a good half hour in the john. Jemma was hesitant; maybe because he was whispering the whole time he was promising her it was no big deal—a side bet with his daughter, he said, a guaranteed win. Jemma acted like she'd heard it all before. Craig tried to keep it light, offered her a cut of the take. She said Craig would owe her, all right, for her discretion.

Craig spots a can of Coke on the end table by the loveseat. He can hear, very softly, its carbonation. Prints may put a person at a scene, but they don't prove when. The bubbles left in the can tell when it couldn't have been too long ago. The timing's just about perfect.

Craig holds the can by its base, brushes the top half. When he finds a latent print, he brushes in the direction of its ridges, to bring it out. Then he unrolls the cellophane tape, keeping it taut, careful not to get air bubbles underneath as he affixes the tape and gently rubs it over the can. He lifts the roll evenly away from the surface and applies the tape to an index card he labels "Coke." It's a good print.

Next, he checks the liquor cabinet. He never wanted to be the schnapps police, so he has always had an open-cabinet-door policy, in order to make a point of the honor system. The unspoken part of his policy, though, is that the honor system only works if you can monitor it, so he'd meticulously positioned the bottles, their labels at particular angles. As a secondary measure, he sealed tight the caps of the light-colored spirits—vodka, gin, and rum—and loosened all the others a quarter turn.

Last time he checked, there were no signs of interference. This time the bottle of Seagram's 7, which is eighty proof and should face eight o'clock, faces forward. Craig removes the bottle carefully, by its base, and holds it up to the light: there are prints all over the neck.

He dusts the bottle, lifts two near-perfect prints, and marks the card "Whiskey." Then he uncaps the bottle—which had been sealed tight, no quarter turn—and takes a drink: a toast to the fucked-up fact that he's spending a night on the lam from a Chinese gang dusting for prints in his own house.

Then he takes another swig, just to verify that the whiskey has been cut with water.

Does everyone think he's a fool?

He puts the bottle back in the cabinet. Alcohol has done nothing to dull his irritation thus far; watered-down whiskey intensifies it. He picks up the Zephyr brush, and like some artist crazed with inspiration, dusts the room top to bottom. Every wood, metal, glass, plastic, Formica, and tile surface gets worked over, except those already coated with an undisturbed layer of dust. Like the piano.

It figures: the untouched baby grand. Leslie had to have it. It had to be this one. And this one had to cost ten grand.

No, Craig had said; but this, but that, she'd said. Leslie had played before they were married, in college, but never since. She'd talked about it, sure—but she talked about doing all kinds of things with the money they had tied up in the house.

Craig knew her passion to play again was exaggerated, her promises to practice thinly veiled. But it was their fifteenth anniversary; she felt like she deserved it, and he felt like he owed her. So he refinanced.

Dummy.

Craig opens the keytop and decides that if he can't lift his wife's prints from the keys, he's selling the fucking thing.

The magnetic dust is like charcoal on the ivory. Smudged, unusable prints cover the keys in the middle octaves. He's a little disappointed; he was hoping for a reason to get rid of it. Ten grand—or five, or whatever it's worth now—would take the crunch off the bank account, especially since he's going to have to make another hefty withdrawal before he shows up at Mr. Moy's tomorrow.

He has to admit it's a little satisfying to imagine Leslie's conflicted reaction when she finally does sit down to play and discovers the leftover dust. If she has any sense, she'll wipe off the keys and pay a little more attention to her so-called passion.

Craig rolls the tape lengthwise over four high notes and comes away with a bunch of decent prints. When he's through, he marks the index card "Piano" and puts it with the others in a manila envelope. He puts the envelope in his briefcase, his briefcase by the door.

He cleans up with a cobweb brush, giving the room a quick once-over, the magnetic dust coming up easily. Then he sneaks into his bedroom, quiet as a burglar, and steals a change of clothes. He'll shower and shut-eye downstairs so he won't disturb Leslie. For now, he'll continue to tiptoe around her.

17

Aside from Mother's Day and Valentine's Day, roses are sold most steadily on Saturday mornings. Leslie hates working this shift; though the time flies, it's because she's suddenly inundated with managing men's apologies. From all over the city they call in orders hoping to "say it with flowers." She's decided this is because none of them know what else to say.

Some customers order the run-of-the-mill red dozen, apologies for last night; others send showy bouquets—as if the woman cares what the damn flowers look like. And then there are other men, the peculiar sort that make Leslie think people want to hurt each other more than they want to make up.

A half-hour ago, someone called in with a delivery for a red rose bouquet. He asked that the card read *I'm sorry for being an asshole but if I ever see you with him again you're dead.* After working here for so long, Leslie doesn't try to read into the personal messages people have no trouble giving over the phone, but when a guy can't keep the edge out of his voice and the name on the credit card is Two-time Malone, she kind of wonders if they should send out the delivery boy with a police escort.

The latest of this morning's orders, yet another dozen red roses, is on its way to a woman named Kim. The guy who called in the order asked Leslie to write *For Kim: Every Rose Has Its Thorn* on the card. She isn't sure if it's supposed to be funny or poetic or if Kim's suitor is admittedly the thorn, but now Leslie can't get the damn song out of her head.

Leslie slips Kim's card into its clip, adds the order to the outbox, and debates whether she should stay up front and pretend to be busy or suck it up and go help Raylene. She locks the register and heads to the back room, wishing her conscience wasn't always her guide.

"Phone finally quit ringing," Leslie tells Raylene.

"Good," she says from somewhere behind an amassment of Pepto-pink helium balloons. "Help."

Leslie makes her way through the balloons and finds Raylene busy as always, simultaneously filling balloons at the helium tank and tying pink ribbon to foil weights.

"Will you double-clip these by six?" she asks Leslie with ribbon between her lips. "We're in trouble: this order should already be on its way to the Radisson."

One of the reasons Leslie doesn't like working with Raylene is because she acts like every task is embarrassingly behind schedule. Another reason is that Raylene is the one who makes the schedule.

Leslie begins to gather the balloons by the half dozen. She wishes there was something she could say that wouldn't sound like a blatant attempt to make conversation. For all their similarities—both hit forty this year, both live with teens and in-laws and potential divorces— Leslie can't think of a single thing they truly have in common. Maybe it's because Raylene's the sort of woman whose optimism is as conspicuously fake as her capped teeth. She sees the bright side, sure, but she's never on it.

The intermittent whoosh of helium from the tank makes the silence in between all the more prominent, and when Leslie can't stand it anymore, she asks, "Do you think the bride is going to regret all of this pink?"

Raylene slips a balloon onto the nozzle. "Bubblegum is the 'in' color this spring."

"Better she regrets the color than the man, I guess."

"I like the color. It pops."

Leslie finds the pun as asinine as any other. Thankfully, it isn't in her job description to pretend Raylene is clever. She tends to her task, deciding the silence isn't so bad.

"I'm nearly finished," Raylene announces. "Will you call Tanner? I don't know what takes him so long."

Of course she fails to factor in the traffic she complained about this morning that made her late. Oh, the gaps in a blameless mind.

Thinking of an early lunch, and the excellent idea of getting out of there for a little while, Leslie says, "I'll take these to Lincolnwood if you'd like."

"Are you kidding? In your little car?"

"I've been known to transport a record number of teenagers."

"Find Tanner. It's what he's paid for."

"Right," Leslie says, marveling at what two bucks more an hour and a manager's tag can do to a person's attitude. Leslie puts the balloon clips on the workbench and heads for the front, glad to be dismissed.

"I'm ten minutes away," Tanner says when he answers his cell.

"It's not me who wants to know, T."

"Tell Raylene to suck air."

"I'd love to."

"I'll be there when I get there," the kid says.

"Works for me."

The clock just shy of noon, Leslie roots through a stack of mail and finds a *Florist's Review* magazine. As she flips through it, her attention is distracted, not that a feature about pod-covered topiaries would mesmerize anyone. What's bothering her is the fact that she has better rapport with a goofy teenager than with any of her peers. Actually, she is more bothered by the fact that she thinks her peers are a bunch of insufferable jerks.

She idly hums *Ev-ry rose has its tho-o-o-orn* as she skims over something about hydroponic home accents. An indoor garden might be good for the house. Maybe she should focus on remodeling again. If Craig is having an affair, she'll take the house in the divorce and use the alimony to remodel. By the time it's official she'll have turned the place around completely. She'll put in skylights, yes—and a window box in the kitchen to grow herbs. Lavender plants in the bathrooms; sea salts and candles. And new artwork on the walls. Something more ethereal and modern. Everything new.

Yes: she will take all things maritime out to the yard and burn them. Out with the ships, the dolphins, anything navy blue. She will paint the walls in all kinds of colors—one, in the dining room, the richest red. She will sell the TV and listen to music. And she will not have to clean up after anyone or wonder where they are; it will be her house, her time: she will take baths, and play the piano. She will plan to travel.

Hydroponics, yes: everything in her house will be lush with life instead of worn, toward death. And everything will be absolutely fine.

She closes the magazine, the rock ballad still humming in her head: *Ev-ry rose has its . . .*

Niko?

Out the shop's window, a metallic black sports sedan that looks exactly like his crawls toward the parking lot from the alley. Leslie's heart revs. The sedan slips into the parking spot in front of hers; nobody gets out.

She combs her fingers through the tangled hair at the nape of her neck and opens the magazine again, but she only looks at the words, so she decides she should busy herself. She gets up, taking the mister from behind the cooler and giving the succulent plants in the front window an extra drink.

Until Niko gets out of the car. When she sees him, she ducks behind an FTD poster.

What is he doing? Maybe he's just here for lunch—next door, East of Edens is popular for its gyros. And there are additional stores on the other side of the building—a cellular store, a Realtor, an attorney. A nail salon.

What is *she* doing? It's none of her business why he's in the parking lot. She should get back to work. Pretend not to see him. Maybe reorganize the greeting cards or wipe down all the vases they haven't sold that are collecting dust.

She should not get this wound up about her daughter's boyfriend.

She peeks around the poster as a gray pickup truck rolls into the lot from Devon and continues on into the alley, but Niko doesn't seem to notice the truck—or Leslie—as he leans on the sedan's doorframe, mindlessly toying with the hands-free cord that runs from his earpiece to his pocket, saying little to whoever's on the other end of the line. He must not think anyone is watching. Or he doesn't care.

Leslie can't stand it. She stows the mister and gets her purse. "Raylene," she calls over her shoulder, "I'm going to lunch."

Outside, Leslie makes like she's headed for her car, and also like she's looking through her purse for the keys that are right there in her hand. When it would seem impossible for her not to notice Niko, let alone trip over him, she looks up and says, "Niko?"

The smile that finds his face upon seeing her could make her lose direction. He closes his car door, says "*Adio*" to his phone conversation, and removes his earpiece so it hangs from where it's clipped to his collar. "*Herete*," he says to Leslie, plants his hands on her arms, kisses her on both cheeks. She clutches her purse and closes her eyes and hopes the friendly hello will linger. She loves his cologne.

"What's the occasion this time?" she asks, her voice too soft for a parking lot, for a boy.

"No occasion," he says like a disclaimer.

Leslie steps back, afraid her question seemed a come-on. She palms her keys, shoulders her purse, explains: "I thought, you know, your mom loved the roses, maybe she sent you for more . . ."

"I don't need flowers," he says.

"Then this is a funny place to park." She shifts on her feet and wonders if her own smile is absurd.

"I came to talk to you," he says. "Do you have a minute?"

"I have sixty of them, but I was planning to get some lunch."

Niko spins his keys around his finger. "How about Psistaria?"

"We can't get in and out of there in less than an hour."

"My cousin works there; he'll hook us up." Niko walks around to his passenger door and keys the lock like the matter is decided.

Leslie glances back at the flower shop, and then at her watch, wondering if her reluctance is a sure sign she thinks there's more to this than lunch.

Niko opens the car door. "Come on, Leslie. *Pinao*," he says, a hand to his empty stomach.

"I'm hungry too," she says, and gets into his car. Her conscience would starve her.

18

Craig isn't a very religious guy, but he figures it doesn't hurt to say a little prayer while he's waiting for Juan to show up at Our Lady of Lourdes. He's going to need all the help he can get this afternoon.

He sits in the very last pew and leafs through the Bible, its pages thin as carbon copies. The church is empty except for a Spanish woman who is changing the hymn numbers on a scroll to the left of the pulpit to match those she's already updated on the right of the lectern. Her clothes are nice, but ill-fitted, like hand-me-downs or donations from North Shore's Goodwill; whoever wore them before probably wore them once and she'll probably wear them for years. The woman works quietly, so as not to disturb the space while it waits for its congregation.

"Craig, so good to see a spirited soul this morning." Father Ferris appears from behind, like maybe he'd been in the confessional.

"Father," Craig says, standing up, a handshake. "Did you come over here to talk me into the confession box? I know I look like *h-e-double-hockey-sticks*, but I'm on a case."

"I know that, Craig. Of course I know that. Please, sit."

Craig resumes his position and the priest joins him, and he doesn't keep his distance. Craig smells the old man's musty breath when he says, "I've got my own case to make. Have you heard about the stained-glass endowment? I'm hoping I can bend your ear."

"I'm not the one with any money, Father. You should be hitting up one of the commanders. Or the super."

"Think of this much like the way a member of this parish would come to me in order to have a dialogue with God."

"I get it, Father," Craig says, breathing through his mouth to avoid the old man's halitosis. "Let's hear your pitch."

The priest leans back, looks around the church like he's taking it in for the first time. "In 1929," he says, his voice grand, "they widened Ashland Avenue. The church was in danger of being torn down. The community was so vested in its place of worship, they vowed to save it themselves. They split the church in half, literally, so they could move it to this side of the street. And when they put it back together, they had to add a thirty-foot extension just to accommodate the burgeoning parish.

"Of course this was back in 'twenty-nine, back when people believed in serving God," he says, the sermon working its way in. "Today, people won't even pay for a couple of windows."

Craig shifts his weight against the hard wood seat. "I hate to tell you, Father, but nicer windows don't change the view."

The old man is silent for some time; every feature on his face so patient, blinking might be optional. Eventually, he says, "I believe that the congregation suffers now because of discordance among community strongholds."

Craig wants to say the real community strongholds around here—the gangs and the so-called merchant associations—are getting along just fine, like bosom buddies, but the church is no place to argue, so instead he says, "You can count on me. I'll talk to my superiors."

"Thank you; thank you, my son. I'll send you the fund's paperwork." He gets up and takes Craig's hand, his steady grip another lesson. "Money," he says, "is not what we sacrifice."

Craig nods, mum, since the thousand dollars he withdrew from the bank just this morning that will most likely wind up in Moy's pocket feels very much like a sacrifice. He pulls his hand away, feels like he should hide it.

"Bless you," the priest says, crossing Craig and then himself.

As Father Ferris hobbles off to the vestibule to prepare for his next sermon, Craig tells himself the lingering pang of guilt is only Catholic; if there is such a thing as divine intervention, he hopes God doesn't want him to give it all up for a window.

The Spanish woman makes her way through the nave now, her hand a support to her lower back as if she's pregnant, or has been too many times. She checks each row of pews and resets the kneelers that had been left down, the hollow sound of weight to wood echoing through the chamber. Watching her, Craig wonders what she considers sacrifice.

A CTA bus strains to a stop outside the church, and Craig hopes Juan is deboarding. He shifts again, his sitting bones stiff, and puts the Bible away, thinking what this place really needs are some cushioned seats.

Right on his own schedule, an hour late, Juan comes into the church. He slips into the pew next to Craig and he smells like he fell off an animal control truck.

"What is that, eau de raccoon?" Craig asks.

"It's cologne. Called Lucky You."

"Lucky who, dogs in heat?"

"It's better than smelling like pig."

"Your words cut deep, kid." Craig lays his briefcase flat and unlocks it, but he leaves it closed while the Spanish woman checks the nearby aisles. He sits back and waits, and he notices Juan's cologne isn't the only thing that seems a bit much: his hair is slicked, and his outfit is as upscale as anything he's ever worn—some high-collared silk suit that should make him look like he walked out of a kung-fu flick. Maybe a young lady might think he looks good, but on that skinny frame, Craig thinks Juan looks like he's wearing pajamas.

And, the kid seems antsy. Craig decides there's something going on in that angular head, and he's probably going to have to bully it out.

Once the Spanish woman moves along, Craig says, "You have trouble finding the place?"

Juan's stiff upper lip slants, a scowl. "I wasn't going to come at all."

"What's the matter, you couldn't find a belt to match that pout?"

"I just came to tell you I'm out," Juan says. He rubs the points at his temples, and Craig is surprised not to have noticed the pinky nail on Juan's left hand sooner. He's let it grow long enough to meet the nail bed of the finger next to it. Some guys do this for style, others for drugs. But Juan?

"What's with the pinky?" Craig asks. "You run out of Q-tips?"

Juan doesn't answer, just shakes his head, his eyes set on Christ at the altar like the fixed parts of a pendulum.

"I need you at Moy's, Juan. I need you in there to translate."

"Then send me in alone."

"I did that yesterday. See how that worked out?"

"They think you're the rat," he says. "If they see me with you, they'll think I'm in on your game. They'll come after me."

"You want to go alone, you wear a wire."

Juan looks at him sideways. "Hell no."

Craig nods to the altar. "A little respect?"

"You make me wear a wire and God better get used to it, because I'll be dead for sure."

Craig leans forward, his hands clasped together on the back of the pew in front of him. "You think I want it this way? You think I want you to risk a wire while I stay behind and listen to a bunch of Chinese mishmash, hoping to hell you make it back out of there so you can translate?"

"You should wait until this blows over. Let them find the rat, and then go back in."

"You said they think it's me, Juan. If I continue to hide, they're only going to come looking. I have to go. Today." Craig gets his cell phone from his pocket. "And if you aren't coming with me, you're going to stay behind and listen. I'll dial you in."

Juan's mouth vees, a smile. "They won't let you in there with that. If they don't take it from you, they'll make sure you don't take it home in one piece."

Craig hands Juan the phone. "So I'll give it to them," he says. Then he opens his briefcase and takes out another phone. "I'll just have this one in my coat pocket dialed to you."

Juan's vee disappears. "Forget it. What if they find it? They'll look at the call log. They'll trace it back to me."

Craig takes another phone from the case and switches it with the one he gave Juan. "No they won't, because you'll use this."

"What is this, another bat phone?"

"These are all burners. Throwaways. I got them at the gas station."

Juan opens the phone and turns it around in his hand. "Doesn't matter: they find yours, they'll kill you."

"I'll take my chances." Craig dumps the other phones in his case and the two of them sit quiet for a while, Craig wondering how many more chances he'll get.

As the early afternoon sun comes around the building it strikes a pane of stained glass that throws a square of light on Craig's pants, and he wonders how many things have to be just so for that to happen.

"Look, Juan. I've got a thousand bucks that says I'm in it to play. I'm going to go in there and show them I'm there for the dough. And

I'm going to do this, I'm going to risk it, because this is our window. People are dying because of these guys, and we're going to have all of them in one place. The Kuang Tian, the Fuxis, the Triad—we're not talking Pai Gow anymore. We're playing a whole new game." He notes Juan's fidgety hands, his own. "You can help me get these guys. All I'm asking you to do is listen."

Juan flips the phone shut. "Fuck the Fuxis."

19

Halfway through Leslie's glass of Boutari Retsina, her grasp on time has become fuzzy. The wine has done one hell of a job on her senses, making the food deliciously irrelevant, the conversation all the more satiating.

Not that she could say for sure what they've been talking about. Everything, nothing. The weather. Whatever; the subtext is the tease. The spaces between their words. The way they catch each other looking.

She savors one last bite of sea bass, the rich fish that Niko's cousin Ammon filleted for them at the table. They were served a veritable feast: broiled octopus, lamb chops, calamari stuffed with spinach; lima beans, taramosalata, tzatziki. Niko ate quickly, and a good amount; still, most of the plates are barely touched.

Niko takes a sip from his coffee, his hand a giant's around the white demitasse cup. A thick layer of froth caps his upper lip and he grins, unbothered by it. Leslie feels invited to watch when he captures the foam with his bottom lip, his tongue.

He sighs, hinges an elbow on the back of his seat. "Did you get enough to eat?"

"If these were ancient times I'd ask where to purge," she says. "I ate too much."

"I don't think you need to worry about it."

Leslie knows she should steer clear of the compliment, though she would hate to argue why. She reaches for her wineglass. She's resisted the urge to ask Niko about his agenda, and he hasn't mentioned it. Anticipation is in the subtext, too, and on Leslie's mind.

His cell phone vibrates when he takes it from his pocket, his attention stolen for the first time since they sat. He checks the display and says, "Excuse me, would you?"

As he gets up, Leslie puts her wineglass back on the table, the world's intrusion a damper. Next to her, a man with an old-world face who looks like he's worked here all the restaurant's thirty-five years takes a plate of chicken from a woman who doesn't seem likely to enjoy anything. Leslie knows how the woman feels, but she doesn't feel it now.

The blue and ocher walls make the spacious room feel cozy, but within them, busyness abounds. A host seats a party of nine, a high chair and the wine list and water requested before the last person reaches the table. The waiters and other patrons zip from here to there doing whatever it is they do; everyone in a hurry to what's next.

But Niko, he had carved out this little piece of time, this here and now, just for Leslie. Why rush when right now is good enough?

Leslie gazes at the mural on the far wall, wistful, like it's a picture window; if only they were truly on Crete or Karpathos, the Aegean Sea against the shore outside. She's only seen such a view in books or paintings. Is this as close as she'll ever be? Is this good enough?

"Sorry," Niko says from behind her, his voice low, in her ear. She bends to the sound of his voice as he comes around the table. "That was the confirmation for my audition Monday. Four p.m. Two selections of my own with contrasting styles, sight reading, and improvisation." He smiles. "Now I know what you mean about throwing up."

"I'm absolutely certain you'll nail it," Leslie says, though her tone skews the comment toward inappropriate. She nurses her wine.

"We're in trouble," Niko says, looking at his watch. "It's ten after one."

"Another glass of this and I would have been ready to blow off the afternoon."

"And I wondered where Ivy gets her impulse."

Mention of the girl's name puts Leslie in her place which is not on some faraway fantasy island but is here, at a chophouse on Touhy Avenue, with her daughter's boyfriend. She is skipping work to spend time with a man half her age on the *pretext* of some conversation they aren't having. What the hell is she thinking? "You're right," she says, "we're in trouble. Let's go."

Niko flags Ammon and says, "*To logariasmo,*" requesting the bill. Ammon, who bares an older, unkind resemblance to Niko, throws a blue towel over his shoulder and shuffles away.

Niko watches his cousin tally the bill at the server's stand. He says, "Would you believe he learned English from the menu? He came to visit my aunt—my mother's sister—about six years ago. He never left."

Leslie nods, half-listening as he goes on about Ammon, the least of her interests. She finishes her wine, the last swallow over her tongue, slipping into her system. Its effects will soon wear off; she will feel sullen, she will think about Niko. But she will not feel naughty. She will feel bad.

". . . says he's saving to return to Korinthos—"

"You know," she interrupts, "I never asked where you live. It's probably something I should know," her tone heavy when she adds, "if you're dating Ivy."

"Berwyn Avenue," he says, no weight to it. "Out toward Cumberland. My mother thinks it's safer out there, don't ask me why—"

"Niko," she cuts him off again, "we're leaving and you still haven't told me what it is you wanted to talk about."

He gets out his wallet, discreetly checks its contents, takes five twenties. "We're having a good time, aren't we?" He folds the bills once, holds them between two fingers, waits for Ammon.

"Yes—sure."

"I don't want to ruin it."

He gives Ammon the cash, says, "*Efharisto.*"

"Yes, thank you, Ammon." Leslie gets up to exchange handshakes and kisses and fond wishes, the good-bye rituals that always seem a pleasure, even with a stranger, or a waiter.

But on the way out, as they pass the woman who had been so disappointed with her lunch, Leslie knows how she feels.

The sunroof is open and Niko's doing seventy-five on the Edens, making a quick trip back to the flower shop. Leslie closes her eyes, feels the sun on her face, and has nothing to say. She can't remember where she heard the phrase *the heart wants what it wants*, but whoever said it must have been miserable.

Niko hasn't said anything, either; maybe he realized what a mistake this was, too.

He turns into the parking lot and pulls into the space behind Leslie's, her car blocking his from the shop's direct view.

"Okay," he says, like an ellipsis follows.

"Ruin it," Leslie says.

"What?"

"You didn't come up here to buy me lunch and I didn't join you because I had a taste for souvlakis. Just ruin it. Tell me why you came."

Niko looks out the driver's side window. "I'm afraid of what you'll say."

Leslie shrinks in the bucket seat. Is it the subtext? Is he going to discuss it right here in the parking lot?

"I just didn't think it would go this far."

No, Leslie thinks: this is all wrong—"Forget it," she says. "I don't want to know."

"Please, Leslie. Listen: the other night. The ecstasy. It was my brother's."

Now Leslie is afraid of what she'll say. She thought this was more than lunch, and it's nothing but an apology. Had she been the one with the agenda?

Niko shuts off the engine, releasing the door locks, and she considers an escape.

"I was afraid he'd get caught," Niko says. "Ivy offered to hide the drugs and I let her. I never meant for her to get in trouble."

"She didn't get in trouble, Niko, because we're both covering for her." Leslie eyes the door handle. She doesn't want to talk about her daughter; she wants out.

"It's my fault," Niko says. "I'm supposed to be looking out for Rios and I'm just letting him get away clean. And it's getting worse; I think he's dealing again. I need help, Leslie. I need you to tell me what to do."

His appeal keeps her there, maybe because she can't remember the last time someone asked her for advice. She wishes she had some. "It sounds to me like your brother will see the judge again before too long. You keep hanging on and you're only going to be called to testify."

"He can't go back to jail."

"You can't serve his time."

"We're family. I have to do what I can."

"Have you spoken to your parents?"

"My mother thinks my brother is poison. I'm supposed to be the antidote. You know how the old Greeks are; she thinks there's an answer for everything in the Holy Scripture. There's no section on drug dealing. I looked."

Leslie appreciates his humor; she can't be angry with him for her own assumptions. She offers a tender laugh, to let him know this is okay. She wishes this were okay.

"My father thinks God is using Rios to teach the family a lesson," Niko says. "Testing our faith. And there's no answer key."

"But there is the truth."

"That's worse."

"It does seem problematic." Leslie looks up through the sunroof, at the wisps of clouds lost in an otherwise cloudless sky. She thinks of all the truths she'll never tell, including this impossible crush. "I have to go," she says, because of it.

Niko starts the car's engine, the automatic locks inadvertently trapping Leslie. He takes her hand, his arm at an awkward angle over the center console. "Thank you for speaking to me like an adult."

"Thank you for lunch," she says, her hand tense in his, ready to draw away. But then he leans over, their hands an anchor, and pulls her close to kiss her on the cheek, a good-bye that is slow and tender and definitely a pleasure, smelling breath-mint sweet, though she never saw him put one in his mouth. When he moves around to kiss her other cheek, their lips brush; her mouth opens, an objection, but she doesn't stop him; not when he kisses her again, this time on her other cheek, his lips so warm. "*Yassou*, Leslie," he whispers, but she does not want to say good-bye, and he doesn't back away, so they are suspended there: her move.

"Do you love my daughter?" she whispers, because it's too late to be appropriate, and she's had enough with the subtext.

He lets go of her hand and sits back, says, "You don't have time for that conversation." He fingers a door switch, releases the locks.

"Give me the short answer."

"The truth?" He shifts in his seat and adjusts his rearview mirror and for the first time seems shy, but then he turns to her and says, "I think I'm interested in someone else."

Leslie doesn't know what to say to that.

"It's nothing against Ivy," he says. "I like her. But if I'm going to play, I want to be keyed in, whether I'm sitting at the piano or in a parking lot."

"I should go." She reaches for the door handle.

"Are you sorry you asked?"

"No. I think I already knew the answer. *Yassou.*"

Leslie gets out of the car and heads toward the shop; before she gets too far he drives up beside her, window down, and says, "The Green Mill. Tonight, midnight. Come see me play."

"I don't think my family would let me get away with a trip into the city in the middle of the night."

"So sneak out. Ivy did."

"Not a chance," she says, defying her smile.

He waits there a moment, like maybe she'll change her mind; he hits the gas a split second before she does. And as he drives away, she walks into the flower shop, still high on the wine, and maybe the fact that she's keyed in.

20

No one's outside Mr. Moy's back door. No problem: Craig has a plan.

He starts his act in the parking lot, pacing back and forth, phone to his ear, dishing out an improvised verbal assault.

"I told you, darlin', from the day we met: what's mine is mine." He turns on his heel, seemingly oblivious, though he is completely aware that it is stupid to walk into a spider's den if he can draw one or two out.

"I don't see you hauling your ass out of bed to collect a paycheck." As far as anyone at Moy's knows, Mickey's a single guy. Works at a machine shop. Lives for lady luck. Juan told Moy he met Mickey at the Grand Victoria riverboat out in Elgin. Said he was a real good loser. Said he might spend a few bucks on gas and lotto tickets at the Oasis on the drive into the city, but would be sure to pony up at the Pai Gow table.

Craig turns again; this time he winds up like he's going to pitch the cell phone at the bricks in front of him. Instead, he brings it to his face like a walkie-talkie and yells: "You were standing behind me bitching about the tight slots and your watered-down drink! I didn't win a goddamned dime because you were there!"

Craig sees movement at Mr. Moy's door; this outburst must be effective. He turns his back and puts the phone to his ear, pretends he's wrapped up in Darlin's response. He's the only one who knows she's giving him the silent treatment; she always does. Sometimes he thinks he could use a real woman like this.

"You've got no sense arguing with me," he says. "I've got the cash and you've got a date with your suitcase." He pivots, says, "Pack your shit and—" and stops.

The little tatted Fuxi who manned the door last time is standing on the landing flanked by two of the biggest Chinese men Craig has ever seen. They watch him with uncurious faces, like insects.

Craig claps the phone shut. "Girlfriend," he explains. "Ex-girlfriend."

The doorman nods to the Fuxi on his left—the one with webbed sleeves tattooed on his arms to his wrists—and the guy comes down the steps, positioning himself behind Craig.

"Look, I didn't mean to make a scene," he says, the phone loose in his hand, almost an offer. It's okay if they take it away; it's not okay if he gives them a reason to search him and they find the one in his boot, the burner holstered where he usually keeps his Walther .380.

The other big man moves to the steps and remains on the landing, looking down at Craig like unswept dirt. He has no visible Fuxi ink, but the Glock in his forty-two-inch waistband paints enough of a picture.

"Something wrong?" Craig asks.

"Silk wants to see you," the doorman says.

"Who the fuck is Silk? I'm here for the game."

"Then let's play," the doorman says, baring sharp teeth.

And then Craig feels a hand around the back of his neck: strong fingers unmerciful at his carotid arteries. He goes down quick.

"Mickey, wake up."

Craig opens his eyes and he's at Mr. Moy's table, but there's no game, no cards, and no Moy.

He tries to turn around, see behind him, but the same hand that knocked him out now rests on his shoulder. This time the fingers find a trigger point that governs his current position and steals the feeling from his right arm. Craig involuntarily complies.

The one they call Silk steps into view and puts a mason jar on the table. Inside, dozens of black spiders tangle and crawl over one another to be the first out of there, given the opportunity.

Silk says, "They only bite when they become trapped."

"So let them go." Craig is not afraid of spiders, but he is terrified he's been made. "What is this about? Where's Mr. Moy?"

Silk sits across from Craig, in Moy's chair. He folds his slender hands on the table, his skin jaundiced by the weak overhead lamp. "Mr. Moy is in the kitchen," he says, "waiting to try a recipe for Irish fried rice."

"Listen, kid, I came here to play cards, not to be pushed around by some asshole with a bug collection."

Silk leans in, his eyes set deep in their sockets, shadowed under the light. "Tse Jin Yuan, he is your friend."

"Yeah, so what?"

"When we asked who he suspected to be an unfaithful player, your friend pointed to you."

"He must not have had the pleasure to play with you."

Silk unfolds his hands and points his index fingers over Craig's shoulders. Reactive, Craig reaches for the invisible shoulder holster where his gun isn't, but the webbed arm that slams into his chest like a human seatbelt stops him. When he tries to escape the restraint, a trigger point humbles him again: one finger dug into his hip socket, and his muscles are in spasm to his toes.

Silk nods. "Venom: check him."

The second big Fuxi comes up on Craig's left.

"Your name is Venom?" Craig asks. "I'm sensing a theme."

Venom doesn't bother to protect his Glock as he goes through Craig's shirt and pants pockets; Craig is effectively bound, words his only weapon. Not that they've worked so far.

"Come on, guys: I lose my money loyally here. What's with the shakedown?"

Venom puts Craig's wallet, keys, and Excedrin on the felt. "He's clean."

Silk asks, "Are you clean, Mickey, or are you hiding something?"

"I don't know what the fuck you're talking about. I didn't cheat and I know Juan wouldn't say so."

Silk cracks a gold-toothed smile. "Let's see what the widows say."

Venom takes the mason jar from the table and unscrews the lid. The big trigger-point-happy Fuxi releases his front restraint at the same time he wedges a finger between Craig's shoulder blades, forcing him to puff his chest and creating an opening for Venom, who pulls Craig's shirt collar forward and turns the jar upside down, releasing the spiders.

"Jesus fuck!"

The Fuxis clear out of the way as Craig stands up, the spiders trapped in his shirt, quick and everywhere and—"Fuck!"—biting, and Craig rips off his shirt, brushing those who didn't latch on to it from the hair on his chest, shaking them out of the hair on his head; at his waistline—

"Fuck!"—another one bites, trapped there, having tried to escape into the dark recesses of his pants; he shuts his mouth, eyes when he feels one skitter over his face, another at his neck. He thrashes about the room stepping on his accidental assailants.

He knocks into the den wall and with nowhere else to go, kicks and throws fists, shaking the spiders from his pants, the hair on his arms.

When Craig is finally rid of the spiders, or thinks he is, he opens his eyes, and realizes the Fuxis are laughing. To them, this has been amusing. A juvenile prank. His skin stings, the joke stings worse. His instinct is to swipe Venom's Glock and teach the three of these motherfuckers what it's like to wonder whether they'll live or die, to regret who they think they are, to find out they've just fucked with the wrong guy.

But he's just Mickey, and they're just spider bites. His seething anger is a joke.

He knows he has to keep his cool if the joke's ever going to be on them.

He doubles over, makes like he's recovering, and gets the epoxy putty from between the laces of his left boot.

"Sit down," Silk says to him. The others go quiet.

Craig takes his seat, shirtless, shamed.

Silk looks him over. "I thought you might be stupid enough to involve the law."

"Are you going to start in with the fucking Chinese water torture now, to see if I involved my optometrist? What is it that you think I did?"

Silk uses his pinky nail, scrapes grime from under his nails. He says, "Someone in Mr. Moy's circle is responsible for our loss the other night."

"Your loss? Why is it your problem? You weren't even here."

"Mr. Moy is indebted to us for a certain amount of money each month. Because of the incident, he is unable to pay. So it is very much our problem."

"If the money's for protection, Mr. Moy should get refund."

"The money is none of your business. The only business you have here is to convince us you are not the one who took it."

Craig puts two fingers to one of the spider bites on his chest, compression to stop the acute pain; with his other hand, he kneads the putty. He says, "Let's be real, here. I'm a white guy. I live in the suburbs. The only ninjas I'd seen before that night were in Kung fu movies. And I was here when they hit us, for Christ's sake. I had my own cash stolen."

"A good cover-up."

"Why would I come back? Go ahead: take a look in my wallet. I got just under a thousand bucks in there—I won it last night at the boat. I'm here to get well again . . ." and as the words are coming out of his mouth he realizes telling them about the money does not help his case, nor does it carry the promise of keeping it.

Venom opens the wallet and lays the hundred-dollar bills out, one by one, on the felt.

Silk folds his yellow hands. "The boat, you say."

"The Grand Victoria. I had a run at the blackjack table." He kneads the putty more forcefully now: it'll only take a little longer—

Venom says something to Silk in Chinese and Craig wishes he could understand the intonation, at least. He hopes his little act in the parking lot is being translated into a credible alibi.

Then he feels the business end of the Glock against his temple.

Craig closes his eyes, but this time there's no mental replay of his life; there's just a black and white list of so many mistakes. Suwanski doesn't know where he is; his family doesn't even know who he is. The only person who knows what's going on can't help him since Craig couldn't slip the phone from his boot, let alone dial it in to Juan. He *is* going to die in this shitty place, his job undone, and it's not fate. It's his own fault.

He opens his eyes. "Please, Silk," he says. "I don't even know how to talk my way out of this."

Silk breaks out his golden smile. "You are lucky you're a white man; people look for you when you are missing." He waves the Fuxi away. "I do not need people looking here."

Venom takes the Glock from Craig's temple and asks, "Does anybody look for a white man's money?"

"Only his woman." Silk leans over the table to pick up Craig's hundreds, one by one. "Let's call this payback, Mickey."

Craig watches, helpless, but he's still alive. And now, there is nothing he wants more than payback.

"Will you leave me a couple bucks, for some Bactine?" he asks, drawing attention to the red mark on his chest while, underneath the table, he lifts the cuff of his pants with his opposite boot. "God, I've got the fucking creepy-crawlies," he says, figuring if he draws their attention while he reaches down between his legs, makes like he's got an itch, they'll never suspect he's reaching just a little farther toward his ankle, lifting his foot—

The door to the den swings open and the Fuxi doorman steps in to give a hand signal that starts with eight fingers splayed and ends in fighting fists.

Silk speaks to him in Chinese, the vowels drawn out and offensive; the doorman responds with equal affront. Venom and the other big Fuxi retreat, flanking Silk, protection.

And as they go back and forth, Craig continues to "itch," his racing heartbeat the only thing that would give him away as he slips the phone from his boot, fingers the send button, and affixes it to the underside of his chair with the epoxy putty. He presses up on it, waiting as long as he can for the epoxy to set.

"Sorry, Mickey," Silk says. "We've got business." He nods to his protectors; they come around to Craig again.

Venom says, "Game's over."

Craig releases his fingers from under the chair, praying to God the phone stays put.

This time when he feels the big Fuxi's hand around his neck and his world goes dark, he hopes these motherfuckers are ready for payback.

21

The Aragon Arms Hotel is not listed in Fodor's, or Frommer's, or Conde Naste, and when Leslie pulls up outside, she knows why. It's a dump.

The building is a typical old brick job similar to the others on Kenmore, but it's the only one on this block that advertises "weekly rates." Leslie parks up the street, where run-down walk-up homes sit back from the sidewalk behind overgrown grass and blistered wood porches. If this is a working-class neighborhood, it must be the sort where people work a lot for a little and the little doesn't go toward upkeep.

Across the street, a chain-link fence borders an empty park. The pavement inside is cracked, the pattern like nature made a hopscotch court. The rusted playground equipment on the backside of the lot doesn't look like much of a place to play. Maybe it's better in the daylight.

A bundled-up black man who's probably wearing everything he owns, including a cowboy hat, makes a point to stop and look in Leslie's car windows, his hands deep in his pockets, like he's got something to hustle. When she ignores him, he returns to the corner just up the way, his transient office.

So the neighborhood is shady; that's not why Leslie can't bring herself to get out of the car. She drove around the block three times just working up the nerve to stop. She drove around, thinking maybe she'd find Craig's car. She'd wait there, talk to him there. But she didn't find his car, and the truth is, she's waited too long already.

She shuts off the engine and checks her lipstick in the rearview mirror, the need to impress looming, and unfair.

She roots through her purse, cursing her hesitation. She's not the one who should feel guilty. She's not the one who withdrew a thousand dollars from their account at the Bridgeview Bank in Uptown this morning.

This afternoon, she called the bank to check the account balance over the automated phone system. There had been money missing, and when she returned from lunch with Niko, she spent the rest of the day at the shop figuring out a way to catch Craig in the wrong. Make herself feel better by default.

The courteous robot on the phone said, "Your savings account, ending in three, three, five, six, has an available balance of, three thousand, nine-hundred eighty-two dollars, seventeen cents." A thousand less than the last time she did the math—just a week before, after she'd paid all the monthly bills. Leslie stayed on the line to listen to the last ten debit transactions, confirming the hefty withdrawal, and confirming her suspicions, as she listened to the nice woman say "withdrawal" nine more times.

Leslie knew there was no mistake, but she drove down to the Bridgeview Bank anyway, her mind so lost on the matter that she forgot they closed at three on Saturday. It was past six when she arrived.

She used the ATM machine to check the balance again and got the same result from the receipt. Less than four grand. Then, as she walked back to her car, the sky falling dark, her thoughts skipping from one terrible thousand-dollar scenario to the next, the Aragon Ballroom's marquee switched on like a beacon.

The Aragon Arms had to be around there somewhere.

She went over and tried the doors to the theater: locked. Inside, the lights were on, but no one was in the lobby. The marquee advertised a show at eight for a band called The String Cheese Incident, but she didn't want to wait.

She backtracked west, looking for another place to inquire; that was when the Green Mill's neon sign winked at her from across Broadway. Niko would be playing there tonight. Right here, on Craig's turf.

The small world in the big city only made her mad. She ducked into the Uptown Lounge, ordered a shot of vodka, and asked the bartender if he'd ever heard of the Aragon Arms. He took one look at her and gave her the shot on the house.

Leslie's conviction was eighty proof until now—until she found the hotel. The place where Craig has been spending his nights. A bed he prefers to his own. And with a woman who is not his wife.

She grabs her purse and takes Rudy's old flat badge from the zipper compartment. She clips it to a lanyard left over from a garden show pass, hangs it around her neck, tucks the badge in her shirt pocket and gets out of the car.

A dead rubber plant hangs in a plastic pot beside the Aragon's front door. Leslie goes inside and finds a second locked entrance. She rings the buzzer, looks in through the glass. The overhead light is burned out, so the only source of light comes from some kind of service window ahead and to her left, where the continuous glow of a television projects alternating blues and whites out into the foyer. Someone must be in there. She rings the buzzer again.

A speaker overhead clicks and scratches and a woman says, "We're all booked up," her voice hollow, like she's communicating through a tin can. Click.

"I don't need a room," Leslie says. "I'm looking for someone."

Click. "Our guests appreciate privacy." Click.

"Do you think they'll appreciate having the entrance blocked by squad cars?"

Click. "Are you the police?" Click.

"You'll find out one way or another."

No click.

"I'm waiting," Leslie says, because cops don't say *please*.

No click, but the door lock releases.

Inside, the stale odor of cigarette smoke reminds Leslie of Craig's dirty laundry. As she approaches the service window, someone turns on a desk lamp that drowns out the blues and whites.

That someone turns out to be a woman who looks like a seasoned carny. Her cut-offs are a few inches too cut off and her tank top doesn't leave much to wonder about; she's covered otherwise by heavy makeup, extra weight. Her hair is teased into a muffin top; the ends are split and haphazardly drawn into a banana clip. She can't be that old, but there's no way her age has kept up with her.

The really disturbing part of the scene is that behind her, on the couch against the opposite wall, there is a shirtless little old Asian man wrapping a loose strand of her hair around his finger. His belt is undone, and—

"You don't look like a cop," the woman says. Smoke from her fresh cigarette drifts toward Leslie and stings her eyes but it is welcome, given the other possible odorous byproducts of the situation back there.

Leslie reminds herself she's supposed to be here on business as usual and none of this should faze her. "The man we're looking for is

Caucasian," she says, using *we* like there's backup outside. "He's forty-five years old, just over six feet tall, two hundred pounds."

"Sounds like your average white man. What's his name?"

"I'm asking the questions," Leslie says, afraid this woman has the answers.

The woman takes a drag of her skinny cigarette, the filter choked between her chubby fingers, the cherry aimed at Leslie like an accusation. "No," she says, "you don't look like a cop. You look more like a wife."

Leslie slips Rudy's badge in and out of her shirt pocket, long enough to make her point without seeming like she wants to. "Are you the owner of this establishment?"

"I'm the manager."

"Do you have a registry?"

The woman drums one hand of fat acrylic nails on the counter. "I told you, our guests value privacy."

"White male," Leslie says. "Brown hair, blue eyes. Wanted for a string of robberies. You let him stay here and you might be next."

"Sooz," the Asian man interrupts.

The woman glances over her shoulder. "Just a minute, Moy honey."

The man shakes his head, impatient.

"Does your friend—Moy? Does he know who I'm talking about?" Leslie asks.

"Moy don't speak much English. I think that's why we get along so well, if you know what I mean."

If you know what I mean? Jesus, is this the woman with open arms?

Leslie steps back as Sooz leans forward and tugs at her bra's underwire, says, "Only been one white guy here lately and that's Mickey."

Anger burns Leslie's cheeks. Some of the guys call the Irish cops Micks; Rudy used to call Craig Mickey, a fonder version of the nickname. Craig has been here, all right.

Sooz wipes perspiration from her face with the back of her hand. "I wouldn't peg him for a thief," she says, cracking a crooked-toothed smile. "Then again, he wouldn't be able to steal a thing from me. I'm happy to give it to him."

Leslie could reach over the counter and pull out Sooz's hair by its four-inch roots. Craig's been with this piece of trash? She widens her stance. "When was Mickey here last?"

"Just last night, actually."

"Did he come alone?"

"Sooz," Moy says, getting up from the couch and, with nowhere else to go, sitting again. Leslie recognizes his voice: he's the one who answered when she called a few days back. Does he know something?

Sooz leans over the counter and says, "Moy was in the middle of stealing a little something of mine, if you know what I mean. How about you give me your card, and if Mickey shows, I'll call you?"

"Sooz," Moy says, this time a demand.

"How do I know you're not going to tip him off?" Leslie asks and immediately rephrases: "We need to find him, not set him on the run."

Sooz looks back at Moy who nods like he has the answer, but as far as Leslie can tell, the nod is to his erection.

Sooz says, "What Mickey does when he's not staying here is none of my business and when he is, I respect his privacy. He does pay for it, if you know what I mean." She blows a stream of smoke in Leslie's direction. "So do you want to leave your card, or what?"

"No. Thanks." Leslie steps back. "We have all we need."

22

When Craig comes to, he's flat on his back in the alley around the corner from Mr. Moy's. The sky above the streetlights is clear and pitch-black, but he feels fuzzy, and he's sweating against the cold night air.

"Mickey."

Craig's nerves are shot, and if he had a gun he'd be pulling down on the little tatted Fuxi doorman he finds sitting on the ledge of the Dumpster to his right.

"Jesus, you now?" He wishes he had the strength to fight.

The doorman jumps off, lands on his feet. "I have something for you."

"My shirt, maybe?" Craig sits up, brushes gravel from his bare skin.

"A gift."

"If it can crawl, I don't want it."

The doorman kneels down, hands Craig his wallet. "Everything is there. Plus what you lost the other night. My elders apologize for any miscommunication."

"They're a little late."

"They mean to handle this diplomatically."

"What, like third-party talks with your friend Silk and his fucking bugs?"

"This is Silk's family. He takes it all very personally. Be assured they spoke to him, and he will not bother you anymore."

"Bother me? What if he killed me? What those guys did to me in there was illegal. You've been standing guard over a crime scene, you know that?"

The doorman sucks spit through his sharp teeth. "They say you can come back and play as soon as you like."

"How thoughtful." Craig leans left to pocket his wallet, feels the sting of his spider bites. "Think I better see a doctor first. Make sure I'm not going to start shitting cobwebs."

"If I had it my way, those spiders would have eaten you alive."

"Let's hope you aren't up for a promotion."

The doorman spits at Craig's feet. "Confident now, are you? You think you're so smart. They only return your money because they know you will come back. Why do you come back?"

"I like to press my luck."

"There's no such thing as luck."

Craig could beg to differ, but he doesn't. He just looks up and smiles, silently thanking whoever invented epoxy putty.

The doorman spits again, tosses Craig's car keys on the pavement, and slinks away.

Craig gets up, uses the Dumpster for balance. He isn't sure if he feels sick because of the gamy garbage or because the spider bites really are affecting him. No matter: he has no idea how long he'd been out and he's got to get the hell out of there before his luck runs out.

He rounds the corner and takes Kenmore, a one-way north, traffic coming toward him. He could skip over to the next street, hope for a cab running south, but he doesn't want anyone sneaking up behind him.

He runs past Wardell, the loony homeless guy who elected himself block sheriff because of, go figure, the homeless problem.

"My man Mickey, what happened to you?" he asks, lifting his thrift-store cowboy hat to watch Craig go by.

"Anybody from Mr. Moy's comes this way," Craig says, passing a Honda Civic that looks just like Leslie's, "you tell them you never saw me."

"You really do got a gambling problem, you lost the shirt off your back!" Wardell says after him, like it's the funniest thing.

Craig stops at Lawrence and tries to hail a Checker taxi; one, then another, passes him by. Out of breath and without a shirt, he figures nobody will dare pick him up. He probably looks worse off than Wardell.

When the light changes he crosses, turns east at Leland. His calves are tight, his quads burning; the cramp in his shoulder is like a knife through his collarbone.

Forget it, he thinks. Five minutes and he'll be there and he hopes Juan will be too.

Craig convinced Juan to stay in the Caprice in the church parking lot, to wait for his call. It's the safest place, far enough from Moy's; plenty of time for Juan to bail if things went bad.

If Juan isn't there, it means someone at Moy's has discovered the phone, and they're fucked. They'll believe Craig's the rat, and he'll have to assume the role and disappear. He'll drive straight to the station, call Suwanski on the way, tell him they've been made. Suwanski will dead-end the report, black out Juan's name in the files, and close the case while Craig will get rid of Mickey Hugh: destroy his fake IDs, strip the piece of shit Caprice, shave his beard. Just like that, his turn in the game will be over.

Juan will be okay: he'll wait a few days, go by Moy's and say he heard Mickey's hiding out in Elgin. They'll send him on a fruitless search that will prove his loyalty and let him slip back into Chinatown's zipped-up world. Craig, on the other hand, will never set foot on Argyle Street again; not without about sixteen Chinese reasons to look over his shoulder. Another sixteen reasons that will take turns waking him up in the middle of the night long after the case is closed.

Craig picks up the pace though he thinks maybe he should be running to the bathroom. His stomach is starting to cramp and threaten worse. He keeps at it, though, through the pain, feeling like he's in the last stretch of the race.

The light changes at Clark and he darts through the intersection, anticipation putting one foot in front of the other. He sprints the last block hoping Juan isn't on the run now.

The church parking lot is jammed with cars for six o'clock Mass. Craig maneuvers between a Volvo and a minivan and heads down the aisle where he parked the Caprice, and when he sees Juan's head through the back window, he could throw open the door, pull the little fucker out, and give him a hug.

He can't trust that Juan remembered to mute the phone, though, so unless he wants to risk broadcasting to the men at Moy's, he's got to keep a lid on it.

Craig opens the driver's-side door real quiet, an index finger to his lips for Juan to get the hint. He doesn't.

"You're never going to believe this; Mick—"

"Shh," Craig whispers, afraid of a glitch in the phone's system.

"Relax. They can't hear. They're all gone anyway. Been nothing on the line for a while. Where you been?"

Craig pulls the door closed. "Look at me, man. Where do you think?" He reaches back to the seat behind him, gets the dirty button-down he forgot to bring in for the wash the last time he was home. "Those fuckers didn't make it easy to plant that phone. Tell me it was worth it."

Juan waves the phone like a hard-won medal. "Chinatown says there will be no retaliation for the robbery."

"Wait—why not? Aren't they supposed to protect Moy?"

"The Night Hawks are the ones who hit Moy's."

"The Vietnamese gang?"

"Yes."

"And Chinatown doesn't want to get rid of their rivals?"

"They are not rivals. They work for the Triad also."

"No shit."

"The Hawks went to the Triad and confessed to the robbery," Juan says. "The Triad came to Moy's to settle the score."

"Chinatown's keeping the peace."

"Trying to. The Hawks say the Fuxis have been bribing their distribution man on the south side, forcing him to tamper with their heroin, to make the Hawks look bad."

"Are we talking China White here? The Fuxis have been making the distributor cut the horse with fentanyl?"

"Didn't say. But the Hawks did say they are sick of looking the other way on account of the Triad."

Craig buttons up his shirt, racks his brain. He'd been building a case on the assumption that the Fuxis were the ones delivering the China White. What the hell kind of case does he have if that assumption is completely wrong?

Outside, a Spanish family approaches from church, the little girls dressed up like it's still Easter. Craig figures they're headed for the custom-painted minivan on the other side of the Caprice: a real bean-mover, probably seats twelve, doubles as a bedroom.

Then the group splits up; one guy unlocks his late-model Beemer;

a woman and three little girls get into the Volvo; another woman climbs into an SUV, and the last two take off in the Lexus that was parked right behind Craig.

Then it hits him: he's been coming at this case all wrong. It's like he's been watching the minivan instead of the parking lot. He's been assuming his options. Limiting his list of suspects.

"So the Hawks are the ones moving the China White," he says. "I don't understand why Chinatown employs rivals. What do they expect? It's the nature of the game: one or the other's got to go."

"The Fuxis are family. The Hawks are the future."

"Yeah, but if the junkies are dying because of a turf war, they're only losing customers. Not much future in that."

"The Triad means to run like a business, but they are burdened by honor."

"Oh you people and your fucking honor. The Triad is burdened, Juan, by gangs and drugs and other illegal shit."

"They gave you your money back, didn't they? I heard them tell Silk to repay you."

"There's no honor in returning what was mine to begin with. Silk wanted to kill me."

"Wait," Juan says, holding the phone between them. "They're back."

Even though Craig doesn't understand the language, he recognizes the voice that comes over on the speakerphone: the harsh tone, the long vowels. "That's Silk. Translate."

"He . . . he says . . . the Triad will not stop him. He says . . . he will cut off the Hawks' distribution entirely."

"Who's he talking to?"

"Wait." Juan listens. Craig's got to give him credit: from the burner's inauspicious position under the chair, the voice is muffled; like someone in another room.

"He says he . . . will go after the Hawks' distributor."

"Why would Silk do that if he's—"

"Wait."

Craig shuts up and listens, like he could understand through sheer will. Not that he understands any of this, even in English. It doesn't make sense for Silk to take out the middleman—not if he's been using the guy to tamper with the Hawks' product. So either the Hawks are full of it, or Silk is full of it, or—

"He says innocent people have died because of the Hawks' product. And now, so will the guilty."

"Translate, Juan: did you just say murder?" Craig gets his own phone from the glove box and dials Suwanski.

"He says the distributor is due a new package tonight. Silk is going to go see the man . . . and show him what his China White has done."

"Halle-fucking-lujah." Craig gets Suwanski's voice mail, waits for the beep, says: "Ronnie, get your ass over to the station. We've got a whole new case."

23

Leslie's mother used to say that a crisis serves as a humbling reminder that there is very little over which anyone has control.

Leslie wonders if a midlife crisis falls into that category or if Craig's behavior just proves, like her father used to say, that her husband is a *malaka*.

"Richter, party of four," the hostess's voice blares from the loudspeaker, over the chaos at Lou Malnati's.

Leslie sits at the end of the bar wishing her iced tea had a little Long Island in it. It's Saturday night, and she's still waiting for the pizza she called in for pickup almost an hour ago. She should have known the place would be packed: it's an absolute circus, the entertainment entirely caloric. *Come one, come all,* Leslie thinks; stuff cheese and sausage and Coke into your fat faces, and choose to remain oblivious to the sad clown in the corner.

In a booster chair pushed into a booth to her right, a toddler tugs at the red plastic barrette that holds a thin bunch of curls up on her head.

"No, honey," her mother says, redirecting the girl's attention to a crayon without missing a beat of the grown-up conversation she's having with the man across the booth. The little girl takes the crayon to her paper place mat, draws a harsh blue line through a friendly-looking duck, and throws the crayon on the floor.

The man takes a deliberate, if not impatient, pause.

"No, honey," the girl's mother says, probably for the hundredth time tonight. She hands the child a purple crayon, as if the color was the problem. The crayon ends up in the girl's mouth, which seems as good a place as any.

Leslie sips her iced tea. She feels like a clown, that's certain. Her visit to the Aragon Arms made it clear. Craig's infidelity clicked into position as a matter of fact right next to the others: his absence, the missing money, the downed lines of rational communication. And Sooz.

That Craig would stoop so low, that he would break the only marriage bond they had left in a seedy hotel like that, with that woman as the welcome mat; it's all enough to cancel any reconciliation she'd been planning and call in the big guns: Hassett and Klein, LLP, Attorneys at Law.

Instead, she called Lou Malnati's. She ordered a pizza. She might as well be wearing a red nose.

"Large butter-crust, extra cheese," a waitress announces, and delivers it to the toddler's table. At once the little girl is out of her chair and on the table belly first, something new to get her hands on.

"No, honey," her mother says, same ineffectual tone. She returns the child to the booster and belts her in. The belt is not a good idea. The girl begins to scream.

Some slice of life.

Around the restaurant, adult patrons shake their heads; some at the poor parent, others the poor child. And as the mother lets her daughter cry it out—at the man's request—Leslie is surprised by her own lucidity. Normally she'd have worked herself into a fit over the mother's laissez-faire command of the situation. She'd have wanted to scream, watching the couple serve themselves, all the while pretending the little banshee disrupting the entire joint doesn't belong to one or both of them. At the very least, Leslie would have included herself among the disapproving spectators.

But Leslie doesn't feel like doing anything at all. Maybe it's because she believes the child might be on to something.

The little girl runs out of tears just as soon as her mother takes her out from the booster chair and into her lap, where she occupies herself quietly, breaking her soggy purple crayon into bits and topping the pie on her mother's plate.

"McHugh order for pickup," the hostess says over the loudspeaker.

Leslie swallows, her throat parched from the tea's tannins. So the pizza is ready. Is she?

She can be a victim. She can act like the world spins too fast and it's all she can do to hold on, at its whim, the tears on her cheeks streaked like raindrops on the windshield of a speeding car.

Or, she can take a cue from that little girl. She can cry out, and make sure everyone hears it.

"Ivy, come eat." Leslie cradles the phone with her shoulder and gets a Diet Coke from the fridge while she waits for Craig to answer. She gets his voice mail. She hangs up.

Ivy comes in, lifts the pizza box's lid. She says, "I won't eat this."

"Why not? It's your favorite."

"Do you know what they do to baby cows?"

"You mean calves. Baby cows are called calves."

"Whatever. You know what they do to them?"

"Raise them in cages on milk-fed diets to prevent muscle growth, so the meat will be tender and delicious with a marsala sauce."

"It's inhuman."

Leslie doesn't feel like correcting the girl again. She rolls a pizza cutter through the pie four ways. "This isn't veal. It's sausage."

"Sausage is worse. It's made from scraps that can come from every part of the animal. Even their buttholes."

"So pick it off."

"I'm not eating it. You can't make me."

"Then I guess you'll starve." Leslie plates a greasy slice and takes it to the counter where Niko's rose, indifferent to her sadness, is still in bloom.

Leslie doesn't really want the pizza. She keeps thinking of Sooz and her sweaty, satisfied face. It makes her sick.

"There's nothing else to eat," Ivy says, the fridge open, moving cartons and containers around like she's strategizing.

Leslie pushes her plate out of the way. "No."

"What do you mean, *no*?" Said snotty.

"Clearly I have failed you as a mother if you don't understand the meaning of the word. I know you're looking for a way out of this house tonight and I'm telling you. No."

"Why?"

"You don't need a reason."

"Unreal." Ivy closes the fridge and returns to the butcher block, her bottom lip stuck out. She picks at the pizza crust. Such a child.

"I am not going to negotiate," Leslie says. She gets up and retrieves the cordless phone. "And you know what else? I am not going to continue to pretend everything's fine."

She moves past the girl without saying another word. She could tell her so much about real disappointment.

She goes into the dining room and looks through the accumulated junk in the hutch for her phone tree. Nobody needs to tell her that information is only as good as its source, nor do they need to point out that Sooz's statement wouldn't hold up on crutches, but luckily, Leslie knows where to seek corroboration. She finds the handwritten list of numbers, photocopied by one of the wives some years ago, tucked into her old address book. It's for emergencies like this: if a cop's wife is desperate, if she needs her fears substantiated, she calls the others to service. Forget the blue line; a man with blue balls will talk.

Leslie updates the phone list whenever someone moves in or out of the picture. Over the years, only four of the seventeen original numbers remain, the McHughs' included; she figures the ratio is about right for cop marriages. New phone numbers—and new wives—are recorded, scribbled out, and revised; still, standard operating procedure remains the same. You need to make a case, a cop's wife has her ways.

Leslie dials Jackie Suwanski first. Since her husband is Craig's current case agent, compassion should be her middle name.

"Jackie, it's Leslie McHugh. I'm calling to find out how late you expect Ron tonight."

"Are you kidding? He went over by the Pagorskis' barbeque a few hours ago. I don't expect him soon or sober."

"Of course," Leslie says, like she knew there was a barbeque. Like she wasn't calling because she assumed they were at work.

"Ron's been itching for a Saturday night since they started this case. I was going to go along, but our youngest is running a hundred-and-two fever."

"Something's going around," Leslie says, since something's always going around.

"Wait a minute: how come you aren't going?"

"Craig and I, we've been having some problems."

The way she says it must be clear because Jackie says, "You're kidding."

"Has Ron mentioned anything to you?"

"Forgive me: I had no idea. When Ron said Craig hadn't been acting like himself, I assumed it had to do with the officer who died. I should have asked. I just didn't think: Craig?"

"Will you check into it?"

"My dear, when Ron comes home loaded, I won't even have to fake it. I just hope he can speak in coherent sentences."

"In the meantime, can you give me Pagorskis' phone number?"

After Jackie relays the number, Leslie says, "I appreciate it. Hope Joey feels better."

Next, and for the hell of it, Leslie dials the Pagorskis.

"I'm looking for Craig McHugh."

"One second," a young man says.

In the beer-soaked background, testosterone and rank compete so every guy has to yell to be heard. It sounds like a cop party, all right. She listens for Craig's stupid laugh.

"Hello," a man's booming voice comes on the line.

"I'm looking for Craig McHugh," she says again.

"Who's calling?"

"His wife."

"Haven't seen him."

"Because this is his wife?"

"Hello? I'm having trouble hearing you."

"I'll bet." To verify the possibility that this guy is full of it, she asks, "What about Ron Suwanski? Is he there?"

"Here and gone."

"Let me guess: he just left."

"As a matter of fact . . ."

Leslie hangs up. No point needling him; to the boys, one pissed-off woman is just like the next. Unless she's waiting at home.

Leslie's next call is to Pam Flagherty, a force her husband Jimmy wouldn't dare reckon with; Leslie figures that makes Pam Craig's boss's boss, and a willing informant.

Pam is also one of the four originals, so Leslie cuts to the chase. "I need you to talk to Jimmy."

"He's over at Pontecore's," Pam says, "helping Donna with some damn thing." Seems like Flagherty always volunteers to check up on widows; probably the only way he ever gets any sympathy. "He'll get his ass home soon. What's going on?"

"It's Craig."

"Seriously?"

"Yeah."

"Miserable prick."

"I need you to check into it."

"Absolutely. I'll call you back if I hear anything."

Just to return the favor, Leslie calls the Pontecore house. There is no answer.

By the time Leslie calls Camille Painter, the phone tree is in bloom.

"Judy Swigart called and told me," Camille says. "My god, Leslie, I'm sorry. I'm already checking into it."

One hour and four more phone calls later, Leslie takes no comfort in the fact that everyone she called was home alone on a Saturday night. By now, though, most everybody's heard that Craig is having an affair. Unfortunately, nobody can verify it. Worse, no one can deny it.

The clock past eleven, Leslie makes one final call. When she gets Craig's voice mail, she doesn't leave a message. She can't think of anything to say.

She goes into the kitchen for the pizza she'd left earlier, the grease now cooled and coagulated so she can pick up the slice and eat it by hand. She sits at the counter in front of Niko's happy rose; the refrigerator's noisy icemaker is her busy, indifferent companion. It does not make her feel any better to know that other women are accustomed to this loneliness, busying themselves so as to be indifferent, distracting themselves as desire slowly dies. They may as well be making ice.

Ivy comes into the kitchen, speaker buds in her ears that trail to the iPod clipped to her pink pajama bottoms. Apparently, Leslie has become invisible since they last spoke: the girl looks right through her on her way to the fridge. Leslie knows Ivy will spend the rest of the night in her room, one of her better tantrums; she's got years on that kid with the purple crayon.

Ivy opens the fridge, gets a Diet Coke, and turns to leave.

Leslie puts on a too-sweet voice and calls after her, "Good night."

Without looking back, Ivy says, "Fuck you."

Leslie doesn't say anything; she just sits there. The sincerity in the girl's voice was as sharp as a slap. Ivy has never spoken to her that way. Not on her life.

Outside, an airplane jets across the night sky on its way out of O'Hare. And Leslie sits there.

Upstairs, Ivy's door slams. Leslie sits there.

Then, the icemaker drops a tray of cubes into its bin, and Leslie cannot sit there. Not anymore.

24

"Craig, are you sure this is it?" Suwanski asks. "This block is so black they could hold the entire NBA draft. I haven't seen a slanted eye since we crossed Throop."

"This is the place," Juan says from the back of the van.

"They don't shit where they eat, Ronnie," Craig says, from next to Juan. He looks out the tinted window at the row of walk-ups nobody's walked up to since Suwanski parked an hour ago. Only action on this street involves a couple of zombie-junkies who've been keeping an eye on a corner kid who's been keeping his wares to himself, and his eye on this van. Doesn't matter. "Juan says this is the place, it's the place."

Behind them, the United Center's lights bounce off the low-lying clouds, a backlight that gives way pretty quickly to the darkness hanging over the train yard in front of them. This section of Wolcott Avenue, south of the el tracks, is nowhere for anybody to spend a Saturday night, unless they're doped to the gills or looking to get that way.

"What do you think, Picky?" Suwanski asks his copilot. "You think this is the place?"

Detective Steve Pickowicz turns around, sticks his head between the two front seats and says to Craig, "I think I left a perfectly cold Budweiser at Pagorski's to come down here and practice for my stress test. You owe me for this, McHugh."

"You got barbeque sauce on your face," Craig says. Seems like he owes a lot of people.

Pickowicz licks his lips and faces front. He's one of the younger guys, but the Job is starting to show the first signs of catching up with him: a few extra pounds, a little less patience.

"McHugh," Suwanski says, "you sure your translator back there didn't get his words mixed up? They say Mandarin is one of the most difficult languages to understand. You can mistake a word simply by its intonation."

"I did not make a mistake," Juan says. "This is where Silk said he would meet the middleman."

"Juan says this is the place," Craig says, feeling like he's some kind of translator, too. He checks his watch, and out the window at the address Juan gave them. It's going on midnight, a good reason for feeling increasingly defensive. Suwanski's right: this doesn't seem like the kind of neighborhood where Chinatown would do business. When Juan said the south side, Craig had visions of a busy street like Wentworth, an easy grab: he and Juan would ID Silk and company, Suwanski and Pickowicz would call in backup for the collars. From there, it'd be Suwanski's pleasure to work over the Fuxi boys: Who wanted to go down for attempt to commit? How about conspiracy? Aiding and abetting? Let them all plead the fifth and face a judge; they'd still be off the street long enough for it to hurt. And Craig would be the unnamed hero, the guy who swept a broom through the web.

The problem is that nothing has gone according to this hopeful plan. Looks like Craig and his boys will be the ones with explaining to do, starting with a legitimate reason for signing out the van, and getting pretty sticky around the impromptu trip out of their jurisdiction—all on a hunch. Maybe private dicks can work that way, but for sworn Chicago detectives, a hunch is about as useful as a dead witness. The extra paperwork is enough to make a guy's brain itch.

"So, Juan," Pickowicz says, "is it true you guys eat dogs?"

"You still hungry, Picky?" Suwanski asks.

"My body is an overworked machine," he says, rubbing the flab above his belt. "It needs regular fuel."

"You could probably give your mouth a rest," Craig says. "Might save your energy."

"What's wrong, McHugh?" Suwanski asks. "Your spidey-suit too tight?"

"Forget Spider-Man," Pickowicz says. "Try Captain Buzzkill."

"Maybe you should both shut up." Craig cracks the window. It's so stuffy in the van, but there's no way he can complain without provoking more banter. No way he can get out, either; he can't risk being seen.

It pisses him off, the way the guys are acting. Like this is any old grab. Pickowicz doesn't seem to understand how delicate the situation is; Suwanski no longer seems to care. They think they're so safe, so certain, on the other side of the law. Who do they think they are?

Pickowicz turns around and looks at Craig. "Man, you do look like shit. You know arachnidism can cause abdominal pain, weakness, dizziness—"

"How'd you get so smart?" Suwanski asks.

"I was an Eagle Scout."

"So tie a knot in it," Craig says.

"He's just trying to help," Suwanski says.

"In severe cases," Pickowicz says, "a bite from a black widow can cause nausea, vomiting, tremors . . ."

Craig looks up at the dark window Juan says is the one to watch, a tattered bedsheet hung in place of curtains. He does feel sick. He's got a sick feeling about this whole thing. So what if the case is about as stale as the van's air? It's still a case. Who are these cocky assholes that are supposed to be his brothers?

Craig stares at the walk-up's window, the yellowed bedsheet, slivers of darkness where it's torn. His eyes go in and out of focus, straining and wishing and—wait—did the sheet move? Is the shape of the darkness different?

". . . chest pain, respiratory difficulties . . ."

"Fuck me," Craig says. The bedsheet moved. Again.

"Are you having respiratory difficulties?"

"No: someone's up there, in the window. I saw the curtain move."

"What if Silk is already inside?" Juan says, shrinking in his bucket seat. "What if he knows we're here?"

Suwanski rechecks the load of his .44 and looks over his shoulder at Craig. "We sticking with the plan? Or do you want me and Picky to go shake it up?"

"I don't want to get out of the vehicle," Juan says, not for the first time tonight.

"You really are a yellow little guy, aren't you?" From Pickowicz.

"You're not getting out of the vehicle, Juan," Suwanski says. "All we need you to do is make a positive ID. All you have to do is look out the window. Say the word, McHugh."

Craig stretches his neck, the tension set there thick. If they go now and Silk isn't inside, best they can hope for is the middleman and a reason to arrest him. If he's got the China White, they'll collar him, get him out of Silk's way, and hope to cut a deal.

Or, they'll go now and find Silk inside with nothing to hide. They won't be able to bust him for having a friendly conversation, so they'll split without a suspect. Two days later the middleman will turn up, an OD, and Silk will be sitting as pretty as a China doll.

There are no truly promising possibilities. The chances of a solid arrest are slim to none. But Craig can't take another loss in this case. He can't go back to Moy's, start over at square one. And if he wants to get at Silk without blowing his cover, this might be the only way. "Do it."

The guys in front bail out and they're at and in the walk-up's door, no time flat.

Craig keeps a safe hand on his holster and watches the window, waiting for the reassuring flip of a switch.

Juan says, "We do eat dog."

"Not now, kid."

"It is not a delicacy. It is because of our economy." So he's being chatty now; probably nerves.

"What's the holdup?" Craig asks the walk-up's window.

"Your culture has its own unsuitable tastes. Every day you put another animal's milk on your Cheerios. Milk meant for their babies."

"No, I don't. I'm lactose intolerant."

Finally: the light comes on upstairs. Craig sits back, finds his breath.

Juan says, "You do not respect me. Because I am a *Hun Xue*."

"That can't be true," Craig says. "I don't know what a hun-soo is."

"I am mixed blood. My mother Chinese, my father American. That is why the Fuxis would not let me join them. They say my blood is bad."

"That's a bit old-fashioned, don't you think? Why would you want to be a part of something like that?"

"Because I want to be a part of *something*." Juan sits back, his face lost in the shadows. "I wish I did not have an American bone in my body."

"You hate it here so much, why don't you go back to China?"

"In Hong Kong it is worse. I am a *gweilo*—a white devil."

"You know what I am? A mutt. My father was Irish. My mother's family came from all over the map. But does that put me on the devil's leash? I don't think so."

"You do not want to understand."

Craig looks over at Juan's shadow. "If you're talking about trying to fit in, I understand better than you think."

Juan extends his arm from the dark, a finger pointed toward the windshield. "There is someone coming."

Craig takes the binoculars from the front console, focuses up the block. "You need to open your eyes all the way, Juan, because I see two someones."

Both dressed in black. Moving fast. Toward the van, toward them. What the fuck? Why didn't they come up with a contingency plan for what happens when Silk shows up behind the detectives?

"Get up," Craig tells Juan.

"I do not want to get out of the car—"

"I know Juan. Jesus. Just get up and move out of the way."

Craig kneels between the seats and refocuses the lenses, which brings the stars on the approaching uniforms into crisp view. "What the hell are they doing here?" It's too early for backup. "Fuck, did Ronnie call the Thirteenth?"

"The Mexican mafia?"

"Not the Thirteen, Juan. The Thirteenth. This is their district."

"What do we do?"

"Be cool," Craig says, "maybe they'll pass us by."

They don't.

The two men are careful as they split up at the front of the van, one left, one right, gun-hands ready. The one on the left taps at the driver's-side window with his billy club.

"Sorry, Juan," Craig says. "Looks like you might be getting out of the van." He climbs into the front seat star-first and rolls down the window.

"You're gonna jam us up," Craig tells the white-haired, rough-faced cop whose nameplate reads *Votchka*.

Votchka steps back, the club loose in his hand. "This is our block, my friend. Step out, let's talk about it."

Craig sees the other officer's flashlight darting into the tinted back windows. "We're UC," he says. "There are two detectives looking for a suspect in the house across the street—the 211B address, upstairs unit. Suppose you talk to them."

"Suppose we don't waste each other's time. We already picked up your man Silk."

"Goddamn it. Suwanski called you."

"Let's say we just happened to run into Silk, otherwise known as Xiang Wen Li, and he happened to match the description of a robbery suspect that hit Popeye's over on Western last night."

"Since when do Chinese guys break the law for chicken and biscuits?"

"We had probable cause."

"That's a bullshit collar and you know it. Suwanski called to give you a heads-up and you decided to fuck us."

"This is our beat, McHugh. We're not going to let our body count go up on account of your hard-on for this guy."

The second officer comes around to the driver's-side door, a black guy the size of a workhorse, nameplate *Ross*. "Vee, you want me to pop in to 211B?"

"Sure." Votchka stows his club. "Tell them the good news."

"This isn't good news," Craig says, watching Ross hustle toward the walk-up. "We've been working this case for months."

"And our man DeSilva has been watching 211B for a year. You think you're the only one trying to catch bad guys?"

"This particular bad guy, yeah."

"Don't worry. Silk is just doing a little deputy time. He'll be out in forty-eight; we'll be sure to drop him off up north so you can chase him around again in your own neighborhood."

"You're a man of limited principle."

"When surrounded by morons." Votchka leans against the van.

"What does this mean?" Juan whispers from behind Craig, his voice thin.

"It means we have to try another angle," Craig says.

"I'm done trying," Juan says. "I'm done, Mick."

"Look," Votchka says, as Pickowicz and Suwanski follow Ross out of the walk-up. "Here come a couple more guys with their dicks bent out of shape."

Pickowicz stops just past the curb, bends over, and pukes.

Votchka sees this and bends over, gut-laughs.

"What the hell happened?" Craig asks Suwanski when he comes over, a little green around the edges himself.

"You saw the curtain in the window move, McHugh, because of the flies."

"Could barely tell the body from the bugs," Ross says, same green.

Craig says, "I guess it's your mess after all, Votchka."

"Bullshit," Votchka says, pushes off the van. "I'm calling Kingman Cade."

25

"Let me see your IDs," the bouncer outside the Green Mill says to the young couple in front of Leslie. Light bounces off the bouncer's bald head from the neon bulbs that tick around the sign above them.

Leslie thought twice about leaving Ivy alone at the house. The first time, she listened at the girl's bedroom door: Ivy had barricaded herself inside and she was clicking away at her Macintosh, probably griping to a friend about being stuck home on a Saturday night. Stuck there, and maybe plotting a way out—if she dared to follow through, though, Leslie had her own built-in alibi: she'd come here, to the Green Mill, looking for her daughter.

The second time Leslie thought about leaving Ivy home, she decided she had nothing to lose. If her daughter stayed locked in her room all night hating her mother and Craig was at that god-awful place in Sooz's open arms, then why shouldn't Leslie do what she wants? It wasn't a big deal, anyway; she was just going to see some live music.

Leslie shivers; goose bumps prickle her bare arms. The night is cool and she knew it, but she didn't have a jacket suitable for the occasion. In fact, the only appropriate top she could find in her closet was the black satin shell she's wearing that's supposed to be layered under an olive sweater. She ditched the sweater when she decided it made her look like a walking tent.

The bouncer checks the couple's IDs, diligent. It's enough to make the young guy fidget, though Leslie doesn't think he's trying to get away with anything. It must be intimidating, being scrutinized by a man twice your size who looks like he just came off a road trip with the Hell's Angels. The bouncer's black leather outfit should be enough to deter underagers: he wears boots, pants, vest, and wrist cuffs like armor. The flamed tattoos up and around his arms are permanent accessories and, in another indelible fashion choice, there are dime-sized holes poked in his earlobes.

"Twenty," the bouncer says to the couple, returning their licenses. He takes a bill from the man and nods them inside. "Quiet during the set." When they enter, the sound of a faint stand-up bass line spills out, gets sealed up again when the door closes.

"ID," the bouncer prompts Leslie.

"Seriously?"

"You're the only one standing here."

Leslie feels nervous, young, as she fumbles with her wallet inside her purse. "I'm flattered," she says. "Here it is. But please tell me I look better than this mug shot." The bouncer checks her license with no discernible opinion on the matter. She's anybody; she's saying whatever. His lack of a reaction makes her feel like she's jabbering.

Zip it, she thinks: old people jabber.

"Ten," he says. Leslie fumbles with her wallet again; they swap, and the bouncer pushes open the door. "Quiet during the set."

When Leslie steps inside, she does feel like she's getting away with something.

It's dark, it's late, it's so cool. The band is working its way through Lee Morgan's "Totem Pole," a trumpet and a sax chasing each other on the 4. And she can hear Niko at the keys, playing in broken time, improvising syncopation like he owns the rhythm section.

The band is on the stand at the back of the joint, past the long, dark wood bar on the left and the crescent-shaped booths to the right, behind the two-top tables beyond them. Leslie can't see the musicians from where she positions herself just inside the door, but she isn't ready to. Not yet. She's got to get a feel for all this.

The décor is just as she remembers, save for the NO CELL PHONES sign over the bar. Ornate landscape murals hang heavy above the subtle gold-specked booths. Votive candles flicker here and there on the white tablecloths, placed to make shadows, not light.

Wooden shells mute the lights overhead; the patrons, dressed mostly in black, seem to absorb the rest. A smoky haze hangs over the art deco bar; behind it, the arrangement of liquor bottles suggests the popularity of whiskey and vodka.

A woman to Leslie's left, at the window, says, "For breakfast I had tomato soup and some lettuce, like a salad, and that was it."

Leslie turns to shush her, because noise policy or not who wants to hear about some woman's diet, but her chump of a male companion blows a stream of smoke at Leslie's face, his own shush.

The woman says, "It's a sad state of affairs when I can't get into my size fourteens." As it is, it looks like she's uncomfortably stuffed into her double-digit denim, but why discuss it now?

"I don't know what it is," she says, "getting older, maybe?"

From midway down the bar, the little pierced-faced bartender tries on a dirty look when she catches wind of the woman's mouth.

The woman's companion says, "Honey, you have a rump a black man like me dreams of."

The bartender bites her lip ring, stows a bottle of Jägermeister, comes down-bar and says, "Hey. Shut up."

Leslie moves away from the window, so as not to risk being affiliated.

She finds an empty seat halfway down the bar, right in front of the old bronze Schlitz statue. Its lighted globe reads *Niema Schlitza niema piwa,* Polish for "When you're out of Schlitz, you're out of beer." Leslie knows this; actually, she knows a lot about this place, because twenty years ago when she was enrolled at Loyola, the Green Mill was taken over by a guy who just happened to be her music theory professor's pal. And since Dr. Collins, said professor, just happened to be fond of holding class in establishments that served alcohol, she spent sixteen Tuesday evenings here, from seven until nine, learning about jazz.

Leslie leans over to get a look at the old piano that still sits behind the bar. Underneath, she can see the glint of the handle for the trapdoor that was used way back when, during Prohibition. Dr. Collins said mob proprietors ran liquor in through the tunnel below on a hydraulic elevator. Must have been the place to be: select patrons would come in, all tuxes and gowns, indulging vanity and vice. Unlike now, when not trying to impress is supposed to be impressive, and alcohol doesn't do the trick unless it's mixed with Red Bull or infused with some fruit flavor.

Leslie figures one thing hasn't changed, though: even way back then, you had to sneak so much of what you really wanted.

The guy sitting to her left snaps her out of her reverie, literally: a real jazzbo in a black beret, he puts down his glass of beer to snap his fingers on the offbeat while the trumpeter plays, his timing elastic over the solid rhythm section. The horn player's range is unbelievable, the notes high and articulate, his embouchure perfect. It sounds like his first time on the horn tonight, though it's going on one a.m., and Leslie would guess he's been at it for hours.

Niko is just as hot as he comps the solo, left hand only, dissonant and heavy on the hammers, playing like he's in charge and out of control at the same time. And every one of his notes is in Leslie's key.

The bartender throws a napkin in front of Leslie and raises her unpierced eyebrow. "Drink?"

"Just water," Leslie whispers.

The bartender bites her lipring, fills a glass with water from the soda gun, and leaves it in front of Leslie with no apparent plans to include ice.

Leslie puts two bucks on the bar; she isn't being stingy, she just doesn't need any alcohol. She's already buzzed from the atmosphere. The anticipation. Her own audacity.

The musicians back off, as they always do, for the bass break, the player sneaking in a quote from "The Man I Love." Mid-solo, the house phone rings at at least eighty-three decibels, the ringer all the way up, loud as one of the horns. The bartender finishes shaking a martini, in no hurry to snatch the phone. The blatant hypocrisy amuses Leslie.

When the tune ends: applause, and Leslie's chance to move closer to the bandstand without bothering the audience. She grabs her water and spins on her seat but is stopped short of making her move by a man wearing a suburbanite smile.

"Hey pretty lady, can I sneak in here?" he asks.

"Go ahead."

Behind him, and now in front of Leslie, three other men round out his geek brigade. All of them wear similar light-blue button-downs, receding hairlines, and paunchy, pale faces. They probably sit around the same office every day and, like a married couple that spends so many years together, have begun to look alike. Leslie decides they all might as well be named Toby.

"You come here often?" Toby number two asks. As if the not-it factor wasn't enough. She might be older than these guys, but she'd like to think she has a clue.

"Probably never again," she says to number two, and she snakes her way around the brigade. She can't deny, though, that the attention puts a little spring in her step.

Until she gets past the bar and sees Niko. He's seated at the piano below the bent-tube neon *Green Mill* sign that throws green tinges on his gray shirt and gunmetal tie. He's leaning to the left, listening to whatever the trumpet player—apparently the bandleader—is telling the band. His facial hair is a shadow, grown in from earlier today.

All the other band members must be decades older; years in the clubs have laid them back, whiskered their black faces. But Niko is no boy; he is as comfortable up there as any of the rest, and his evident confidence is a turn-on. When he laughs at whatever the trumpeter says, Leslie is aroused.

She ducks around a black-and-white-tiled column and goes to the jukebox that sits next to the exit, a quick way out in case she follows the urge to bail. She pretends she's interested in the antique player, its handwritten song selections, the 45s. That's why she's here, right: the music.

"What's that?" The mic picks up the trumpet player's time-scratched voice.

Leslie decides she'll turn around, find an empty table, when they start playing. She just wants to watch Niko play. *Just see him play.*

"Aw-right, awl right, ladies and gentleman," the trumpeter says, into the mic now. "I'ma sit this one out, because the rest a the fellas got something special for you." The audience responds, a few in front whooping it up. The trumpeter lowers his voice to a baritone when he says, "This one's for Leslie."

Jesus. Niko must have seen her.

She tells herself *it's no big deal*—a friendly gesture, it doesn't mean anything, he's just a sweet kid—but she doesn't believe it. And she's acting like she thinks otherwise, if she doesn't turn around. She grips her water glass, afraid it'll slip through her fingers, and turns, hesitant. The trumpeter, who's moved off to the side now, counts out, "A-one, two, three, four . . ."

Niko begins the tune, a slow intro Leslie doesn't recognize; then the band joins in, the brush on the snare and a slow bass line. She can't place it, but it sounds amazing.

Then the sax player comes in playing a smooth, drawn-out version of the melody, and Leslie can name the tune straightaway: it's Duke Ellington's "I Got It Bad (and That Ain't Good)."

Jesus. She feels like she's been found out.

Her feet manage to take her to the nearest empty seat at the end of the bar where it curves around the old piano. She sits with her back to the bandstand, sets down her water glass. She's shaking; can the people next to her tell she's actually shaking? Will they know she's Leslie, the one the band plays for?

Her furtive glances around the room are met—by the jazzbo, the loudmouth woman, each of the Tobys. Is it because she's the only one who isn't watching the band?

She closes her eyes, listening to the melody; the unsung lyrics performed by the voice in her head: *I'm so mad about him / I can't live without him . . .*

Jesus. She's been found out, indeed.

Niko plays his own melodic line behind the sax, complementing the player's languid phrasing and timbre, and soon enough Leslie doesn't care so much about who knows what. It feels like Niko's every gentle keystroke gets at her, inside, everywhere.

My poor heart is sentimental . . .

The trumpeter gets back on the mic and says slow, with the rhythm, "Take a walk around the keys, Niko."

Leslie opens her eyes. Time to face the music.

The band follows Niko when he picks up the tempo and begins his solo a half-step up, slamming chords with his left hand. His connection to the keys makes everyone in the room feel the groove; the other players, too—they're all in it.

The trumpet player shakes his head like he can't believe it, says, "Ya."

Niko backs off the chords, a thumb line, while he runs alternating scales with his right hand, the tune fluttery now, upbeat, as Leslie remembers the lyrics: *Lord above me, make him love me / The way he should.*

She's mouthing the words when Niko looks right at her, a flash of that divine smile.

Jesus.

"Hey," from behind Leslie, the bartender. She puts a cherry-garnished cocktail in front of Leslie. "A Manhattan. From your admirers."

Leslie would ask who that might be, but the bartender is already on her way to fix the next drink.

Her first guess is the Tobys, but they're right where she left them—drinking, of all things, salt-rimmed margaritas—and none of them are paying any attention to her. They're too caught up in trying to be caught up in the music, heads bobbing, none of them to the beat.

Nobody else at the bar seems interested and she wonders if it's Niko who bought her the drink but then, she spots her admirers on the other side of the room: they're toasting her from Al Capone's old booth, the one he picked so he could always see both ins and outs.

Leslie guesses the man on the left is Asian, judging by his flawless pale skin and his precise features. His hair is pulled back into a tight, short ponytail that accents the new-moon shape of his black-on-black eyes. He is younger than Leslie but older than his seatmate: an unkempt-looking man with mussed hair, a goatee, thick eyebrows. He is not Asian; his long, strong nose suggests Greek heritage. Could he be one of Niko's friends, or relatives?

The Asian sets his drink on the table without taking a sip; the other finishes his—both with their eyes on her.

Unnerved, she returns the silent toast, takes a sip, and wonders why they do not smile.

The drink is strong, its potential unsettling. She shouldn't be accepting it. She shouldn't be enjoying this. She shouldn't even be here.

Or maybe she should. She reminds herself she isn't doing anything wrong. Maybe if she drinks this, the sick feeling will subside.

She takes another long sip, decides no.

The tune goes on, but the momentary interruption has taken her out of the moment. Those two guys must know who she is. Did she think coming out tonight, with all these people, would be her little secret?

The sax player solos now, and she tries to get back into the groove, but he plays too loud and she feels too close and this is too much; she should go to the bathroom, look at herself in mirror. Look herself in the eye.

She won't get up, though; the bathrooms are on the other side of the stand, and if they're occupied, she'll be standing there, part of the performance, front and center for her admirers.

"Awl, lord," the trumpeter says. Leslie agrees. How in God's name did she think this would be okay?

She glances back toward Capone's booth. Ignoring the rule, the

Asian man is on his cell phone, clearly dissatisfied with whoever is on the other end. Leslie can't hear him speaking, but the couple at the table nearest his obviously can because they're exchanging aggravated glances. The Asian's seatmate flips his fingers out from under his chin, a fuck-you to the couple and anyone in their general direction with a problem.

Great, Leslie thinks: the guys are jerks. And so is she for taking them up on the drink.

Niko raises his left hand in the air, indicating to the band that this is the final chorus, and Leslie decides that's her cue. As the band goes out, the trumpeter gets on the mic and says, over the applause, "The kid's been shedding, ain't he? Better every night. Keep the love going . . . clap your hands . . . "

Leslie leaves her drink and makes for the exit; on her way out the trumpeter says, "Aw right, awl right, we're gonna let you stroll on this one, boy . . . "

The exit door sticks open an inch, and as Leslie makes tracks down Lawrence, she can still hear the band as it starts in on Miles Davis's "So What."

26

"You gotta go," a broad-shouldered bouncer yells at the crowd; they finally disperse, like schools of student-fish, when their Bud Light–soaked brains register the grown men with badges slung around their necks who are standing at the entrance. The young ones swim over and around each other, trying to get out of Hamilton's and back to their dorm rooms without being scooped up by the police.

It's after two: closing time, as per the bar's license—and so thirsty cops can drink in peace, or some semblance of it.

"Good evening, Detective McHugh, Detective Suwanski," the beat cop Swigart says with a British accent, even though he's from Milwaukee. "Tell me your mission was a success." The collection of empty shot glasses in front of him is an indication as to why he's speaking like he just hopped the pond.

"The mission was cock-blocked by the Thirteenth," Craig says, waiting for two frat boys in Northwestern baseball caps to vacate the premises before he takes a seat at the bar.

"Mutiny," Swigart proclaims.

"Not exactly," Suwanski says, bellying up next to Craig. "It's their district, their body, their problem."

"It's our case," Craig says.

"We no longer have a case."

"Thanks to you."

"Forgive me for finally following a little thing they call procedure."

"Commander," Swigart calls to Dean, their favorite bartender, "pour these men of valor whatever spirits work to quell the need to bicker."

"Heineken. Bottle," Suwanski says, though he didn't need to clarify, because none of the cops ever drink draft.

The Commander uncaps a Heineken with the opener mounted on the bar. He looks like the kind of guy who used to open bottles with his teeth, back when he was the life of the party. Before Vietnam did its thing. The Commander puts the Heineken in front of Suwanski and sizes up Craig. "You aren't joining the revelry, McHugh?"

"You think this is revelry, I think you've been swilling from the tap." The running joke is that the taps haven't been changed out since the bar opened in 1933. It's no joke that the beer tastes like it.

Craig sits back, sighs. He doesn't want a drink; he doesn't want to bullshit with these guys, either. But this is how it works when a cop can never completely wind down. He just keeps going.

"Look who's here," Jed Pagorski says on his way in from the restaurant side of the bar. He's carrying a paper plate that buckles under wings, curly fries, ribs. "What happened to Picky?"

"Mrs. Picky," Suwanski says. "She wanted some face time."

"There's something up tonight," Swigart says. "My wife left me a voice mail, said, 'Come home, Squiggy.' She only calls me that when she wants sex and she only wants sex when she wants something else."

"Like what, tennis lessons?" asks the Commander.

"Like dirt on one of the boys."

Pagorski says, "McHugh, your wife called by my house. Sounded like she was doing recon."

"Someone broke out the phone tree," Suwanski says.

"So which one of you's in trouble?" From the Commander.

All four cops shrug, blameless.

"Does this mean we could all go home and get some?" Swigart asks. "Guilt-free?"

"It's two-thirty and I'm sweating alcohol," Pagorski says. "At this point, you're talking about a roll of some very touchy dice."

"Give me a Heineken," Craig says, figuring in his case there are no dice.

"Jed," Suwanski says, "how's the grub?"

"Cold, greasy, worth the price."

"I'm sold." Suwanski gets up.

Craig waits for his beer and follows his boss to the restaurant side of the bar. If he's going to stay, he's going to keep working.

Under heat lamps, the buffet has been pretty well decimated since Midnight Madness, the Saturday night tradition offered free, to sober up the kids. Suwanski plates the last quarter of a quesadilla, considers what little else remains.

When Craig steps up next to him, Suwanski shakes his head. "You can follow me home if you like, McHugh, but my answer's still no. You can't win them all. Some, you only survive."

Even though Suwanski already pegged his objective, Craig takes a paper plate and looks over the buffet. "Ronnie," he says, "you can bring in the other agencies. You can set up a full-court press. All I'm asking is that you keep me on."

Suwanski absently fills his plate with celery from a bin next to the leftover wings that sit in barbequed grease. "Nope." He yanks a drumstick by its bone; the skin sticks to the bottom of the pan.

"What about all the people who are dying?" Craig asks. "Shooting bad China White and dying, because of the pissing match between these gangs?"

"What about the people getting killed because of the Latin Kings' beef with the Conservative Disciples over on Winthrop? I don't see you all worked up about that." Suwanski steps to the right, assesses what's left of the fries.

"We've had roadblocks before, Ronnie."

"Roadblocks. Not land mines. You fucked us when you left that phone at Moy's. How do you know Silk's story was legit? He might have found out about the phone and staged a setup—said he was going to kill the middleman to draw you and Juan out."

"If he knows about the phone and he pegs me for it, he wouldn't have sent me on a dry run to find a dead body—he would have sent someone else to try to turn me into one. He doesn't know it's me. I can go back."

"You've already gone too far. You were tortured—you risked worse—to obtain information you can't verify and I can't document. You let your snitch take us outside our jurisdiction to catch a guy who was already in jail and another who was already dead. Now we don't have a target, we don't have a lead, we no longer have a willing informant—"

"Juan will come around, Ronnie. He's just scared."

"We don't need the snitch, McHugh. We don't even have a crime. We have wasted the city's time and money on this; we have kept them in the dark, and we have come up with nothing more than the clear indication that this is over our heads and out of our hands."

"We were looking at the wrong guys. We want the China White, we need to go after the Night Hawks."

Suwanski eyes Craig's empty plate. "Craig, have you looked at yourself lately?"

His own first name is awkward from Suwanski's mouth. "Don't make this personal."

"That's all this case is anymore is personal. You're like one of the junkies, and this case is your fix."

"That's real great coming from you, the one running it."

Craig hates the way Suwanski looks at him: unaffected. Objective. In control.

Suwanski puts down his plate, says, "I'm at my son's first ball game yesterday. I'm in the stands, kids are running around, it's a regular day in the life. But Craig, I'm losing it. You know why? Because they're up against some south-side team that's half Asian. It's a tie game from the first inning, and I'm more interested in the other parents. What if they're connected? And then I start worrying what my son knows. What does he tell his friends about me? And what about that little Asian shortstop: what's my son saying to him? So what if he's actually Korean, I don't know that. He could know someone who knows someone. And every time my son gets up to bat, I'm secretly hoping he strikes out, just so nobody will remember his name. This is personal. And it's over."

"Did you spend all day in your office polishing that speech?"

Suwanski picks up his plate and starts back toward the bar. "You're done gambling."

"Wait, Ronnie: you're right. I'm getting nowhere at Moy's. And I've already lost—the thing with Silk, the money—there are so many other things. But you can't let those fuckers take my dignity. I lose that, and then what? Please, let's get a new angle on these guys. Take a look at the Hawks. I'll work with the Thirteenth. Don't shut me out."

Suwanski looks at his plate like it's full of more stuff he doesn't want. "You want to keep your dignity," he says, "you walk away."

"This is my job, and you're asking me to quit?"

"Craig, this is also your life." He starts for the bar, stops short, says, "This case is over. Come finish your beer, shoot the shit for a while. Then go home, see your family. Make love to your wife."

It's impossible, but it's happening: Leslie keeps crossing Peterson Avenue. She thought she was on Peterson Avenue. And then she hits Peterson Avenue.

She turns left, and an oncoming car's headlights are blinding white and coming straight at her so she cuts the wheel and slams on the brakes, tires squealing, eyes closed, waiting for impact. There isn't one.

She opens her eyes and sees her own hands in front of her, then the dashboard, the windshield, and Peterson Avenue. In the rearview mirror, the other car's taillights wink and disappear.

She pulls over in front of a rehabbed condo, turns on her hazards and double parks. Just breathe, someone says. Or echoes. Did she turn on the radio? Just breathe. Who said that? The hazard lights tick, relentless, like they're counting down.

Leslie thinks this weirdness is because of that Manhattan, the cocktail from those monster-men at the gin-Green Mill. Why did they have to do that? Buy her a mean drink. And now it's in her system: but what is it? Is it toxic? Is it deadly? She doesn't feel sick, but she has to get it out.

"Wasted," she hears herself say, and it's kind of funny.

She watches herself open the car door and throw up on the street. What comes out is a citrus surprise, yellow and orange and pungent, and now she feels so light. In the rearview mirror, she thinks she looks much better now.

Leslie closes the door and she wants to continue on, here on Peterson Avenue, but it's like someone has pulled the bill of a baseball cap down over her brow. There's nobody in the car but her; it's the damnedest thing. She pushes the bill back up off her forehead, but it won't stay. She's got to get home, but this cap keeps restricting her vision.

Headlights strike her rearview mirror and sneak around the car. She waits for the car to pass, hits the gas and follows the twinkle of its taillights, hoping whoever is in front of her is headed toward Forest Glen Avenue.

She drives one-handed—the other dealing with the godforsaken cap—and the road bends this way and that; she's lucky that hand of hers knows how to steer the wheel. She follows the taillights as they breeze through a green light. Leslie checks the sign at the intersection: she's crossing Peterson Avenue. Again.

She giggles, tells herself, "Be quiet."

In her distinct peripheral vision, all kinds of shooting stars burn out too quickly to catch in glances. She focuses on the red taillights ahead, little points of concentration.

"Where am I going?" she asks. She sees Starbucks, Borders, Olive Garden; she could be in Rockford or Addison—or Iowa or Anywhere, USA.

She thinks about pulling over, closing her eyes until she can make sense of this. But what if a cop finds her? One of Craig's pals who isn't so understanding.

The hazards go tick, tick, and she feels like she's running out of time. "Shit," she says, because she's been driving with them flashing. She slows down enough to take her eyes from the road and turn them off.

A block later, she comes up on pink lights that run around a building she instantly recognizes: the Lincoln Village movie theater.

Thank God she's had plenty of chances to familiarize herself with the outside of the building, all the times she'd been stuck in the crummy parking lot waiting for Ivy.

"Tell me this is Devon," she says, and when she pulls up, the sign reads right at the intersection. More confident now that she knows where she is, she slips into the left turn lane and waits for a green arrow.

On Devon, cars whiz past her, dangerously fast. Or maybe she's driving dangerously slow; she can't read her speedometer—it yo-yos like a cartoon compass. There is one car that stays behind her, satisfied with the speed, so she decides to stick with it.

She makes an unprotected left into her neighborhood, headlights from oncoming cars in slow motion, as if they're waiting for her, courteous.

"Almost there," she says, her ingrained homing device kicking in.

Left, right, slight right, left, and she's in her driveway. The Caprice Craig has been driving isn't there, so she pops the door to the detached garage, pulls in next to Craig's Tacoma and shuts off the engine.

"Wasted," she says again, relieved, though no less confused, because she is not the one who closes the garage door.

Nor is she the one who opens her car door.

And she is definitely not the one who invited the monster-men home.

"Did you enjoy the ride?" the Asian man says, standing over Leslie, blocking her from getting out of the car. A slick black strand of hair falls around his face like the tail of a snake.

"I know who you are," Leslie says. "You were at the Green Mill. You followed me?"

"Had to make sure you got home safe," the other man says, slipping into the passenger seat. He rubs his gloved hands together, then takes the keys from the ignition, killing the door-ajar indicator and any chance Leslie had of driving out of this, right through the garage wall if she had to.

The Asian man pulls Leslie up and out of the car by her hair and braces her against the doorframe.

"Please," she says, "I'll give you all the money I have—you can take my purse, take the car—"

"Shut your mouth," he says, his breath hot, like cinnamon. "You smell like vomit."

"I told you my shit was good," the other one says, out of the car now. "Tasteless, odorless, just a couple drops when nobody's looking and Mom's all freaky."

"Plze," Leslie says, through her teeth.

"If you do not shut up, I am going to drag you into your own house and do this in front of your family."

"I'll bet she would like that," the other one says, coming around the hood. "You want everyone to watch, Mom?" When he smiles, his goatee seems to move like a thousand antennae on his chin. Why does he call her Mom? Why does he act like he knows her?

The overhead light clicks off, its timer run out. The car's dome light does little; all Leslie can see are the tiny whites of the Asian's eyes when he says, "Listen to me, Leslie. I don't want your money. I don't want your car. I just want you to know what silk feels like."

"Right," the other one says, a greedy laugh. "Silk."

"Shut up," the Asian snaps.

Leslie knows what silk feels like but it's nothing like the pain that burns the base of her neck as he grips her hair too tight in his glove and tears away a chunk of hair. She closes her eyes, wishing this were another hallucination. She will not fight; she cannot risk giving them any incentive to go to the house, where Ivy sleeps, all alone.

"Get the lights," the Asian says.

The goateed one finds the switch by the side door. There is only one window in the garage from which any light can escape, and it faces the back tree line. No one will know they are there. She prays her daughter will never know.

Leslie's eyes tear at the corners as the Asian drags her around to the hood of the car and splays her flat on her back, her calves pressed against the front grille.

He leans over her, his hand around her throat; she can feel his erection against her inner thigh. "You want me to tell you how this is going to go? Or do you want to make it easy, and tell me what it is you want to do to me."

"My husband is on his way home. He will find us—"

"That's why I brought a friend. One for him, and one for you."

The goateed one leans over the hood from the side and says, "Or maybe both of us for you." He touches her face with the back of his fingers and his hands smell like menthol cigarettes.

"Please, let me go," she says. "You can take whatever else you want—"

"The only other thing I want is your daughter."

He knows about Ivy. Did she say her thoughts out loud? How much of this is really happening? The Asian's grip around her neck is the only thing that keeps her from throwing up again.

"Mom wants all the action for herself," the goateed one says, positioning himself just behind the Asian.

"Convince me you want this action," the Asian says, pressing his black pants around his erection with the fingers of his free hand.

Leslie tries to clear her throat.

"Tell us what you can do that your daughter can't," the goateed one says. "Because I would love to get my hands on some young, tight ass."

"I—" Leslie coughs; she doesn't know how to talk dirty. She doesn't know what to say besides, "I can make you feel good."

The Asian backs off and she curls to one side, trying to get her breath, knowing this is nowhere near over.

"Get on your knees," he orders.

Leslie slides off the hood and buckles to the cement floor, so hard, more forgiving than all this.

The Asian stands over her. "Tell me how bad you want to suck my silky cock."

"I want to. I will."

"Say it."

She looks up at them: the Asian man wears no expression at all; the goateed one looks down his long nose at her, like she's a disgrace. If she has any hope of saving Ivy from this, she has to say it.

She looks down, ashamed, says, "I want to suck your s-silky cock." Like the words are foreign.

"Leslie, I do not think you mean it."

"I want to suck your silky cock." Said again, desperately this time.

The Asian takes a gun from the back of his waistband and hands it to the other one. Then he steps up to Leslie, unbuckles his belt, and says, "Show me."

"I'm just saying, fat's one thing." Pagorski sucks the last shred of meat from a chicken wing, licks his thumb, says, "Cellulite is another thing entirely. I can't stand it, and my wife's ass has more dimples than a bucket of golf balls."

Swigart nods to the detectives as they return to the bar. "What do you think, guys: cellulite? Cover it up or learn to love it?"

Suwanski shakes his head, settles into his stool. "You guys hit my age, you'll be begging to see the skin on your wife's kneecaps."

"God help me if Katie's knees get fat," Pagorski says, working on his last chicken wing.

Nobody points out the fact that God helped him plenty just finding a woman who'd put up with him and his fat mouth.

"Commander," Swigart says, slipping back into his British lilt, "may I request another round so we may toast to this occasion, wherein men debate matters of such significance . . ."

At the other end of the bar, the men's bathroom door swings open, and John Roscoe stumbles out.

"Strike that," Swigart says, no accent.

People feel one of two ways about Roscoe. Most people, like Swigart, feel the second way.

"How long has he been in there?" Craig asks.

"I didn't even know he was here," Pagorski says.

Roscoe makes his way toward the men, interesting on his feet. His right eye blinks independently of his left, calibrating his approach. Craig is surprised to see him drunk; he usually stays under his limit, so as not to undermine his self-appointed position of moral authority.

"Well if it isn't the Twentieth's finest," Roscoe says, his speech impressively exact.

"Never a pleasure," Suwanski says.

"Crack me open a cold Bud, Commander," Roscoe says, and attempts to climb up on the stool on the other side of Pagorski. Roscoe's a short, compact guy, and the move is so awkward that one would think he was trying to mount a spooked horse.

Craig sips his own beer, a little embarrassed for the guy. He's annihilated all right, but nobody cuts off a cop. No matter how hammered, no matter how unlikable a drunk. This is his one reprieve. Another beer, however bad an idea, is his right.

There are techniques, however, to get a drunk to call it a night; if well executed, he might even believe he's a man of good judgment and cut himself off. It doesn't always work, but the Commander has proven to be a master of this technique.

He opens a Bud, sets it on the bar, and shoots it down the wood. Roscoe reaches for the bottle while it's on the move, comes at it hard and a second too late, and redirects its course. The bottle cracks open when it hits the tile floor at the end of the bar.

It takes Roscoe a little while to process the scene. He looks at the other guys' beers, the space where his should be. He looks at the other guys: blind eyewitnesses. The Commander pleads the fifth, disposes the broken bottle.

"What the hell?" Roscoe asks, like his Bud up and disappeared.

The reason a technique like this doesn't always work is because guys like Craig can't resist saying something, like: "You missed."

The Commander is the only one who keeps a straight face.

Roscoe turns, his right eye dead-set on Craig. "Yeah, McHugh, I missed," he says, "but I won't miss if I come over there and punch you in the face."

Craig turns back to his own beer. He's not going to go at it with a beat cop who's about 160 pounds of self-righteousness on a good day.

"Relax, Roscoe," Suwanski says. "McHugh wasn't picking a fight."

"Oh, I get it: you're the boss, covering for him."

"I'm just telling you fighting is a bad idea."

"You want to end it, tell McHugh to buy me another beer."

Craig turns his near-empty Heineken around in his hands. "Wasn't me that served you, Roscoe, and it wasn't me that knocked over the Bud, either. I don't owe you anything."

Roscoe slips off his stool, steadies a hand on the bar. "You know, McHugh, you might be a decent cop, but you're a shitty person."

"I always liked you," Craig says.

Suwanski extends a forearm to stop Roscoe's clumsy advance. "Not smart."

Roscoe wobbles against Suwanski's arm, his right eye on Craig. "Guys like you, you can't take the heat."

"You're the one who's steamed."

"You two have a way with words," Suwanski says. "Maybe make up, take a poetry class."

Roscoe teeters back from Suwanski, points a finger at Craig. "You listening, McHugh? Because I wanna tell you something about responsibility."

"What rhymes with asshole?" Craig asks Suwanski.

"Go ahead, be glib," Roscoe says. "But know this: the only reason your daughter isn't in jail right now is because of me."

Craig swivels his stool to the guy. "I'm listening."

"We busted a rave a few nights back and picked up your daughter. She was doing ecstasy. Offered me the pills she had tucked into her bra. I had to beg her to keep her little black dress on, and to keep her hands off me. How does that make you feel, Dad?"

Craig is on Roscoe in a heartbeat. He tackles him and they're on the floor, Roscoe sloppy, flailing. Craig gets in a few quick punches to his ribs, gut, before Suwanski says—"Stop it"—and the other cops pull them apart.

Suwanski holds on to Craig by the back of his shirt while Pagorski and Swigart stand guard, linebackers waiting for another snap. The Commander makes his way around the bar to cover Roscoe.

"If you're going to handle this like men, take it outside," the Commander says.

Humiliation flushes Craig's face. He doesn't want to handle this at all, because if Roscoe picked up Ivy and kept it a secret, both Craig's families have defied him. Who's left?

On the floor, Roscoe rolls to his side, wipes his mouth. "You should be thanking me, McHugh. I got your little girl home before she spread her legs to the city."

"You don't talk about another man's daughter that way," Pagorski says, and Craig is grateful for some loyalty.

Roscoe gets up on an elbow, his one good eye squinting, defiant. "You want to know what's really going to get at you, McHugh? It was your wife who asked us not to tell you. Said you couldn't handle it, you were stressed, the usual B.S. Denniwitz says the real trouble is that you two are splitting. I guess she doesn't like you, either."

The men circle Craig, the Commander included, all ready to huddle to prevent him from going after Roscoe again, but Craig drops his fists. "Roscoe, we're supposed to be brothers."

Then, in each of the cops' faces, Craig recognizes the same practiced bluff they'd shared a few minutes ago, when the Commander tried to trick Roscoe out of his beer. Suwanski, Swigart, Pagorski: "You all knew about this?"

"Rumors," Swigart says.

"I didn't believe them," Pagorski says.

"I figured you knew," Suwanski says.

Craig steps back, and he wonders why the truth always winds up so awful. He finds his keys in his pocket and walks out of the bar. He knows no one will follow; now he knows there is no one on his side at all.

"Step outside," the Asian man tells his friend, who nods, checks the load of the gun, and slips out the side door.

The Asian looks down at Leslie, there on her knees. "Now, no one will bother us."

He unzips his pants, and Leslie sees the black ink of a tattoo just above his fly, the outline like the tips of an angel's wings spread across his groin.

He is no angel.

He steps forward, to her, his erection apparent through his boxer briefs; Leslie leans back on her heels.

"Come here," he orders. He grabs her by her hair again and pulls her up; she resists, a hand against his hipbone. Her knees, already scraped so close to the bone, rock hard over the pavement.

She tries to push away but has no leverage; even as she tugs at his waistband, she only manages to expose more of his tattoo. Wings, yes: black and feathered over his skin, the tips spiked like a falcon's or a bat's.

He steps around her left leg with his right to secure her position. Then, with his free hand, he gently slips his stiff penis through the access flap of his underwear. Thin tufts of pubic hair peek out at its base; purple veins pulsate underneath the shaft's yellow-white skin.

The foul chemical smells of cologne and urine and semen overwhelm her. Leslie closes her eyes as her mouth waters, sour and fast. She begins to shake from so much pain, and from the awful realization that the only other way out of this would be worse. It would include Ivy.

He pulls her closer, relentless, and she can't help it: she immediately begins to retch—her body fighting, trying to rid itself of the pain. She feels strands of hair being ripped from her head as she convulses but she can't stop heaving, sobbing.

He yanks her head back and looks down at her, pitiless. "I have not given you anything to cry about."

"I'm sorry," she says, her voice small, "it's the drug—whatever you put in my drink—it made me sick."

"You make me sick." He pushes her down with so much force that she has no time to protect herself. Her forearms slide on the pavement and when she tries to keep her face from doing the same, her elbows take the brunt of the impact.

She tries to push herself up on her hands but he forces her back down with his boot. If she could crawl away, out of reach, there are tools on the workbench on the other side of the Tacoma; if she could make it there, she could get ahold of a hammer, something sharp—

She tries to get up again but he steps around her, blocking her path. He looks down at himself, at his erection becoming flaccid. And then he reaches into his front pocket and with a flick of his wrist, opens a tiny shiv. The weapon is toothed on one side and razored on the other, and he is showing it to her, a possibility.

It's a doable crime: she has no connection to these men. Only Niko knows where she was tonight. No one will save her; no one even knows to look. He could kill her, just like that, a flick of the wrist.

He opens and closes the shiv, flick-flick, playing with her, and Leslie knows her only chance to live through this is to play back.

"Silk," she says, slowly pushing herself up on her hands again, testing him. "Please, you said you would show me what silk feels like."

"I do not want your dirty mouth. I think I want your daughter's clean mouth instead."

"She's just a girl." Leslie gets up on her knees; they burn, wet with blood, but the pain is irrelevant now. It has to be. He watches her, expressionless. She says, "I am a woman."

She stands up; the muscles in her legs tremble. She takes off her shirt, the material catching on her arms where the wounds have already begun to pus. The cool air stuns the skin above her navel; the hair on her arms stands on end, and her nipples turn hard against her lace bra.

If he suspects she's doing this on purpose, his erection is coming back, and it's preventing him from doing anything about it.

Her breasts are full and heavy, and she can tell the way his eyes fall on her body that he's interested. She unhooks her bra and cups her breasts in her hands, an offer.

He closes the shiv.

"I am a woman," she says again, to hear herself.

"What do you want from me, woman?"

She lets her hands fall away from her breasts, submission her only defense. "I want you to show me what silk feels like."

"Turn around," he says. When she does, he pushes her to the front of the car and bends her over the hood.

He reaches around and unbuttons her jeans. Tears blur her eyes but she cannot cry out; she can only hope to satisfy him, to suppress his urge to use the shiv.

The car hood is warm against her torso. The only warmth, she thinks, as his unkind hands go after what they want.

He tears at her underwear but they are caught by the crotch of her jeans; her muscles tense and she cannot separate her legs though he tries to force them apart with his knees. As before, when she was convulsing, her body is trying to stop this.

But there's no stopping him. One hand on her back, he flicks open the shiv and slashes at her panties on one side, then the other. The elastic snaps her skin like a rubber band and when he rips them off from the back, the cotton burns her inner thighs.

He tosses the panties into the bed of Craig's Tacoma.

Craig. If she lives through this, she will never tell him.

Tears flood from her eyes; her nose runs. But there is nothing she can do. Because this is what rape is: it is not being able to say no.

She should have said no to so many things before now.

Leslie hears the man's gold belt buckle clank as he removes his pants. No more barriers now.

He puts his right hand on the hood, holding the shiv close to her face, a threat. The metal handle scratches the car's paint as he drags his hand back at the same time he forces himself inside her.

Feeling him as he begins to thrust, machinelike, she is enraged. He has already violated her. Made her fear for her life. She will not let him do more. She arches her back and cranes her neck to see him: his eyes are closed. He is uncaring, and unprotected, but he is also unaware. She could get the shiv and kill this monster. Or at least make him bleed. Make him leave evidence. Make him regret this. She might die trying, but at least she'd be trying.

She reaches for the shiv, pinching one of its teeth between her fingers; because of his glove, he doesn't notice. She tries to pull it away by the blade, but his hand goes back and forth as he thrusts and the blade cuts her.

Fuck it, she thinks, and moves her whole body to the right, her weight pulling him the same way and turning his knife hand thumb-up, just enough for her to take the shiv, again by the blade, but it's the only way. It slices through the skin on her fingers at the knuckle creases but she keeps holding on and jams the tip into his arm; he makes no sound as he pulls out and backs away from her, but she cries out as the blade slices her deeper and she has to let go of the shiv. It dings the hood and clatters to the floor.

Leslie slides off the car, her hand warm and pulsing and suddenly wet and it feels like she is holding her own heart, and she is dizzy, but this could be her only chance to get away. She sees him, pants down, checking his forearm; there is blood, but it could be hers. She starts toward the Tacoma, forgetting her jeans are at her knees and shortening her stride, and she doesn't get very far before she feels the Asian's familiar grip: he wraps his gloved hands around her throat and pushes her down to the pavement again. When her knees hit the hard floor, her body gives way and he straddles her from behind, his fingers pressing at her windpipe.

She does not fight. She has no more fight left. This is her fault. Her fault, and no one can save her.

"Remember this, you cunt," the Asian says.

He will not let go of her throat; she can't breathe, and she no longer tries. She does not believe she will live to remember.

Consciousness comes and goes. Then it just goes.

Craig had planned to use the money he got back from Moy's on something nice. He thought he'd give it to Leslie, let her get a good start on her plans for the house. He'd look through her stupid catalogues, agree to the unnecessary updates. Rebuild the home like the relationship, and all that.

But what's wrong with the house, really, has nothing to do with the goddamned decorating. What's wrong with the house is that Craig hasn't spent enough time putting it in order. He'd counted on Leslie. Now, he knows he can't count on anyone.

Craig switches off the lamp and pulls the warm sailboat afghan his mother made for him up to his neck. When he turns on his side, he hears the change he forgot to take out of his pocket fall between the couch cushions. He doesn't bother to retrieve it.

There's going to be a hell of a lot more change around here, he thinks as he dozes off. *Soon enough.*

27

Before she opens her eyes, Leslie evens her breathing and listens. She has to make sure the men are gone.

The overlapping sounds of far-off engines of cars and airplanes on highways and skyways fill in each other's spaces; the constant hum of the city, even in the wee hours, is a muted soundtrack. But beyond that, she hears nothing. She thinks she is alone. For the first time in her life, she prays she is alone.

She opens her eyes just enough to recognize a pattern of blood spattered on the pavement, dried and leading to her hand, which is swollen, palm crusted, scabbed nearly black. She must have been out for a while.

She turns to push herself upright, the pain in her side excruciating, forcing her to cough. Her head swims; her skin is cold where it rested on the pavement. For how long?

Gray light comes through the single garage window; there's no sun. It must be morning. No one has come looking for her.

Unless . . . oh god, what if the men went looking for Ivy? What if they found her?

Leslie's shirt lies crumpled by her car's front tire, her bra close beside. She crawls over, her jeans stuck to her knees; the fabric too thick to have bled through completely, but adhered to her skin. She clasps her bra, pulls her satin top over the raw pavement burns on her arms.

She pulls herself up by the car door handle and buttons her jeans. She cannot remember what happened to her underwear.

Through the car window, she sees her keys on the passenger seat. The men wouldn't have been able to get inside the house without them, would they? She gets in, keys the ignition a click to the right, and reads the digital clock on the dash: it's 5:38. Jesus, why hasn't anyone found her here?

The garage's side door hangs open on its hinges; after the men left, the light must have spilled out to the lawn, a slice of day before dawn. It would have been out of the ordinary. Something to wonder about, had anyone seen it.

Two steps out of the garage, Leslie stops: the Caprice is parked at the end of the drive. Craig is home. The men couldn't have gone in the house; he would have discovered the break-in. He would have known something was wrong. He would have come looking for Leslie. Wouldn't he?

The men must have left once the Asian finished with Leslie. Or maybe they were chased away. Maybe they saw Craig's headlights, took off when he drove up. Then he let himself into the house, half drunk, half asleep. Yes: she can see that the front blinds are pulled. He probably went inside, went straight to the couch. And now, he'll sleep until noon, expecting Leslie and Ivy to prepare for their Sundays with light feet and whispers. He will wake up when Ivy slams the door, angry to find him on the couch again when she would have loved to breeze through the house on her way to work, just angry in general.

Had he been looking for Leslie, he would have found her. Now, she cannot go home. What the hell will she do?

She slips back into the garage and sits in the car. In the rearview mirror, red marks and purple bursts of broken blood vessels ring her neck. Her eyes are hollow, her skin sick-white. There are no visible marks on her face, but it is plain to see her tough façade is broken, revealing that secret someone underneath. Who did she think she was? Someone she can never let her family see.

She pops the trunk and retrieves the olive sweater she decided against wearing the night before. She thought it made her look like too much of a mom. She'd wanted to look sexy.

She goes to the workbench, where the hammer or the screwdriver or the goddamned hacksaw might have given her a chance. She removes a pair of gardening gloves from a cubbyhole underneath and carefully slips the right one over her hand; she decides to wear the left one, too, in case anyone sees her when she leaves. She'll stop, pull some weeds in the yard, wave and smile. She'll wear her hair down, around her neck; they won't see the swelling, the marks that will become bruises, turn brown and fade to yellow. But where is she going to hide?

Craig is a light sleeper; there is no way she can take off in her car. He'll be at the door before she's out of the driveway. She's got to get somewhere on foot. She could make it all the way to Swedish Covenant Hospital, but they won't treat her without knowing what happened. She can't call on a neighbor, either—just let the Women's Identity League hear of this. She can't blame them: who would stay quiet about such a crime on the very street they block off with little yellow cones so their children can play dodgeball?

There is no one she can trust in walking distance. Really, she has no one to drive to, either. Even if she did, what parent, what cop's wife would keep this secret? Who can she ever tell?

Blood seeps through her glove: her hand is bleeding again. She may have broken open the cut, or maybe it never quite closed. She has to do something.

She goes back into the garage and retrieves Craig's old hunting coat—the heavy camouflage he wears during pheasant season when he takes day trips to Kankakee and comes back a different man, more of a man, after the kill. Leslie has never understood the so-called sport. Craig hunts in controlled areas. The birds don't have a chance in hell.

She puts on the coat. She still has a chance.

She hurries down the driveway and out of sight from the house. She rounds Thome Avenue; though this route is less direct, she doesn't want to walk past the Rellingers' or any of the other gossips on the street.

She keeps her head down, moving as quickly as she can. She's in no rush: she's just some woman, out for a brisk morning walk, albeit in camouflage and bright yellow gloves. She hopes she'll go unnoticed, as she always has.

As she turns up Sauganash, her head aches through its fog; probably from dehydration, or from whatever the goateed man slipped in her drink. Just a little farther now, a few blocks.

When she has the church in sight, a wave of panic breaks at her chest. She has sinned, hasn't she?

She stops at the corner across the street from the Queen of All Saints Basilica, its tall steeple poking heaven. In front of the church, the sky opens up over vast lawn that sprawls toward the place of worship, a massive introduction.

On the other side of the lawn, light traffic flits back and forth on Devon. Soon enough, cars will turn toward the church, parish members arriving for their weekly dose of spirit. Right now, the church sits, a quiet giant. This is Leslie's time to confess.

As she approaches the church, the lump that rises in her throat couples with the swelling and makes her wheeze. She pulls at one of the gigantic door handles, but the door is locked. She tries another, the next, the last. All locked.

Tears are hot in her eyes. It's Sunday morning. Where is God?

She tries each door again, yanking at the handles to no result. The locks rattle; the sound must echo through the cavernous chapel. Will no one hear her?

The physical effort drains her, and too soon, she can't catch her breath. She looks up, at the building and the bell tower and the big blue sky.

And then it all goes black.

"Miss, are you okay?"

A tall man with soft, gray hair stands over her. He is dressed in black slacks, a windbreaker.

"I think I fainted," she says.

"Worse than that," he says, pointing to her yellow glove—blood has stained it brown. She knew the exertion made her lightheaded; she did not think about the fact that it would speed her circulation—through her arteries and veins, out her hand.

"I cut myself," she says.

The man helps her up; she leans into him and he takes her good arm over his shoulder, supporting her weak legs and practically carrying her along.

"I'll call an ambulance."

"No—really," she says, resisting his forward movement. "I'm okay; I just need a bandage."

"At least come inside. We have a first-aid kit."

He leads her around the chapel to an adjacent building nestled in between the church and the school.

"Here we are." He helps her up two steps; she leans on the railing as he opens the door.

When he turns and offers his hand, his warm, hazel eyes a second invitation, she feels like she should explain herself.

"I was . . . gardening," she says. "Working in the yard."

His smile has nothing to do with the truth. "Spring is bringing beautiful flowers this year."

What if he thinks she's nuts? Or that she's lying. What if he has some ethical duty to tell the authorities? "I locked myself out," she explains. "My husband is out of town, and no one else has a key."

"You're only human. Please, come inside."

She takes his hand.

"We'll have to be quiet," he says, in a voice that is already soft, "there are five of us priests here, and we usually don't receive callers until after eight." He leads her inside through a small, marbled foyer that is noticeably warm and smells of brewed coffee. Then, through a bigger hall with honey-colored walls, he takes her through a mahogany-framed doorway past two closed doors and into a bathroom.

He turns on the bathroom lights by a heavy, old-fashioned switch. The room is tiny and pale blue; a high, glass-blocked window above the shower throws chunks of daylight onto the adjacent tile.

He sits her down on the toilet lid and runs water in the pedestal sink. "Takes a while to get warm," he tells her. "I'll go and get the first-aid kit."

Leslie sits and waits. The air in the room is moist and just as warm as the others, and the wall opposite the toilet is beaded with condensation, though there are no towels in sight. No towels, no toothbrushes, no lotions or the like; only a brand-new bar of Ivory soap sits on the back of the sink. Nothing fancy; only necessary.

When the priest returns with the first-aid kit, his face is solemn, and he does not speak. Instead he kneels on the tile before her, puts on a pair of thin-framed rectangular glasses, reaches for her hand, and gently removes the blood-soaked glove.

He turns her hand over, palm side up, and examines the wound.

"I'm so embarrassed," she says.

His deep eyes are magnified by the glasses. "It is warm in here. Do you want to remove your coat?"

"I'm cold," she says, because the collar of the jacket hides the marks on her neck. She pulls the coat together by the zipper's teeth, covering herself.

"Chilly mornings," he says. "They still keep most of the parish from coming to the early service."

"Does Mass begin soon? Will you be late?"

"I do not conduct services; I am the vicar. I am responsible for overseeing all the priests in the diocese, so I have the weekends off. It's a bit like being God's secretary." He takes her arm by the heavy coat and turns her toward the sink. "The water is warm."

He pulls back her sleeve so it doesn't get wet and Leslie puts her hand under the faucet. The water runs red but it does not hurt her. The priest stands up and shares the water, lathering the bar of Ivory, and then tenderly assists her, his hands soft and soapy, no hesitation over her blood.

"This is not as bad as it looks," he says.

Her fingers are swollen; the shiv sliced her skin one way and then another, but the cuts are fairly shallow, and it seems they only bled again because her hand had been curled into a fist. When she'd inadvertently flexed her fingers, she split open the scabs.

Once finished, the priest opens the cabinet next to the door and retrieves a plain white towel.

"I will stain it," she says.

"I will wash it," he says.

He helps her dry her hands and then kneels again to dress each finger, first with alcohol, then with salve, then with gauze and tape. He is meticulous, as though he is fixing the fragile hand of a doll, though his hands are the ones that are pale and soft and hairless.

"There you are." He takes off his glasses and nods, proud of the job.

"I can't go home," she says, a confession.

The priest sits back on his heels. "May I ask you something?"

Leslie nods while what's left of her defenses shoot up around her, thin as an eggshell. She realizes her coat has fallen open again, and she knows he's seen her neck.

"You can ask me," she says, her voice so small.

He looks down at his hands, hesitating, as though he's mentally rewording the question. Then he looks up and she feels like her pain is absorbed in his eyes. He asks, "Are you a Roman Catholic?"

Defenseless, Leslie says, "No."

His face concedes nothing: no disappointment or agenda. He says, "I just thought you might want to come to Mass. I like to be there to welcome the parishioners."

"I need some time to rest."

His smile is a solace. "You need time to heal."

He helps her up from the toilet and takes her back into the front room, a great red room with a grand piano and bookcases and photographs and all kinds of couches and chairs; still, it seems like a peaceful place where someone might sit and listen to the clock tick. He leads her to a red-and-white-printed couch that backs up against a bay window.

"Please sit," the priest says, almost under his breath. "I'll just be a moment."

He leaves her there, entering an archway that boasts a huge dining table. She wonders if that's the room where the Catholic Neighbors' Association holds their monthly brunch. She sits, feeling like a pauper in some valiant stranger's mansion. On the wall opposite, a large gold-framed painting hangs, a wisp-drawn angel reaching down toward a dark-shrouded woman below. The background is also dark, making the light detail exquisite: it seems the angel's wings could lift them both up and away, if not for their withdrawn expressions.

The priest returns momentarily with a glass of water, which he sets on the end table next to Leslie.

"Ah," he says, "you're looking at our little treasure."

"It's beautiful."

"I found that in the basement last year. We'd been doing some cleaning—making more room for more things we didn't have room for—when I found it. It was unframed and covered in dust; nobody thought it was worth a dime. It spoke to me, though. So I had it cleaned up. The man who restored it contacted an appraiser, and we discovered it was painted in the late eighteenth century."

"It must be very valuable."

He sits down next to her, close, like they've known one another a long time; it makes her nervous, but at the same time his calm is affecting. "Value," he says, "does not influence my appreciation. It's human nature, though, isn't it? To take for granted those things we believe have no value?"

Leslie looks down at her bandaged hand. She feels like he's talking about her. About the fact she took her whole life for granted, just for one night.

He puts his hand on his chin, like he's thinking about the right way to phrase his next thought; Leslie is afraid it will come in the form of a question.

"Thank you," she says, hoping he won't ask.

He smiles, warm as the room. "If you decide to go home before I return," he says, "please know my door is always open."

He leans over and takes her good hand, a meaningful squeeze. "Peace be with you." He gets up, heading the direction they came.

"What is your name, Father?" Leslie asks, after him.

He stops near the piano and turns to her. "Grace. Father Michael Grace."

He leaves without asking hers.

Before he opens his eyes, Craig reaches for his gun. He never knows where he's going to wake up these days, but one thing remains the same: he keeps his .380 in reach at three o'clock. Most times, his gun is ready to go before he figures out which room he's in at the Aragon, or who woke him up.

Usually he's coaxed from dreaming by someone bitching at someone else out on Kenmore Street. Or by Leslie bitching at him. This morning, though, it's the lack of a rude awakening that rouses him, and he immediately wonders what he's late for, where he's supposed to be.

He puts his gun back on the table and flips open his phone: clock says it's just after eight. Despite the shitty, sagging couch cushions, this might have been the best six hours he's had in months.

He sits up. Why is it so quiet?

He gets a glass of orange juice from the fridge, sucks it down, pours another. He feels sluggish; that's what late nights do to a guy. He's got to be short on Vitamin C, D, probably all the rest. He can't remember the last time he ate three squares. He needs to tell Leslie to get him some multivitamins.

Leslie. Sleeping upstairs, probably ticked off, even in her dreams. Upset with him for some damn thing, for not talking about his feelings, probably, even though she knows he's got to keep things separate. She knows that his identity, as a police officer and a husband and a father, depends on the strength of silence. She knows, and apparently she no longer gives a shit.

Point taken, though in no way accepted.

Craig climbs the stairs. He'll tell Leslie what she did: how she trashed the entire foundation of trust he'd built on the force with one fell swoop. How she made him the laughingstock; undermined his authority, sullied his star.

If she did this to get his attention, she's about to get it. And then some.

Craig reaches the end of the hall and quietly opens the bedroom door. Not because he doesn't want to disturb her—he plans to disturb her, all right.

Inside, though, the bed is made, blinds open; his bride is nowhere in sight. Various outfits are strewn from the closet to her vanity: pantyhose and that long black skirt he thinks is too tight and every damn blouse that was on a hanger last time he got dressed in here. The vanity is covered with makeup, brushes, woman-clutter. And she is gone.

So she must have heard from one of the other wives: she found out that word got back to him, got herself together and got the hell out of here without so much as a peep. She was probably so paranoid she'd wake him and start a fight that she put her car in neutral and let it roll down the driveway. Smart move.

Craig strips naked and runs the shower. While he lets the bathroom steam up, he shaves off the scruffy beard he hadn't so much as trimmed since the case started. It was unruly, and itchy, and it always smelled like whatever he ate last. It feels so good to get it off of his face, even if his jawline has grown soft underneath.

Once clean and dressed, he goes downstairs, makes himself some peanut butter toast. He wonders what the deal is with the rose Leslie put back on the counter after he threw it across the room the other night. It sits there, same place, new vase. She must be making some other point, though he couldn't care less what.

He takes his toast, settles into the recliner and flips through the Sunday morning shows. He doesn't feel like hearing about the war on terror, or the latest opinion polls; he can't stand the latest opinions. Guys wearing makeup telling him what's wrong with the world. He might as well find a cartoon.

He winds up watching some dumb thing on Nickelodeon with super-annoying kids teaching each other life lessons. The show is nothing like the one he and Ivy'd watch when she was a young girl: she'd get him out of bed at the crack every Saturday morning, her sweetest voice her secret weapon. She'd do the same routine every time: a little dance, a made-up jingle advertising her favorite treats from Swedish's. She'd have her order ready, drawn up in a list: cream-cheese doughnuts and chocolate-iced rings, glazed long johns and sugar twists—more than a little girl could ever eat, though she always promised otherwise. He'd run down to the bakery—he had a stand-ing bribe with the girls behind the counter so he could skip the line— and he'd speed home to make it back in time to join Ivy in front of the television for the newest *Animaniacs* adventure. It was a crappy show, but that wasn't the point.

When Craig would pull up in the drive, the white bakery package on the seat next to him, Ivy would throw open the front door and race to meet him, all bright-eyed and bushy-tailed, anticipating the delivery. She'd bring the box into the house and carefully untie the red string as though what was inside was the biggest, most fragile surprise. And she'd smile at him. Through every powdery, jelly-filled bite.

Now, on the weekends, Ivy sleeps until at least noon; she's not interested in cartoons or doughnuts, or in sharing much of anything with her father. And Craig can't remember the last time she smiled at him. The last time she smiled at all.

But Leslie is the one who insisted the girl grow up, isn't she? She'd implored Craig to quit babying her; to invest in important things instead of good times. A computer for research, Leslie argued; "Send her to the library," Craig argued back, and lost. A cell phone for safety, Leslie said; 563 text messages to friends, the bill said. Ivy never said anything. She just took whatever they handed out.

And now she's up there in her room—in her cyber-world, door locked, her lifeline a DSL cable. And her father is silly and pointless.

Craig hesitates when the incoming call on his cell display is a general number from the station. He was starting to get antsy and hoped Suwanski would call with a change of heart, but he knew that chance was slim, so he'd been thinking about driving out to the suburbs to see his buddy "Limestone" Kenny Naylor. Limestone owns a couple gravel pits; he lets Craig and some of the cops in the burbs use the digs for target practice. All Limestone asks is that the guys clean up after themselves and look the other way when one of his trucks is a little heavy. Craig thought he could drive out, unload that way.

As appealing as firing his gun sounds, he answers the call.

"Craig, it's Jemma Rowe. I thought you'd like to know I matched your prints."

"I didn't expect to hear from you so soon."

"I was stuck here on a rush job matching latents against the IAFIS. The judge knows our system is slow, and he didn't want to chance losing a day and letting the perp skip. I'm sitting here twiddling my thumbs while the computer does my work for me, so I thought I'd cash in on that bet."

Craig doesn't want to seem anxious, or like he had any question about the results, but if Jemma's heard any of the rumors about him, she's doing him another favor by playing along.

He shuts off the T.V.

"I'm on my way."

28

Leslie wakes to the sounds of the playground outside: the creaking chains of a swing as a child rocks back and forth; little footsteps charging across the sandy gravel; another young someone testing the resiliency of the jiggly bridge.

Through the window, the sun warms Leslie's face. Craig's hunting coat is pungent with mildew; the smell is foul, as out of place in the warm, linen-fresh room as the woman wearing it. She sits up, faces the long-lost painting: the angel's wings luminous on a dark earth, her arm extended toward the shrouded woman, hope suspended.

"Mommy, watch!"

Out the window behind Leslie, a girl of no more than five wearing a spring-green knee-length coat stands at the top of the curly slide, a daredevil. Her mother waves, a proud spectator; the girl disappears into the tube.

When Ivy was the girl's age, she spent Sundays at church, too, though there was no playground at Assumption. Leslie would put her in a dress and drive her down to Bridgeport where they'd pick up Leslie's parents; the four of them would attend Divine Liturgy.

Craig always said that church at such an early age didn't do a child any good, but Craig didn't understand the Greek Orthodox Church. Nor did he understand his in-laws, Mr. and Mrs. Georgio and Anastasia Kastanis.

Since Leslie was an only child, Ivy was the only grandchild. Pappous and Yiayia, as Ivy called them, were never thrilled with Leslie's decision to marry outside the faith, but it was either that or Ivy come into the world without legally bound parents.

They never said anything about Leslie, but her mother declared, "The child needs God." And back then, with a toddler and with a husband working violent crimes, Leslie needed her parents.

Yiayia would prepare Ivy, tying ribbons around her pigtails, re-straightening her Sunday dress, promising her feasts of sugar-coated goodies if she behaved at the service. Once at church, Pappous would take over, parading the girl around and showering her with kisses as though she were one of the icons. Pappous would hold her in his arms for the entire hour and a half, and she wouldn't so much as squirm. Between the expressive faithfuls and the singing and the general commotion, there was so much sensory overload that Ivy had no time to misbehave.

Her parents' watching Ivy gave Leslie a rare reprieve, time she would use to pray. She'd let the hundreds of voices envelop her spirit, and her mind would drift through the service, a sort of meditation that would bring simple solutions to so many of her troubles. She would find contentment and thank God for keeping her family together, her little girl on the right path, and her husband safe.

Then, shortly after Ivy turned five, Pappous and Yiayia both fell ill. They died within months of each other: Yiayia of lymphoma, and Pappous of congestive heart failure. And Leslie didn't feel much like praying anymore.

Maybe that's where she went wrong.

Father Michael's mantel clock softly chimes the Westminster Quarters. It's 8:30 a.m. and he hasn't returned. He must sit through every Mass.

At home, Craig is probably waking up, wondering where Leslie is. He'll loaf around while Ivy sleeps, glad to have the house to himself, until he gets hungry and needs Leslie to make his peanut butter toast. He'll start to get annoyed—he might even try to call her when he can't find another roll of toilet paper, or his favorite Levi's. When he can't reach her, he'll make do with paper towels, a dirty pair of jeans. He'll be ticked, he'll be antsy, and he'll be gone by noon.

And Ivy: she'll hit the snooze button six times after her alarm goes off. She'll sleepwalk to the shower, ignore her father, and spend too much time finding the right outfit. She'll only realize how late she's running when her ride honks a third time, and she'll blame her mother—assuming she's in the house somewhere—for not waking her up. She might even yell something snotty on her way out the door. She'll be gone by noon, also, and at least a half-hour late to work, since her ride will still stop at Starbucks on the way.

Leslie knows both Craig and Ivy will be irritated by her absence in their Sunday schedules, but neither one of them will ever believe she went to Mass.

Outside the Queen of All Saints, one of the church's side doors is open, and Leslie hears the call and response, priest to parish, as she passes by on her way around to the front doors to enter from the main entrance. Inside the doorway, she finds a statue of the blessed Virgin Mary to which she makes a *metania*—crossing herself with her right hand and bowing to the floor twice. She kisses the icon and, feeling silly when she catches the eye of an altar boy who's hanging around the foyer, moves on.

In the nave she slips into the last aisle although the pews are empty nearly a quarter of the way toward the front. She sits, feeling affected by the grandeur in front of her. She hasn't been in here in years, not since Craig's old captain Jackowski was married, and she'd forgotten just how breathtaking it is: stone pillars reach up between the stained-glass windows and spread like strong branches to support the red, star-studded arched ceiling, narrow and high; sunlight shines through the windows, as golden as the lamps overhead. And in front of her the parishioners sit, miniature, before the altar.

The priest, a gentleman of about fifty whose robe billows over his huge stomach, rounds the pulpit and says, "Through him, with him and in him, in the unity of the Holy Spirit, all glory and honor is yours, almighty Father, forever and ever."

Everyone stands up, and the heavy hymnal chords of the pipe organ spill out in waves, surrounding the giant space like spirits.

The parishioners sing, their chins held high, to the giant mosaic of Jesus above the front altar.

Amen, Amen . . .

Leslie can hear the high-pitched sopranos of older ladies, the certain, monotone voices of the older men. The chorus fills in the harmony, blending the parishioners' sharps and flats. Leslie watches them, the backs of their heads, each taller or shorter with different-shaped ears, but all of them moving in unison, with the music.

Except one man. He's standing in the middle of the last occupied pew to Leslie's right, looking over his shoulder, right at her. He seems unhappily surprised to see her. Leslie would guess him to be about her age, his face framed by a full head of dark hair and thick, rounded glasses. He is singing, and forcefully, as though he could shoo her away; in doing so, he attracts the attention of the man to his left, and the woman beside him, and the man beside him; pretty soon it seems like everyone in the nave has turned to check her out.

She doesn't recognize the man. Could he be from the neighborhood? She lowers her head and pretends to pray.

As the organist plays the final notes, Leslie reaches for the missal in the box in front of her to figure out what's next. By the time she finds the date and the section, the parishioners begin:

Our Father, who art in heaven . . .

And Leslie knows this part; she's said it a million times. She joins the recitation, confident, but she can still feel the man with glasses staring at her. She looks a mess, and she is, but isn't church a place of acceptance? What's his problem?

Feeling lightheaded, Leslie closes the catalogue. She figures these people are bound to sit again soon enough, so she crosses herself and takes a seat.

. . . *For the kingdom, the power, and the glory are yours, now and forever.*

The priest says, "The Peace of the Lord be with you always."

Everyone answers: *And also with you.*

Leslie folds her hands at her heart, in prayer. Maybe it was a mistake to come here; she hasn't prayed for anything except for that man with the staring problem to mind his own business.

The priest says, "Let us offer each other a sign of peace."

She shuts her eyes and prays: *please, God, have I fallen so far? I have sinned and been sinned against, can't we call it even?*

"Peace be with you."

Leslie feels a hand on her shoulder and she nearly jumps out of her skin. She opens her eyes, and the man with glasses is standing over her, his hand out.

"Peace be with you," he says again.

She doesn't move.

He lowers his hand. "Forgive me," he says, "I didn't mean to startle you."

"Why were you looking back here?"

"I thought I knew you."

"I think you need new glasses."

"You're probably right."

The parishioners in front of them kneel, the priest and his helpers preparing for Communion.

"Will you take Communion?" the man asks, pulling out the kneeler.

"I don't think so," Leslie says, thinking of her knees.

"Only say the words and you shall be healed," he says to her, reciting with the rest of the parishioners.

"I don't think that's going to work, in my case."

"You're here. God understands." He tucks the kneeler away, gets up and goes back to his pew.

Leslie closes her eyes and prays, hoping the man is right.

Jemma doesn't pay any attention to Craig when he walks into the lab's main office. She's the only one there, feet kicked up on her desk, reading glasses low on her nose, scanning an issue of *People.*

"Jemma."

She looks up, lifts and lowers her glasses like she's switching the magnification on a microscope. "Cray-ig: you look like a different man."

"Got rid of the beard. I clean up nice, don't I?"

Jemma tucks her glasses into her lab coat pocket. "I wasn't talking about the beard." She tosses the magazine on the desk, gets up and comes around to offer him a hand tipped with long, hot-pink nails. "Latest case get to you?"

"Nah."

"Liar." She smiles, her two front teeth crossed over one another, the only two things Craig can find out of line about the woman. She presses a flat hand against the edges of her ironed afro, says, "Come with me."

Craig follows Jemma as she walks real slow, just like she talks. Her hips lead, every step a statement, into the next room.

On the desk in the corner, she has two computer screens running: one searching prints, probably her IAFIS latents case, and the other playing piano-led jazz, a digital slinky bouncing around the screen to the beat.

"Dave Brubeck?" Craig asks.

"Yeah. Hey, I didn't figure you for a guy who likes jazz."

"You thought I was more of a classical guy?"

"Classic, that's for sure." She opens a file cabinet, reaches to the back, retrieves a file.

"It's my wife, actually. She's the jazz expert."

"Makes sense." Jemma doesn't say why. She opens the file and places a plastic sleeve suspending glass slides on the backlit work-table, flips on the light.

"So, on the level: is this about your daughter, or your wife?"

"You heard."

"I *heard* nothing. Look at this." She pushes the sleeve toward him. "Samples brought back four people." She traces a line with one hot-pink nail from top to bottom of the first sleeve. "You, Leslie, your mother, and Nikodemus Stavrakos."

"Niko—what? What's his last name?"

"Read it," she says, and runs a fingernail between her eyelids, fishing something out. "Sounds like some kinda Greek dignitary or something."

"Stavrakos. He's my daughter's boyfriend."

"So he's in the house," she says. "But where's Ivy?"

"You didn't match her prints?"

"Nope." She bats her fat eyelashes. "So what kinda bet are you running, Craig? With a girl who never set foot in the room."

"It's more like a bet against her. I heard she had a little party while I was at work, and I'm betting she's not as smart as she thinks she is."

"She's certainly smart enough to clean up after herself."

Craig wonders if Leslie gave her any help.

Jemma takes out another sleeve and slides it to Craig. "Must have been some party, anyway. Based on the samples you gave me, it seems your mother was the one who had her hands on the whiskey."

Craig wishes he still had the beard to hide his reaction. "She's not supposed to drink with her medication," he says.

"My mama says, the older she gets, the more she believes in the healing power of a brandy press."

Craig is thankful that Jemma's playing along, making him feel okay about all this, but tension is still thick from his side, because she knows something he doesn't. The something she didn't say when he'd mentioned Leslie.

"Tell me about this kid Niko," he says, the easier line of questioning. "How'd you match him?"

"I checked the local databases. He worked at one of those convenience kiosks out at O'Hare last year. I matched him to his smart card."

"But SecuGen doesn't keep employee records online—it's a violation of privacy."

"Violation of *huh*? This is wartime, Craig. And he's no longer an employee. So you know what that makes him, in the eyes of the TSA? Another potential threat."

"But is he a threat to Ivy?"

Jemma takes out two more plastic sleeves and hands them to Craig. "Here's the thing, hun. These slides? All from the piano. Some Niko. The rest, Leslie. I don't think the kid's a threat to anyone but you."

Craig compares the prints, seeing Niko's name next to Leslie's, next to Niko's, next to Leslie's—

"He could be trying to get into your wife's good graces," Jemma says, while Craig is caught up in the memory of lifting prints from the piano: they were everywhere, overlapping—"And you do know," Jemma says, "that these prints tell us who was there, but they don't tell us when. Maybe Niko was playing for Ivy."

Craig puts both sheets down on the worktable, studying one of Niko's prints through the light, its perfect loops, its defined ridges. Ivy never took to the piano. This kid was playing with his wife.

"SecuGen keep pictures?" he asks.

"No, but look." Jemma goes over to the second computer and moves the mouse: the slinky bounces away and a Web page fills the screen. At the top, the Green Mill Cocktail Lounge's lights blink, just like the sign out on Broadway.

"What's this?" he asks.

"This," she says, "is the first thing you find when you Google Nikodemus Stavrakos."

Jemma clicks on the home page's calendar link and brings up the month of May; then she clicks on "Jay Jones's Quartet Jam Session," which brings up a slide show of photos. She clicks through, stopping on one in particular: the band.

Two black guys frame a third at the drums, each one older than the next; a white kid sits to their right at the piano, smiling for the camera, real sure of himself. The caption underneath: *Sammy "the Tramp" Lewis, Tom Blackwell, Jay Jones, Niko Stavrakos.*

Craig says, "Print it."

Jemma hits the drop-down menu to print the page and they stand there, the awkward silence between them filled by Brubeck and his band doing "There'll Be Some Changes Made."

While Craig waits for the printer he imagines them, Leslie and Niko, at the piano in *his* house, the one *he* bought for his wife: their heads toward one another as they play, Leslie smiling as Niko reaches over—

Jemma hands him the photo, says, "Look at the bright side. The kid doesn't have a rap sheet."

Leslie has never asked God for answers, but she's starting to feel like he's trying to make a point when the priest who conducts the nine-thirty Mass just happens to be the man with the glasses who asked her to take Communion at the last service.

With no sign of Father Michael, Leslie decided to stay; it was too soon to go home, and she didn't want to return to the priest's residence, give him an opportunity to ask more questions.

Instead, she sat in the last row and pretended to pray while the parishioners from the previous Mass filed out and the new ones came in. Then everyone stood and the priest came in behind the altar boys, a generous smile in her direction.

The church is packed this time, all the way to the last pew. Just before the service began, a twenty-something mom ushered in three young brothers, each about a year apart, no older than six. They took their seats in front of Leslie, similar polo shirts, same buzz cuts, and began the service on their best behavior. Leslie was impressed.

Now, though, as Mass drags on, the promise of whatever reward they'll receive for such behavior—a Happy Meal, maybe, or a new video game—has become a distant memory, and all three are fidgety, more interested in what the one next to him is doing that he shouldn't be.

Leslie can't blame them; the service barely holds her attention. She's just glad they aren't interested in the strange woman behind them who looks crazy or homeless or worse: Leslie, the woman Mom clearly wonders about, stealing just as many glances at her behavior as at her own boys'.

After the second reading, the parishioners stand up again, and Leslie wonders where they got this formal routine. In the Greek Orthodox Church, everyone stands all the time: there are people up and down the aisles, coming and going, praying and singing, each one on their own personal prayer schedule. Here, people are by the Book, singing "Alleluia" from their missals instead of their hearts. It feels more like being in the Army than in the spirit of things. If God did have an army, wouldn't he want them to show some enthusiasm?

Figuring the thought is sacrilegious, Leslie crosses herself, shuts her eyes and prays with everyone else.

The priest goes to the pulpit and says, "A reading from the Holy Gospel according to Luke."

The parishioners respond: *Glory to you, Lord.*

The priest leans over his Bible; even from the very back, Leslie can tell he's squinting. He reads, "And He spoke a parable unto them, saying, 'The ground of a certain rich man brought forth plentifully.'

"And he thought within himself, saying, 'What shall I do, because I have no room where to bestow my fruits?'

"And he said, 'This will I do: I will pull down my barns, and build greater; and there will I bestow all my fruits and my goods.'

"'And I will say to my soul, Soul, thou hast much goods laid up for many years; take thine ease, eat, drink, and be merry.'

"But God said unto him, 'Fool, this night thy soul shall be required of thee: then whose shall those things be, which thou hast provided?'

"So is he that layeth up treasure for himself, and is not rich toward God."

The priest bookmarks his Bible, closes it, and says, "The Gospel of the Lord."

The parishioners say: *Praise to you, Lord Jesus Christ.*

Leslie says "Amen" all by herself, acknowledging another of God's lessons. In front of her, Mom shoots her oldest boy a dirty look for looking at Leslie. It's only then that she realizes she's the only one still standing.

She sits as the priest comes around the pulpit.

"Now, you may ask yourselves, what do we take from the Word of the Lord today? But, my friends, if you listened to the passage, you might suspect this is not the right question. Today, I call on you to ask yourselves, not what do we take, but what do we do to *take care* of the Word of the Lord?"

Having been pinched by his brother, the youngest boy in front of Leslie squirms. She tries to ignore them now; she wants to hear this.

"We are here on a beautiful Sunday morning," the priest says. "How many of you are sitting out there, anticipating the end of this service? How many of your minds fast-forward to your child's next activity, or today's baseball game, or this afternoon's trip to the mall?"

A good number of the parishioners lower their heads, embarking on their Catholic guilt trips.

The priest asks, "How many of you are thinking about brunch?" which gets a few laughs.

The brothers in front of Leslie look at one another like they missed a joke. After a second pinch from older to younger, this one caught by Mom, she intervenes, moving one boy to the other side and scooting into his seat.

The priest steps down, into the nave. "Isn't it true that God has given us everything we need?"

A handful of lowered heads nod.

"And in doing so, he has asked only that we live in Him. But we do not, do we? Just as Luke tells us, when we have all we need, we want more. We want the next thing: a bigger home. A better job. A more passionate spouse." He starts down the aisle; a few parishioners watch him, but most remain face-forward.

The two boys make faces at the third, on the other side of Mom, every single moment she isn't looking.

"Who of us hasn't wished for something more?" the priest asks. "And how many of us take all we are afforded, without taking care of what we already have?"

When he reaches the center of the nave he stops, turning back toward the altar, quiet for a moment, maybe ordering his thoughts.

In the silence, Leslie's sure just about everyone can hear the two older boys in front of her whisper nonsense to one another, hands over their giggles.

The priest turns around again and continues down the aisle. "The real question, my friends, is how many, if any of us, expect what we have to be taken away?"

He stops when he reaches the back of the church, standing before Mom and her three boys. "There are those of us in need," he says, and it sounds scolding. "Those who are afraid God has turned away. What should a person in need believe when the rest of our daily lives are so filled up with our own taking that we fail to reach out to them? That we fail to *give*?"

It's clear to Leslie the priest is speaking to her; the boys, however, shrink in fear. They've forgotten McDonald's and Nintendo, and they'll never forget this. They don't need to know the priest can't see past his nose.

"Let me assure you," he says, smiling at Leslie, "God is not preoccupied with playdates or dinner parties or with the Cubs—don't we know he's not. God makes each and every one of us his first priority.

He only asks that we live in Him. And to do so, we must be grateful for all we have, and we must *take care* of it."

He turns back up the aisle, and it isn't until he reaches the altar and faces the parishioners that he says, "I ask you all today to *take care* of God's Word, not to take from it."

The parishioners stand, and begin to recite: *I believe in God the Father Almighty, Maker of heaven and earth . . .*

A few lines into the Apostle's Creed, Leslie is out of there. The priest is right: she's got to take care of what she has left.

29

Usually when a case is over, Craig has no problem returning to life as usual. It's like the day after Halloween, when he dismantles his old standard vampire costume, and in the daylight it's just the black suit he wears to civilian funerals, a silver wig, and one of Leslie's tablecloths doubling as a cape.

He gets into the Caprice. He was going to turn it in, find a beat cop, catch a ride back to his house to get the Tacoma. How nice it would be to give it a wash and a wax, drive it up to the state line and find some mud, kick it into four-wheel, get it dirty again.

But Craig knows he can't take a day off when there isn't much left of his life beneath the dismantled costume.

He pulls out of the station's lot and goes down to Foster, heads out to the Edens. At a stoplight, he rolls down the windows. The day is warming up, and quick; spring is finally making its move.

And so is Craig. He thought about calling Denniwitz, doing this over the phone. But sometimes you have to read a man: his eyes, what he does with his hands. Craig doesn't know why Denniwitz covered for Ivy—and for Leslie—or when. But the guy was acting funny at Rudy's funeral, and now Craig knows the reason.

Craig shoots up the Edens, gets off at Touhy, makes his way back south to Estes. Denniwitz's house is the last one on the left, backed up against the expressway's on-ramp. It's a decent one-story, single-family; he and Annabelle and her daughter, Lindsey, moved in just before they were married. The place would be a dump if it were built in some suburban cul-de-sac, but here, on the outskirts of the city, it sits proud.

Craig parks in the drive and rings the bell.

"Craig," Annabelle says, like she didn't want to find him on her doorstep.

"Hi, Annie. Stan home?"

"Where else would he be?" She jerks her head back, chin-first, like she tasted something sour. She doesn't make a move to open the screen door.

"Something smells good," Craig says, since she's wearing an apron that says *I love cooking with wine . . . sometimes I even put it in the food!*

"It's dinner," she says, no invitation.

"I won't stay long," he says. "Just need a word with your husband."

"Staa-an!" she yells over her shoulder, and goes back into the kitchen, leaving Craig standing there.

Craig folds his hands in front of his waist, decides it makes him look submissive, crosses his arms instead. By the time Stan comes to the door, Craig's got his hands on his hips, head cocked, a regular cowboy.

"Craig," Denniwitz says, the Cars section of the *Trib* tucked under his arm. "I figured you'd come around." He opens the screen door; Craig steps inside.

They walk through the front room, down the steps into the finished basement where *Planes, Trains and Automobiles* is playing on the twenty-seven-inch TV.

Denniwitz goes for his easy chair, the leather so old it's cracked around the cushions' buttons. The rest of the *Trib* is spread out on the carpet next to the chair, a fat gray and white housecat sitting on the front page. Stan shoos the cat and sits, raising the leg rest; from behind the chair another, bigger cat, this one orange, abruptly jumps up and joins him. "Have a seat," Denniwitz says.

Craig says, "I don't want to have a seat, man."

John Candy says, "God you're a tightwad."

"Tight *ass*," Denniwitz says. "This dubbed-for-TV baloney. Tightwad doesn't even make sense."

"I didn't come here to watch basic cable," Craig says.

Denniwitz reaches for the remote, temporarily disturbing the gray and white cat who has repositioned itself underneath the leg rest. Denniwitz shuts off the TV and says to Craig, "You're in my house. Sit." The orange cat blinks, slow motion, watching Craig from its lap-throne.

"Maa-am!" Annabelle's daughter, Lindsey, yells, appearing from the basement bathroom, same flat a's as her mother. She has half the hair on her head straightened, the other still in its natural, frizzy curl.

"Go upstairs, Linz," Denniwitz tells her.

Lindsey folds her arms and kicks out a bony, prepubescent hip. "I need five bucks."

"Go ask your mother."

"That's what I was try-ying to do."

"What do you need five bucks for? A hat?"

"I ran out of hairspray."

"I like your curls. Why do you have to do that to your hair?"

"Because I'm white, Stanley."

By the look on Denniwitz's face, Craig thinks taking a seat and getting out of the way is a real wise idea.

"What's all the fuss?" Annabelle asks when she reaches the bottom step, a can of creamed corn in her hand.

"I need five bucks," Lindsey says.

Annabelle says, "You haven't done your chores. Or your homework."

"Any chance you girls can take this negotiation upstairs?" Denniwitz asks, petting the orange cat with considerable force, the cat pressing up, its spine stiff against his hand. Below them, the gray and white cat locates an invisible enemy and attacks the newspaper, clawing the paper's Home section.

"It's time for Caitlin to go, honey," Annabelle says.

A girl about Lindsey's age, presumably Caitlin, shows up in the bathroom doorway; her smile is fake behind blue-banded braces.

With backup, Lindsey stands a little taller. "Caitlin isn't going anywhere. Not with my hair half-done."

Craig takes a seat on the far end of the high-backed plaid couch, figuring none of them are going anywhere, but Denniwitz pushes the orange cat from his lap and says, "Let's go." He gets up out of his easy chair.

"Where are you going?" Annabelle asks as he passes her on the steps.

"Out," Denniwitz says. "For a beer."

"Staa-an . . ." Annabelle starts—

"Zip it, Annie. One beer."

Craig shrugs at Annabelle as he follows Denniwitz up the steps.

"Maa-am, I can't go to school tomorrow looking like this," Lindsey says behind them.

Denniwitz shakes his head, keeps moving.

.   .   .

Everything according to plan.

Leslie hangs up Craig's hunting coat and fills a bucket with two parts water, one part bleach, a much stronger solution than she's ever used at the shop. First, she tries removing the blood on the garage floor in front of her car with a mop, but she can't get up the stains, so she pours the diluted bleach over the area and lets it sit. Then she pulls on latex gloves, positions an unopened bag of potter's soil right next to the stains, and rests her shins against the softer surface to protect her knees while she goes to work with a scrub brush.

It takes her a long time, using her left hand, and when she can't scrub anymore, she's sure she can still see the stains. Maybe because she knows where to look. Or maybe because they are too deep.

The fumes are harsh: they burn her eyes, dry her throat. It isn't until after she mops again and dumps the dirty water out back, along the property line, that she realizes she is sweating, and she feels ill from the overwhelming chemical smell. She wishes she could open the garage doors, but someone might see her and wonder why on earth she's the one waxing the car. Craig would be the one they'd expect to find out in the drive, both vehicles soapy, water running out to the street.

She uses Turtle Wax and a chamois to rub out the damage the Asian did with his shiv on the hood of her car. She goes over the scratches again and again, but she can't buff them out. She decides she'll have to take it to a body shop: the scratches are too deep.

She collects the scrub brush, the head of the mop, the garden gloves: all of it goes into a trash bag. Once the floor is dry she sweeps up dust, spilled soil, strands of her hair. She shakes the dustpan into the trash bag and goes over the area once more, checking for anything she may have left behind.

She finds her underwear in the bed of Craig's truck.

Finally, when she's exhausted every angle, and herself, she puts the trash bag in her trunk and opens the electronic garage door. She steps out onto the drive and feels the sun on her face. It's become warm outside; the faint breeze chases the humidity, tickles new leaves on the trees in the front yard. The garage should air out quickly, and soon; there will be no visible evidence of a crime.

Everything according to plan.

Inside the house, the jagged edges of her nerves soften once she is certain she is alone. Still, she sneaks through the house, afraid she'll give herself away. She stops in the kitchen for another, smaller trash bag and her conscience follows, a threat.

The bedroom is just as she left it last night: clothes strewn here and there because she didn't have a clue what to wear. Back and forth between a skirt, jeans. *What's the big deal?* she'd wondered, though she knew the answer had something to do with the flutter of excitement in her chest. Nothing was really going to happen between them, she'd told herself; anything could, she knew.

In the daylight, there is nothing so exciting. In the daylight, there is only the mess.

She puts away the clothes, her makeup, the necklaces she couldn't decide between. She tidies. Straightens. This mess, she can clean.

In the bathroom, panic momentarily blinds her and lingers like a camera's flash when she finds Craig's hair all over the sink. A wet towel hangs over the tub. A *Sports Illustrated* sits on the tile next to the toilet, the cover warped by water spots.

Craig must have been in here, just a little while ago. Did he notice anything amiss? Did he bother to look?

Did he wonder about his wife?

Incensed, Leslie runs the shower and prepares to wash away the last of the evidence. No one will ever know what happened to her. It'll be easy, she guesses, because no one will ask.

She strips off her olive sweater, and then her black satin shell—the top she wore to the Green Mill that was supposed to be sexy, understated—the one she thought would help her blend into the crowd and still show enough skin to make her stand out. The pavement burns on her forearms wouldn't have been so bad if she'd covered herself up from the beginning.

She sits on the toilet, careful of her knees as she pulls off her jeans but as soon as she does, she remembers: the Asian man, what he did to her. She can still smell him.

Her body twists to the floor; she lifts the toilet seat and dry-heaves, her stomach tight, the rest of her completely unraveling. There is no plan that will cover this. The wounds run too deep.

"I tell ya, it's been a living hell," Denniwitz says. "Lindsey turned ten and her wings fell off." He cracks open a Bud, hands it to Craig.

Craig hands the beer back to Denniwitz, says, "That's too bad Stan, but I think you know I'm here about *my* daughter, and why you wanted me to think she still had hers."

Denniwitz takes a sip of Bud, looks out over the empty basketball court like he's nostalgic. Like he used to play. Like he didn't just put a sixer of beer in the backseat of his old Jeep Wrangler, drive two blocks from his house, and stop here at this crummy park on Greenleaf just to get away.

"Why didn't you tell me about Ivy, Stan?"

Denniwitz leans against the Jeep. "You remember when I got married?"

"Of course I remember. I stood up at the wedding."

"You didn't want to."

"I never said that."

"You didn't have to say it."

Craig leans against the Jeep, too, because it's hard to face a man when he's right. "Lucy had just died," he says. "I thought you and Annabelle were rushing it."

"You and everybody else." Denniwitz sips hard on his beer. "Maybe you were right." He walks off toward the basketball court, the sound barrier that separates the park from the highway an ugly backdrop.

"I still wore the tux," Craig calls after him.

Denniwitz stops, turns around. "You know why? Because you respected me. You respected what I was going through. You think it would have done any good to tell me what you knew? That my sons were hurting, and they didn't need a replacement? That Annie's a control freak? That here I'd be, five years later, closing my eyes just to get a glimpse of what I had before?" He fishes a pack of Marlboros from his shirt pocket.

"I thought you quit."

"Don't worry. My marriage will be the thing that kills me."

Craig snags a beer from the back of the Jeep, follows Denniwitz across the court to a picnic bench.

Denniwitz sits on the tabletop, lights a cigarette, exhales hard. He says, "I'm sorry. I kept my mouth shut because I thought you needed me to."

Craig climbs up, sits beside him. "I guess we're even."

Denniwitz spits a flake of tobacco from his tongue. "You know, toward the end, when Lucy was real sick, she sat me down one night. Told me she didn't want everybody coming over, bringing casseroles, trying to make it okay. She knew it wasn't going to be. But she wanted the chance to make it okay by me. Those last days, it was just Lucy and me and our sons. And in those days? I realized that sometimes you have to stop being the police and be a goddamned human being. That's what I was trying to do for you: I was trying to give you the chance to make it okay."

"It's not okay. Not between Leslie and me."

"She know you heard about Ivy?"

"Shit, Stan, who cares? The entire department knows. I'm a complete brown eye."

"I didn't think it would blow up like this."

"You lied to me, Stan. Even when I came to you about my snitch—"

"—About your case, Craig. At Rudy's memorial service—at your best friend's memorial service, for Christ's sake, you came to me about your case. Not your family."

Craig puts his Bud on the picnic table. He reaches into his back pocket, unfolds the photo printout Jemma made from the Green Mill Web site. "Well, now, Stan? I'm coming to you about my family."

Denniwitz stows his cigarette between his lips and takes the photo.

"Distant relatives?" he asks, squinting at the picture through smoke.

"The kid on the right," Craig says. "Ivy's boyfriend."

Denniwitz runs his finger along the listed names, stops and says, "Niko. Yeah."

"You know him?"

"Never seen him before."

"So how come it sounds like you know him?"

"Because when Ivy was in Roscoe's backseat, she kept asking about him. Said she showed up there with him and she wanted us to find him. Unfortunately, I had about five hundred other kids to collar."

"Like my snitch."

Denniwitz hands back the photo, takes the cigarette from his mouth, stiff-fingered. "Craig, you act like I wanted to jam you up. We had every beat cop in the district trying to wrangle those kids, and any one of us could have arrested any one of them. It was like flushing pheasants. I just happened to pick off your man."

"And my daughter."

"Wasn't me who found her. I didn't even know she was there till Roscoe told me. He said when he went into the warehouse, she's the one who approached him. He put her in his squad and came over to ask if I'd ride with him. Said she was acting real inappropriate, and he wanted me to come along, since he knows you and me are buddies. I couldn't leave right away, so I checked on her; that's when she was on about her boy Niko. She offered Roscoe the ecstasy she had in exchange for finding him."

"What did Roscoe do with the drugs?"

"What do you think he did with them? He waited till we got far enough away from the scene and threw them out the fuckin' squad window."

Craig picks up his beer, turns it around in his hands. "Roscoe wasn't exaggerating. Ivy was that bad."

Denniwitz studies the cherry of his smoke, maybe trying to word his answer nicely. "I only know what I saw in his backseat," he says, flicking ashes into the grass. "By the time we drove her home, she was jabbering like a kindergartener. 'The love bug, the love drug' she kept singing, like it was some kind of nursery rhyme. It could have been worse, man. At least she was coherent."

Craig takes his first drink of beer, a long one. "I can't believe she turned up, same place as my snitch."

"You know what I can't believe? The fact that you *still* keep trying to make this a case. If you're worried about your snitch, go read his arrest report." He takes the photo, dangles it in front of Craig's face. "You're worried about Ivy, you deal with this kid Niko."

Denniwitz turns the photo around and looks at it again; this time, he flicks the whole cigarette away. "Wait a minute: I know this name, Stavrakos. Remember last year, January? That guy who went down for stealing ketamine from a string of veterinary clinics down on the near west side? Name was Stavrakos."

Craig takes the photo back, his gut feeling twisted. "Why the hell does that stick in your head?"

"Because one of the places was PAWS Chicago. You know: Pets Are Worth Saving?"

"Again: why in the hell does that stick?"

"PAWS promotes fostering from birth. Last year Christmas, Santa let Lindsey take a trip to PAWS for a kitten. She found the one she had to have, but the shelter wouldn't let her split the litter. Lindsey conned Annabelle into letting her foster four. She was supposed to keep them until they were old enough for adoption. We figured it would be a good responsibility lesson for Linz. Six weeks later, somebody cleaned out PAWS's ketamine supply. They couldn't spay or neuter. A month after that, the city's cat population practically doubled and the shelter couldn't take any of the fostered ones back."

"How come you didn't put the cats up for adoption?"

"We did. You ever tried giving away a cat?"

"You could've taken them to a shelter that euthanizes."

"Some lesson that would've turned out to be for Lindsey. Your new daddy can't stand your cats: he's going to take them on a little trip. To die. Say good-bye!" Denniwitz picks up his beer and guzzles until it's empty. He burps, says, "I left at least one door open accidentally every single day last year."

"So now you're down to what, two cats?"

"Two you saw." He gets up, tosses his bottle toward a trashcan, and misses; then he jogs in huge strides to the Jeep. Being out of the house for just a little while has apparently done wonders for the guy.

"Couldn't have been Niko Stavrakos who took the ketamine," Craig says when Denniwitz returns, a fresh beer in hand. "The kid doesn't have a record."

"Guy's name wasn't Niko," Denniwitz says. "It was Soterios. Capital *S-o-t-e-r-i-o-s*." Denniwitz finds another smoke in his pocket.

"Jesus, you remember the spelling?"

"A guy doesn't forget the reason he winds up with four fucking cats." He tips his bottle to Craig, a toast. "If they're related? Call me, I'd like to neuter them both."

The reason one flower dies more quickly than another once it's cut from its mother plant has to do with how it is preserved. If no care is taken to prevent air embolisms or bacteria from blocking the stem's conducting tubes, the flower will begin to wilt; in effect, dying from the inside out. If, on the other hand, acidified water is used, the temperature is controlled, and rehydration is assured, the flower can bloom beautifully for a very long time. It will be beautiful, yes, even though it is still dying.

Leslie stands at the kitchen counter before Niko's rose, blooming in its full glory. Dressed now in a camel-colored turtleneck that is a nice contrast to her chocolate-black hair, she looks like the same woman who's always been able to keep up appearances, no matter how much she feels herself dying inside.

She's done a fine job with her makeup, particularly the concealer; she's bandaged her hand very discreetly, a skin-toned Ace bandage over the gauze. No one will see what she doesn't want them to see.

"Everything's fine," she says out loud. All she has to do to preserve the lie is find the strength to cover up her mistakes. Starting with Niko.

She plucks the rose from its vase and drops it into the trashcan.

Upstairs, she straightens a paper clip, shoves it into the lock on Ivy's bedroom door.

The room looks much the same as it did last time Leslie was allowed inside: piles of unworn clothes, stacks of unread books; the unmade bed, the unopened college applications.

Leslie sits at the computer, moves the mouse to wake it. Ivy keeps everything on her hard drive, so it's the most logical place to look for Niko's phone number.

Unfortunately, the screen that greets Leslie requests a username and password. Leslie's fingers stop short of the keys: this is not such an easy lock to pick.

For the username, Leslie tries Ivy and all variations she's seen on school papers: Eyevee, Eye-V, IV. Next, she tries the girl's old nicknames—Poison Ivy, Ives, Navy Bean. No luck.

Her beloved chinchilla Frosty and all the morphed variants of his name are possibilities. She tries Frosto, Roberto, Rob, Bobby, and six other names he had in the years before his premature death. Still no luck.

Finally, she types *Niko* into the box. The girl no longer decorates her notebooks with doodled advertisements about her love life, but that doesn't mean she hasn't put Niko's name to use in other meaningful ways. A multicolored disk spins on the screen while the computer checks the username. Does Ivy have it bad for Niko?

The screen resets, reads *incorrect username*. Even though Leslie can't crack the code, she's relieved Niko isn't part of it.

She spins in the swivel chair. If she can't figure out the username, she'll never guess the password. There's got to be another place Leslie can look for Niko's number.

In the corner, Ivy's school backpack sits, untouched since Friday.

Untouched until now.

Ivy's day planner doesn't tell her much. It seems like everything recorded recently was written in the same sitting: her classes and her work schedule appear through June in the same ink, same slanted handwriting. There are no other events listed.

The back address pages are empty, save for the last page where someone scrawled BRINKMAN HAS NO BALLS and sketched a picture of a naked man, apparently Mr. Brinkman, sans testicles. The fact that her math teacher's unimpressive genitalia is featured in place of telephone numbers speaks to Ivy's reliance on technology: all her contact information, like every other teenager's, is stored on her cell phone.

Leslie tucks the day planner away. There is one place she knows Ivy still writes, and that's in her poetry notebook.

It's on her nightstand. There's one new entry.

> *Orange, black*
> *Another night*
> *Viceroy, on a roll*
> *Sweetness: your sustenance*
> *Memories: mine*
> *Orange, black*
> *On my tongue*
> *I close my eyes, dance*
> *You: straight*
> *Me: sprung*
> *Orange, black*
> *Watch me*
> *Touch me*
> *I bloom*
> *Black*

Leslie reads it twice, remembering the night Ivy came home high, using all her rave lingo. Said Niko was "straight." Said she wasn't yet "sprung."

Apparently things have changed. Her daughter has bloomed, all right—just like Leslie had wanted to, and for the same man.

It's a shame neither one of them will ever have him.

30

The wind has picked up, dragging late-afternoon clouds toward the city and threatening to bring a light shower from the west. Trash blows around the Green Mill's entrance, which is closed up tight like it's ready for the storm.

Leslie'd taken a chance, thinking somebody might be here. She'd summoned her courage and planned a repeat performance with Rudy's badge: she'd ask the bouncer or the bartender about Niko, say he was in a little trouble, find out how to get in touch with him. If they remembered her she'd say Yeah, I was here, we've got the kid under surveillance. They won't think she's covering her own tracks if she says she's covering his.

In the lounge's window, the new week's calendar advertises an organ trio, a swing-shift orchestra, a Mother's Day show. Next to it hangs a flyer for an Uptown poetry slam. She wonders if Niko told Ivy about it.

The wind kicks up again, blowing hair in her eyes and a Styrofoam cup past her feet. She steps into the recessed doorway, unsure of her next move.

"*Streetwise,*" a grubby black man says when he walks by, flashes a newspaper.

"I don't have any cash," she lies.

"You neither?" His smile is real—the way it has to be when you have nothing left to lose.

"Do you know what time this place opens?" she asks.

"Round about nine I suppose. Can't say for sure, though—I take my business down to Boystown at night. They's more polite. You could check the *Reader,*" he says, pointing down Broadway toward the Riviera Theater. "They got some sittin' outside the door there. And them's free."

A quick burst of wind ruffles his papers. "Storm's coming," he says. "Best find someplace."

"Hold on." Leslie reaches into her purse. "I might have some change."

She gives him a dollar sixteen, all the coins she has. "Keep the paper."

"God bless you, ma'am." He takes the money and nods before he turns to follow a mark headed in the other direction. "*Streetwise.*"

Under the Riviera's marquee, Leslie finds a short stack of *Reader*s. She opens a copy to section three, turns to Jazz, and finds the Green Mill. The hours aren't listed, but under Saturday night, it reads, *The Jay Jones Quartet, midnight; see Calendar.*

She turns back to the Calendar page and finds:

Jay Jones Quartet. **For those of you who think the Green Mill's lineup is as old as Stella by Starlight, check out the new kid who's sitting in. Though he only just turned 21, pianist Niko Stavrakos can almost pass as a jazz vet—if he didn't stun us *and* the real cats on stage— with refreshing approaches that show his chops and remind us what's great about the old stuff. See him now because, as Jay Jones says,**

"He'll be bored of us in no time." *Midnight, Green Mill, 4802 N. Broadway, 773-555-5555, or for booking, 312-555-4013. $10.*

"Jay Jones," is who answers on the first ring.

Leslie is surprised to hear the trumpeter's voice. She'd expected some manager or answering service; she was going to pretend to be hosting a private party, say she saw Niko play, request to speak with him directly.

"'Lo?"

"Hello, Mr. Jones, my name is Stephanie Smith," she lies. "I'm calling about Niko Stavrakos."

"Stephanie who?"

"I'm from Columbia College," she says, her backup plan. "I was hoping you'd help me get in touch with Niko."

"Ya, Columbia, sure."

"We're processing his application," she says, shielding her mouthpiece from the wind as she heads up the street toward her car. "He listed you as a reference."

"That's funny, cause I keep telling the boy he don't need school. He just needs to play in front of the right people."

"We have some great opportunities to offer, Mr. Jones, and we're glad he's interested in our program."

"Well, I can tell you, I've been playing with him a few months now, and the kid's as disciplined as a cadet."

"He's very serious, for a boy."

"There's not much boy left in him, far as I can tell. Besides, I thought you liked 'em young."

Leslie stops, key in her car's door lock. "I don't know what you mean, Mr. Jones."

"I thought all you college types wanted kids who hadn't been around. Fewer bad habits to break."

"Of course," she says, "it's hard to break bad habits."

"I'll tell you, Niko's improv is a little fancy sometimes, but that don't bother me none. He knows the rules. I have to say, the kid is good, and he's going to be great, with or without you."

"You're absolutely right," she says, the simplicity of that truth comforting. "On that note, excuse the pun, do you happen to have Niko's cell phone number? I've tried to reach him at home, but he hasn't returned my calls."

"If it's his mama you're talking to, he's not getting the message. Jazz ain't a real job, don'tcha know? Hold on a minute."

She gets into the car and waits to write the number on the *Reader*.

Some twenty blocks and as many hang-ups later, Leslie sits in her car in Dominick's parking lot and works up the nerve to call Niko. She punches in his number again and tucks the newspaper page where she wrote it into her purse. She knows she could just hit *redial*. She knows she's stalling.

The line rings once and goes to voice mail.

"Hello, *yassou,* you've reached, Niko. Wish I was available."

Leslie wishes his smooth voice didn't catch her breath. She tugs at her turtleneck, tight at her throat.

"Leave a message," Niko says, "we'll talk."

At the beep, she says, "Niko: Leslie McHugh. It's important that I speak to you. Please call me on my cell." She leaves the number and hangs up, hoping she's keyed in well enough to get a quick call back.

"Mrs. Stavrakos," Craig calls out, the third time. He knows she's in there: he saw her peek out the front window after he rang the bell. Behind him, water trickles from a cherub's jug in the fountain that sits in the perfectly manicured patch of lawn. Reminds him he has to take a leak.

"Mrs. Stavrakos, I'm from the police department. I need to speak to your son."

"He did nothing," she says through the door.

"Let me hear that from him."

"He does not live here," she says.

Craig steps back, surveys the house. It's a tiny A-frame lined up along a street full of others, all variations on a theme. On this stretch of Berwyn Avenue, most of the other houses are built sturdy with wheat-colored brick, plain concrete steps. This one has a softer face: the brick is whitewashed; the Corinthian columns supporting the porch are painted to match.

Not such a soft face peeking out the window, though: the woman looks like she took the long way from Athens. When Craig waves, the lace curtains fall back into place.

"Mrs. Stavrakos," he says, "I'm a detective. This is your son's listed address. If he doesn't live here, you need to give me his current address. If you can't, then I'll assume that he does in fact live here, and that you're lying. Then you'll be the one in trouble."

The front door opens just enough for little Mrs. Stavrakos to look him up and down, one beady black eye. "Do you not know today is a holy day? You may come here and order my death before you will come in and take my boy away on Easter Sunday."

"I'm not taking anybody anywhere," he says, "I just want to talk to Niko."

Her eye bulges. "Nikodemus?"

"Yes."

She lets go of the door to cross herself a bunch of times, repeating "*The'Mou, The'Mou, The'Mou—*" and giving Craig the chance to step inside.

"It's okay," he says, an unconvincing hand on her shoulder. She's got to be less than five feet tall, so Craig addresses the top of her head. "Just let me talk to him, and then you can get back to your lamb—"

From outside, the roar of an engine swallows his words. He turns around, sees a black Trans Am peel out from the space in front of the Caprice.

When he turns back, Mrs. Stavrakos stands there, the kind of grin that should come with feathers caught in her wrinkled lips.

"Was that Niko?" he asks.

She shakes her head no, but that's not what her face says.

"If it was, Mrs. Stavrakos, I already took the plate number. I can just run out to the car, call it in, have one of my boys pick him up. You do know the penalty for evasion is considerably stiff."

She takes ahold of his arm. "No, please, do not do that. Niko is not in that car." Her hands fall from his arm, take his hand. "Please. I will talk to you. Sit down."

"I think you're lying."

"I do not lie," she says, pushing him toward her plastic-covered couch. "That was my son—yes—but it was Soterios. Nikodemus is not here, on God's name."

She sits him down and the couch covering crinkles like a shower curtain. She sits in the adjacent rocking chair, her feet together. When she rocks back and forth, short and quick, light catches the silver in her wiry black hair.

"Mrs. Stavrakos," Craig says, "what is Soterios running from?"

"He has done nothing. I do not lie. But since he was in jail, he is afraid of the police."

"So you were covering for him."

"I am his mother."

"I know how it works," he says. All too well.

On the mantel, cheap gold-framed photographs overlap one

another, an extended Greek family on prudent display. Craig gets up to have a look; instantly, Mrs. Stavrakos is at his side, her hands thumb-forward on her hips, her steps mimicking his.

"If it's Greek Easter," he says, "where are all these people?"

"My sister Adonia holds the celebration this year. With Soterios returning home, I did not have time to get the house in proper order. We just came back a little while ago to rest—my husband was feeling tired after the Easter meal. We go to his sister's this evening."

"So I should follow you to your husband's sister's? To find Niko?"

"No," she says, her tiny fists held up close to her heart.

"Maybe I should talk to your husband."

"No! He is asleep. I will not wake him."

"I can wait." Craig crosses his arms, surveys the mantel. Most of the pictures are of older folks and children; everyone posed in front of one holiday scene or another. In the center, there's a panoramic of about thirty people, probably the Stavrakos clan. He finds Niko seated at the front, two small girls on either side of his lap. Certain smile.

Craig picks up a circular-framed photo of Niko with his arm around a taller kid who looks like him, save for a long nose that distorts his face and spoils his chance at handsome. "Is this Soterios, here?"

"No," Mrs. Stavrakos says, taking the frame from his hands and wiping off his prints with a dust cloth from her cardigan. "Ammon. My nephew."

"Show me Soterios."

"You are here about Nikodemus."

"I know what Niko looks like." He produces the Green Mill photo, shows it to her. "If you're not going to tell me where he is, maybe I'll find his brother, ask him."

"What has he done? My boy . . . Niko, he is a good boy." Her shoulders wilt and curl inward so that this time, when she crosses herself, her hand is like a claw.

"If he's such a good boy," Craig says, "what's with the runaround?" He takes a square-framed photo from the mantel, this one of Mrs. Stavrakos and a kid with eyebrows thick as fur. "Is this Soterios?"

She snatches the picture from him. "Nikodemus is by Greektown. Playing cards with his cousins."

"There are lots of places to play cards in Greektown. I'm not driving all the way down there on that tip."

"Nine Muses is where he goes these days."

"These days, or today?"

"I tell you the truth," she says. "You tell me what he has done."

Craig stuffs the photo back in his pocket. "I'll get back to you on that." He heads for the door, says, over his shoulder, "Happy Easter."

Leslie loads the last of the groceries into her trunk right next to the garbage bag full of last night's evidence. She knows she should get rid of the bag, maybe ditch it in a city can, but she hasn't had the opportunity. Before she shopped, she drove around behind Dominick's, thinking she'd leave it in one of their Dumpsters. There was a kid outside, taking a smoke break. She didn't stop.

She filled her shopping cart with a head of iceberg lettuce, tomatoes and olive oil, baking potatoes. The New York strip steaks were on sale, so she bought three, thinking Ivy might change her mind about meat if she got a whiff of the barbeque. She also bought some zucchini and eggplant, to slice up and grill, just in case.

She rounded out the purchase with milk, a block of sharp cheddar, and a bottle of cabernet; if no one comes home tonight, wine and cheese will be the extent of the menu. She hasn't eaten all day, and she's still not hungry.

If Ivy and Craig do show up, firing up the grill will make for a casual Sunday meal and give Leslie a good excuse to stay out of the bright kitchen light. Her wounds are covered, but her face won't be, and she isn't sure she's quite prepared to look either of them in the eye.

She heads west on Foster, the inevitable trip home feeling like surrender. She could go back to the Green Mill, wait for someone to open the doors, but there's no guarantee anyone will help her, and the risk isn't worth taking—not when her family will expect her. Better just to go home, be there, in the thick and thin of it.

While she's stopped at the light at Pulaski, her cell phone buzzes, and the vibration goes straight to her chest. She pulls over at the corner, traffic blowing by, and opens the phone. It's Niko.

"Leslie, it's me," he says, as though she should be so familiar. "*Kalo Pascha.*"

"Niko," she says, tears immediate. She wipes her eyes, but they keep coming. "I forgot what day it is."

"It's okay," he says. "I didn't recognize the number when you called; I thought it was my mother calling again. She's still upset that I missed church last night, even though I told her about my show well in advance. I had to say twice as many prayers for repentance at the service this morning. What did you think, anyway? You cut out of the club pretty quick—"

"I need to talk to you," she says, her voice wet.

"You want to come down?" he asks, no indication he senses trouble. "I'm playing Plakoto with my cousins. I was getting creamed until the last game—I just barely made my money back. Why don't you come? I have to go by my aunt's house tonight, but I would love to see you."

She's got milk in the trunk. Cheese. Steaks. She's got a family.

She's also got to end this. Now.

"Where are you?"

"Nine Muses."

She hits the gas and drives through Pulaski, on toward the Edens. "Wait for me."

31

Despite the weird weather, the storefront windows at Nine Muses are propped open, challenging the wind to come inside and blow out the candles on the tables and in the wall sconces. Craig rolls past on Halsted and spots Niko seated in plain view at a low bar table playing cards with two other guys, presumably his cousins.

Craig sees a string of open spaces on the other side of the street so he flips a bitch, parks in front of another Greektown joint with a misspelled sign that advertises *Late Night Dinning*. Most of the other restaurants are closed, probably because of the holiday. It would follow that Nine Muses would be packed but here it sits, all lit up and mostly empty. Craig gets his binoculars from the pocket behind the driver's seat and settles in to get familiar with the guys in the window.

The first one, to Niko's left, is built strong. Mid-twenties. Long legs he barely fits under the table put him over six feet; moussed black hair gets him another inch. The guy next to him is older. Paunchy. A real guido: gold, silk, leather; his money making the impression now.

And then there's Niko: bigger than he looks in his pictures; maybe it's confidence, come to life. The cuffs of his smooth black button-down are rolled up to make way for his hands, which he uses like he's directing his audience. It works: he sits there flapping his jaws about who knows what and his bar mates are interested—not to mention the slight young Greek thing who's hanging around their table re-lighting candles on the tabletops, the weather also such a tease.

Craig puts down the binoculars and checks the load of his .380, then he stows the gun in the glove box under the Gambler's Anony-mous handbook. No reason to go into the bar in a huff. Better to be understated with a kid like this: to walk in, introduce himself, let Niko do the talking. See if he's as confident with his girlfriend's dad—or husband—at the table.

If Niko plays it cool, Craig will ask about the card game. What are they playing? Do they have any money on it? Is Niko a gambling man?

Maybe they'll ask if he wants to play. He'll say no: he doesn't much like games. He'll be looking at Niko when he says it.

It'll be awkward, but Craig will stick around. He'll order a coffee. Talk about bullshit. See what kind of response he gets. See how much Niko will bend before he breaks.

Could be that the kid sees Craig and breaks right away. In that case, they'll come to a quick and quiet understanding: he'll put the thousand dollars he won't be spending at Mr. Moy's on the table. He'll tell Niko that the money takes Ivy off the market. Tell him Leslie was never on it.

Inside Nine Muses's window, the guido throws a gold-heavy hand in Niko's general direction like he's had enough of the kid. Craig can side with that. He pockets his keys and gets out of the car.

He's crossing Halsted against traffic when his phone rings. Comes up a city number he doesn't recognize. Could be a break in the case:

maybe someone at the Thirteenth got Silk to talk. Could be a lot of things, doesn't mean he should answer.

Then again, it could be Juan. Kid stuck his neck out for him, and case or not, Craig owes him. He answers.

"Craig McHugh? This is Kingman Cade, from the Thirteenth. I caught the body you and your boys turned up last night. You got a minute?"

"Sure, now that our case is closed." Craig turns around, heads back to his car since it's probably going to take more than a minute. "What's up?"

"Votchka says you were the man in charge. How about you come down south, tell me about it?"

"Not much to tell. You should probably talk to Ron Suwanski. He's the case agent."

"You're going to send me to the guy who's writing the case's obit? Listen. Bodies been popping up so fast I don't have time to look at their toe tags. About the only thing I could use more paperwork for is to use the backside to tender myself a letter of resignation."

Craig gets in the passenger side, lets the door hang open, his feet on the curb. He says, "You can't quit because of the desks. You just have to work around them."

"That's why I'm calling. I understand you have a connection in Chinatown."

The wind sneaks up, blows at the phone's mouthpiece, so Craig closes the car door. He shouldn't have answered; this is a colossal waste of time. Just like the case. "My connection is weak," he says, "at best."

"Votchka said you were down here eyeballing with an informant," Cade says. "He's your inside man?"

"More like my interpreter. And like I said, he's weak. The guy your boys picked up—Silk? That's who we were after. He's a Fuxi. Snitch told me Silk claimed he was going to kill the Night Hawks' middleman, on account of the feud they have going on over a rat in the ranks. Problem was, among others, that I came by this information because I planted a bug in their den without a warrant."

"Working around the desks, as you say."

"It was the only way. We had to jump. We ran down to Wolcott, banking on grabbing Silk on an in-progress, but your guys picked him up first. You know what that means? I have a case agent who's a better snitch than my snitch."

"What about the timing? The vic's been dead too long—the way you tell it, he kicked before Silk said he was going to kill him."

"I wish it meant I have a lousy interpreter. Suwanski thinks the Fuxis found the bug, staged a setup to draw me out."

"You think your cover's blown?"

"Not a chance. My guess? Silk thinks the rat is working from deep inside, maybe Chinatown—maybe even one of the guys in Moy's den yesterday. Whether Silk killed the Hawks' middleman or not, he told them he was going after the guy as a test, to see if there was a leak. And now he knows he's right. Only reason he'll be concerned about the police is because of his bullshit arrest—he'll think that the rat has a friend or two in blue."

"And you want to go back in."

"Doesn't matter what I want. We had no chance of saving that middleman, and I've got no chance of saving the case."

"You think you might have a chance saving mine?"

Over at Nine Muses, Niko is up out of his chair, maybe taking off. Craig decides it's time to plug up Cade's pipe dream. "I told you what I know, Cade. Getting me involved is only going to make it complicated."

"Look," Cade says. "It's not just one body. Junkies have been OD'-ing: south side, west side, lake side. I know Chinatown, and I know that putting this body on the murder blotter could change everything.

I just need someone who's been in deep to take a look, you know, around. Around the desks."

"I couldn't get past a crappy Pai Gow den in Uptown. I can't help you in Chinatown."

Across the way, Niko is at the bar talking to the slight Greek waitress. Craig gets the binoculars and focuses on the waitress as she puts two espresso cups on the bar.

"Listen," Cade says," I'm waiting on the tox reports, but my narc guy is ninety-nine percent sure we're talking China White. Wasn't that your case?"

"Uh-huh." Craig refocuses the lenses, sees Niko close-up: his young, unblemished face, arrogant smile. Then the kid turns, opens his arms, and goes out of frame. When Craig follows, he thinks his focus must be off, because he could swear the next person he finds in the sights is Leslie.

Cade says, "All I'm asking is for you to take a look. See if anything makes your trigger finger itch."

Craig adjusts the lenses, but the same thing is clear: it's Leslie in there, approaching Niko, her body language coy as he's ever seen it.

What the fuck? What is she doing here?

"I'm sorry, I can't help you," Craig says into the phone. "I'm already on another case."

Craig hangs up just in time to watch Niko kiss his wife.

For the first time, Niko's kisses feel so boyish, so wishful. Leslie accepts his greeting as amicably as she can, though she tenses at his touch and she is unnerved by the fact that the young waitress behind the bar is reading into the gesture no matter how Leslie handles it.

"Can we sit somewhere private?"

Niko's smile makes her wonder what, exactly, he's reading into this. He turns to the girl at the bar. "Alexis, is the other side open?"

She nods, eyes cold.

He throws a twenty on the bar and takes both espressos. "Come on."

Through the doorway, the adjacent room is lighter; the white tablecloths and place settings on all the tables and booths indicate this is the dining area. Leslie assumes nobody's dining on a late Sunday afternoon because it's Easter. What is Niko doing here?

He puts the saucers down on a table for two in the front window, which is open, a display for the bypassers. "I love this weather. 'Fleeting' is what the *Sun Times* called it. I like that: *fleeting*. It's a good English word."

"It's going to rain," she says.

He pulls out a chair for her to sit.

"I hope you like Turkish coffee. I think this is the best in town."

"It's fine, Niko," she says, though the thought of drinking bitter espresso makes her stomach curl. She takes the lemon twist from her saucer, twirls it nervously in the fingers of her good hand.

"I probably should have ordered something else. I felt like I was losing my edge after dinner so I've had two of these and now I think I might be able to fly." His smile, the one she'd thought could inspire the world, seems so simple to her now. Uncurious. He doesn't even ask about her bandaged hand when she uses it to pick up the coffee cup.

Leslie brings the cup to her lips, but the strong aroma alone is nauseating. There's no way she can drink it.

Humidity sits on the wind all of a sudden, quieting their surroundings. The temporary stillness makes her more nervous. She plates the coffee cup and chews at the lemon rind with her front teeth.

"What's the matter?" he asks. "You don't want it?"

"I'm sorry." She fingers the collar of her turtleneck, her throat sore. "The coffee is fine. It's you, Niko. You're the problem."

Concern—not discouragement—ruins his smile. He reaches over, touches her arm. "What's wrong?"

"It was a mistake for me to see you last night. I shouldn't be pursuing something that's completely impossible."

"Improbable," he says, "but not impossible."

She leans back, out of reach. "It's impossible."

"Leslie, come on. We haven't done anything wrong."

"You and I are not 'we.'" She swallows, her throat tight.

"You're saying you're troubled by semantics?"

"I'm saying I am married. I have a family—a daughter. And she is in love with you."

Niko leans back now, finds his smile. "Now *that* is impossible. She didn't tell you? She broke up with me last night, Leslie. Says she's going with this guy Viceroy."

"Viceroy," Leslie repeats. She remembers the butterfly-wing poem Ivy wrote a few months ago. Was it about him? "What kind of name is Viceroy?"

"I have no idea. He's Asian. Japanese, maybe."

"Asian," Leslie repeats, her hands suddenly cold.

"I think so. I only met him once—at the rave. Ivy introduced us. I hate to say this, but I think she was stringing me along because of him. Viceroy is the one who wanted to see Rios about the ecstasy."

"You're telling me my daughter is involved with a drug dealer?"

"I'm just telling you she says she's going with him now."

She palms her petite coffee cup, tries to warm her hands. "Jesus."

Niko throws up his hands, a thank-you. "That's what I said. Never in a million years would I have guessed somebody would dump a guy like me for a guy like that. He's about five feet tall, no lie."

"That's not what I meant." But Leslie doesn't explain; he's on a completely different page, a boy's, and she has bigger things to deal with now. Bigger, and so much more important than all this.

She moves her coffee aside. She has to tell him that this—whatever this is—is over.

"It's okay," he says, "I told her no hard feelings. As you know, I'm interested in someone else."

"No, Niko," she says. It's almost ridiculous, how differently she sees him now. "I'm sorry, but I have to tell you that I can't be part of the equation."

His clueless reaction shows no contempt. "What is it you've added up in your head, Leslie?"

Her heartbeat feels amplified. Did she simply imagine the attraction? Had she misinterpreted his friendly gestures because she'd been so warped by loneliness?

All this was nothing?

She was raped for nothing?

"Nothing," is what she manages to say before a rush of tears tells the real truth. She covers her face and sobs.

"Leslie," Niko says, out of his chair, crouched next to her.

She recoils, her good hand up in defense. "Don't—"

"You're pushing me away, okay," he says, but he stays where he is. "You've been crying, Leslie. I knew it the second I saw you. And your hand—what happened to it? This isn't because of me. Please, tell me what's wrong."

"This is because of you," she insists. "Because you played for me last night."

"No," Niko says, and reaches out to her, his hand on her shoulder. When she places her hand over his, it is an admission: the one she had craved for so long; still, the one she always knew would never, ever add up to anything.

"Leslie, please," he says, pain in his voice at seeing hers. "*Ela*," he says softly, asking her to come as he reaches up and takes her in his arms and she lets him: she leans into him. This is what she has needed—this safe human warmth.

She closes her eyes, hears the rain start to fall outside. She wishes she could shut out the world and just feel him, the compassion in his embrace. But her scabbed knees press sharp against her slacks, and her raw arms burn under her sleeves. She cannot wish any of what she hides away.

"I'm sorry," she says.

He rocks her in his arms. "There's nothing to be sorry for."

She squeezes her eyes shut tight, trapping her tears, once again wishing she were oblivious.

"This is a touching moment." At the sound of Craig's voice, Leslie pushes Niko away and gets to her feet.

"Did I make it in time for the farewell kiss?" Craig stands there, clean-shaven, his thin hair and his windbreaker shiny with rain.

"Craig," Leslie says. "This is Niko. Ivy's boyfriend."

"Your daughter would be proud."

"We have nothing to hide," Niko says, standing up next to her.

Leslie sees Craig's fists, tight. She moves in front of Niko, to protect him. "We were just talking," she says. "About Ivy."

"Don't give me your bullshit, Leslie. I saw the whole thing, since you walked in. You know what's good for you, you'll walk back out."

"You won't let me explain?"

"You mean lie?"

"That's fitting, coming from you."

"Ivy broke up with me," Niko cuts in from behind. "Leslie was worried about her—that's why she's here."

"Ivy broke up with you," Craig says, "and now you're after my wife?"

"It's nothing like that," Leslie attempts, though she hears the insincerity in her own voice.

"Go ahead, Leslie," Craig says. "Tell me what it's like."

She knows this hurts him, even if he doesn't show it. She can't find words.

He steps up close, so close she can smell his familiar, stale breath. "Come on, Leslie: tell me what it's like when I'm not there. When Niko and his friends come over to the house—"

"Those guys weren't my friends at Ivy's party," Niko cuts in. "Ivy was using me—"

Craig ignores him—"Tell me what it's like, Leslie, when Niko plays the piano."

"What party?" Leslie asks, of both of them.

"I'm not a fool, goddamn it." Craig wipes the rain from his face, now mixed with sweat. "I thought you were covering for Ivy and now I know this has been about *him*." He points at Niko.

"You're wrong," Niko says. "Leslie didn't know Ivy had any of us over."

"Stop calling her Leslie," Craig says, through a clenched jaw. "I already know you two are friendly. I found your fucking fingerprints all over her piano."

"I play the piano," Niko says, so young.

Craig says, "You know what happens when you lie to a police officer?"

Leslie braces herself, sure she's the only thing standing between a fight.

Niko doesn't back down. "I'm telling the truth, Mr. McHugh."

Craig pushes Leslie aside. "You know what happens when you fuck with a cop?" He shows Niko the handle of the gun sticking out of his waistband under his coat. "If I ever see you anywhere near my family again, you can bet you'll find out."

"Are you threatening me?"

"I'm promising you." Craig steps back, looks at Leslie. "You too."

He zips his coat, covering the gun, and goes out the way he came in.

Niko follows suit, following orders. He doesn't answer, doesn't even look back, when Leslie asks again, "What party?"

And Leslie is the only one who remains. She stays long after they're both gone and the Turkish coffee has gone cold, and long after the rain has stopped.

32

When Leslie finally arrives home, the driveway is empty. Isn't that just like Craig: to make a bust and let his suspect squirm. He could be sitting in his car, parked down the street; she might've gone right past him without noticing. Or, he's at Hamilton's, preaching to his choir. Leslie parks in the driveway, pops the trunk. For all she cares, he could be hiding in the bushes.

Could be, Craig's already been here. He came home, packed a bag, and went back to the Aragon and his easy city-trash. Maybe he thinks that finding Leslie with Niko gave him the evidence he needed to make a clean moral break, and now he can argue that his behavior is justified. If that's the case, he's right: it's no longer a matter of who is wrong. It's a matter of who is worse.

Leslie gets the groceries from the trunk. The real evidence of a crime is gone: she'd exited the Edens early at Foster, found a Dumpster behind Taco City and ditched the garbage bag. If the next step is divorce court, let Craig try and build a case against her on suspicion alone. He will never find out Leslie and Niko shared anything more than a cup of Turkish coffee, and he will never know she was raped. She's already paid for her mistakes; she always will. As long as Ivy never has to.

Inside the house, techno music pulsates, muted, from Ivy's room. It's nearing eight o'clock, so she's been home for a while, and the empty Lou Malnati's pizza box on the kitchen counter means she must have been starving and decided cow parts weren't so bad. For once, Leslie's glad the girl is tucked away upstairs, keeping to herself.

She unbags the groceries: the sweating cheese, the tepid milk. She cuts a few slices of cheddar and plates them with butterfly-shaped crackers, the only remaining variety in the Pepperidge Farm Quartet. She knows she should eat. She tries. She just can't.

She goes upstairs, lingering outside Ivy's door, thinking about knocking. They're going to have to have a talk about this party, and this new boyfriend, but because the news came from Niko, Leslie decides it best to wait—to find out a few things on her own first. She doesn't have the energy to start another war without proper ammunition.

As the techno music changes, the bass line becoming monotone and mellow, Leslie can hear Ivy chatting intermittently; she must be on the phone with one of her pals. She wonders if Ivy heard her come home, or if she cares.

Leslie goes into her own bedroom and takes off her turtleneck, finally letting her wounds breathe. She removes her hand bandage and washes with antibacterial soap; then she gets into the shower, letting the water fall around the tight muscles in her neck and shoulders until it runs cold.

She dabs peroxide on her scraped arms and knees. The wounds bubble at the edges; the scab on her right knee opens again and bleeds. She tapes her knee and rewraps her hand, hoping she'll heal quickly on the outside.

In the closet, she ties a dry-cleaning bag at one end and collects every silk garment she owns from drawers and hangers: most of her underwear, three of her blouses. The knee-length evergreen nightgown Craig bought her last Christmas is the last to go in. It is not something she will ever wear again.

Instead, she'll wear the hideous yellow flannel pajama set Ivy gave her in February, for her fortieth birthday. It was the most thoughtful gift she received: the week before the big four-oh, Leslie had been searching the Carson's sale racks while she waited for Ivy to clock out. As a joke, Leslie held them up and asked what Ivy thought; Ivy said she feared her mother was going blind. The joke, as it turned out, was gift-wrapped. Ivy'd said the color was an old person's, and appropriate in case Leslie turned senile as well, so she'd be easy to find if she started wandering the streets at night.

It wasn't funny, but the gift was more thoughtful than Craig's stop at the Jewel for a twenty-dollar bottle of merlot, a bouquet of blue daisies, and a cake with a tombstone candle. Blue daisies, for God's sake. For a woman who works at a flower shop. That was supposed to be his joke. Leslie drank nearly all the merlot and still didn't crack a smile.

The flannel pajama shirt buttons up the front, and if Leslie folds the collar inward, it covers her neck. Not that it matters; Craig hasn't come home and she doubts she will. At least this time, when she shuts off the light just before nine and drifts toward sleep, she's relieved to be alone.

"Leslie."

She hears Craig's voice. She doesn't answer. He woke her up, but she can pretend he didn't.

"Leslie," he says again, and then she feels the mattress give under his weight. She sighs and turns over, her back to him, like he's merely disrupted a dream.

He tugs at the covers, pulling them tight against her, and positions himself just behind her. She senses his body heat, his cold bare feet on hers. She inches away.

"Leslie."

"Wha?" she says, irritated. More irritated when he presses against her, and she feels his erection touch the back of her thigh.

"You must be kidding," she says, completely awake.

"I'm not."

"What time is it?" Not that there can be a good answer.

"After midnight."

She turns and tries to push him away, but when he doesn't budge she only succeeds in pushing herself to the edge of the bed. In the dark, she can barely make out his silhouette, through she can certainly smell the beer on his breath.

"Jesus, Craig."

"Remember how we used to be, Leslie? I'd come home and wake you up, we'd have a little fun—"

"There's nothing fun about this. Not anymore."

He takes her by the forearm, right on the pavement burn, and pulls her close. "You're right. But you're my wife. And if you say there's nothing going on between you and that kid, prove it."

"This is the first time you've come to bed in two months. I'm not proving anything to you. Let go of me."

She slips off the bed, but he follows right behind her and he grabs her wrist, spins her around and forces her against the wall. Fierce pain, like shards of glass, tears through her arms when he takes her wrists up overhead. She hangs there, at his will.

"I remember my favorite late nights," he says, "when you'd play hard to get."

"I'm not playing hard to get" she says, voice breaking. "I don't want you."

He must not believe her because he comes at her, more intense, kissing her neck, sloppy and angry. She yields to him, but only because of the pain.

His sweaty hand slides up her thin wrist and catches at the bandage. He looks up. "What happened?" he asks, like there's a time-out.

She knows how to stop this, to stop him before he wants the truth: she has to confirm his fear. "Niko did it," she says. "He likes to play games, too."

Craig releases his right hand and tears her flannel top open at the buttons. The pressure of the collar against her neck cuts short her breath.

He covers her mouth and says, "You're a liar."

She gasps through his fingers.

"Look at me," he says, and between the slats of moonlight through the horizontal blinds she can see his eyes, wide and righteous. "Haven't I done everything I could for you?"

With his hand over her mouth, there's no way she can argue.

"All these years I've tried to protect you. And now you want to hurt me? Now you want to rip this family apart over some fucking kid?" He steps back, naked in front of her, red marks inflamed in spots on his torso like bug bites. His penis has gone flaccid, the only indication she's stalled him. Now, she has to stop him. Get him out of there, before he wants to talk.

"You're the one who hurt me," she says. "You left me here. Alone." She pulls her shirt closed and brings her hair forward, around her neck. "Please go."

"No." He steps toward her, his approach softer this time. He reaches out, but she stops him—

"I know where you've been spending your nights," she says, shaking, now afraid she's taking this too far. Still, she hears herself say, "I know you're having an affair. I've been there—the Aragon Arms."

"Are you crazy? Leslie, I was on a case."

"I was alone," she says, feeling hard now, feeling hate. She will not tell him. She will be so mean. She will do whatever it takes.

"When have I ever talked to you about work? It's dangerous for you. For both of us. If I can't keep things separate I'll lose my head." He comes toward her again, more comfortable, like he is when they begin to see things the same. "Is this why you've been so cold to me?" he asks. "Because of the Job? Leslie, we've been through this before—"

"Don't," she says, because there are some things he can never see.

"We can work this out."

"No, we can't."

"This isn't because of Niko. You can't tell me that. I won't believe it." Another step forward and he's got her trapped; panic, now so familiar, sets her mind on the only way out.

She pulls the collar of her pajamas together and faces him. "You shouldn't believe me, because I've been lying to you."

"I know about Ivy," he says. "I already know." His voice is forgiving, and maddening.

"You think you know everything. What about this? When Denniwitz and Roscoe brought Ivy home, there was a moment I thought they were here because of you. I thought something happened to you." She lifts her head to look at him, and it's almost impossible to do so when she says, "The thing is, I hoped so, Craig. I actually wished you were dead."

Craig steps back, his face unreadable before he disappears in the shadows. He goes around to his side of the bed, sits. This must be the end of it, for now.

Leslie regathers her pajama top, hugs herself as she sits on the other side of the bed, her back to him, waiting for him to leave.

But then she hears Craig pull the slide back to load and cock his .380.

"Craig," she says.

"Craig," she says again.

"Come here," he says.

She makes her way around the bed to find him there, naked, the gun in his hands.

"Please don't." The words tremble with her. She cannot tell him. Not now.

He looks up, blank-eyed. "You don't love me anymore."

"Give me the gun."

"You don't know what it's like, Leslie. To risk everything you are."

"Give me the gun."

"I go undercover," he says, slipping his forefinger around the trigger, the gun flat against his thigh, his gaze on the wall behind her. "I stay at that shithole motel; I play the role. I am a gambler. I throw money at this Chinese poker den. My own money after a while. And the whole time, they treat me like I'm stupid. Like I'm no more than the cash I walk in with. But I stick around, because it is my job."

When he looks at Leslie, she feels like he sees right through her.

He says, "One night it all goes to hell. Gang comes in, and a Chinese kid who thinks he's got the world by the balls wants to take mine too. You see what he did?" He points to the marks on his torso with the tip of the .380.

"These wanna-be bangers," he says, "they think I'm a worn-out joke. And they're right. Because all I come away with, after I give my fucking life for this case, is the simple fact that I can't get to Chinatown. I can't even get past this motherfucking kid Silk. And now, apparently, I can't get to you."

A shiver takes hold of Leslie, through her. She lunges at him and grabs the gun by its barrel; he lets her take it—

"Fuck, Leslie, be careful—"

—but she steps back, gun heavy in her hands. "What did you say?"

"Be careful—I said be careful."

"Tell me the name again."

"What?"

"The name."

"Of the kid? Silk?"

She has to tell him. Leslie's hands shake almost uncontrollably as she thumbs the gun's hammer back, clicks the safety into place, and tosses the gun on the floor behind her.

"What are you doing?" Craig asks, self-pity gone from his voice, concern there now.

Leslie finds her breath, and her nerve, and turns on the bedside lamp.

She stands in front of Craig and opens her pajama top. She shows him her neck.

Craig's face goes white. "What happened?"

She lifts the top over and off her shoulders, drops it to the floor, and shows him the bloodied scabs on her forearms.

She says, "He said he wanted me to know what silk felt like." She unties the yellow ribbon that bunches her waistband, removes the bottoms to show him her knees. "I thought it was my fault." She hooks her thumbs inside the band of her cotton underwear to remove them—

"Don't," he says, shaking his head, eyes glazed like shields. "Don't." His head falls into his hands.

She takes off her underwear anyway. She says, "They got to *me.*"

When Craig lifts his head, tears fall from his eyes. In twenty years, Leslie has never actually seen him cry. As all the emotion he'd shelved comes crashing down around him, she falls to her wounded knees, reaches for her husband, and tries to find enough strength to share the pain.

33

Craig's conscience jerks him awake. After Leslie's exhaustion got the best of her, he spent the early morning hours watching her sleep. Watching over her. He told her he would.

Gray light fills in the spaces between the blinds, the sun on its way. Clock says it's ten to six. Craig remembers so many mornings just like this, waking before the alarm, his wife next to him.

Well, not just like this.

Back when Craig worked days, the mornings were a well-oiled routine, thanks to Leslie. He'd get up and hit the shower while she made coffee and poured orange juice for him to drink after he used his Tilade allergy inhaler, because it tasted like shit. Then she'd wake Ivy, assuming her role as their daughter's human snooze button. Sometime in between Craig's shave and shoeshine, Leslie would make his peanut butter toast, pack Ivy's lunch, and solve the latest teenage wardrobe crisis. And somehow, by the time Leslie would coax Ivy out to the bus stop and Craig to his car with his travel mug, she'd be ready to go, too.

The minutes were always quick those mornings, after the alarm went off, and waking up just before the rush had been Craig's secret: just a few minutes of quiet to clear the sleep-haze from his head and to thank God that everything in their lives really was fine.

He rolls over, shuts off the alarm. Leslie doesn't need to wake up so early this morning. The shadows below her eyes are dark, her face thin. She looks so tired. He hopes she'll sleep in. He hopes she's dreaming of something better than this.

She begged him to keep the rape a secret. They'd suffered enough embarrassment these past months, she said, and she couldn't bear turning their lives into an investigation. She'd gotten rid of the evidence; she'd refused to see a doctor. No matter why the men came after her, the damage had been done, and it would never be as black and white as a police report.

Craig held her in his arms and promised her there would be no investigation. It was because of an investigation that she was raped.

He also promised he would find the man with the wing-tipped tattoo. He would find him, and the other man who did this. They would pay.

Out the door now, no shower or shave, no coffee or toast, Craig sees the unmarked car parked across the way. He called in a favor and asked Dan Poole, the watch commander on duty last night at the Seventeenth, to put a unit outside the house for a few days. Said there'd been some suspicious circumstances. Didn't elaborate, and told Poole to tell his beat cop not to either, if the neighbors came asking questions.

He waves to the unmarked when he cruises past in the Caprice. He can't tell who's inside, but the guy waves back, so at least he's awake.

On his way east, he calls the Thirteenth to find Kingman Cade. Silk was in jail Saturday night at the same time he'd been made for the murder on Wolcott, and Leslie's description of her attacker doesn't fit Silk, either. Could be that someone's dropping his name, hoping he'll fall because of it. Then again, could be that Juan's right and Silk's behind all this, getting Craig tangled up.

The one thing Craig knows for sure, though, the thing that scares the shit out of him, is that someone out there knows he's a cop. So before he walks back into Mr. Moy's looking for Silk, he has to be certain it isn't a setup for him to fall, too.

"Hey, Craig," Cade says, "I knew you'd come around. Case got to you like MSG on your insides, did it? Chop suey keep you up all night, make you dream in high definition? Let me guess, you can't shake that funny feeling you got about our dead junkie."

Craig's never met Cade, but right now he can picture his smile.

"Listen, Cade, the funny feeling I have is about the guy they call Silk."

"Give me something good, because his forty-eight is up today, and we can't hold him for his late fees at Bangkok Video."

"He's still in jail?"

"Until the state's attorney figures out he doesn't match the description of a cholo pushing two-fifty who doesn't like to pay for popcorn shrimp."

So he was right: Silk couldn't have been Leslie's attacker. But that doesn't mean the Fuxi didn't set it up, to show Craig how long his legs are. "Has he spoken to anyone?"

"Are you kidding? He even refused his phone call. I don't know how much you know about the Chinese around here, but anything happens, they won't even take a piss if they have to 'cause they're afraid they'd give us a clue."

"Nothing back on the body yet? Nothing you can link to Silk?"

"There's some talk among the junkies in the neighborhood, but nothing sounds like Silk. The vic's name was Desmond Cline, called D-Cline on the street. You're right: he was a middleman, just cut the junk together. He didn't deal, though he was known to keep a couple of the locals happily horsed so they'd keep watch on the stash house. They call him Mr. Magic."

"Magic," Craig says, thinking of the junk that killed Rudy.

"Yeah, you know, suppliers put out the same shit, different name, to get a buzz on the product; junkies remember the product that hits hardest, and they wake up every day looking for the same fix. Magic was big down here a few months back; junkies started calling our man D-Cline by the 'magic' moniker, hoping he'd re-up."

"Magic killed my best friend."

"I'm sorry for you, man. Doesn't matter what you call the shit: it does make people disappear quick."

It's cool, Mickey. Craig tries to shake the memory of Rudy jonesing, his stretched smile, gummy mouth. "I couldn't stop it," he tells Kingman.

"Nobody can stop it," Cade says. "We can only stop it up, once in a while."

Craig blinks away the burn in his eyes, tells himself Cade's right. "You were talking about the neighborhood. Anybody shed light on D-Cline?"

"The junkie who did the most talking was fiercely loyal. He says D-Cline wasn't much of a heroin guy himself; he liked his club drugs."

"Ecstasy?"

"That's mostly what we found at the stash house. My narc guy recognized a couple tabs he's seen floating around the Redeye Lounge in Chinatown—disco biscuits, white doves, love bugs—"

"Love bugs," Craig remembers. Shit.

"Yeah. Isn't it great: they're marketing this stuff to kids like candy. The influx of use in the city is practically immeasurable, since the big boys only want us to go after the drugs that run up the stats. We've got the tabs at the lab, since my guy says not all of them are straight

MDMA, but nothing short of a teen death in Glencoe will get any-body to make a case over the stuff."

"You know what killed D-Cline?"

"Still waiting on the tox reports. Coroner's initial guess is an over-dose, which probably means he took a little of this, a little too much of that. What I want to know is where it all came from. So, your feel-ing about Silk? What's he got to do with this?"

Craig had planned to get the skinny on Silk and blow off Cade, but, "Some ecstasy turned up on the north side last week—same kind of tabs you're talking about. There's got to be a connection. I've got a guy here in Uptown I can talk to. Let me see what falls out and I'll get back to you."

"How about dim sum at the Royal Dragon on Wentworth, noon?"

"Chinatown? Are you nuts?"

"You got me in the mood for cashew chicken."

"They already think I'm a rat, I don't need to be seen anywhere near a cop."

"Trust me, you won't be."

"You pull weight down there?"

"I *am* weight."

Cade did say he knew Chinatown. If he has connections, one of them might be to the Asian with the winged tattoo. "Noon, then."

Craig hangs up and honks at the delivery truck that's blocking the alley beside Mr. Moy's. The diesel engine coughs and knocks in re-sponse, and the truck kicks forward, but not so that there's enough room for Craig to get by. The driver waves Craig around, the gesture gruff, like Craig's the one parked illegally. Craig honks again; this time, the response is the driver's middle finger. Any other day Craig would call in the truck's plates, jam up the guy's delivery schedule while he explains himself to a beat cop, but Craig doesn't have time for regular assholes today. He backs out and leaves the Caprice in a no-parking zone on Argyle.

In the alley, the delivery truck's refrigeration compressor chugs along, drowning out the rest of the city noise. Craig walks up, directly behind so the driver can't catch him in his mirrors, and kicks out the back right taillight.

He ignores the driver when he rounds the cab of the truck. He figures they've both made their points.

In the lot behind Mr. Moy's, a beefy white tow-truck operator starts a winch that pulls a broken-down U-Haul onto the flatbed of his wrecker. He lights a cigarette—he's in no rush: there are plenty of other people with car trouble who aren't going anywhere. They're just going to have to wait.

Upstairs in the apartments kitty-corner to Moy's place, an old Hispanic woman shakes a rug out over the railing. Craig is thankful for all this Monday morning activity: if anything goes down at Moy's, at least he has witnesses.

He knows it's risky, coming here, but it's the only way he can think of to get to Silk.

Mr. Moy's screen door is propped open by a freestanding box fan that blows air back on itself. Inside, the door to the Pai Gow den is closed.

Craig steps inside. "Mr. Moy?"

Moy appears in the kitchen doorway wearing an apron, a pencil behind his ear.

"Mickey, what (are you doing here)?"

"No game today?"

Moy shakes his head no and, like he's through with the conversation they barely started, turns back into the kitchen.

Craig wasn't invited, but he follows.

"Everybody want(s) something from Mr. Moy," Moy tells the guy in the Halsted Packing House uniform who's unloading heavy-duty waxed cardboard boxes marked *Pork Shoulder* and *Pork Ribs* from his handcart onto a metal counter.

Craig knows better than to talk Pai Gow in front of outsiders, but that doesn't mean he won't play his own game. He leans against the doorframe, asks the delivery guy, "That your truck parked in the alley?"

"Nope, I'm out front," he says. "Why?"

"Driver gave me the third degree just now," he lies. "Like he was some kind of cop."

Moy shoots Craig a look sharper than any of the knives stuck in the wood block on the adjacent counter.

The delivery guy puts up the last box, says, "Next time you want to change the order, Mr. Moy, you have to call the main office the week before." He speaks slow, like Moy will get it this time. "Do you understand? We can't split what's on the truck."

"Okaay . . . okaaay," Moy says, like their conversation is also prematurely finished. He licks the tip of his pencil, signs off on the order form and waves, a dismissal.

"I pay too much for too much," Moy says, the complete sentence unprecedented. The delivery guy shrugs and rolls his empty handcart around a standing wire rack full of industrial-sized containers of cornstarch, soy sauce, a supersized can of baby corn. At the kitchen door, he switches his grip and pulls the cart through it.

Craig waits until the guy's gone to ask, "Mr. Moy, what's happening here?"

Moy walks around to the other counter where a whole chicken sits in between a bottom-bloodied box and an empty plastic bin.

"Mickey," he says, dislodging a huge cleaver from the wood block. He turns the whole chicken on its back and in one swift chop, hacks the bird in two. "Game (is) over."

"I didn't come to play," Craig says. "I came to get even."

"You got your money." Moy selects a sizable paring knife from the block and goes at half the bird with short, sharp strokes. He cuts close to the bone, pulling flesh away from the carcass.

"I'm not talking about the money. I want to settle up with the spiders. The one they call Silk."

The merciless way Moy cuts through the ball-and-socket joints of the bird and disconnects the wing and thigh makes Craig wonder if Moy might enjoy seeing Silk against the ropes. But he doesn't say anything; just starts on the other half of the bird.

"They gave me my money back, Mr. Moy, but what about my honor? Those guys tortured me—they humiliated me. And I'm not even asking you to tell me why. I just want to know where he is. I've been loyal—don't *you* owe me?"

Moy says nothing, though the thin lines of his face are drawn at conflicted angles as he slices pieces of meat from the bird and tosses them into the plastic bin.

Craig steps into the room, finally. He says, "I saw that act you pulled with the delivery guy, Mr. Moy. You can't get away with it now. I know you understand me."

Moy grips the knife's handle upside down and stabs the blade into the wood block.

"You do not understand me," he says. "I run Pai Gow for Chinatown. Gangs fight, I lose. Chinatown say(s) I pay more. Fuxis do not protect." He takes the cleaver to the bird's leg bones, chop-chop. He looks at Craig and says, "They (have) no respect. I am finish(ed)."

"We can help each other, Mr. Moy. Silk disrespected both of us. Tell me where he is."

"Mickey, I have honor. I get out of (the) game. I go with Sooz. Be legitimate."

"That's one word you obviously don't understand."

Moy throws the stripped carcass in the trash underneath the counter. "You have (a) better offer?"

Craig feels the handle of his gun in its shoulder holster when he gets his keys from his inside coat pocket. "Not yet."

"Mom, what's wrong with you?"

When Leslie rolls over and opens her eyes, Ivy is standing there, hands on her hips, snotty pout on her lips. "This is the second day in a row you haven't gotten me up. I'm totally late for school." She finds herself in Leslie's vanity mirror and crosses the room to primp.

Shaking off sleep, Leslie remembers what the hell she looks like and pulls the covers up over her neck. "I'm sick."

Ivy fingers her glossed lip line. "How am I supposed to get to school?"

"Take my car."

Ivy's mouth drops open and she looks at her mother through the mirror. "Wow. You are sick."

"Keys are in my purse," Leslie says, turning over. "Will you call Sauganash? Tell them I'm not coming?"

"Yeah, hold on."

Leslie listens as Ivy unzips her purse, roots through it. Then, for a moment, it's completely quiet.

"Ivy? Did you find them?"

"Why, in the hell, do you have Niko's phone number?"

"What?" Uh-oh: she'd forgotten she tucked the *Reader* page into her purse.

"Did he call you?"

"No," Leslie says, wondering if she should have said yes.

"Don't lie to me, Mother."

"It's not what you think."

"You don't know what I think." Leslie hears her purse hit the floor. "Answer me: he called you, didn't he?"

Leslie wishes she could disappear under the covers. She has to tell her, doesn't she? "I'm not going to lie—"

"I fucking knew it," Ivy cuts in. "He's so pathetic: calling my mother? Did he tell you I said I don't want to see him anymore? He's such a geek. He's a total fucking downer—"

"Watch your mouth," Leslie says, hoping she sounds anything but relieved.

"Isn't that just like you to stick up for him? Unreal. You know, you should just stay out of my life, Mom, because you don't have a clue, and you make me want to leave here and never come back."

Leslie hears Ivy rip the paper in two; then her keys clink together when Ivy finds them and storms out.

Leslie listens as the girl tears off downstairs, slams the front door, revs the engine and speeds away. Talk about hell on wheels. Unreal is right.

She sits up, looks at the clock. It's just after nine; she can't believe she slept so long. She knew Craig wouldn't wake her, even though she asked him to. His cop-brain must have kicked in when he woke up, and he's probably out there right now with his gun in some Asian's face.

The thought is strangely comforting; it recalls something she'd thought was long lost: after last night, she remembers what it feels like to respect her husband.

He had been so strong, all this time, and she hadn't seen it. She chose to doubt him. Resent him. To betray him, for temporary dreams. For a boy.

And still, he remained a man, strong as ever until he realized she'd been hurt. That was what broke him, because he blamed himself.

They'd come after her because of his case, he said; someone must have blown his cover and come after her to get to him. Someone found him out, and made him pay with what he held most dear.

It broke him. After all these years, seeing her hurt was what finally made him cry.

Though she should have, she didn't tell him that the men followed her from the Green Mill. She couldn't bring herself to tell him she'd been there to see Niko. Craig couldn't have handled that blow, not after everything else. He wouldn't have been able to get back up.

She knew, last night, that she had to go on as planned. She would cover up her mistakes; now she had to, for her husband.

Leslie gets the cordless phone from the nightstand and dials work.

"Raylene," she says, "I can't come in."

"Since when does part-time mean anytime you want? What's going on with you?"

"I'm sick."

"You figured that out a half hour before you're supposed to be here?"

"I'm *that* sick."

"I'm fresh out of sympathy cards," Raylene says. "Blow your nose and be here tomorrow."

"Thanks." Leslie hangs up and crawls to the foot of the bed. She takes the torn *Reader* pages from her purse, amazed at how desperate she'd felt calling Niko, just a day ago. She wonders if she'll feel different tomorrow.

She crumples up the pages and throws them into the trash can next to the vanity. She didn't say good-bye, but really, there's nothing more to say than that.

The burns on her arms itch beneath the bandages. She should get up, shower, redress the wounds.

Instead, she slips a bobby pin from its card on the vanity and heads for Ivy's room. Her daughter says she doesn't have a clue? She's about to get one.

She picks the lock and tucks the bobby pin into her hair.

In Ivy's room, there's the same mess, but no backpack. She switches on the Macintosh.

When the computer asks for Ivy's username and password, Leslie types *Ivy,* but it doesn't work, so she tries *Viceroy* for both and the system accepts. Leslie should have known: when the girl's got it, she's always got it bad.

Once the Mac's programs appear across the bottom of the screen, in the dock, Leslie double-clicks the Firefox Internet icon and waits for the connection.

A mailbox sweeps out from the corner, and then a Web page that loads MySpace.com, Ivy's home page, which advertises itself as a "place for friends." At the member login prompt, Ivy's email address and password are already keyed, provided by the auto-fill. Leslie hits return.

The new page says, *Hello, Ivy!* Underneath, a close-up photograph of a butterfly tattoo is positioned amidst sixty-two different options, top friends, a block of "cool new people," and a few select ads. Leslie chooses Ivy's profile link.

The decision renders another photo of the tattoo. The butterfly's wings are orange and black, the ink so new it appears iridescent; the tattoo's detail is so precise it looks like someone pressed a live monarch to someone's skin. The caption next to it says: *Check out my tattoo. Who wants to see it in the flesh?*

The flesh, that is, of her daughter's inner thigh.

Leslie scrolls the page, afraid this is just the beginning.

34

It wouldn't take a detective to find Kingman Cade: he's the only black man in the Royal Dragon, and he's seated in the back at a table for six that seems just about his size. His suit looks so expensive the pinstripes could be real platinum. A fat gold ring weighs down his little finger as he raises his teacup to his pink lips. As Craig approaches, he doesn't seem to notice: his eyes are glued to the soap opera playing on the TV rigged up in the corner.

When Craig reaches the table Cade says, "You're late."

"Sorry, Cade. Traffic."

"I was talking to the girl," he says, his gray-brown eyes still on the TV. "Lily. She's been sweet-talking this kid Jonathan, but look at her body language. She's dancing that pretty dance around him and he doesn't see it coming: she's holding something back. I'll bet she's pregnant."

Craig pulls out a chair across from him. "You watch this crap?"

"For the purpose of research," he says. "Difference between acting and lying depends on whether your audience is willing to believe you. Actors lie for a living. Just like criminals."

"Helloo," a short, young Chinese man in an apron sidles up to the table and collects the extra plates. He asks Craig, "Something to drink?"

"Water's fine."

Cade opens his menu, says, "Let me get an order of the sautéed water convolvulus with chili and black bean sauce. And some of that seaweed soup."

The waiter bows, angles his head toward Craig. "For you?"

Cade passes him the menu; without opening it, Craig passes it to the waiter. "Sweet-and-sour pork?"

"Lunch special?"

"That's fine."

The waiter nods, rib cage up, and moves off.

"Bold choice," Cade says.

"If I can't pronounce it, I don't want it," Craig says. "Anyway, what happened to cashew chicken, Cade?"

"I'm a vegetarian. Didn't think I could sell you on bean curds and bamboo shoots, though." He grins, his bone-white teeth straight and narrow. "Call me Kingman, by the way. I don't dig on the pseudo-formal bit."

"Then what's with the suit? You trying to pass for a gangster or a politician?"

"There's a difference? Truth is—" He stops, his attention back on the TV.

Lily says, "I took a pregnancy test."

Jonathan says, "What?" Music swells, and the screen cuts to a diaper commercial.

"Poor kid." Kingman shakes his head at the TV, pours himself more tea. "Truth is, my wife works for Neiman Marcus. She might not make me a better man, but she sure makes me look good."

Craig thinks of Leslie, and wonders if Kingman can tell he's acting when he smiles.

"So," Kingman says, "what went down in Uptown?"

"Nothing. There's dissention in the ranks over this whole Hawks-Spiders feud, so my guy decided to close his Pai Gow den, and his mouth along with it."

"That's how it works. It's even worse, here in the Ninth. You see all the CAPS signs in the windows: 'We Know Our Police'? That stream doesn't flow both ways. Place is so sealed up, cops down here have no idea who's who. They probably think a Night Hawk is a high school mascot. And they like it that way. You talk to any guy in this district about gang activity and they'll act like you're the one speaking Chinese. They have the lowest crime rate going, and they think those little signs are doing the trick. Trick is behind those little signs. Back behind the businesses. That's where Chinatown handles the real stuff."

"I know it. I've been there." Craig watches Kingman sip his tea, wondering if he'll be a willing audience. "Listen," he says, "that feeling I had about Silk? A while back I ran into an Asian guy. Long hair. Tattoo on his groin, some kind of black wings—a bird or a bat, who knows. Mean motherfucker. Carries a shiv."

"Keep talking."

"He sounds familiar?"

"He sounds like a Hawk."

"From what I hear, he's been tearing up some players, dropping Silk's name."

"These guys don't name names."

"Unless they're trying to get Silk out of the picture."

"They wanted Silk out of the picture, he'd be gone."

"Not if Silk is the nephew of one of the men who runs Chinatown."

"No kidding?"

"He'd have to do something pretty fucked up to get gone."

"So what? This funny feeling you have about Silk is more of a soft spot?"

"I'm just saying, maybe Silk is being set up."

"What did this guy do, exactly? The wingding."

"He stole."

"Stole what?"

"Nothing anybody's going to admit." Craig knows his detached expression is getting thin.

Kingman eyes him. "Is there something you aren't telling me? Why do I feel like Jonathan up in this episode?"

"I just think this guy needs to be found."

The waiter brings Craig's water and Kingman's soup.

Kingman uses his napkin to clean his soup spoon, waits until the waiter's gone to say, "You want to know the grislies on D-Cline now, or do you have a delicate stomach?"

"I'm not the one eating seaweed."

Kingman puts down the spoon. "Body was found sitting upright against a wall, needle stuck in his arm. We figured overdose, like I said, but we couldn't tell whether the fluid coming out of his nose and mouth was blood from trauma, or just plain old purge fluid. Rigor mortis already came and went, and he broke down pretty quick: skin was going black from green from the black he started out with, and he was so bloated we were afraid he'd pop."

"Sounds like any guy who kicks and doesn't get a date with the mortician."

"It isn't what was dead that bothered us."

The waiter brings Craig's sweet-and-sour pork and whatever the hell Kingman ordered.

"Enjoy."

"I will," Kingman says, and starts into his soup.

Craig looks down at his plate: glazed pork and peppers, flecks of egg and carrot in his rice.

"Flesh flies, maggots, beetles," Kingman says. "Ants, there for the maggots. Wasps—the ME got bit. It was a mess."

"A mess, maybe, but nothing that doesn't love a corpse." Craig shoves a forkful of stir-fry into his mouth.

"You didn't let me get to the spiders."

Craig thinks about spitting his food back onto his plate. He can hardly chew, let alone swallow. "Spiders," he says, through the mouthful.

"Of the orb-weaving variety. Not the kind that set up camp indoors, unless the season is rainy, and we're out somewhere past Huntley."

Craig forces himself to swallow. "You think it's the Fuxis?"

"That's why I was waiting to hear what you had on Silk."

Craig pushes the rice around his plate. If he fesses up about his spider bites, Kingman will want to use him—maybe even get him to show his face—to hang the murder on Silk. But if Kingman can't find the tattooed guy, Silk might be the only one who can.

Craig hopes he's convincing when he says, "I wish I could tell you I had something on him."

Kingman drizzles soy sauce over his stir-fry, not-so-casual glances back at his lunch date. "A shame we have to let him go this afternoon."

"You've got to have other leads. What about the cause of death? The tox reports?"

"D-Cline died due to a lethal combination of heroin, fentanyl, MDMA, and ketamine. Like I said, a little of this, too much of that. Can't say he meant to do it, but I've got no proof otherwise. That's why I called you."

"Heroin and fentanyl: that's the China White. And you said he had an ecstasy habit. Where does the ketamine fit in?"

"Remember I told you about the tabs we were testing? There were these blue ones with dog bones stamped on, called disco biscuits. They're manufactured with ketamine. They're just like China White: cheaper to make, harder to take." Kingman picks up his soup, drains the bowl.

"We know we can't get to the China White," Craig says, and points his fork at Kingman. "That means we need to find out where the ecstasy comes from."

Kingman picks up his chopsticks, flashes his perfect whites. "So what? You want to go clubbing?"

Almost an hour later, after reading every last word of Ivy's MySpace profile, Leslie feels like she birthed the Antichrist. There is hardly anything recognizable about the girl; despite all her references to philosophers and artists, there is nothing poetic about her online image.

On the main page, a song called "Submission" plays like ambient torture, over and over. The distressing beat fits perfectly with Ivy's stated interests: she is a fan of Nietzsche's nihilism, as she understands it to suggest she "Fuck Faith," and she is an advocate for Arthur Schopenhauer's pessimism, particularly the notion that desire exists prior to thought.

Her own philosophy: "say no and you're missing out."

Ivy's highlighted favorites are foreign to Leslie: music by DJ

Tiësto and Dieselboy, movies like *24 Hour Party People* and *Freaks*. Under books, it says HA HA HA; under heroes: Persephone.

Why would anyone admire the goddess who was stuck in hell?

When Leslie scrolls past the favorites and various photos of Ivy's tattoo, she finds something more disturbing: the only "friend" she recognizes in Ivy's top ten is Viceroy.

Viceroy. His picture is a cartoon—Asian anime of a character with porcelain skin, wild spiked hair, and buglike sunglasses that reflect nothing. Leslie scrolls down to "Ivy's Friends Comments" and finds Viceroy has posted the majority of them.

His most recent post compliments her tattoo, assuming *sick* is a compliment.

As she goes back through the posts, Leslie traces his preceding comments, deciding the boy lacks a decent vocabulary. How could someone like Ivy be impressed by the comment *iv youre so hot*?

She finds the answer when she reaches his post about the rave:

finally i meet u IV. hot. and u were right, rios is a legend. thanks for the intro, disco biscuits will happen, and youre in if you can lose niko. we will be rolling—in ca$h too. love me, VI

And before that:

thanks IV, sounds sick. tell your friend rios to come and hook me up with LBs. i have connections and we can talk DBs. and hey, leave niko at home. lets dance. love me, VI

Leslie can't believe it. Niko said Viceroy was trouble, but the way this reads, Ivy is just as bad.

"Submission" starts yet again, its beat offering a continuous supply of anxiety. Leslie logs off Ivy's MySpace, goes to Google, and types in *disco biscuits.* There are more than a million results, and all the links on the first page go to an electronica-jam band. On the second page, though, Leslie finds a link called "The A to Z of Drugs." Clicking through brings her to *E. E* for ecstasy.

The little bitch. Ivy wasn't only experimenting with the drug at the rave, she was trying her hand at selling it.

And she just got rid of Niko, so it looks like Viceroy's plan succeeded.

Leslie types *find address* into the Google Search box. From there, she links to a digital switchboard directory and does a reverse search for Stavrakos in Chicago. There are four addresses; she finds the one on Berwyn Avenue, out on the city's edge, where Niko's mother says it's safe.

If Niko wanted to be safe, Leslie decides, he shouldn't have introduced his brother, "the legend," to Ivy.

Craig steps out onto Wentworth Avenue and leans against the storefront window while he waits for Kingman, who hit the can after lunch.

Across the way, four white guys in black suits come out of the Bowman Funeral Home and tune up their brass horns. Shortly thereafter, droves of Asians come out from the home, all in black, white bands tied at their elbows. The quiet that surrounds death follows them. They gather in groups on the sidewalk; nobody seems upset, which doesn't surprise Craig, though he doesn't expect the horns to begin playing "Amazing Grace" when the coffin is carried out to the hearse.

"Some Americana," Kingman says, stepping out next to Craig. He smells like mouthwash. "Come on—I want to show you something."

Craig follows him up past the Chinatown gate to the corner.

"You heard about that station?" Kingman asks, sunglasses aimed across the street at the red-bricked Chinatown fire station.

"Yeah," Craig says, "they filmed *Backdraft* there."

"I'm not taking you on a sightseeing tour, here, Craig. You see that bench, sitting between the garage doors?"

"Better if I had glasses."

"A couple months ago, somebody left a guy named Yu Bo Tuo on that bench."

"So?"

"He was on fire."

"No shit. Did he live?"

"Nope. And the way he went out? I think he was the lucky one. Found his wife and kids at the home, tied up, scalped, each of them holding the weapons they were killed with."

"No kidding? I worked a case like that a couple years back. Vietnamese family."

"The Min Los. I know: I looked up the case file to see if you'd turned up something that would help me."

Kingman looks back down Wentworth into the heart of Chinatown, where a director organizes the funeral procession. "The Yus lived over off of Ogden, so I caught the case. Came down here and asked around, since Mr. Yu was active in the Chinese community."

"Nobody talked."

"Somebody talked: Mr. Yu. Apparently that's what got him a customized trip to hell before he sat down on that bench." He takes the handkerchief from his suit pocket, removes his sunglasses, wipes them down. "Something struck me, though, when I went back through the cases: yours, and others like it, were all ethnically matched—all Vietnamese. The Yus were the first Chinese victims. It fits in quite nicely with the new color scheme in Chinatown, don't you think?"

"What do you mean?"

"The violence. The brutality. Home invasions, rapes, robberies. It's all worse since the Night Hawks started their run for the regime."

"It's getting to be the same up north. You think the Hawks were behind the Yu murders?"

Kingman nods, says, "I know it. Doesn't mean I could prove it. Felt like I was like trying to solve an urban legend. I had a name—guy who goes by Viceroy—but I couldn't find anybody who'd ever actually seen him. Looking for the guy was like trying to catch darts. I got pricked once or twice, case went cold. You know how it goes."

"They go cold quick."

Kingman says, "Excuse me." He walks away, sunglasses hooked on his pinky finger, and answers his cell.

Down the street, traffic is stopped as the hearse and its procession make U-turns to head north. Craig wonders what kind of funeral Mr. Yu had. If anyone played "Amazing Grace." His stomach churns, gassy: the sweet-and-sour pork wasn't so sweet.

Kingman comes back, says, "That was my tox man. He traced the fentanyl we found at D-Cline's place—the stuff he was cutting with the heroin. Turns out it was pharmaceutical grade, and based on the makeup, my man found the lab: Mallinckrodt, a drug company down in St. Louis. Mallinckrodt supplies a bunch of old folks' homes up here, and my man did a check, found a place that just happens to be coming up short on its fentanyl supply. It's a convalescent home in Uptown called the Lawrence House. You know it?"

Fucking Juan. Craig burps, says, "Yeah, I know it, and I bet I know who lifted the fentanyl. How about this: I'll find your thief, you find mine."

"Can't pay for that deal." Kingman puts on his sunglasses, and neither man says anything else as the funeral procession passes by, the line of limos following the hearse, their black-tinted windows shielding grief.

. . .

Leslie parks the Tacoma outside the white-bricked home on Berwyn Avenue and debates her approach. It's early afternoon and there aren't any cars out front, so she doubts Rios is there, but she might be able to catch Mrs. Stavrakos alone.

She adjusts her turtleneck and checks her appearance in the rearview mirror. What will she say? Niko said his mother is overprotective, and that she already believes Rios to be a problem. Leslie won't get answers by telling the woman what she already knows, so telling the woman things she'll love to hear is probably the only guaranteed way to get answers.

"Mrs. Stavrakos?" she says after she rings the doorbell. "I'm Leslie McHugh, Ivy's mom?"

"Who?"

"Your son Niko is a friend of my daughter Ivy's."

A woman at least ten years Leslie's elder opens the door, her gray-streaked hair pulled back tight into a bun, making her long nose and tough jaw look all the more old-country. "What is your name?"

"Leslie," she says.

"You are Greek?"

"I am."

"I can tell." Her tough jaw grants a smile that creases her face. "But Nikodemus says nothing about a girlfriend."

"I was under the impression you knew—he brought us some of the tsoureki you made last week."

"I suppose he is afraid to bring girls around. He knows I would like to see him married to a nice Greek girl. What did you say is your last name?"

"Kastanis," she says, figuring it isn't a total lie, and that her maiden name gives her a better chance of getting in the door.

Mrs. Stavrakos studies her, smiling, probably wondering what Ivy Kastanis looks like.

"I was just in the neighborhood, actually, and wanted to thank you in person—the tsoureki was wonderful."

"I'm making kourambiethes this afternoon, would you like to come in?"

"I would love to."

Mrs. Stavrakos offers her hand and notices the bandage covering Leslie's. "*The'Mou,* what happened to you?"

"Oh—it's nothing—I burnt myself roasting the lamb yesterday."

Mrs. Stavrakos crosses herself. "*The'Mou,* Leslie. Come inside."

The aroma of shortbread is the first thing that's appealed to Leslie since the rape. She follows Mrs. Stavrakos into the kitchen, the woman's gait burly, duteous. "You want coffee?" she asks, over her shoulder.

"No need to go to the trouble," Leslie says.

"Going to the trouble is the point. Sit." She fills a narrow-topped boiling pot with water. "Did you have a nice Easter?"

"So nice," Leslie lies.

"I'm glad we still have today to recover," she says, referring to Easter Monday, a hangover day on the Orthodox calendar.

"I agree—I'm still recovering," Leslie says, which is no lie. She pulls out a chair at the kitchen table, a round four-top with a lace-embellished tablecloth. A bouquet of fake lilies sits, the centerpiece. Everything from the tile to the ceiling is some shade of white. There are no red Rio Madame DelBard roses to speak of.

"You have a lovely home," Leslie says. "So light."

"Imagine keeping it this way with three men in the house." Mrs. Stavrakos measures four heaping spoonfuls of coffee into the pot and turns on the stove.

"You've done well with Niko, he's a very polite young man."

She pulls on a hot pad and opens the oven. "Some you win, some you lose. I'm still fighting for both my sons." She removes a tray of kourambiethes and uses quick hands to place the oven-hot oval cookies on wax paper spread over the counter.

"Your Ivy, she's a good girl?"

"She has her moments."

"Greek women are always the feistier of the two," she says, sparkles in her black eyes as she uses a sifter to sprinkle powdered sugar over the cookies.

"I haven't met your other son," Leslie says, like it's incidental. "What's his name?"

Mrs. Stavrakos's black eyes go flat. She puts down the sifter and crosses herself, says, "Soterios." She picks up the sifter again and works more vigorously. "I love both my sons, but be thankful Niko is the one suited for her."

"I'm sure Soterios will find his way."

"He could be a good man—a working man," she says, using a spatula to move some of the cookies onto a white plate. "But American boys, they don't receive the work ethic like they do in Greece." She takes two tiny white cups from the overhead cabinet and pours the coffee just before it boils. "Nikodemus, he has a good work ethic. I wish he was interested in real work, something useful, but at least he is committed."

"I understand he's trying to get into Columbia—you should be proud. College is a very important step for any career."

She hands Leslie one of the coffees. "No one in my family went to college, and we are all just as well." She picks up the plate of cookies. "Let's go into the sitting room."

"Wow: you have a truly Greek family," Leslie says, when she sees the sitting room's mantel packed full of gold-rimmed photographs.

"There are only a few of us here in the States," Mrs. Stavrakos says. "Most of my side of the family is still in Korinthos. Rios is on his way there as we speak—I'm sending him to work for my brother. I am hoping he will turn a corner there. The route he is on here will lead him nowhere . . ."

Leslie surveys the mantel like a polite guest, though she's only half-listening to Mrs. Stavrakos because she's looking for a photo of Niko—hoping to see him differently, maybe when he was younger. It never occurred to her that seeing him through his mother's eyes might help her turn what happened between them—or didn't happen—into something she can hold dear, like the fond feeling anyone has for a child.

". . . worries me, especially this boy he was going around with. He does not hold a job, and he has a liar's eyes . . ."

In each photo, different family members stand among one another, united. She holds her coffee by the cup's rim, close to her nose, and anticipates its strength. In the center of the mantel, she finds Niko in a panoramic family photo, probably taken just a few years back. His smile still hits her the way it shouldn't.

". . . I think it is because he is Oriental . . ."

This, Leslie registers. "What?"

"I am not speaking against their culture. But full-blooded Greeks, we know we have to stay true, to ourselves and to our principles."

Leslie nods, agreeing, until she comes across a square-framed photo of Mrs. Stavrakos with her arm around the goateed man. The one who bought the spiked drink at the Green Mill. The one who leered at her from across the bar. And the one who followed her home and stood guard the night she was raped. "Is this . . . Soterios?"

"Yes: you see? He is a handsome boy . . ."

And he is the one who is on his way to Greece.

Leslie's coffee is suddenly too hot to handle. No matter which way she holds it, it burns.

"... I don't know why he is so troubled. I truly think it is this friend of his—"

"What, exactly, did your son do, that you're sending him away?"

Mrs. Stavrakos's black eyes go cold again. "Try the kourambiethes."

"No thank you, Mrs. Stavrakos." She puts her coffee cup on the mantel, says, "I need to get home. My husband is expecting me."

35

Craig shows his star to the young Spanish receptionist dressed in a cheap pants suit who sits at the front desk. He says, "I'm here about the fentanyl theft."

She looks up from her computer, points a fat fake nail toward the cafeteria door. "Another officer is talking to the residents in there."

Through the doorway, Craig spots Johnny Giantolli putting the screws to a threesome of old women who are in the middle of four o'clock dinner.

Shit, Craig thinks. Since Giantolli was promoted, he's been a one-man show. If he finds out Craig's here to snoop around, he'll throw a fit that starts here and only gets uglier on its way to the lieutenant's office. And anyway, Craig can't show his hand—he's supposed to be off the Fuxi case. Being here on Kingman's is a jurisdictionary no-no.

"Please, be considerate," the receptionist says. "Some of the residents are scared."

Craig pockets his star. "I wonder why."

At the table, only one woman is talking to Giantolli, though she looks like the sort who's always talked about everything all the time. Giantolli follows along, scribbling in his spiral notepad. The second woman stares off into space. She probably has no idea what she's doing there, let alone why there's lasagna in front of her. The third woman eats very busily, like she's trying to act normal: she's guilty, all right. Probably of stealing an extra piece of French bread.

There are at least fifty other men and women in there right now, which means he's got to collate as many stories. Should keep him occupied, though, give Craig plenty of time to look for Juan.

"I'll be following a lead upstairs, room 316," he tells the receptionist, but he doesn't get more than one foot forward when Giantolli looks up from his notepad, sees Craig at the desk, and waves him in.

Damn.

The cafeteria smells like canned tomatoes and ripe cheese; equally ripe old people are buttered with topical creams for their skin conditions, glazed with medications for their aches, fooled by their dwindling taste buds.

Giantolli smells pretty ripe himself when he gets up close, his mouth at Craig's ear, real confidential: " What, they give me a half a day and then they turn it over to you? Are they running me off the case?"

"Relax, G. I'm just here to see a friend."

Giantolli tucks his pen in his shirt pocket. "Oh yeah? Who?"

Craig looks around, but he doesn't see Vergil. He wasn't sitting in the window, either.

"Name's Vergil Walsh."

"Walsh?" Giantolli turns pages over in his notepad, reads: "Walsh. Vergil—I got him right here. Room 316. Claims he doesn't know the suspect."

"Who's the suspect?"

"If I knew that, would I be here?"

"What's the crime?"

"Somebody jacked painkillers from the nurses' station."

"Why aren't you talking to the nurses? Or the orderlies?"

"You're suggesting I talk to the people who have every reason to lie, be it liability, or job security, or guilt, instead of the people who are stuck here, treated like inconveniences, wishing there was some justice left?"

"A valiant effort, G."

"I thought so."

Giantolli steps aside for a man who rolls by in a wheelchair toward the cafeteria line. Back at his table of informants, the woman who'd been jabbering is still at it, though she lost most of her audience: the only woman left is the one who was in nowhere-land; now, she rests comfortably in dreamland, her own breastbone a pillow.

"Better get back to your interview," Craig says to Giantolli, "you might miss something."

Halfway home, Leslie realizes it is almost four o'clock, and before she can talk herself out of it, she's on the Kennedy headed into the Loop for Columbia College. She decided on the major detour because her feelings flipped at least ten times since she left the Stavrakos house.

Since the rape, she'd tried to tell herself Niko was no longer a governing force. She wanted to look back on her feelings for him without guilt: he wasn't a catalyst for what had happened as a result of her trip to the Green Mill. He's just a boy. It was just a crush.

But then she saw the photograph of Rios. And she couldn't shake the feeling that Niko knows what happened and that he's been covering for his brother. Maybe he's no boy, and he's been knowingly taking advantage of the situation. He could have faked his feelings for Leslie, just like Ivy had feigned interest in him, all for Rios. The man who watched the door.

So Rios is gone. But if Niko knows who raped her, he might be the only one left who does, and he is going to tell her. Or else he can forget about Columbia College. He can forget about playing the piano. Hell, he can forget about his goddamned fingers.

Leslie pays eight bucks at a lot on Wabash, leaves the Tacoma, and hustles over to Michigan Avenue. It's just turned four, so students are headed in and out of buildings, with books and bags, coffee and cigarettes.

She finds a kid carrying a guitar case who looks like a future roadie and asks, "Do you know where they hold auditions?"

The kids flips up his fat sunglasses, jerks a thumb behind him and says, "Music Center. Third floor."

Leslie goes into the building, takes the stairs to the third floor and pushes open a door marked RECEPTION. Inside, an older woman walks her fingers through a file cabinet. Her muted blond hair is styled so precisely it has to be a wig. Seated at the desk next to her, a gorgeous young black woman clicks away at a keyboard, a headset wrapped around the scarf that ties back her dreadlocks. Behind the nameplate on her desk that reads *Africa Lanier,* Niko's eleven Rio Madame DelBard roses sit proud, still blooming.

"Hello," Leslie says.

The blond puts on the eyeglasses that hang from a chain around her neck. "Can I help you?"

"Niko Stavrakos is auditioning today for jazz studies," Leslie says. "Can you tell me where? I'd like to be there when he's finished."

Africa cuts her a curious look so Leslie says, "I'm his mother."

The blond looks at Africa, who juts her jaw to one side, skewing her pretty face. "If you're his mother," she says, "then you should know why he canceled."

"I didn't know he canceled."

"Said he had a family emergency," the blond says.

Africa's head juts with her jaw now. She stands up, takes off her headset, and breezes past Leslie. "Follow me."

Outside the office, the sound of a single violin being played in one of the classrooms echoes through the hall. Africa closes the office door behind Leslie and says, real soft so her voice won't echo, "This isn't cool."

Africa stands at least six inches over Leslie, if her intended position wasn't obvious. "You know," she says, "I'm the one who got Niko the audition."

Leslie notices Africa is tapping her foot too fast to the violin's détaché, and instantly she realizes what the young woman is really saying: she got Niko the audition, and she must be getting more than flowers in return.

"He did have a family emergency," Leslie says.

Africa double-blinks her pretty black eyes. "Who the hell are you?" she asks, combative.

That's where Leslie's need to play Mom stops. She juts her head, just like Africa, exaggerated. "Niko's brother is implicated as an accessory to rape. Niko skipped the audition to give him a ride to the airport."

Africa shrinks, an inch at least. "He never said anything to me about a brother . . ." She trails off, her jealous tone too revealing.

"Niko never said anything about you, either. Good luck to you both." Leslie leaves Africa, the violin playing just for her.

Upstairs, Vergil sits in his wheelchair in the hallway outside room 316, watching nothing go by the mint-colored wall in front of him.

"Verge," Craig says, "what happened to your window seat?"

Vergil throws a hand toward him. "Lupe said I had to go to my room so there'd be some kind of order to this so-called investigation."

"Forget the nurse: I know the detective. I can pull rank. You want me to take you back down?"

"Lupe said I'd be in the way. But isn't that what I am? In the way."

"What's wrong, Verge? You feeling okay?"

"I know you didn't come here to check up on me, Craig. I know why you're here."

"Yeah? Then let's go." Craig unlocks his wheelchair brake and pushes him down the hall.

"Where we going?"

Craig leans over, does his best Dr. Strangelove: "Ve have vays of making you talk."

At the back end of the building Craig turns the corner and calls the service elevator. When it arrives he wheels Vergil inside, presses twelve.

"Cubs won yesterday," Craig says, elevator on the rise.

"Don't let 'em fool ya." Vergil squints at the floor numbers ticking by on the panel in front of him. "Who's that yahoo cop, anyhow? Coming in here, looking for justice, he says. From a bunch of prisoners."

"He's just doing his job."

"Spoke to me like I was hard of hearing, so I decided I was."

"I had a feeling he wouldn't get much out of you."

The elevator door opens and Craig wheels Vergil out, down the hall to a stairwell. Craig turns Vergil around, says, "Hold on," and drags him up, step by step, backward.

On the landing, the door says EMERGENCY EXIT—ALARM WILL SOUND.

When Craig turns Vergil's chair around, Vergil asks, "You being the law, that cancels out the fact that this is illegal?"

"We all gotta live a little. Lean to the left."

Craig takes out his Swiss Army locksmith knife, climbs up on the wheelchair's armrest, opens the alarm control box, and clips the wires.

Back on his feet, he asks, "You going to be warm enough?"

"I'm old," Vergil says, "I'm not a pansy."

Craig pushes open the door and shuttles Vergil through.

It's a clear afternoon, a light wind off the lake. Craig wheels Vergil across the rooftop, back toward the south end. Pigeons scatter, surprised.

At the southwest corner, Craig stops and sets the brake. Up here, in between all the high and higher rises, he can just make out a sliver of a section of Wrigley's lights. The way the sun drops in the sky, the backs of the gigantic lights glint like the lights themselves. "Can you see, Verge? Can you see Wrigley?"

"Are you kidding? I can't see my hands in front of my face."

"Well I can see it. And I'll bet you can picture it."

An epic smile spans Vergil's face, from boyish wonder to an old man's fond memories.

Craig asks, "What time's the game?"

"Six oh-five."

"I'll bet, if we wait, we can hear the crowd."

Vergil doesn't say anything. Not for a long time. Craig stands beside him, listening as the wind carries city sounds of construction and transportation and business, everything on the move, except what's been left to stand on its own.

Finally, Vergil says, "I'm not going to go and get an old man in trouble. We're all just trying to stay alive—to feel alive."

"I know that. But I need to know what's going on with Juan."

Vergil takes out a hankie, wipes his nose. "I've been thinking about my early days in the service. Did I ever tell you about Tony Tessoni?"

"Tell me again."

"Tessoni was an Italian from Brooklyn. A big guy who drew enemy lines quick. Tessoni had a problem with me the day I set foot on the base. I'd faked my identification and enlisted when I was seventeen, you see, so that made me the youngest pilot in the Twenty-First. I was also the smallest. And I was also the best.

"We were stationed down in Memphis after the war; there wasn't much of anything for us to do. Tessoni, he used the down time trying to get me into trouble; I used the time to steal his girl."

"I'd expect no less from you, Verge."

"Tessoni did. One night, he rounded up three of his cronies, came into the barracks to teach me a lesson. He didn't know I stayed awake in the dark most nights: it's the only time I could cry—and I did—hell, I was trying real hard to be a man, but I still missed my mama. When Tessoni came in, he didn't know he was catching me at a bad time. And he didn't know I was a featherweight fighter, either. I got up and beat the daylights out of every last one of them."

"Four guys? Verge: you never told me that."

"I'm not proud of it." Vergil looks over in Craig's general direction. The afternoon sun shines white in his eyes. "I don't suppose I'm very proud of what I did on Friday night, either."

"What happened?"

"Juan came into my room. He thought I was asleep. But hell, late at night, in the dark? It's still the only time I can cry. And lately I leave my hearing aids in, because someone's been stealing my clean towels. So I heard Juan come in, plain as a bagel."

"How'd you know it was him?"

"When he got inside and shut the door, he made a phone call."

"Did you hear it?"

"I don't know what he was saying—he was speaking Chinglish. But then he cranked open my window, and he dropped something out."

"The fentanyl."

Vergil stews in his chair. "I can't see, I can't walk, hell, I piss in a pan. I couldn't fight this time, Craig. I just lay there and pretended to be asleep."

Craig puts a hand on his shoulder. "It's okay, Verge."

Vergil shakes his head. "After Juan closed the window, he made another call. This time he spoke in English, and he said he had what they wanted." Vergil looks back out over the city, his blind eyes empty. "And then he promised that he had the cop on his side. Juan said, 'Now, he has to be.'"

Craig takes his hand from Vergil's shoulder, balls it into a fist. Juan only speaks English when he can't speak Chinese. Like when he's speaking to Craig. Or maybe to another Fuxi rival. Whoever was on the other end of that call definitely wasn't a Fuxi and he certainly wasn't a friend of Craig's. Sounds like Juan's the one who's been trying to get Craig tangled up.

"You're the one who doubted his loyalty, Verge. I should have listened. Hell, he said it himself: he's a half-breed devil."

"I'm ashamed, Craig. I thought both of us—you and I—did the right thing by Juan. I thought we got through to him; I thought he was cleaning up his act. But after Friday night, it dawned on me that language—English or otherwise—isn't his barrier; it just isn't what he values. And in this place, words aren't worth a damn thing to anyone, either, unless you got something behind them. Juan understands we've heard it all before. You want to know who helped him steal those drugs? Look for the old man who has no trouble sleeping at night."

Craig notices a faint shift in the sky's illumination over Wrigley: the stadium lights have been turned on.

"I should have spoken up," Vergil says. "I might've stopped Juan. But I'm afraid I don't have that kind of fight left in me."

"Don't worry, Vergil. I do."

· · ·

Driving up Cicero Avenue, Leslie doesn't think much of the squad in front of her. Until she realizes she's following it home.

When she turns on Forest Glen, she finds another squad blocking the street outside her house. Craig's Caprice isn't in the drive, nor is Leslie's car; no one should be home. The unmarked car Craig requested last night is still parked across the street, but Leslie can't tell if anyone is inside.

Every frayed nerve in her system misfires, makes her numb. She knows Ivy's on her way to big trouble, but what if she's already there?

She parks the Tacoma curbside behind the squad as a tall young beat cop with a baby face and a black shock of a buzz cut gets out and pulls on his duty cap. She doesn't recognize him, so she rolls down the window and waits for him to come to her.

"I'm Leslie McHugh. I live here. What's going on, Officer Wood?" she asks, reading his nameplate.

"McHugh—right," Wood says, a pertinent nod. "We've got a bit of a misunderstanding, is all." He puts his hand on the truck's window ledge and points a subtle finger toward the Rellinger house, behind her.

Leslie turns around and there is Meghan Rellinger, the source of the so-called misunderstanding. She's out the door and on her way through the yard like she's on a warpath, a second young beat cop in tow. The way Meghan moves, the big glass beads of her necklace bounce so hard against her chest they'll probably leave bruises. The cop can hardly keep up.

"Oh boy," Leslie says.

"She was concerned about our surveillance," Wood says.

"She called the cops on the cops?" It figures.

"We were hoping to take care of this without disturbing our man's position, but Officer Hollister called for backup when he got here. Your neighbour is pretty upset."

"She's probably been watching your surveillance guy closer than he's been watching my house. Why didn't your officer tell her it's an unmarked surveillance car?"

"We didn't know he was here when the call came in," Wood says. "The watch commander works the swing shift, so he must've put a new guy out before he left, forgot to put it on the books."

Forgot, Leslie thinks: favor's interchangeable word. "I'll talk to her."

Wood gets out of the way and she jumps out of the truck, rounds the Tacoma, and meets Meghan at the curb.

"Leslie, did you know about this?" Meghan pats her forehead like she's checking to see if she broke a sweat getting here. She did.

"It's not a big deal, Meghan, really—"

"Are you kidding? You know they just broke up a car theft ring a few blocks over? How was I supposed to know that man wasn't watching our homes"—she waves a floppy arm toward the unmarked car—"keeping track of when we come and go? He could have been sitting out here looking for the right make and model to add to his collection."

"He wasn't."

"Then I demand to know why he's here." Meghan folds her arms, her chin cocked, waiting for Leslie's answer.

"Everything's fine. It's just a simple safety measure."

"Oh no you don't, Leslie. I'm not buying simple, so don't bother to sell it." She puts a manicured finger in Leslie's face. "Your house is in shambles—you told me so. Your cheating husband, your promiscuous daughter—and don't think I haven't seen the people *you* have coming around. The young men with their souped-up cars and their rampant libidos. You should be ashamed."

The hint of satisfaction on Meghan's face turns Leslie's frayed nerves to steel. Meghan, out of her perfect, remodeled world: out here like she has some ethical duty.

"Mrs. Rellinger," Hollister says, "please calm down."

Meghan reels around to the young cop. "What are you, twelve? I'm supposed to listen to a twelve-year-old?"

"We're here for your protection," Wood tells her, so she turns around to him and says—

"I shouldn't need protection. I shouldn't have to fear for my own safety because my neighbor is a whore."

That does it: Leslie is goddamned tired of living in Meghan's moral shadow.

Leslie lunges forward, but Wood manages to grab her before she gets ahold of Meghan. Rage works on Leslie like a command, and she tries to get away from the officer to take the woman down on her perfect, fertilized lawn. She wants to wreck Meghan's expensive boutique necklace, her salon hairdo. And she can feel Wood, and Hollister now, holding her back, but she just keeps fighting, grasping for Meghan's light angora sweater, for her slim Italian leather belt; for everything that's right about her, to show her what the hell is wrong.

"Broadway Bonds, Peter speaking."

"Is Simon in?" Craig asks.

"One sec." The on-hold music is Gary Glitter's "Rock and Roll Part Two," the anthem that used to remind Craig of the old Chicago Stadium, the Bulls' three-peat, the sweet taste of hometown victory. Used to, that is, until Gary Glitter went to jail for possessing thousands of photos of hard-core child porn.

Craig hits the gas and shoots through a very yellow light at Kedzie. Now that he knows Juan isn't who he says he is, either, he's got to pull out all the stops.

"Simon here."

"It's Craig McHugh."

"You promised me your man Yoo-an would show up for court, McHugh. I'm losing money and my brother Peter's out of patience."

"Juan's on the lam again. This time from me. He fucked up good, Simon. I need you to get your bounties out there."

"They already are."

"Call me first, when they pick him up?"

"I'm thinking I need tickets for the Cubs–Red Birds series."

"You find Juan, I'll find tickets."

Craig hangs up, dials Kingman.

"Craig: how'd you do?"

"Depends how you look at it. I was right about the fentanyl. A Chinese kid lifted it—his name's Tse Jin Yuan. He's on the run—maybe from the Fuxis, definitely from me. I've got a buddy—a bail bondsman—who's got bounties on him now."

"What's the downside?"

"The kid was my CI."

"Aww, man. That's the trouble with snitches. You can trap an animal, but that don't make it a pet."

Craig cuts up Elston and takes Cicero, the quickest way home this time of day. He says, "I'm going to need some time with him before I bring him to you. I think he compromised my cover."

"Any chance he did D-Cline?"

"Yesterday I would have said no way. Today I'm not saying anything. You have any luck on your end?"

"I've got one of my detectives, Jenny Ling, canvassing the tattoo shops down here that are known for inking the Asian persuasion. Haven't heard anything yet, but Ling's good. Give her time."

"Kingman, if my snitch sold me out, we don't have much time."

"If you want me to wait on those bounties, I don't know what else I can do from here."

"I do."

"I'm listening."

"I think I figured another way into Chinatown. My instinct before—to gamble with these guys—was right; I just wasn't playing with the right currency. But I've got it now—we've got it—sitting in your jail. And if you can keep Silk locked up, he can be my trump."

"I can't do that, man."

"If you want to find out what happened to D-Cline, you'll find a way."

"I work murder. I'd have to charge him. And with the evidence I have right now, only thing that I can say caused D-Cline's de-cline was the needle in his arm."

Craig blows the red light at Peterson, turns right. "Kingman, what if I told you that I knew something about those bugs at the scene? About the spiders?"

"Depends what the something is."

"The spiders were Silk's."

"How do you know?"

"Check my Fuxi case files. I've got the bites to prove it." Craig turns onto Forest Glen, sees two squads parked in front of his house, uniforms in the yard.

What the fuck? "Check on it, Kingman. Call me back."

36

Craig tries to wrap his afghan blanket around Leslie, but she shrugs it off. "I'm not a victim."

He sits down next to her. "No, you certainly aren't. You're lucky Wood stopped you; he said you looked like you would've killed Meghan."

"She said terrible things."

Craig pulls her to him and she senses a strength she hasn't felt from him in a long time, but she resists, guilt spiraling. Has she completely lost control?

"Don't worry about Meghan," he says. "Hollister told me she had it coming. There's nothing she can do about a neighbor who didn't touch her, anyway. Or the unmarked car. I told Wood to have the UC move it around the corner, so she should shut her trap for a while."

Leslie fingers the wide stitches around a life preserver on one of the afghan panels. "Meghan's right," she says. "We shouldn't have to live this way. In fear." She knows she has to tell him about Rios. And the truth about Niko. But then how will they live? In shame? Apart? Alone.

"I know this is all fucked up, Les. It's my fault."

Suddenly cold, suddenly wanting the blanket around her, Leslie threads her fingers through the afghan's holes and pulls it up and around her. She's got to tell him. "This is not your fault."

"Please," he interrupts. "Let me come clean with you." He slips off the couch, gets down on his knees beside her. "I kept all this from you before, Les, but now I know I'm in too deep to keep things separate. It's important that you know the truth." He rests a hand on her thigh, his palm warm through the afghan. "I think my informant sold me out. That's why the men came here. That's why you were raped."

Leslie shakes her head: it doesn't make sense. What about Rios?

"I should have known," Craig says. "My informant said he wanted to get back at the Fuxis because they wouldn't let him join. He's a half-breed, Chinese-American. The Chinese think that makes him some kind of devil. They don't trust him, and I shouldn't have, either. But Juan, he was my connection, and we were in so deep, we had to trust each other. I thought I understood him: I mean, I was running out of department backing, we were thin on the case, and Suwanski wanted me to quit. I was an outsider, just like Juan. I guess I thought that put us on the same side. I couldn't see that he was just looking for another, darker place to fit in."

Leslie reaches out from underneath the afghan and takes his hand. "He fooled you." If only he knew how deeply she understands.

He comes up onto the couch then, and they sit quietly, holding hands.

Leslie nestles into the afghan, smelling Craig on its fabric. Mona crocheted the tacky thing, with its boats and its anchors, because Craig and his father used to sail. She'd given it to Craig as a gift for his fortieth birthday—a few years before her husband, Ian, dropped dead of a heart attack, and hobbies were no longer a comfort. Ian passed three years ago. Nothing has comforted Mona since.

As they sit, hands entwined, she realizes that maybe Mona is the way she is because she lost her husband so suddenly. She never had the final chance to tell him her truths, her lies, her good-bye.

Leslie can't take that risk.

She squeezes Craig's hand, tears threatening, when she finally says, "This is my fault, too."

"Don't say that, Les." Craig's cell phone buzzes, the vibration moving it across the table until it knocks against his gun. He reaches for it—

"Craig. Not now. I have to talk to you."

He checks the display. "I have to take this."

"It's about Niko. And his brother."

"It's the detective down south calling—the one I have looking for the man who . . ." He stumbles around the way to say—

"Raped me?"

"He might have found him."

The phone vibrates in his hand, the call light blinking, Craig waiting—this could be his chance to fix this. What can she say?

"Answer it."

He flips open the phone. "Kingman, give me good news." He listens, says, "No kidding. Hold on." He finds a yellow receipt in his front jeans pocket, a pen from his shirt. "Okay, shoot."

Leslie tries to make out the words as he writes them down: first, he writes *Gold Rush*.

"Gold Rush, uh-huh." Next, he writes *Black Wings*. Underneath: *Girl? But*—"He said what?" His hand turns to a fist around the pen. "The guy heard him say that?"

Craig doesn't write that down, but he finishes: *But . . . terfly.*

Then he writes *Viceroy*. Underlines it twice and says, "Your urban legend."

Leslie throws off the afghan and gets up from the couch. Craig says, "That's fantastic. Can Ling get me the pictures?" He nods at Leslie, who's pacing the other side of the coffee table, completely horrified: Viceroy? Ivy's Viceroy?

"Use my home address," Craig says. "From the database."

Leslie doesn't have to play worst-case scenario for this. She's afraid it's worse.

"How much time can you give me?" Craig asks. "Come on," he says, dissatisfied with the answer. He crumples the receipt, tosses it on the table, says, "If I have to deal with the desks instead of China-town I'm putting myself and my family in danger."

Leslie stops in front of him and shakes her head. Danger? He's got no idea.

"You can't hold on to Silk without it?" he asks, then says, to the answer, "But I can get this guy."

Viceroy. Leslie can't believe it.

"No, haven't heard back yet. Yeah: Tse Jin Yoo-an. Juan's what we call him. Spelled capital *T*, *s-e*. With a *J*. Yep. Yoo-an." Craig looks up at Leslie, no indication he notices she's completely beside herself. "Okay, that's fair. I'll call you back."

Craig hangs up and says, "Les, I was right. The detective down south found an artist who inked the tattoo that fits the description you gave. Just last Friday, the suspect was back at the parlor having his girlfriend get work done. One of the regulars heard him outside on the phone—he remembers this guy saying they had a 'sure-fire con-nection to the cop.' Juan must be his connection." Craig takes his gun from the coffee table, checks the load.

"Do they have him—Viceroy—in custody?" Leslie hopes.

"All they have to go on right now is a photo of the tattoo—the artists take pictures of their work to display at the parlor, and the detective snapped some digitals from those. I'm having this guy Viceroy's sent here for you to verify, but between his black wings and his big mouth, we've got enough to collar him." He puts his gun in his ankle holster and gets up.

"Viceroy," is all Leslie says.

Craig takes her by her arms. "I need you to listen very carefully. This guy Viceroy might also be involved in a murder. My guy in the Thirteenth is going to hold another suspect as long as he can while I get a meeting with the men who run Chinatown, but I don't have much time. When you get the photos, I need you to call me and verify a match. And you need to be absolutely certain, because I only have one chance with these men, and I can only make one trade."

"I know it's him," she says. "It's Viceroy."

"What? How?"

She takes the crumpled receipt from the coffee table, peels it open. "Niko told me Ivy broke up with him for someone named Viceroy. He sounded like trouble, so I went online this morning, into Ivy's computer. I saw pictures—this is her butterfly tattoo. Viceroy must be the one who took her to get it. His sure-fire connection to you is not your snitch. It's our daughter."

Craig steps back. "Jesus, who is this guy?"

"Go find him before he gets to you, too." she says. "I'll get Ivy."

Before Craig spent a dime in Mr. Moy's Pai Gow den, he spent a week doing surveillance on the little Chinaman. There were only three places Moy ever spent time. Usually, he'd be at Chu's China Delight, doing business. Sometimes he'd be at the Aragon Arms

Hotel, doing Suzanne. And, once in a great while, he'd be at his little shitbox apartment over on Glenwood—the place where he keeps his wife holed up—doing nothing.

When the little counter girl at Chu's bows and says, "He come back after ten," Craig heads for Suzanne's.

On Kenmore, Wardell is sitting spread-eagle in the middle of the sidewalk, his cowboy hat turned upside down between his legs. "Mickey," he says, "you got some change?"

"None to spare," Craig says, stepping over his legs. "I'm about to go all in with Mr. Moy."

"You're crazy, tempting fate."

Craig turns, says, "I'm not tempting fate, I'm deciding it."

Outside the Aragon Arms, a new jade plant hangs in the plastic potholder beside the entrance. *Suzanne,* he thinks: such a green thumb.

"It's Mickey," Craig says to the call box inside the first set of doors. Through the second set, smoke sits on changing streams of light beamed from Suzanne's TV.

Moy pokes his head out the service window cigarette-first, sees Craig, buzzes the door.

"Where's Sooz?" Craig asks.

"Upstairs. You need (a) room?"

"Nope. I'm here to see you."

Moy looks like an anemic dragon when he exhales smoke from his nose.

Craig places a fresh deck of cards on the counter in front of Moy. "You wouldn't tell me where Silk was, so I'm thinking maybe China-town will."

Moy shakes his head slow enough that the long ash dangling from his cigarette holds on.

"You can't say no yet, Mr. Moy: I haven't told you the bet." Craig takes the cards out of the box. "You're going legit, fine. And you don't want any more trouble, I hear you. But if there's one thing I know about you, Mr. Moy, it's that you can't turn down a guaranteed win."

Moy presses his cigarette between yellow fingers, a thumb to his temple. He watches Craig's hands as he shuffles the cards, slow and steady.

"One hand," Craig says. "If you win? You get one thousand dollars." He shuffles a bit more, lets the dollar amount sink in to Moy's brain. Then he says, "If I win, I'll still give you the thousand dollars. After you take me to Chinatown."

Moy sticks the cigarette back in his face. "Chinatown (will) laugh at you."

"What do you care?"

"Chinatown (will) not laugh at me. No way I (can) bring a white man."

"Come on, Mr. Moy, a good man honors his bets. Chinatown knows that. You lose, you honor the bet and get me a sit-down. It's no skin off your dick. Either way, you get the money."

Moy blows another stream of smoke from his nose, his eyes on the cards. "You pay one thousand for Silk," he says, not believing it.

Craig puts the deck on the counter, looks Moy in the eye. "Yes, I'll pay one thousand for Silk. I thought he was going to kill me." He takes out his wallet and counts out ten hundred-dollar bills, placing them next to the cards while he says, "I don't care about the money. Chinatown is the way to Silk, and Silk is the only one who can really repay me."

Moy considers the spread on the counter, his cigarette burning down to its filter. "What if you push?"

"Same as the game, Mr. Moy: we'll play another hand. Come on. You know you want the money."

Moy's head disappears under the counter, cigarette smoke indicating his position. When he comes back up, he extinguishes the cigarette, shows another deck, says, "We play (with) my cards."

It feels like it takes twenty minutes for Moy to shuffle, to deal all seven hands out, four cards to the dungeon. The ritual, as usual, is painfully pointless; then again, Craig would have been satisfied playing a hand of Indian Poker. But he's got to get through to Moy, and the language he understands best just happens to be this damn game.

Finally, Moy rattles his dice cup; he'll tip them out to decide who goes first, and also to signal permission to turn up the cards. Anticipation works on Craig's nerves—not that he cares what the cards turn up; it's just that if he loses, he's going to have to resort to communicating with Moy in a way everyone understands: using his Walther .380.

"Moy," Suzanne says, out from the elevator, her plump bod testing the elasticity of a purple velour jogging outfit. "Don't you be playing cards with a criminal."

Moy's cup is poised over the counter. "What?"

"You remember that woman-cop who came in here the other night, asking about Mickey?"

"What?" From Craig now.

"Yeah: she told us you were wanted for robbery. That true? Is that what you do, Mickey? Steal from people?" She steps up next to Craig, a waft of smoke and sweat and powdered perfume following, and looks over the situation as its presented on the counter. "Be careful, Moy. This looks like some kind of trick."

Moy clutches the cup of dice to his chest. "A trick?"

"No—Mr. Moy—she doesn't know what she's talking about."

"Come on, Moy honey, how do you know he didn't steal all that cash?"

"I don't know why you're trying to jam me up, Sooz."

"Looks to me like you're already in a jam. What's a guy like you going to wager that kind of money for, anyhow? You don't seem like much of a risk-taker, if you know what I mean."

"Mr. Moy," Craig says, "this is none of her business. Tip the cup."

"This is very much my business, Mickey. I can't have gambling here—what if one of my other guests sees you?"

"I'm about to make your boyfriend a bunch of money. Can't you wait one minute?"

"Moy is not my boyfriend."

That's it, Craig thinks: enough. Time is short; his patience shorter. He bends over to get the .380 from his ankle holster and be done with this.

But then, while he's down there, he feels Suzanne brush her hand along the side of his ribs, a caress that neither tickles or entices, though there's no doubt it's supposed to. Moy can't see what she's doing from the other side of the counter: she's coming on to Craig.

"No," Suzanne says from up there, "Mickey isn't a risk-taker."

Truth is, Craig doesn't want to draw his weapon. It'll scare Moy; it'll blow any chance of a friendly trip to Chinatown. He leaves the .380 where it is, stands up, sucks it up.

"Listen, Sooz," he says, "I know what this is about: you're pissed because I never took a look at that problem you have with the elevator lights. You know what I mean? Since Mr. Moy can't reach?"

Suzanne's sweaty face shimmers with promise.

Moy says, "Sooz—"

"Just a minute, Moy," she says. "Someone has to take care of things around here." She winks at Craig.

He shrugs. "I guess the lady's in charge."

He follows Suzanne across the lobby. She presses the elevator call button and beams at Craig like they're headed to the penthouse suite. Craig would smile back if he could.

All he has to do is get Suzanne alone, promise her a few sweet nothings—emphasis on nothing—and get her out of the way. He'll tell her he's uncomfortable with Moy there. He'll say she deserves to be treated like a lady. He'll ask her out on a date. Whatever it takes.

The elevator door opens, the overhead fluorescents inside like intermittent flashbulbs. Craig steps into the car, says to Suzanne, "Come in and hold the run-stop, will you?"

Suzanne comes in while he reaches up to remove the plastic panel cover where the light shorts out. "You've got a bad ballast," he says, making relevant conversation until she hits the run-stop button, which will sound a ringing alarm they can talk underneath.

Instead, the door closes, because floor number six's button is the one she pressed.

She curls her fingers in his belt loops, pulls him close, looks down at his package while she asks, "Going up?"

Before he can tell her otherwise, she gets her hands around his neck and jumps up, straddling his legs. Her weight knocks him off balance and he staggers forward until she's pressed against the elevator door.

"Oh baby," she says to the position, her body rocked against his.

With so much of her weight hanging from his neck, gravity assists when she pulls his face to hers and she lays on a thick, sweaty kiss. Her lips are like warm, wet ashtrays; her tongue darts into his mouth like a lizard's.

The elevator dips when it pauses at each floor, the movement like a bad wave; the lights flicker, and the cables above them strain against the car's loose weight. But the laws of physics are no match for Suzanne's thighs, a meaty flesh-vise, and Craig is trapped.

"Sooz," he says, angling his chin at her lips. "Mr. Moy will kill us." He pushes off the doors and pivots so he's the one pinned, in the corner now.

"I don't care. I've got you." She comes at him again with that tongue and it's all he can do not to gag.

He reaches for the control panel, his fingers searching for the protruding red alarm button. When he moves, she puts a leg down for balance—it's all he needs to get a firm slap at the button.

The alarm sounds and the car stops: the disruption of movement forces Suzanne to both feet, giving Craig just the space he needs to push her away.

"Mickey," she whines over the alarm as he pries open the elevator door, preventing the car from moving further. The fourth floor sits two feet from the top: he can climb out; without his help, Suzanne probably can't.

He pulls himself up and out of the elevator and wipes his mouth. Then he drags the hallway's metal trash can into Suzanne's view.

"I like you, Sooz," he shouts over the alarm, "but you just left that Chinaman downstairs with a thousand dollars of my money. I didn't come here to get fucked twice. So either you agree to stay up here and wait until I'm through, or," he knocks on the side of the trash can, "I block the door and make you wait."

Suzanne extends her hand, says, "Shit, Mickey, I like it when you're bossy. Help me up: I'll make us a bed."

Back downstairs, Craig finds everything as he left it: the cards, the money, Moy and his cup of dice.

Craig wipes his mouth again, tells Moy, "I think Sooz is going to need a professional. Job's too much for me."

Moy blows smoke through his nose; this time, the ashes of his cigarette fall to the counter when he shakes his head. "Where (is) Sooz?"

"Are we talking about a woman or are we talking about a thousand dollars? I didn't come here to play repairman, Mr. Moy, and I could give a shit where Sooz ran off to. Tip the cup."

Moy puts out his cigarette and turns the dice out onto the counter. Craig flips his cards: he's got a pair of eights and a pair of queens, king high. He sets his cards and crosses his fingers: if he doesn't win, after all this, he's going to have to take another look at that Gambler's Anonymous pamphlet. Admittedly, he could have just cut to the chase with his .380.

Moy sets a pair of fours and an ace high.

Craig pockets the grand, says, "Mr. Moy, my friend, it looks like we're going to Chinatown."

"Can I help you?" Leslie hears Ivy ask.

She rounds a rack of control-top briefs and finds her daughter with a large-breasted older woman who's comparing about six Maidenform full-support D-cup bras.

"Which of these has underwire?" the woman asks. "I need better support."

"You might want to try a T-back," Ivy says, polite as Leslie's heard her in months—yet another side of the girl she's been missing.

Leslie approaches as Ivy searches the rack for the woman's size. "Ivy. I need to speak with you."

Ivy's eyes roll so far back in her head Leslie's sure she can see her own brain. "I'm helping a customer."

"I'm your mother. Help me for once." Leslie takes her by the elbow, steering her away.

"This is my job," she whines. "You're embarrassing me."

"That is my job." Leslie directs her down an aisle topped by nylon-covered mannequin legs and into the dressing room.

Ding-dong.

Inside, Leslie takes Ivy into an empty stall and slides the lock on the slatted door closed. "Take off your skirt."

Ivy's cheeks go red under the yellow lighting. "What?"

Leslie moves the cushioned stool from the corner to block the door and sits. "I want to see the tattoo."

Ivy cowers four ways, three in the angled mirrors.

"Is this how you behaved," Leslie asks, "when you went down to the Gold Rush tattoo shop and spread yourself out in front of a stranger? Did you act like a scared little girl while he put that Viceroy butterfly on your inner thigh?"

Ivy eyes the spaces between the stalls like she wants to crawl out, though those on either side of them are occupied: a woman's bare feet stand on tiptoes on one side; black-soled heels pivot, modeling, on the other.

Ding-dong. Someone else comes or goes.

Leslie says, "Show me the tattoo."

Ivy undoes her ribbon-trimmed belt, her cheeks full-red now. She untucks her thin blouse, the *Carson Pirie Scott* nametag getting caught in her hair when she leans over to pull down her black pencil skirt, and then her black nylons.

She turns her left leg out, showing stubs of pubic hair grown in around the elastic of her black thong, and the orange and black butterfly, a permanent mistake on her inner thigh.

Ding-dong.

Leslie asks, "Who's Viceroy?"

Ivy pulls her nylons back up, turning flip when she says, "My boyfriend."

"He convinced you to get this done?"

"I wanted to. I was going to tell you—"

"Bullshit."

337

"—but I knew you would overreact. I was right, wasn't I?"

"What's Viceroy's real name?"

"I don't know."

Leslie stands up, taller over her shrinking daughter. "He's your boyfriend, and you only know him by his gang moniker?"

Ding-dong.

"Did you have him over to the house when we weren't home?"

"What," Ivy says, "now I can't even have friends over?"

"Does Viceroy know your father is a police officer?"

"Who cares?"

"Does he have any of his own tattoos? A bird, or a bat—anything like that?"

"My boyfriend's skin is none of your business, Mother."

"You're seventeen: you don't get to determine my business."

In another stall, a plastic hanger hits the floor. *Ding-dong.*

Ivy straightens her skirt. "You *would* interfere the very first time I fall in love. You can't just be happy for me—you never have been."

"This has nothing to do with love."

"How do you know? You don't know the first thing about Viceroy. He's different. Cultured. He wants more out of life—more than some dead-end job, or this boring suburban existence. He's smart, he supports himself, and he wants to travel the world. And he says he'll take me with him."

"Viceroy is about to be implicated in drug-dealing, assault, rape, and possibly murder. The only place he's headed is jail—you planning on accompanying him there?"

Another customer's stall door swings open. *Ding-dong. Ding-dong.*

"Viceroy is a criminal," Leslie says. "This romance is over."

Ivy buckles her belt. Same with her mouth.

Leslie moves the stool away from the door. If she can't get straight answers, she's going to have to use Ivy's MySpace page like a polygraph. She turns back to the girl and very quietly says, "Tell your boss you have a family emergency and get your ass home."

Ding-dong.

When Leslie pulls up in the Tacoma, Ivy right behind her in the Civic, she spots a manila envelope stuck in the door: the messengered photo. Nothing could prepare her.

She hurries to the door and takes the envelope. It's just a picture, she knows; but her body calls up pain and adrenaline and fear, just the same as the night she was raped.

And an additional feeling creeps through her heart: shame. If this is the same winged tattoo, how will she tell Ivy the truth? How will she tell her daughter that the man she's in love with raped her?

Leslie can't bring herself to open the envelope until she hears Ivy on her way up the walk. There's no time left now.

In the photo, there are black wings, yes: but Leslie does not recognize them. They surround the same Asian anime cartoon figure Leslie saw on Viceroy's MySpace profile. Relief considers making an appearance: she'll call off Craig, and they'll find another, safer way to sort through this mess.

She pushes open the door as she digs through her bag for her cell phone, pausing as Ivy storms past, arms crossed, the world so cruel.

"Ivy, I'm not trying to be the bad guy."

"You don't have to try."

"Come back here and look at this." Leslie passes her the photo. "Is this Viceroy's tattoo?"

"God, what are you, the tattoo police now? Unreal."

Leslie takes that as a yes, and dials Craig.

Ivy says, "Let me guess: now you think he worships the devil or something."

"I don't care what he worships. I'm calling your father." The line rings once.

"It's not satanic or anything," Ivy says. "It signifies his mixed race."

"I'm sure your dad will be impressed." Second ring.

"He drew the character himself. It's anime: it's a *gweilo*. That's what the Chinese people call Chinese Americans."

Third ring.

"Translated," Ivy says, "it means white devil."

Leslie takes back the photo of the tattoo: the little white gremlin boy surrounded by big black wings.

A half-breed devil. Craig's snitch. No.

Craig's phone keeps ringing.

"Ivy: is Viceroy's real name Juan?"

"God, Mom. He's not Mexican. It's pronounced Yoo-an."

Leslie hangs up. Craig's in trouble: he doesn't need a phone call. He needs backup.

She runs into the dining room, gets Ron Suwanski's cell number from the phone tree.

"Hello."

"Ron, this is Leslie McHugh. Craig needs you right away—he's on his way to Chinatown and he's after someone he thinks is named Viceroy. But he's got the wrong man, and he's going to wind up blowing his cover and his informant's, too—Yoo-an or Juan? Craig's going down there and he doesn't know he's got the wrong guy—"

"Slow down, Leslie: the case is closed. Juan took off. Why is Craig after this guy Viceroy?"

"Because I thought he raped me."

"My God, Leslie—"

"Ron, Craig doesn't answer his cell. Please, call the Thirteenth district and find someone named Kingman—he's a murder detective. He

was working with Craig to find Viceroy. I don't know how else to find
him—"

"Did he drive the Caprice?"

"Yes."

"I can track it. I'm on my way—"

"Thank you, Ron."

"Don't thank me yet."

Ron hangs up, and Leslie redials Craig. Why did they rush this?
How could they have assumed they had the right man? Why isn't
Craig answering?

"Mom?" When Ivy's voice cuts through the chatter in Leslie's
head, she realizes her daughter is there, in the room.

Ivy's expression is at once hard and fragile; she is a child who is just
beginning to understand.

Leslie isn't sure how much of the phone conversation Ivy heard
and she doesn't have to ask when the girl comes to her, and crumbles
in her arms.

Craig's phone rings, and rings.

37

"You're kidding me," Craig says to Moy. "Right here on Cermak? Right across from the fire station?"

"No," Moy says, but he proceeds to shuffle toward the last business on the block: its metal-lettered sign reads *Overseas Art and Travel*.

"So what," Craig says, "we're taking a trip?"

The building is a two-story; the first floor has a red-and-white-tiled face, the second is brown-bricked with wide-open, empty windows.

Moy comes to two entrances: on the left, a glass door opens to the business, and on the right, a red door with a tiny, blacked-out window sits like an invitation to an underworld.

"Oh, I get it," Craig says, but he doesn't, because Moy chooses the glass door instead of the red one and goes into the travel agency.

The office is bright and busy: a half-dozen young Chinese women work their phones like stockbrokers in a trading room. Their desks are displays for brochures to sunny, exotic getaways; one wall exhibits maps of different parts of the world, destinations marked by red flashing lights; on another, clocks tell the time in London, Tokyo, and Hong Kong. A digital register keeps track of changing currency rates Everything ticks and shifts and blinks, on the move.

A young woman in a cobalt-blue suit waves the men over to her desk, invites them to sit. She speaks to Moy in long, unfriendly vowels, though the pleasant look on her face suggests she's offering him an all-expense-paid trip to Kathmandu.

She tilts her head back and forth like some kind of robot while she listens to Moy, and a smile jerks to her lips every time she looks at Craig. Every time she smiles, Craig nods, feeling like it's his function in this machine.

Across the room, Craig notices another young woman wearing a similar blue suit, this one like a stewardess from the 1960's, her head topped with a pillbox hat. She's come through the single doorway at the back of the office and she sits at the only open desk: ruler-straight spine, narrow shoulders, equally narrow glances. Craig wonders if she's the one in charge; seems like her only job is to watch everyone else. He wonders if he looks suspicious to her, or if he looks like any other white man, affecting confidence in an unfamiliar situation. He wonders if she thinks he's nervous because he was told not to bring his phone. Or if she thinks that he worries about being forced to leave his wallet, the thousand dollars, and his identification in the car.

Craig feels the handle of his .380 against his leg, beneath his faded Levi's. The metal points of his star are warm against his bare chest—on a lanyard underneath his plain old white tee, his oxford shirt, his down vest. He half-smiles at the woman. He can be nervous. He can be any other white man.

Moy says something to the robot-woman that results in agreeably toned communication between them. The woman takes a blank slip from a drawer, marks it with precise Chinese characters, folds it in two and tucks it into a ticket envelope. She bows to Moy as she hands it to him.

"We go, Mickey," Moy says, gets up; Craig follows him past the watchful woman with the pillbox hat and out the back door.

"What the hell was that about?" Craig asks, once outside. "Did you just book us a flight to Cleveland?"

"Appointment," Moy says, shuffling on toward the backs of the buildings whose storefronts face Wentworth. The night sky weighs heavy here, between the el tracks and the busy lights over Chinatown's main drag. It's like walking into a void. Craig can't find the moon.

"Where are we going?"

"Chinatown always changing," Moy says, holding up the ticket envelope like an answer.

Over the bushes that weave in and out of the chain-link fence on the left, Craig hears cars come and go on the Stevenson Expressway ramps. He looks back, following the fence from where they came, and realizes the alley is completely closed off: Chinatown's back doors provide the only access.

Fifty yards down, the darkness is pierced by light from a back door that's propped open by a concrete bucket. When they pass it, Craig sees the inner workings of a kitchen much like Moy's: two Chinese men tending to their cigarettes and their woks simultaneously, their attention and bets placed on the TV's horse races.

"You say it's changing, Mr. Moy, but nothing much seems different to me."

"You stay (in) one place, you get stuck."

"You're a regular fortune cookie."

Another fifty yards later, Moy cuts in toward the back of a dark building with no visible signage or sign of activity. He raps on the steel door and waits.

Craig wishes he were wearing his shoulder holster instead of carrying his gun way down there, on his ankle; standing here in the dark without the weapon in his hand is almost worse than standing here without having a weapon at all.

After a minute or so, a compact Chinese man dressed in a black jumpsuit answers. Craig can just barely make out the man's slim face in the dim light inside. Moy hands the man the ticket envelope; he tucks it into his black belt and ushers them inside.

As they follow him through the back room stocked with boxes of who knows what, all Craig can see of the man in black are his bare white feet. He hopes the guy won't make him remove his boots; he'd surely discover the gun holstered there.

When Craig's eyes adjust to the well-lit store, he is immediately unnerved: swords, nunchucks, throwing stars, staffs, fighting fans: if it kills, it's on display in this shop.

Shit, Craig thinks: he's got seven rounds loaded at his ankle and he thinks he's going to negotiate with Bruce Lee and company?

The guy in the jumpsuit ducks underneath a divider and comes up on the other side of the service counter. He opens the envelope and reads its message; then he takes a deep breath, and does nothing.

The shop is completely silent, everything held there like the guy's breath, so Craig does what he figures any white-knuckled white guy would do, and that's to comment on the arsenal around him. "The Art of War," he says, "no kidding."

Neither of the other men says a word, so Craig takes a dragon-handled sword from its stand and acts like he's examining the gold inlay. It makes him feel better, to hold something lethal in his hands. Like he has some control here.

After much too long, the guy in the jumpsuit says something to Moy that sounds too calm to be promising.

Moy responds, a firm: "*Bu dui!*" thus beginning a temperamental verbal battle, each man arguing his case.

Juan once explained to Craig that the Chinese have no direct words for yes or no; Craig figures this must be the reason for the haggling. How can a guy argue when he can't say no?

Eventually, the guy in the jumpsuit opens his cash register, and Craig figures they're getting somewhere—until the guy takes out a lighter and sets the slip from Overseas Art and Travel on fire.

Moy says something that sounds like an objection, but then the guy marks up another slip of paper and puts it into the ticket envelope, and just like that, Moy takes it and makes for the front door.

Craig returns the sword to its stand and follows Moy.

Outside, he asks again, "What the hell was that about?"

Moy looks both ways on Wentworth Avenue, and then up at Craig, and says, "That guy (is) always an asshole."

At a break in traffic, Moy and Craig jaywalk across the street. The main drag of Chinatown is abuzz, all lit up like the set of a Broadway musical. Moy approaches a storefront window painted with red Chinese characters and block letters that read SUN SUN SEAFOOD. In the window, a neon-red tube light runs around a murky fish tank, tinting the whitish-colored fish that float in the water into sickly pink ghosts.

Craig follows Moy inside, past the fish tank and a wall of uncooked rice stacked like bags of potting soil. When they round the corner, the pungent odor of all things fish immediately reminds Craig of his father. They never talked much, but they sure did fish.

On their way through the store, bins of clams and mussels and crab legs on ice set a chill in the air, and Craig gets the feeling this is finally the place.

At the back counter, behind a rack of dishes, a Chinese man about

Craig's age is snapping photographs of a lobster he has trapped on a sushi boat, its tail curled toward the bow, its claws clipping at the air, angry and ineffective. To the man taking the photos, this seems like a wildly entertaining adventure.

Seeing Moy and Craig, he grins and raises the camera for an action shot of the approaching men, asking, "Okay?" though he takes the picture before either of them can answer.

Craig blinks away the flash as Moy hands the ticket envelope to the man, who considers the contents. Then he hands it back to Moy, a pleasant smile, and refocuses his camera.

He takes a final picture of the pissed-off lobster, checks the shot on the camera's digital display, and then, "Okay?" He's apparently satisfied.

He moves the sushi boat to make way for a cutting board and removes the lobster from the boat, holding it by its tail and moving with it to avoid getting pinched, another entertaining exploit.

Until he retrieves a large Santoku knife. The lobster goes to the board, the tip of the knife goes between the lobster's eyes, and with one swift plunge, the lobster goes to his afterworld.

The man grins, "Okay?" and invites them to come around back as the lobster's little legs spasm and a claw twitches, good-bye.

The man takes off his apron; underneath, he wears a Navy Pier sweatshirt. With the camera around his neck, his white tennis shoes, and that inquiring grin across his face, he's a fanny pack short of passing as a tourist.

The back room is empty, save for a card table and chairs, to which the man says, "Okay?" and signals them to sit.

They do, but Craig quickly realizes it's not okay, because back here, it smells less like fish and more like burnt human hair.

Mr. "Okay" opens a door adjacent to the back exit, permitting the escape of a man's shrieking, terrified screams. Mr. Okay bows at them, then disappears, muting the screaming when he closes the door.

A lump rises in Craig's throat. What the hell's going on down there? He looks at Moy: as usual, his face conveys nothing more than general disappointment.

Craig resists the urge to get his gun and stow it in the back of his waistband. He prays these men understand honor, because even if he had the gun in his hand, it wouldn't give him the same power to negotiate.

The next time the door by the exit opens, another man appears. This one looks like some kind of professor, wearing a V-neck sweater over a pale yellow collar and plaid pants. He greets the men with a single bow and strolls to a position by the exit, though the look on his face is one of such poised concentration it seems as though he's about to make a very strategic move.

"I understand you're looking for Silk," he says, his English smooth, ordinary.

"It's not that simple," Craig says.

"It never is."

"Do you run Chinatown?"

The professor brushes lint from his sweater. "I'm as close as you're going to get."

The door near the exit opens again, and this time Mr. Okay comes out with a narrow-headed Asian man who is dressed in all black, a round gold medallion at his neck. He moves easily and doesn't appear to be in any sort of pain; he finishes his cigarette quickly and stamps it out underfoot.

"Mr. Moy," the professor says, "I trust you'll wait up here with Ngoc Minh while we speak with your friend in the basement."

Ngoc Minh doesn't wait for Moy's answer: he takes a seat and finds a pack of Viceroys in his shirt pocket.

God damn it, Craig thinks, having put himself here to find a man who goes by a name as common as a cheap cigarette.

Ngoc Minh sits close enough for Craig to smell the smoke he's carried with him, but it isn't from his latest cigarette. It is much worse. And when Craig makes out the raised gold hawk on his medallion, he realizes why Ngoc Minh isn't in pain: he is a Night Hawk. He is most likely the one who has been inflicting it.

"Join us, at our table?" the professor says to Craig.

"Okay?" is his partner's duplicate request, from the basement doorway.

"We can lay all this out on whatever table you like," Craig says. "You're not going to scare me."

"We don't mean to scare you," the professor says. "We are simply interested in privacy."

When Craig gets up, the professor's face suggests a smile, like he just moved a chess piece into checkmate.

Craig leads the way, his empty gun-hand twitching like the lobster's as he descends the stairway into a dark cloud of smoke.

"We would turn on the lights," the professor says, from behind him, "but our friend Bei Du Nu seems to prefer a nice fire."

Craig reaches the bottom of the steps, none too happy about being grouped into the "friend" category, because the man called Bei Du Nu doesn't look like it's helping him any. He sits next to a burnt-out fire pit built from concrete blocks; only thing that looks like it's been on fire, though, is Bei Du Nu's head. Almost all his hair is gone, his skin scorched. The man is passed out now, restrained by a single band of rope; he must have been in too much pain to fight. He must have been screaming when the fire crawled up his arm, melted his skin, caught his hair.

"What the hell did he ever do to you?" Craig asks.

"Perhaps you've heard of Yu Bo Tuo?"

"The guy who burnt up outside the firehouse on Cermak?"

"Yes."

"He's the one who did it?" Craig asks, of Bei Du Nu.

"No," the professor says, kicking aside a piece of kindling. "I just like that story. Come on."

The smoke gets thick as they move deeper into the room; it burns at Craig's lungs and he tells them, "This is dangerous. There are no windows down here—hardly any ventilation—we all could die from smoke inhalation."

The professor takes the lead toward the far end of the basement. "We come from Hong Kong," he says. "I can assure you we'll be fine."

Craig isn't claustrophobic and he isn't stupid, either. He knows these men brought him down here to show him Bei Du Nu—to illustrate what bad business looks like. They don't have to tell him his .380 will get him nothing but a seat next to his so-called friend.

Mr. Okay pulls the chain on a light over a big round table where a deck of cards sits at six o'clock. He selects a seat for Craig at twelve, "Okay?"

As the professor stands before the cards, Craig waits for him to sit; he waits for Craig, and Craig continues to wait.

Now, the professor's smile is more competitive. He must like this game, since Craig has to let him win.

Craig sits.

Mr. Okay hangs back, on the edge of the light, between them and Bei Du Nu.

"You are looking for Silk," the professor says again.

"That's what I told Mr. Moy."

"I agreed to meet with you because Mr. Moy is a loyal member of the Kuang Tian. Despite his old-fashioned opinions, he has done well for us. He is an honorable man."

"That's why he brought me here. He lost a bet: it was the only honorable thing he could do."

"It is not Mr. Moy whose motive I find problematic. You can't possibly think we will entertain your interests. Silk is, to his bones, one of us."

"And when he attacked me, he was protecting you."

"I am sure you would have done the same for your family."

"You're right. That's why I'm here."

The professor takes the deck of cards in his left hand and does a Charlier cut, turning half the deck around with his thumb. "You must be holding some very high cards, Mickey."

Craig takes off his down vest, unbuttons his oxford, says, "I will show you my hand, because I think you and I have the same problem." He steadies his hand as he pulls his star from under his T-shirt. He sits up straight when he hangs it on his chest.

When Mr. Okay sees the star, he produces a Russian Stechkin APS automatic from under his Navy Pier sweatshirt and he's at Craig's side, the gun to his head. "Okay?"

The professor says nothing; cuts the deck again. It's still Craig's move.

He says, "I'm a police officer. I shouldn't have to tell you what will happen if Mr. 'Okay' uses his firearm. I've got enough on Silk to bring the feds in for one of these sit-downs, and his file is sitting in my office, waiting to be found if I'm not."

"We do not deal in threat."

"That's not a threat: it's a reason to listen."

The professor hooks a finger toward Mr. Okay, and he backs off.

Craig says, "Our shared problem is this: Silk is being set up. We both know he didn't kill Desmond Cline."

The professor cuts the deck. "He will do his time, if he has to."

"Solves half the problem. The other half is the guy who set him up in the first place."

"Why is this of your concern?"

351

"I was put on the Fuxi case to find out who was in charge of the China White. I went into Mr. Moy's undercover, I tried to make friends." Craig lifts up his T-shirt and shows his spider bites. "I got these instead."

From beside him, Craig can see the teeth between Mr. Okay's grin.

"Case closed," Craig says. "As far as I'm concerned? I did my job. And Silk did his. No honor lost. But this other guy—the one who's framing Silk? Who the fuck hired him?"

The professor cuts the cards one more time, and then begins flipping the top card around over the rest, just like he must be turning this whole thing around in his head.

"You don't care if Silk goes down, he'll go down," Craig says. "The guys in the Thirteenth are about to nail the D-Cline case to his name six ways. But then, where's the honor in letting someone else get away with murder?"

"We do not know who killed Mr. Cline. How do you propose we resolve the situation?"

"Make *me* a trade."

The professor fans the deck of cards from one hand to the other, his face like the game's been a scratch. "We do not make deals with the police."

Craig unfastens his star's lanyard. "I believe the man who set up Silk for D-Cline's murder is the same one who claimed he was Silk the night he raped my wife. I don't want to arrest him, I want to kill the motherfucker." He tosses his star on the table. "Honor that."

The cards fall away from the professor's hands as he looks at Craig's star, his honor, lying there. He takes a moment, straightening the deck on the table, putting his thoughts in order.

Finally he says, "You know who this man is."

"He goes by Viceroy."

Forget the chess face: the professor's smile grows as broad as a Cheshire cat's. "Viceroy," he says, like it's a joke.

Mr. Okay laughs.

The professor stands up. "Please, make yourself comfortable. We will be back momentarily."

Mr. Okay holsters his Stechkin APS. "Okay?"

Craig waits: long enough for Bei Du Nu to regain consciousness, and to cry out in fear, and then in anger; his words are unknown, but the excruciating desperation in his voice is clear.

Craig waits: long enough for Bei Du Nu to wonder if the men have left him there to die, and to beg for help in repetitive, stressed tones. Sometimes it sounds like prayer.

Still longer, Craig waits; the man weeps.

Craig does not say anything: even if he spoke Bei Du Nu's language, he knows he could offer no comfort, and no reprieve. The men will be back. Their business is unfinished.

When Bei Du Nu grows agitated again, Craig knows the men are returning. He stands up, his head fuzzy from the stagnant smoke-filled air, and the echoes of Bei Du Nu's screams. He is sweating, not only at his hairline: he feels it run down between his shoulder blades, and from behind his knees to his ankle holster.

Craig can't see the men from where he is behind the light, and as he moves forward, Bei Du Nu's screams are cut short by what sounds like kindling splitting over his blistered head.

Then a match is lit and tossed into the fire pit, and by the expanding light Craig sees the professor, and Mr. Okay, and Mr. Okay's gun held to Juan's head.

"Here is your man," the professor says. "Viceroy."

Juan is so paralyzed by the sight of Bei Du Nu that he doesn't seem to register Craig's presence.

"What is this," Craig says, "some kind of trick?"

"This is Viceroy."

"No: this is Yoo-an. I know him from Moy's table. He's not a player in your world—he's just a pawn. I'm telling you, this isn't Viceroy."

"Perhaps we should ask him," the professor says.

Mr. Okay takes Juan by the hair and puts him on his knees.

"Viceroy," the professor says to Juan. "That's what you like to be called, isn't it?"

Juan closes his eyes and slowly nods.

"Maybe you're the one pulling some kind of trick," the professor says. "You made quite a case for Viceroy, and now we bring him to you and you change your mind."

"This is no trick—it's a mistake. This can't be the man who raped my wife. If I went by a name, I could just as easily blame Silk. This isn't him."

"I suppose you are correct," the professor says. "Perhaps we should ask him. Viceroy, did you rape this man's wife?"

"No."

Mr. Okay turns his gun around and uses it to crack Juan in the head.

"Viceroy," the professor says again, "did you rape this man's wife?"

Juan shakes his head; Mr. Okay raises his gun—

"Stop," Craig says—"You know he'll say whatever you want him to say. There's another way to prove it. The man who raped my wife has a tattoo."

Juan objects—his head shaking no: don't—but Craig says—

"If this is the man who raped my wife, he has a tattoo of a bird or a bat on his torso. My wife remembers a winged tattoo—that's how she identified him, by his tattoo."

"I suppose you are right," the professor says. "A policeman needs his evidence."

Mr. Okay grabs Juan by the hair while the professor rips his buttoned shirt off. There is no tattoo on Juan's stomach.

"See? It's not him."

But then, Mr. Okay pulls Juan up by his hair and puts the business end of the gun against his head.

The professor says, "Viceroy: your pants, please."

Juan looks at Craig, dead-eyed, as he undoes his pants.

Mr. Okay takes a look, says, "Okay," but this time, with no question. He knocks Juan to the concrete floor in front of the fire and steps on his neck and there, on Juan's pubic bone, Craig sees a tattoo of a cartoon devil with black wings.

"Wings," the professor says.

"No," Craig says.

"Oh yes," the professor says, and hooks his finger toward Mr. Okay, who disappears into the darkness and returns with a second chair, just like Bei Du Nu's.

On the floor, Juan grabs at his neck, gasping for air.

"If you do not believe it," the professor says, "we will make him confess on his own."

Mr. Okay drags Juan to the chair and ties a simple rope around his waist. Juan does not resist and Craig realizes the restraint must be symbolic, as men like this are supposed to have too much honor to fight.

Craig stands by. What the fuck is he supposed to do? He can't tell them Juan is his snitch: it'll get them both killed. He can't pay his way out of this. He can't play his way out of this. He can't talk his way out of this—

"Being burned," the professor says, "is the most painful torture a human can experience. If it is done correctly."

"I'm not here to torture him," Craig says. "There is no honor in that chair. Let me handle this myself." He bends down and retrieves his gun from its holster. It's the only chance he's got.

At the sight of Craig's .380, Mr. Okay takes aim at him with his Stechkin APS.

The professor hooks his finger again, says, "Leave the officer to his law."

Craig steps around in front of Juan and looks down at him. "What is your name?"

"Tse Jin Yuan."

"Do you call yourself Viceroy?"

"Yes."

Craig pulls back the .380's hammer. This is it: if the professor carries a weapon also, this is it.

Craig asks Juan: "Did you rape my wife?"

Juan looks up at him, the truth: "No."

Craig turns his gun on Mr. Okay and he looks nothing like a tourist now: just a man with an automatic weapon who is waiting for the "okay."

"Well," the professor says, "this is another confounding turn: a policeman who is standing in his own line of fire."

"Juan says he didn't do it. I want to let him go."

The professor says nothing.

"Okay?"

Nothing.

"Okay?"

A nod. "Okay."

Mr. Okay turns his weapon on Juan and fires.

At the gunshot, Craig drops to the floor, rolls to his left and shoots—once, twice, aiming anywhere, getting the hell away from there—

Mr. Okay fires back, he must, because Craig hears another gunshot and another and another—and then there's shouting; people are shouting, but Craig just keeps firing.

Craig pulls the .380's trigger until Ron Suwanski pries the gun from his hands.

38

The call comes in shortly after ten. Leslie has been waiting by the phone, Ivy at her side, for nearly four hours: the girl too afraid to ask questions, and all Leslie's answers hanging on this one phone call.

Leslie never felt so helpless there, the phone in hand, the display reading *Suwanski, Ronald,* her life literally waiting on the line.

"Ron," she says, a hopeful hello.

"Leslie," Ron Suwanski says, not so hopeful.

"Where's Craig?"

"Getting stitched up at Presbyterian St. Luke's. He'd have called you himself, but one of the detectives from the Ninth accompanied him to the hospital, and I get the feeling she'd admit a sneeze into evidence if she could. Can you come rescue him? I've got to stick around for damage control."

"I'm on my way."

"He's at the Bowman Center on Paulina. We've got a suspect on his way to surgery, three others who need lockers at the main hospital, and we're trying to keep Craig off Channel Two's radar."

"Is he okay?"

"He's pretty messed up, Leslie. His informant was killed."

If Ivy's face is a mirror, Leslie's tells the heart-breaking truth. She takes her daughter's hand, a reassurance, and says to Ron, "Thank God you found him."

"Thank Kingman Cade. You were right: I called him on my way. That man knows Chinatown like he drew the map. When we found the Caprice, only thing our guys could do was blanket the neighborhood, but Kingman—he knew who to corner to get a lead on Craig. He found somebody who saw Craig on Wentworth with Mr. Moy, and then he found Moy. We were questioning him at Sun Sun Seafood when we heard a gunshot in the basement."

"Was Craig—was he hurt?"

"Bullet caught his arm. Nothing serious, given the could-have-been's. I'll tell you, the Ninth has one hell of a cleanup ahead of them—between my guys and the Thirteenth, we had at least thirty uniforms responding. The Ninth came after the fact, caused a complete clusterfuck. They're going to need a team just to take statements."

"What's going to happen to Craig?"

"He's being released on his own recognizance. Like I said, they've got a lot to sort through. I have to tell you, though, I was at the scene, and if they don't call what Craig did down there self-defense, they can have my star, too."

"Thank you, Ron. You saved his life."

"No, Leslie: you did."

Ivy waits in the car when Leslie leaves it in a no-parking zone and runs into Pres St. Luke's.

"Craig McHugh?" she asks the nurse with a fresh night-shift face at the front desk.

"Are you his wife?"

Leslie nods.

"He's been waiting. One moment." She picks up the telephone and dials an extension, says, "Mr. McHugh's wife is in the lobby."

An old woman in a bathrobe exits the lobby elevator and approaches the desk. Leslie steps back to move out of her way; though there is clearly enough space for both of them, the woman chooses to stand immediately beside her.

"They will be here," she tells the nurse.

"Tomorrow, Margaret, remember?"

Margaret looks over at Leslie—a suspicious once-over that reminds her of Mona—and asks, "Tomorrow?"

Leslie says, "That's what I hear," and wonders why her tone is so much more tolerant with a stranger than with her own mother-in-law.

Margaret nods. "Tomorrow. Then everything will be fine." She turns and pads back to the elevator.

The nurse shakes her head, says, "Tomorrow never seems to come in this place." She points a Bic pen toward the lobby's tan and turquoise foam-cushioned couch. "You can wait right there."

Leslie nods, though she doesn't feel like sitting. She goes over to the elevator and stands outside, watching the floor number rise from one, to two, to three, and stop on four.

The directory placard on the wall lists fourth floor geriatric specialists' offices, an Alzheimer's Disease Center, and a physical rehabilitation clinic. So many things to look forward to, Leslie thinks, though she isn't being snide: she has no idea how she'd live another day without Craig.

She finds a loose corner of the tape that secures the dirtied bandage to her hand and removes it completely, discarding the bandage in the trash can next to the elevator. Wounds, she decides, are impossible to hide from the ones you love.

The elevator decends to three and stops. Outside, the Civic idles; her daughter sits in the passenger seat doing the same.

The elevator moves down to two, then one, and as the door opens, Margaret's telling Craig, "They will be here."

Before he has a chance to move, Leslie is in the elevator with him, her arms around him; she turns a cheek against his chest, toward the sling around his right arm, and he embraces her, his chin resting on top of her head.

"They will be here," Margaret says again.

"Tomorrow," Leslie says, closing her eyes, hugging her husband.

Margaret says, "Then everything will be fine."

Ivy loses it about ten minutes into the ride home. Before they left the Bowman Center, Leslie and Craig agreed to discuss what happened once they were alone, because no matter how grown up Ivy thinks she is, Craig thought it'd be too much. So, once in the car, Craig claimed he needed to rest. They made this much of the trip in silence.

But then Ivy asks, "Daddy, are you okay?"

Leslie merges onto 90/94 and checks the rearview mirror: Ivy's in tears. Leslie can't remember the last time she called him Daddy.

"I'm fine," Craig says. "Bullet grazed my arm is all. To tell you the truth, I think you got more stitches that time you fell down the basement steps—you remember that?"

"I do," Leslie says, following Craig's lead. "Twenty-six stitches across her beautiful forehead—the day before second-grade class pictures."

"I think you were more upset than she was, Les."

"I was afraid she had a concussion."

"You were afraid DCFS would want to use her as a poster child."

"She was beautiful anyway. That's still my favorite school photo." When Leslie checks the rearview mirror again and sees Ivy's fat tears show no sign of letting up, she knows that forcing idle conversation, however thoughtful, won't make it past the Loop.

"I'm sorry, Daddy," Ivy says. "This is my fault."

Leslie glances over at Craig. His face has turned hard, a reluctant interrogator's, and Leslie realizes the reason he didn't want to discuss what happened in front of Ivy is because it would be too much for *him*.

"How is this your fault?" Craig asks, his heart pulling his inflection away from angry.

"I wanted Viceroy to like me."

"Is that why you got the tattoo?" Leslie asks.

"I thought it was cool."

"You didn't know," Craig says, "that in his culture, tattoos on young women are meant to be demeaning? To show they've lost," he starts, "that they've lost," he starts again—

—but Leslie knows what he's trying to say so she cuts him off–

"Ivy's already lost plenty. If it wasn't for that tattoo, we never would have found *you*."

Craig pinches his lips, looks down at his hands. He must know she's right.

Leslie cracks her window, to let in a little air and a little distraction she thinks they'll all welcome, but Ivy says—

"Viceroy said he was falling in love with me. He never asked me to do anything. It was my idea to introduce him to Rios. Viceroy knew someone who makes ecstasy, and Rios knew how to get ketamine. They were going to cut it together and sell it to some people in Chinatown."

"Why would you want to get mixed up in something like that?" Craig asks.

"I don't know," she says, the words pushed out in sobs.

"You knew what you were doing was illegal."

"I didn't know." Ivy says, her only defense.

"Viceroy was my informant," Craig tells her. "He was using you. Just like I was using him." Craig turns away from Leslie, gazes out his window at the skyline that shoots up around them, the city's big shoulders carrying less weight than his.

Leslie rolls up her window. "It's my fault," she says, wanting it to be completely true. "I covered for Ivy when I knew she was lying. And it was because of a crush."

"Niko," Craig says.

"What?" Ivy asks, her teenaged brain unable to make the connection. "I don't have a crush on Niko."

"He was a person of interest," Craig says, covering for Leslie now.

"Niko didn't have anything to do with this," Ivy says.

Leslie thinks of that god damned Madame Del Bard rose. She is no flower and she won't let it kill her, inside-out. She has to tell them.

"The night I was raped," she says, "I went to the Green Mill to see Niko play. Rios and the man I thought was Viceroy were there. They followed me home."

"You went to see Niko?" Ivy says, getting a clue.

"Rios knows who raped you?" Craig says, getting a suspect.

"Rios went back to Greece," Leslie says. "Niko made sure of it."

"Niko?" Ivy asks, her tears stopped up in disbelief. "Does he know?"

"I don't know, Ivy. But I do know family secrets run deep."

"They have to," Craig says.

Leslie doesn't know what else to say. She hits the gas, speeding home now, wishing they were leaving all this behind, in Chinatown.

"This is my fault," Craig says. "I let this family fall apart."

No one says anything after that. They are all to blame.

.   .   .

Over the years, being a cop's wife has conditioned Leslie: to anticipate, to accommodate, and to acquiesce—in short, to be prepared for the worst and still manage to get a good night's sleep. Tonight is different. The worst is supposed to have come and gone, and she can't sleep at all.

Shortly after they shut out the lights, both she and Craig too tired to say more than good night, she hasn't been able to give in to her exhaustion. She'd nestled in: her head on his chest, his good arm around her, her one leg draped over his two. She lay there, listening as his breathing became even and heavy, moving in fast on sleep. And as she lay there, her own breathing became irregular, her thoughts too aware. How can she play house with an unmarked car out front?

She gets out of bed and sits in the chair at her vanity, but in the darkness, panic fills in the quiet spaces between Craig's slow breathing. She does not feel safe. She does not know what safe feels like.

Downstairs, she checks the locks on all the doors and sits on the couch in the front room, Craig's blanket around her shoulders. Out the window, the middle of the night waits for morning. Around the corner, the cop in the unmarked car is probably bored as all hell. He's keeping up with the real action on his police radio, or ping-ponging jokes with the other beat cops on their MDTs. He's probably a rookie. He doesn't know why he's here and he doesn't care: he's on shit detail. He'll complain about it tomorrow.

Because he doesn't yet know the Job. What it will do to him.

And in the meantime, his girlfriend or his young wife or whoever shares his future is learning to live this way: to be alone in the middle of the night. It will be the one thing she never gets used to.

The phone rings: an alarm. Leslie dashes for the phone: the call display reads *Private*.

If Craig were at work, the call would mean bad news. Since he's upstairs, sleeping, it still means bad news; it also means he'll have to go out and deal with it.

Leslie answers on the second ring but says nothing, because she hears Craig on the line in their bedroom; the static as he fumbles with the cordless.

"Yeah," he says.

"Craig McHugh," a low voice says, drawn-out vowels.

"Yeah," he says again.

"I am the one looking for you now."

"Silk?"

"Come to Mr. Moy's. Alone."

"No way. You want to talk, we meet on my turf."

"You would like me to come to your home? I don't think that is such a good idea: there is an officer sleeping in a car outside. He could wake up."

Craig is silent.

"Moy's," Silk says. "Now."

Leslie is stationed by the front door, lights off, when Craig comes downstairs. He's nearly fully dressed, including a backward baseball cap, though his sling hangs loose around his neck and his tennis shoes are untied. The butt of his old .44 Magnum sticks out of his Levi's.

"Help me," he says.

"I can't let you go," Leslie says.

Craig comes to her, his face gray by the streetlight in through the window. "I'm going, Leslie. You want me to walk in there with my fly open?"

"Going out there won't fix what happened," she says.

"They've got my number, Leslie. Our number."

Craig secures the .44 as he bends over, tries to tie his shoes with his left hand.

"You can't go like this," she says. "You need help."

Craig stands up. "You're right. I do need help. I need you to tie my shoes, and to zip my pants. And I need you to be my alibi." He takes her hand with his good one. "I know I can't fix this, but I have to finish it."

Leslie double-knots his shoelaces.

Craig sneaks out the back, the sling doubling as a carrying case for the .44. He catches a cab after he's well into the Indo-Pak neighborhood on Devon; he keeps conversation with the Indian driver generic: the weather, the Cubs. He keeps his baseball cap low over his eyes until they reach a nowhere corner ten blocks from Moy's. He pays his fare and an extra buck, and disappears.

The cabbie said the weather is supposed to be very warm come morning, but right now, Craig thinks it's much colder than it has been in a while. He wonders if it's just him, minus the blood he lost tonight.

Since Silk called, he figures he lost more than that. Down at Sun Sun Seafood, Moy must have slipped through the cracks; he probably got away with his confused-Chinaman act, skipped the scene. And Kingman couldn't keep Silk in jail, not on a murder he didn't commit.

So they're out and about, and they want more.

They're going to get it.

He crosses over to Moy's on Winnemac, a residential, tree-lined street. At Broadway, he waits for a near-empty CTA bus to pass, the only traffic: this is the city's dead of night.

He keeps a casual pace on Argyle until he ducks into the alley past Moy's. There he crouches behind a Dumpster, puts the .44 between his knees, and slings his arm. The revolver is too heavy to hold with his right hand so he has to depend on his left; the advantage to carrying this big gun, though, is that he doesn't have to aim so much as he just has to fire.

The lot behind Moy's is quiet, dark. Craig sticks to the perimeter, aims around the single old Buick Regal that's parked there, makes his way closer to Moy's back door.

When he gets the door in direct sight, he sees it hanging open on its hinges, the light in the Pai Gow den burning. He knows Silk won't be waiting inside, though: a spider doesn't wait for his prey in the center of his web.

"I know you're out here," Craig says, making no effort to hide himself now, or his gun. "You watched me come down the street." He takes six long steps into the middle of the lot, says, "If you're going to strike, do it: you already know my defense."

From the upstairs porch where the old Spanish woman's laundry still hangs to dry, Craig sees the cherry of a cigarette drop to the ground and smolder on the pavement. The .44 won't do much but make noise at this range, and he can't see anybody up there, but he aims the gun anyway.

The wooden steps at the inside corner of the building creak underfoot, but Craig doesn't get a visual on Silk until he's standing out on the pavement in front of Moy's porch, lighting another cigarette.

Silk takes a drag, says, "You are going to be the one to strike," and heads into Moy's, disappearing into the Pai Gow den.

Craig follows, his .44 leading; he maintains distance and aims around the doorways, but inside, Silk is alone. He's seated, apparently unarmed, since there's a gun sitting on the table.

He says, "I have been sent here to speak to you on behalf of Chinatown."

"Already spoke to them," Craig says. "I didn't like what they had to say." He positions himself against the den wall so he can keep an eye on Silk and the doorway at the same time. He lowers the .44, heavy in his weak left hand. "How did you find me?"

Silk reaches into his shirt pocket, tosses Craig's wallet on the table. "Mr. Moy told my family the location of your car shortly after you arrived in Chinatown. My uncle sent a man out to search the car before you met with Nguyen Van Duc and Zhu Le Rong."

"The guys at Sun Sun Seafood? They knew I was a cop before I told them?"

"I'm sorry, your cell phone was confiscated."

Craig gets his wallet from the table, flips it open. "So was all my money."

"You had promised that money to Mr. Moy."

Craig pockets his wallet. "The house wins again."

"My uncle was impressed that you told Mr. Duc and Mr. Rong the truth. Doing so made a strong statement when word came from Mr. Rong that you wanted to make a trade for Viceroy."

"I thought Viceroy raped my wife. I didn't know he was Juan—my goddamned snitch. I didn't know he was my daughter's boyfriend, either. Me: that's who he wanted to fuck."

"My uncle is aware, now, that Viceroy was indeed working for the police. For you."

"Is that why you're here?"

"No." Silk takes a long drag from his cigarette and blows the smoke between his gold teeth. Then he says, "I am here because my uncle believes you are right: we have a shared problem. His name is Chieu Chin Bo."

"Wonderful: another problem I've never heard of."

"He is the newest leader of the Night Hawks. When he took over, he offered my uncle an alliance. Big business has been hurting Chinatown, and Bo offered a sort of co-op. My uncle did not realize that the co-op would result in pressure for profit, violence, and takeover."

"Sounds like the cost of doing business in America."

"This is no business. Bo has insisted on integration—one of his men with one of ours—but it is not integration. It is his strategy to limit the power of our men. He has done it in Chinatown. You have seen the result: tonight, when you met Mr. Duc and Mr. Rong."

"The professor and the gun."

"Mr. Duc was a Night Hawk. He was the one who ordered the fate of Bei Du Nu."

"The man they lit on fire?"

Silk nods once. "Bo has divided Chinatown. He has been setting many fires."

"Did he kill that guy Yu outside the firehouse on Cermak? And his family?"

Silk says nothing, and his even expression is no answer, either.

"What about the Min Los, up here? Was it a Night Hawk job?"

Silk's answer: "My uncle wants the violence to stop."

"Then work with me," Craig says, putting the .44 down on the table. "I can make a case. We can take these guys down. Just give me names— or a way in—I can show this guy Bo how Americans really do business."

"I am not here to go into business with you. I am just here to offer a solution to our problem."

"This isn't my problem. It's just my job."

Silk licks his fingers to extinguish his cigarette. "I was supposed to be Bo's partner, but I fought against him: I wanted the Fuxis to remain independent. By that time, Bo had too much power, and my uncle could no longer support me. If you hadn't put me in jail, I would have been convicted of D-Cline's murder, and of your wife's rape. That was how I was supposed to be integrated: Bo was digging me a hole I would never climb out of."

"He's the one who set you up."

"He is the one who raped your wife."

Craig backs up until he hits the wall. "I don't believe you," he says. "You know I'll kill the man who raped her. This is the real reason you're here: to get me to do your dirty work."

"As I said, I am just here to offer a solution. Chinatown cannot retaliate against itself, but my uncle, unlike Bo, still believes in honor. And I have come to you because I think you do too."

"How do you know Bo raped my wife?"

"Mr. Rong spoke of a winged tattoo. Bo has a hawk tattooed on his stomach."

"Juan got killed over a tattoo. That's not good enough."

"Viceroy enticed Bo with his connection to a Greek man who wanted to distribute ecstasy in Chinatown. The night I was put in jail, Bo told my uncle of the meeting at the Green Mill. Now that we know of Viceroy's connection to you, we understand why Bo went after your wife: he must have believed he could get rid of you and me at the same time."

Silk takes out his cigarettes, lights one, and tosses the matches on the table.

"My uncle says this is how to find Bo. I can assure you he is alone."

"I go after Bo, everybody loses—everybody but Chinatown."

Silk says nothing. Lets Craig find his own answer.

"What about the men I killed in Chinatown?" Craig asks.

"If Bo should happen to disappear, my uncle will call this game a push."

"A push," Craig says. "Like a Pai Gow tie."

Craig picks up his .44. And then the matchbook. He says, "I've been pushed plenty."

39

Leslie cannot resist. Not when he sneaks up behind her, confident; his intention clear. Not when he turns her around and backs her up against the butcher block, a hand at her breast and the other, oh, God—is he serious?

He knows they shouldn't be doing this here, now—what if Ivy comes downstairs?

He answers with an urgent kiss that says he doesn't care. He's prepared to take her. Now. She cannot say no: he is a man made weak only by her mistakes. He needs this.

The oven timer buzzes, the world's rude intrusion as it goes on around them: the same world, as ever; only they are different.

Different, since the marriage crumbled. Since Craig got lost in his work. And since Leslie sought a way out of the loneliness. The routine.

There had been nothing wrong, really, with the routine.

This morning, she had been glad to get back to it. She'd whistled Billy Strayhorn's "Lush Life" while she went through a load of darks, the Maytags keeping time to her tune. She did the usual: she checked the pockets.

She found the matchbook. It was tucked into the fifth pocket of Craig's Levi's: a plain white matchbook, just like the one she found from the Aragon Arms. Inside, precise lettering. She wouldn't say anything about it. Not this time.

Sometime later, a chicken in the oven, she was reading the *Sun Times*. She came across a story in the Local section. A man, a suspected Night Hawk named Chieu Chin Bo, was killed. The reporter wrote that it was another case the police wouldn't crack; the Vietnamese community would not cooperate, and the police department suffered from a lack of multilingual officers. The article came down hard on the department's need for racial sensitivity training.

Leslie threw the paper away.

Craig pushes her up onto the butcher block. She is still sore in places; it still hurts. But she remembers desire. He reminds her.

She kisses him, wishing he could be better, stronger by the years between them. Wishing she could have been better all along.

Still, he wraps his arms around her, strong as he can be, his right arm healing. She bends to his embrace. He has done all he can to fix this. She is ready to give him what he wants.

But Craig doesn't go any further: he just holds her there. He is hurting, too; this is all that he wants.

And Leslie knows they'll tell anyone who asks that everything is fine, because she knows they'll both heal, eventually, best they can together.